MIDLOTHIAN

THE SPEAR

NOVELS BY JAMES HERBERT

JAMES HERBERT

THE SPEAR

BCA

LONDON · NEW YORK · SYDNEY · TORONTO

The author and publisher wish to thank Hugh Trevor-Roper and Weidenfeld & Nicolson Ltd, and Hermann Rauschning and Eyre & Spottiswoode (Publishers) Ltd (as successors to Thornton Butterworth Ltd) for their kind permission to quote from *Hitler's Table Talk* and *Hitler Speaks* respectively.

This edition published 1992 by BCA by
arrangement with Hodder and Stoughton Ltd

First published in Great Britain in 1978
by New English Library
First published by Hodder & Stoughton 1991

CN 1739

Photoset by Rowland Phototypesetting Ltd,
Bury St Edmunds, Suffolk.

Printed in Great Britain by St Edmundsbury Press Ltd,
Bury St Edmunds, Suffolk.

'A deathly cry! I rushed in:
Klingsor, laughing, was vanishing from there,
having stolen the holy Spear.'

RICHARD WAGNER: *PARSIFAL*

'For myself, I have the most intimate familiarity with Wagner's mental processes. At every stage in my life I come back to him. Only a new nobility can introduce the new civilization for us. If we strip "Parsifal" of every poetic element, we learn from it that selection and renewal are possible only amid the continuous tension of a lasting struggle. A world-wide process of segregation is going on before our eyes. Those who see in struggle the meaning of life, gradually mount the steps of a new nobility. Those who are in search of peace and order through dependence, sink, whatever their origin, to the inert masses. The masses, however, are doomed to decay and self-destruction. In our world-revolutionary turning-point the masses are the sum total of the sinking civilization and its dying representatives. We must allow them to die with their kings, like Amfortas.'

ADOLF HITLER

'You realize now what anxieties I have. The world regards Adolf Hitler as a strongman – and that's how his name must go down in history. The greater German Reich will stretch from the Urals to the North Sea after the war. That will be the Führer's greatest achievement. He's the greatest man who ever lived and without him it would never have been possible. So what does it matter that he should be ill now, when his work is almost complete.'

HEINRICH HIMMLER

33 AD

. . . So the soldiers came and broke the legs of the first, and of the other who had been crucified with him; but when they came to Jesus and saw that he was already dead, they did not break his legs. But one of the soldiers pierced his side with a spear, and at once there came out blood and water . . .

John 19:32
(RSV)

23rd May, 1945

Sergeant-Major Edwin Austin almost smiled in pity for the pathetic figure who sat huddled on the couch, with a blanket wrapped round his trembling body. Almost, but not quite, for they said this innocuous little man had caused the deaths of millions in the vicious war that had just ended. His persecution of the Jews in his own country, then in other captured territories, had horrified the world, and even now, more atrocities were coming to light. Could this be the man who had instigated such evil, this timid creature wearing only shirt, pants and socks beneath the army blanket? Was he really the person he claimed to be? Without the moustache, weak chin and bloated neck unshaven, without the military uniform, without the arrogance of his kind, it was difficult to tell. When he'd been captured, the German had been wearing a black eye-patch and a uniform with all the insignia removed. He'd claimed to be a member of the Secret Field Police, but under interrogation had announced a different – a more sinister – identity.

When he'd torn off the eye-patch and donned a pair of rimless spectacles, the likeness was evident, despite his bearing, his nervous affability.

Colonel Murphy, the Chief of Intelligence on Montgomery's

staff, had accepted the German's claimed identity, so why should he, a mere sergeant-major, doubt it? They had insisted the prisoner be watched every moment of the day; that's how seriously they were treating the matter. The sergeant had already lost one prisoner who'd been put in his charge: SS General Pruetzmann had crushed a cyanide capsule between his teeth. He'd make no mistakes with this one.

Through the German's interpreter, the sergeant informed him the couch was to be his bed, and he was to undress and lie down. The prisoner began to protest but became silent when he saw the resolution on the Englishman's face. He unwrapped the blanket from his shoulders and began to take off his underpants.

It was at that moment that Colonel Murphy, followed by another uniformed officer, entered the room. The Intelligence Chief brusquely introduced his companion as Captain Wells, an army doctor, then ordered the German to strip completely.

The sergeant knew what was about to happen, for a small phial had been found hidden in the lining of the prisoner's jacket two days before and they suspected he had another secreted somewhere on his person. They were taking no chances with a prisoner of this importance.

They began to search him, running their fingers through the hair on his head and pubic regions; they examined his ears and the cracks between each toe; they spread his buttocks and checked his anal passage. Nothing was found but there was still one area unsearched, and this was the most obvious hiding place. The doctor ordered the prisoner to open his mouth.

Captain Wells saw the black phial immediately, between a gap in the German's teeth on the right-hand side of his lower jaw, and with a shout of alarm thrust his fingers into the open mouth. But the German was too quick. He wrenched his head to one side biting down hard on the medic's fingers as he did so. Colonel Murphy and Sergeant-Major Austin leapt forward and threw the struggling prisoner to the floor, the doctor holding him by the throat, squeezing with both hands, trying to force him to spit the capsule out. It was too late though; the phial had been cracked and the poison was already finding its way into the man's system. His death was inevitable but still they fought to prevent it.

Colonel Murphy told the sergeant to find a needle and cotton as quickly as possible and valuable minutes were lost as the interrogation centre was turned upside down in the search for such trivial articles. The doctor kept his pressure on the prisoner's throat, but the death spasms were already beginning. The sergeant soon returned and it was the steady hands of the Intelligence Chief that had to thread the needle and cotton. While Sergeant-Major Austin forced the dying man's mouth open, the colonel grasped the slippery tongue and pierced it with the needle; by pulling on the thread they were able to hold the tongue out from the mouth, preventing it from blocking the throat. For fifteen minutes they used emetics, a stomach-pump and every method of artificial respiration. It was no use; the three men had prevented the cyanide from killing with its usual swiftness, but they had only delayed death.

The prisoner's body contorted into one last spasm of agony, his face hideous in its torment, then his body slumped into stillness.

Two days later, Sergeant-Major Austin wrapped the corpse in army blankets, wound camouflage netting tied with telephone wire around it, and buried the body in an unmarked grave near Lüneburg. The final resting place of Reichsführer SS Heinrich Himmler was never recorded.

1

'The struggle for world domination will be fought entirely between us, between German and Jew. All else is façade and illusion. Behind England stands Israel, and behind France, and behind the United States. Even when we have driven the Jew out of Germany, he remains our world enemy.'

ADOLF HITLER

Harry Steadman locked the door of his grey Celica and glanced around the wide, grass-middled square. The majority of other parking spaces were filled, forming a many-coloured, machine fringe around the green lawns. Most of the square's working inhabitants of solicitors and accountants had arrived, and were already easing their mental gears into the Monday morning pace. He'd noticed the couple sitting in their Cortina when he had driven towards his allocated parking space and would have paid them no mind had not the man's eyes snapped to attention on seeing Steadman; the forced casualness as the eyes glanced away again had not deceived the investigator. The man had recognized him, but Steadman had not recognized the man. Nor his female companion.

Both appeared to be in deep conversation as he looked

across the roof of his car towards them. It was a small thing, for there was nothing unusual about clients waiting in their cars until their appointment with solicitor, accountant – or even private investigator – in Gray's Inn Square, but Steadman felt an unease he hadn't experienced for a long time. A throwback from the time he'd lived with that unease for weeks, sometimes months, on end. And it had been triggered off just by the meeting of eyes.

He crossed the smooth roadway and entered the gloomy interior of the red-bricked terraced building that contained his small agency, along with three company accountants' offices. It was a prime position for an enquiry agency, in the midst of the legal 'ghetto', Lincoln's Inn and Bloomsbury on the doorstep, the law courts and the Old Bailey ten minutes away. The address gave respectability to a profession that was often looked upon as seedy, even sordid. Harry Steadman, along with his partner, Maggie Wyeth, had worked long and hard to establish an agency of high repute, beginning with the principle that no case, provided there were no illegalities involved, was too big or too small. Fortunately, over the past two years, because of their growing reputation, most of their cases were for big companies, involving anything from industrial espionage to fraud or embezzlement within a company, though they still handled matrimonial enquiries, traced missing persons and carried out the service of legal process, delivering writs or warnings of prosecution to debtors. Their staff consisted of three: a retired police officer named Blake, whom they naturally called Sexton; a young trainee detective, Steve, who would leave them soon to set up on his own; and Sue, their receptionist/typist and general runaround, twenty-nine, plump, unmarried and an absolute godsend.

Steadman ignored the small and generally unreliable lift, and climbed the three flights of stairs to the agency, his breathing becoming sharper and his strides less agile as he neared the top. At thirty-eight, his condition could be described as 'fair but wearing'.

The clatter of Sue's typing met him in the hallway, and her smile greeted him when he pushed open the office door.

'Hello, Sue,' he said, returning her smile.

'Morning, Mr Steadman. Good trip?'

'Good enough. One more week should cover it.'

Steadman had spent the previous week in the North, setting up a complete security system for a manufacturer of electrical goods. The company's innovations in refining communications systems had a nasty habit of being 'innovated' by a rival company just weeks ahead of their own; coincidence was one thing, but almost identical patents over a period of eighteen months stretched credibility too far.

'Is Maggie in yet?' Steadman asked, taking the letters Sue slid towards him.

'Yes, she's got someone with her at the moment. I'll let her know you're back as soon as she's free.'

'Fine. I'll have to leave again about eleven so we'll need to talk soon.' He headed towards his office, waving a hand towards Steve who was frowning over a booklet outlining the Laws of Evidence and Procedure.

'Stick with it, Steve,' Steadman grinned. 'In ten years it will all be crystal clear.'

Steve smiled weakly back.

Steadman paused in the doorway of his office. 'Is Sexton around?' he asked Sue. 'I may need him this week to help find me some good security people.' As an ex-policeman, his employee still had good connections with the Force and knew who was soon to retire, or sick of the job and considering leaving. These men usually made excellent security staff.

'He's Process Server for Collins and Tullis this morning,' Sue replied.

'Okay, I'll ring him from Salford if I miss him.' Before he could close the door, Sue stopped him by waving a piece of paper in her hand.

'This gentleman wants to see you this morning, Mr Steadman,' she said apologetically.

'Oh, come on, Sue. You know I won't have time,' Steadman said in an exasperated tone. 'Can't he see Maggie?'

'I tried to get him to, but he insisted on seeing you. He rang last week and wanted to get in touch with you up North when I told him you were away. I didn't let him know where you were, of course, but he said it was very important that he saw you personally the moment you got back. He wouldn't even *talk* to Mrs Wyeth.'

Steadman walked back to the reception desk and took the folded piece of paper from the girl's fleshy hand. His stomach muscles tightened when he unfolded the paper and read the message. His earlier unease had been instinctively correct.

'Dark hair, dark complexion? In his early thirties?' he asked, still looking at the handwritten message.

'Yes,' Sue replied, puzzled by her employer's reaction. 'Goldblatt, he said his name was. I can put him off when he arrives, if you like? He did make it sound important, though, so I thought you might just fit him in before you went back to Salford.'

'No, it's all right, Sue. He's already downstairs sitting in his car. I'll give him ten minutes.'

As Steadman went into his office Sue stared across at Steve, who had been watching the brief exchange with interest. He shrugged his shoulders and turned his attention back to the intricacies of the Law.

Steadman sat at his desk and reread the message on the piece of paper. 'Zwi sends his regards' was all it said, but it stirred up memories of emotions and actions governed by a passionate vengeance. 'Zwi Zamir,' he said softly, then screwed the paper into a tight ball on his desk. He swivelled his chair and gazed at the grey autumn sky outside his window, the image of Zwi Zamir, ex-Director of Mossad Aliyah Beth, the Israeli Secret Service, clear in his mind.

Ten minutes later, Sue buzzed him on the intercom. 'Mr Goldblatt for you, Mr Steadman.'

With a weary sigh, Steadman said, 'Send him in.'

He reached forward and picked up the crinkled ball of paper still lying on his desk and tossed it into the waste-bin, just as the door opened and Sue ushered in the man he had spotted earlier in the car. Goldblatt was alone, his companion presumably still waiting below.

'Mr Goldblatt,' Steadman acknowledged, standing and stretching his hand forward across the desk.

Goldblatt shook it, his grip hard and dry. He was a short, stocky man, his hair black and crinkly, cut short, his features not as dark as Steadman had at first thought. It must have been the darkness of the car deepening the man's natural swarthiness.

'David Goldblatt, Mr Steadman. Thank you for seeing me.' There was barely a trace of accent, except for a slight American inflection on certain words. His eyes searched Steadman's as though looking for some sign of recognition, not personal; perhaps a recognition of shared beliefs.

Steadman's eyes remained cold.

'I'll bring you some coffee.' Sue's words interrupted the awkward silence. She closed the door, nervous of the coldness she felt emanating from her employer. He seemed angry at this little Jewish man.

'You saw the note?' Goldblatt asked, taking the seat the investigator had indicated.

Steadman nodded, sitting himself and lounging back in his chair to study the other man. 'How is Zwi?'

Goldblatt smiled across at him. 'He's well. He retired from the Service, you know. He's Chairman of a big construction company now. It's owned by the Israeli confederation of trade unions, so his interests are still for the good of our country – as are the interests of all of us. They used to be yours too, even though you're not a Jew.'

Steadman dropped his gaze. 'Things change,' he said.

There was a silence between them. Goldblatt broke it by saying softly, 'We need your help again.'

'Forget it,' Steadman snapped. 'I told you, things change. Mossad changed. Ideals were replaced by vengeance.'

'Only by revenge can we achieve our ideals!' Goldblatt's voice was angry now. 'We have to avenge the persecution of our people. There must be retaliation for every Israeli man, woman and child killed by terrorists! Only then can they respect our strength. Only then will they realize we will never be beaten. You know that!'

'And I know you've murdered innocent people.' Steadman's anger matched the Jew's, but his voice was quieter, more steady.

'Innocent people? And the massacre at Lod Airport? Munich? Entebbe? Every time the PFLP or PLO guerrillas strike, innocent people are murdered.'

'Does that give you cause to act in the same way?'

'We have made mistakes, Mr Steadman. But they *were* mistakes, not deliberate acts of aggression against innocent bystanders! We have never hijacked a plane, nor planted bombs in crowded airports. How can you compare us with these animals?'

Steadman's voice had lost its anger now. 'I don't, Mr Goldblatt,' he said wearily. 'But I'd had enough of The Institute. I had to get out or be tainted by what we were doing. As you said, we made mistakes.'

A gentle tapping at the door brought a brief halt to their exchange. Sue entered bearing a tray containing two cups of coffee. She smiled nervously at Goldblatt and placed the coffee and sugar on the table between them. The two men were quiet until she'd left the room again. Goldblatt sipped his coffee and, as an afterthought, added sugar. Steadman ignored his.

'I'm sorry, Mr Steadman,' Goldblatt began again. 'I did not come here to argue with you. Israeli feelings run high, but then you understand that. Mossad needs your help again, and so far I have only succeeded in making you angry. Please accept my apology.'

'Accept mine too, Mr Goldblatt. I meant no disrespect to

you, or your cause, but Zwi Zamir must have explained why I left the Israeli Intelligence Organization.'

Goldblatt nodded. 'Yes, he did. He also said you probably would not help us. But you did before; you left the British Army to join us. Perhaps you will find that sympathy for our cause once again.'

'No, I don't think so. I had a stronger reason then.'

'Lilla Kanaan?'

Her name, after so many years, still caused the old grief to flood through him, its intensity almost causing a panic within him. He said nothing.

'Listen to me first, then if you still will not help us, so be it. We'll find other ways.'

Goldblatt took Steadman's silence as approval for him to go on. 'Everyone is well aware of the escalation of terrorism throughout the world. At first, we Israelis defended our country from the inside but, as you well know, we were forced to fight our war beyond our own boundaries. We did not wish it, but we had no choice . . .'

Steadman's thoughts were racing back to that blood-filled night, Tuesday, May 30th, 1972. Lod International Airport. He and Lilla had been waiting for the flight that would take him back to England, his assignment in the Middle East over – his orders now to return to his regiment. Gunshots had startled them from the sadness of parting, and exploding grenades had made him hurl Lilla to the floor and push her beneath a row of seats. When he saw the three Japanese with their Kalashnikov carbines and laden with hand-grenades, he covered her body with his, pulling a discarded suitcase in front of them as feeble protection against the hail of bullets and shrapnel. People were screaming, running in terror from the lethal fire; others threw themselves to the floor, too frightened to move, praying they would be spared. Steadman had looked up to see if there was any way to reach the gunmen and he had seen a grenade explode in the hand of one of the Japanese, tearing off the terrorist's head.

A second died as he carelessly strayed into his companion's line of fire. The third then seemed to lose his nerve and had begun to run; Steadman saw him disappear under a crush of border police and civilian police officers.

He pulled Lilla to him and they had sat there stunned at the violence and the carnage it had caused. The wailing began and the hall came alive with the dying.

Twenty-eight people had been slaughtered, most of them innocent Puerto Rican pilgrims, and seventy had been wounded. The surviving terrorist, Kozo Okamoto, later confessed he was a member of the Japanese Red Army and had been trained for the suicide mission by the Black September group.

Three months later, Steadman had returned to Israel and the Central Institute for Information and Espionage, no longer as an adviser on loan from British Military Intelligence, but as a member of the organization . . .

'. . . It was not long before we realized we were not fighting just one terrorist group but many.' Steadman's attention was drawn back to Goldblatt. 'In Ireland, the IRA; in Spain, the Basque; in South America, the Tupamaros; in Turkey, the Turkish Liberation Army; in Japan, the Red Army; in West Germany, the Baader-Meinhof. All are now aiding and abetting each other, a terrorist alliance brought about by the Russian KGB. They have even narrowed the split between the Arab factions, the PFLP and PLO. But the people we least expected to give succour to our enemies were the British.'

Steadman raised his eyebrows in surprise. 'The British? How are we helping such people?' he asked.

'By supplying them with arms; new, advanced weapons. Training the terrorists to use them effectively.'

'Nonsense. Sure, the Middle East and Iran are big customers of the British Government itself, but it doesn't deal with terrorist groups. Nor does it allow private armament companies to. Licences are strictly controlled.'

Goldblatt smiled without humour. 'Come now, Mr Steadman. As an ex-military man and as one who has negotiated the sale of arms to Israel yourself, you know just how far the arms business can be "strictly controlled".' He drew out the last two words scornfully. 'It's no longer just Russian weapons we find in the hands of our assassins. There are certain highly sophisticated weapons we have traced back to your country.'

'They may have been paid for and passed on by another source.'

'Having worked for Israeli Intelligence yourself, do you doubt our efficiency in these matters?'

Steadman had to shake his head, for he knew Israel had one of the most respected and feared Intelligence organizations in the world. On his return to that country he had joined Mossad, which was responsible for external Intelligence, and he soon appreciated the strength of Shin Beth, which was responsible for internal security and counter-espionage. No, he didn't doubt their efficiency.

'We know for certain that the PLO bought direct from a British company. Unfortunately, our source of information died under interrogation so we have no proof, no first-person confession.'

Steadman also knew how ruthless Israeli interrogations could be and shuddered inwardly.

. 'What do you know of Edward Gant?' the Mossad agent asked.

'Gant? You think he's the supplier?'

Goldblatt nodded.

'He's not one of the big dealers, but his weapons are of the sophisticated kind. Did your informant tell you it was him?'

'No, our informant didn't know. We believed him.'

I'll bet you did, Steadman thought. Torture has a way of making people want to be honest. 'So what makes you think he's your man?' he said.

'Let's just say several roads lead back to him. Now, what do you know of him?'

'Not much – he keeps out of the limelight. I know he's

wealthy, respectable and, as I said, deals in the sale of arms on a small scale. He seems to move in high circles.'

'Appeared on the scene in the United States around the late fifties,' Goldblatt continued. 'His record shows he was an emigrant from Canada. He married a wealthy American widow and began his activity in the armament field, his innovations in light weaponry outstanding at that time. His wife's connections and money helped him approach top-ranking Army personnel as well as the odd senator here and there, and he soon became a steady supplier to the US Forces. He seemed to have some influence himself at the time, even though he was new to the country, and he was by no means a *poor* immigrant. He came to England in 1963 after his wife's death and opened up a weapons development plant here, warding off any state control when he became successful. He's now a considerable force in the industry and, like many arms dealers, has kept away from publicity – until recently, that is.

'By all accounts he is a remarkable man, hardly looking his age, extremely fit, shrewd and quite ruthless in business. Three weeks ago, one of our agents investigating Edward Gant's activities in this country disappeared. We have not heard from him since.'

The last words were made to sound as though they were part of the arms dealer's biography. Steadman leaned forward across the desk. 'You want me to find your man,' he said as a statement.

Goldblatt nodded.

'And if I can dig up some evidence against Gant at the same time, that would be useful.'

'Yes. Very.'

'And what would you do with that evidence?'

'Turn it over to your government, of course.'

Steadman sat back in his chair and stared coldly into the Mossad agent's eyes. 'Goodbye, Mr Goldblatt.'

The Israeli sighed deeply. 'Do you have no feelings for us any more?'

'None.'

'What changed you? What turned you against us?'

'Zwi Zamir knows. I'm sure he told you.'

'Did Lilla's death mean nothing to you?'

Steadman's hands clenched into fists on the desk-top. 'It meant everything to me,' he said evenly.

'And would her brother's death mean anything?'

Puzzlement showed in the investigator's eyes. 'What do you mean?'

'Her brother, Baruch, was the agent sent in to contact Gant.'

Baruch. Young. Anxious to serve his country. Even more so after the death of Lilla. They'd used him, just as they'd used his sister. Just as they used up the lives of so many of their young.

'I had no idea he'd joined the Institute.'

'Our country needs such fine young men to survive, Mr Steadman. Baruch Kanaan was conscripted into the Air Force and flew helicopter missions into enemy territory, giving support to GHQ assault groups on the ground, covering their retreat from Arab strongholds. I understand you, yourself, were recipient of such cover on several occasions when you were with us.'

Steadman nodded and thought of the nightmare raids into Beirut, the hasty retreats through hostile streets, silenced Parabellums, hot from use, burning their hands. The welcoming sound of rotor blades, the huge dragonflies dropping from the night sky with guns blazing to disrupt enemy pursuit. Grenades and spikes dropped into the roads to thwart enemy vehicles. It all seemed a long time ago.

'Baruch eventually became a member of the GHQ, himself,' Goldblatt continued, and allowed himself a brief smile. 'He walked to Petra twice.'

Steadman raised his eyebrows. The GHQ was a secret paramilitary outfit of the Israeli Defence Forces, its members specially chosen officers or sergeants from other units, an ability to fight in small groups against heavy odds an essential requirement. One of the initiation rites into the unit was a voluntary trip by foot from the Israeli border, across a stretch of the Jordanian desert to the abandoned city of Petra, only cunning and endurance keeping the lone traveller out of the hands of the prowling Bedouin battalion guarding the area. Some initiates declined to take the trip and these were considered unfit for future highly dangerous or solitary missions, while many others who accepted the challenge were never seen again. 'He must be very special,' the investigator said.

'Very special,' the Israeli agreed. 'It was not long before he became an agent for Mossad. He speaks French, German, and his English is particularly good. He is cool and resourceful under pressure, and quite ruthless where our enemies are concerned. He also has an excellent knowledge of the armaments market, much of it learnt from you, I gather.'

'Baruch liked to know everything about everything.'

'You were a good teacher. Baruch Kanaan was chosen for this mission because of these qualities and because his face was unknown to our enemies. He hoped to contact you, by the way, to enlist your help. We forbade it. We did not want to involve you in any way, but now I am afraid we have little choice.'

'What was his cover?'

'He contacted Gant as a representative of our government. He was to buy arms for us.'

'And?'

'He made the contact and reported back that Gant was interested. Then we heard no more from him. We learned he had checked out of his hotel and left no forwarding address. Baruch left no message for us, nor did he try to contact any of our "safe" houses. He just disappeared.'

'Three weeks ago.'

'Yes.'

'And you've heard nothing since?'

'Nothing.'

It was Steadman's turn to sigh. 'Just how did you expect me to find him?'

'You could approach Gant in the same way, as a buyer for a Middle East power. You would not have to reveal your employer's identity at first – not until negotiations were underway.'

'But Baruch let Gant know he was working for Israel.'

'Yes. A mistake, we think.'

Steadman smiled wryly. 'Some mistake. If Gant is supplying arms to Arab terrorists, he may have some sympathy for their cause.'

'It is not unusual for an arms dealer to supply both sides in a war.'

'No. It can be an embarrassment sometimes though.'

'An embarrassed arms dealer? An amusing thought.' Goldblatt's smile was cynical. 'However, our point was this: if Gant showed any reluctance to deal with us, that would at least give some indication our information was correct.'

'Indicate, but hardly prove.'

'No, but that would only have been our first step. Surveillance, enquiries, bribery here and there would have confirmed the rest. Proof would have followed.'

'And if it hadn't? If you couldn't get the proof to hand to my government, what then? Eliminate Gant?'

'Probably.' There was no hesitation.

'But you can't fight your war in this country.' Steadman's anger was rising again.

'We have no choice.'

'I have. I won't help you.'

'We are not asking you to take any risks, Mr Steadman. We merely want you to get close to Gant, to find out if Baruch saw him again. If not, then trace Baruch's movements from the last time he contacted us. That's all we ask: a straightforward investigator's commission. No involvement with Mossad.'

'Why don't you go to the police?'

'That could prove rather embarrassing. Besides, we have no faith in the co-operation of foreign governments in Israeli affairs. You remember how France let the assassin Abu Daoud go free after arresting him in Paris in 1977? The French were worried that their sale of two hundred Mirage jets to Egypt would fall through because of it. No, justice is governed by self-interest in all countries. I think your government would not be too concerned with the whereabouts of one missing Israeli spy.'

'Then why not use another private investigator? Why me?'

'Because of your connections. You were with the military, you dealt in arms. You negotiated deals for arms for Israel in the past, and there is no reason why you should not be believed as a freelance now. You have the perfect cover; and you also know Baruch. You are suited for the job in every way.'

'Except one.'

'And that is?'

'I'm not interested.'

'Not even for Baruch's sake?'

'No.'

There was disgust in Goldblatt's eyes now. 'Will nothing I say persuade you?'

'Nothing. Find another agency, or do your own dirty work.'

The Mossad agent stood and looked coldly down at Steadman. 'You've lost your beliefs,' he said.

'No, they're just different now.' Steadman sat back in his chair, his face expressionless. 'I hope you find Baruch.'

With a shake of his head, Goldblatt turned and walked to the door. He stood there as if to say something further, then walked out, closing the door quietly behind him.

Steadman sighed deeply and drummed his fingers on the desk-top. The past never wants to let go, he mused. He wondered about Lilla's younger brother, Baruch: always smiling, so easily excited, yet so intense when conversation turned to the political struggles of his nation. Had he been sacrificed now like his sister, all in the cause of his country's fight for freedom? The gentle tap at the door was a welcome relief from his brooding thoughts.

'Hello, Harry. That sounded heavy.' Maggie Wyeth's head peered round the door.

He grinned. 'Listening at keyholes again?'

Maggie entered the room and perched herself on the corner of his desk. Forty, elegant, she was attractive in the special way older women can be. A certain firmness in her lips and jawline gave her a slightly intimidating aura, and Steadman had frequently seen this turned to good use in many of the cases they had handled. Her husband had owned the agency and Maggie had helped run it, until a heart attack had killed him five years before. She had continued to run the business, having learned much from her late husband, but the prejudices of clients against a woman handling their affairs were difficult to overcome. Although not unusual for a woman to be a private investigator, she soon realized the agency needed a masculine influence and image, so 'feelers' were put out for the right man. Steadman had just returned to England having resigned from Mossad, and a mutual acquaintance had brought the two together. They were cautious of each other at first, but a reciprocal respect had soon grown between them. They had both lost something, but they were determined not to wallow in self-pity. They recognized the need in each other.

After a three-month trial, Steadman bought himself in as a full partner and the agency's client list had steadily begun to grow again. It was inevitable their relationship should develop beyond that of a business partnership, but their affair was brief, both realizing they could only offer each other a shallow comfort. There was genuine fondness between them, but love was something they'd used up on others. It had lasted for three months, then, by mutual consent, they'd reverted to their business relationship, although a strong bond of friendship had grown between them.

Steadman glanced appreciatively at the smooth line of Maggie's thigh and felt some of the tension drain from him. They hadn't seen each other for a week and both found it good to be in contact again.

'Who was he?' Maggie asked.

'A voice from the past, you could say,' Steadman replied casually.

'From Israel?'

'Yes.'

'Mossad?' She knew of Steadman's past associations.

He nodded.

'Do they want you to work for them again?'

'In a way. They wanted to commission the agency to find a man.'

'He wouldn't speak to me last week when you were away.'

'I have special connections, it seems.'

'But you didn't take the job on.'

'No. I want nothing to do with them.'

'But if it was just a straightforward case we could have handled it. We're not that busy that we can turn down work.'

Steadman frowned. 'With Mossad it's never that straightforward. We don't need it.'

'We could have discussed it first.' Maggie's tone was soft, but he recognized the firmness behind it. 'We could have given it to Sexton, or I could have handled it.'

'I told you, Maggie, they wanted me. Let's drop it, eh?'

This time Maggie recognized the firmness in *his* tone.

'Sorry, Harry. It's the businesswoman in me. I hate to let one get away.'

'Okay.' He smiled and patted her thigh. 'Now, what's been happening?'

'Well, we've still got a few cases on the go, nothing that Sexton and Steve can't handle, though. Sexton has a couple of writs to serve this week although we'll probably let Steve have a go at one of them – he can run faster than Sexton. I'm in court giving evidence tomorrow and Thursday, and a client I've just seen this morning wants to investigate pilfering in his chain of hardware stores. He's losing several hundred a week and suspects it's an organized ring working in his shops.'

'Is he losing stock or money from the till?'

'Oh, it's straight from the till. We'll check receipt books and till rolls in the evening and if we find too many "No Sale" marks we'll try some test purchases.'

Steadman nodded. Test purchases were an easy way of checking the honesty of suspect shop salesmen.

'You'll check on regular tradesmen to the shop, too?'

'Naturally. There might just be conspiracy involved. It shouldn't take too long to find the culprits, but after that, we're pretty clear for work. That's why I was interested in your visitor.'

'Oh come on, Maggie. You know what happens when we begin to slack off. People go missing, couples want a divorce after twenty years of marriage, debtors do a bunk, blackmailers start blackmailing – we're up to our ears in it again. And they're just the little cases. We've always our main diet of company jobs: industrial espionage, embezzlement, security.'

Maggie laughed aloud. 'It's my insecurity showing. There's no reason why things should suddenly go bad for us – not now.'

'Right. Look, I've got to get back up to Salford and there's a few things to tidy up before I go.'

Maggie stood. 'Is it going well?'

'The usual problem of old Joe retiring soon so why can't we put him in charge of security? Fortunately, they're seeing it my way and I want Sexton to select some good men and send them up to see me this week. Then it's just a matter of setting up systems and hiring and training the security.'

'All right, Harry, I'll let you get on. I'll give you a ring if anything important crops up while you're away.' She gave him an affectionate smile and walked to the door. 'Maggie,' he called after her. She turned, the door half-open. 'Forget about our Israeli friend,' he said.

'Forgotten.' She blew him a kiss, then left the office.

Sue looked up from her typewriter as Maggie approached.

Maggie's voice was low when she said, 'Sue, did Harry's visitor leave an address where he could be contacted?'

2

'. . . *it is the tragedy of the élite to have to participate in acts of violence for the glory of the Fatherland.'*

HEINRICH HIMMLER

'The world can only be ruled by fear.'

ADOLF HITLER

Steadman threw his suitcase on the floor and slumped on to the bed. The night drive from Salford had been long and wearing, but he'd wanted to be home on Sunday evening. That way, he could be in the office the following day after a good night's sleep. His client had insisted he stay over for the weekend as his guest, after the long hours he'd put in during the week. Steadman had accepted gladly, for there were still a few loose ends to be tied up before he returned to London and these would be more easily concluded with his client in a congenial and relaxed mood.

Steadman was pleased with the way things had gone. Over the past two weeks he'd thoroughly screened all of the company's employees and had found nothing amiss; but from now on, every member of the firm would possess a Works Pass, numerically marked and containing a photograph of the employee over-stamped with the company name. A daily report would be submitted by security on any unusual happenings during the day or any early or late visits to the company by employees (even if the reports were negative they would still be submitted). All documents would be classified, the more important of which would receive special markings and closer attention. A better system of floodlighting was already being installed, and in future no windows or doors would be left in shadows; even the roof was to be illuminated. All locks and safe combinations had been changed, and ground-floor windows had been fitted with thin but sturdy bars. Steadman had been in favour of a silent alarm system so that the security guards and police could be alerted of illegal entry without actually warning the trespasser; he wanted the intruder to be caught, not merely frightened away. His client had wanted clanging bells and sirens at first, to show the power of his alarm system to would-be thieves so that they would be deterred from ever attempting a break-in again, but he had given way to Steadman's argument that the best deterrent to them, and any other villains who might have their eyes on the plant, was for them to be caught and made an example of. Steadman had also argued against the manufacturer's request for guard dogs; correctly trained dogs were expensive and required handlers. He also had a personal abhorrence of any animal being trained to attack a man. Besides which they could easily be drugged.

He had spent the weekend coaxing a higher salary for the Chief of Security out of the manufacturer, for Sexton had provided Steadman with the ideal man for the job. A soon-to-retire police officer, the man needed more persuading to move from London up to Salford, and only a good wage and financial help in moving would do it. The manufacturer argued that there were plenty of suitable men locally, but Steadman had not been totally happy with any he'd interviewed; they would be fine as guards, but were not sufficiently qualified in the key role of Chief of Security. The client finally succumbed to Steadman's wishes and the investigator pressed home his advantage by persuading him to employ his own maintenance men and even his own window cleaners rather than use outside tradesmen. It was a smaller issue, but as far as Steadman was concerned, of vital importance if strict security were to be maintained, so he was particularly pleased at the outcome and had allowed himself to relax for the rest of the weekend.

He flexed his shoulder blades against the softness of the bed and eased his shoes off with his toes. He had enjoyed the last two weeks' work even though it had been arduous and frustrating at times. If his client stuck to the agreed plan for security, then the plant should become thief-proof and, hopefully, spy-proof, which would be good for the agency's reputation and could lead on to similar commissions from other companies. Steadman had set up four such security systems in the past, with variations for the particular needs of each individual company, and it had proved to be highly lucrative work. It beat the hell out of runaway debtors or stay-away husbands.

He briefly considered ringing Maggie to let her know he was back, but on glancing at his watch and seeing it was well after eleven, he dismissed the thought. He had spoken to her a few times during the week and there had been no crises at the office, so there was little point in disturbing her at such a late hour. Tomorrow morning would be time enough to catch up on any news.

Steadman stretched his limbs but resisted the urge to let himself sink into sleep. He was hungry and a stiff drink would do wonders for his metabolism. The investigator rolled off the bed and padded over to the window. He peered into the darkness, seeing little of the small church grounds opposite, a dark reflection of himself in the glass obscuring the view.

Steadman lived in a small terraced house in a quiet mews off Knightsbridge. It had cost a small fortune, but the cul-de-sac was central and its peaceful position in the thriving city was something to be relished. The tiny park that surrounded the church across the narrow road, made an ideal spot to relax over the Sunday papers during the summer months; even the occasional gravestones, grey and white with age and bird droppings, gave the grounds a peaceful stability. A few benches were scattered at random in the grounds and his neighbours all seemed to have their allocated spot, their dogs their allocated trees. The money Steadman had acquired through working for Mossad, and the commissions he had received on negotiating arms deals for the Israelis, had been enough to pay for the house as well as buy himself into Maggie's business, and now his earnings came purely from the agency. It gave him a comfortable life and a busy one which, he reflected, was the most one could expect. You had more, once, he told himself, and you foolishly expected it to last. Foolishly, because danger was all around you both then, but you still thought it couldn't touch you. It had though, and it had killed Lilla. So never expect too much again. That way, you'll never be disappointed. He closed the curtains on his dark, brooding image.

He went downstairs, his stockinged feet silent on the heavy carpets, and along the short hallway to the tiny kitchen, where he poured himself a large vodka with a small tonic. Deciding it was too late to eat out, he took a pizza from the fridge, unwrapped it and put it into the oven. His cleaning-lady, who came in twice a week, had thoughtfully stocked up his food supply during his absence, but he rarely cooked elaborate meals for himself – women friends could be relied on for that.

Steadman padded back down the hallway to the front door and retrieved the week's mail that was lying there. He took the letters and his drink into the lounge and settled into the armchair. He sipped at his vodka tonic, then began to open the envelopes on his lap. The only bills he paid any attention to were the red ones; the others he crumpled and dropped on the floor. A letter from an ex-girlfriend made him groan aloud. She had grown tired of being an ex- just as quickly as she had of being current and now thought it would be 'super' if they got together again. That letter, too, soon lay crumpled at his feet. An invitation to a security exhibition followed by a series of lectures on the subject interested him and he placed this one with the Final Demands resting on the arm of his chair. The rest were advertising circulars and these found their rightful place on the floor.

He ate his supper at the breakfast bar in his kitchen, the cool voice and records of a late-night DJ keeping him company. A hot shower and another large vodka eased the remaining stiffness from his muscles and left him pleasantly drowsy. He fell naked into his bed and was asleep within seconds.

The hammering woke him with a start. He lay on his back staring up into the darkness wondering what had dragged him from his slumber with such suddenness. Then the banging came again. It came from downstairs – his front door. Who the hell could want him at this time of night? And why not use the doorbell? But this was hammering, not knocking. With a curse, he leapt from the bed and pulled back the curtains, pressing his face close to the glass of the window in order to see directly below. The banging stopped almost immediately.

Steadman blinked his eyes as he tried to see into the gloom. He thought he saw movement in the shadows below, but couldn't be sure. As he turned from the window, about to find his discarded trousers and dash downstairs, he thought he saw a black shape scurry across the narrow road into the darkness of the churchyard opposite. Again, he couldn't be sure, nothing was distinct in the poor light.

As he pulled on his trousers, he snatched a quick look at the luminous digital clock by his bedside. Two twenty-three. If someone was playing a joke, he'd kill them. He ran down the stairs, angry now, but when he reached the hallway, he halted. Something made him hesitate. He stared at the door, for some reason reluctant to open it. There was a stillness in the air. A chill. And he could hear a strange muffled sound coming from the other side of the door.

He moved slowly along the hallway, his breathing held in check, his footsteps quiet and deliberate. He pressed his ear against the wood and listened.

Something was scraping itself against the door and he thought he heard a low murmuring. The sound wasn't human; it was like the whimpering of an animal in pain. He considered going back for his gun which was locked away upstairs, but dismissed the thought as being over-dramatic. A sudden thump against the door made him draw away.

Then he realized how ridiculously he was behaving, standing there in the dark like an old woman, afraid to open the front door. He reached for the latch and swung the door inwards with a jerk.

A figure stood spread-eagled in the doorway, arms out-stretched, holding on to the doorframe. The head hung down and a dark liquid seemed to be drooling from its mouth. The figure seemed strangely slumped, for the knees were bent as if giving no support to the body. A low moaning noise came from it, occasionally rising to the animal-like whimper Stead-man had heard from the other side of the door; but the noise had a strange gurgling to it, as though blood were running down the person's throat.

Steadman could see nothing beyond the feebly twisting body except blackness. He reached for the hallway light switch and flicked it down, blinking his eyes rapidly against the sudden light. When he finally focused them, he saw that the figure in the doorway was that of a woman. And there was something familiar about the slumped head.

'Maggie.' The name came from Steadman's lips in a whisper. He reached forward and raised her head; blood ran from her mouth on to his hand. Her eyes were glazed and red-rimmed but he thought he saw a flicker of recognition there.

'Maggie, what's happened to you?' He moved forward to take her in his arms. For some reason, her arms remained stretched outwards as though unwilling to let go of the door-frame. Her head moved and she tried to speak, but the blood in her throat choked her words.

'Oh God, Maggie! Who did this?' He pulled her forward, wanting to carry her to the sofa in the lounge, but a weak scream came from her.

'Maggie, let go of the door. Let me take you in,' he pleaded.

She tried to speak again and her head slumped forward as she lost consciousness. This time Steadman tugged a little more firmly, but still she clung to the doorframe. Then he noticed the trails of blood running down from her arms. He pushed his head past her shoulder and his eyes widened in horror as he saw the nail protruding from the back of her hand.

He grabbed her to support her weight and saw her other hand also had been nailed to the doorframe. 'Maggie, Maggie,' he said over and over again, holding her close, lifting her to prevent her hands from tearing. He called out, hoping a neighbour would hear, but no lights came on from the other houses. It was the dead of night; they were either in deep sleep or just didn't want to hear. He made up his mind quickly, sensing he had no time to lose. Someone would come eventually if he kept shouting, but by then it might be too late.

He eased Maggie's body down as gently as he could, then ran into the kitchen and threw open a cupboard where he kept his work tools. He found a hammer and raced back down the hallway, his heart pounding, his fear rising. Her torn clothes were covered in blood, most of which seemed to have come from her mouth. Steadman eased himself past her and with one arm around her body, pushed the forked end of the hammer underneath the nailhead with his free hand. He tried to pull the nail out without using the back of her hand as a lever, but it was deeply embedded. He had to let her go and use both hands. Maggie's body slumped again and he pulled at the hammer with all his strength, a cry of relief escaping him as he finally wrenched the bloody nail clear. He tried to catch her as her body fell sideways, prevented from falling completely to the ground by the nail in her other hand. Steadman let her go and again gave all his energy to yanking out the other nail. It was embedded deep into her hand and he had to push the hammer's fork into the skin to gain a grip. It made him nauseous to do so but he knew he had no choice; he had to get her free as quickly as possible.

The three-inch nail loosened, then came out smoothly and clinked into the road. Steadman dropped the hammer and carried the still figure into the house, gently laying it on the sofa in his lounge. He snapped on the light, then knelt beside her, wondering if there was anything he could do before he called an ambulance. Her head lolled to one side and her open, unseeing eyes told him the worst. Frantically, he ripped open her jacket and placed his hand over her heart. He couldn't trust his trembling hand to give him an answer so he put his ear to her breast and listened. There was no heartbeat.

He cried out her name again and took her head in his hands, looking at her still face, pleading with her to be alive. Her mouth had dropped open and he saw it was thick with blood. Perhaps she was choking, perhaps if he laid her with her head down. Then his muscles froze as he stared into the blood-filled cavity. He fought against the sudden upheaval in his stomach and, as steadily as possible, rested her head back against the arm of the sofa.

He knew that she was dead. But he wondered why her tongue had been ripped out.

3

'This time our sacred soil will not be spared. But I am not afraid of this. We shall clench our teeth and go on fighting. Germany will emerge from those ruins lovelier and greater than any country in the world has ever been.'

ADOLF HITLER

Steadman sat at Maggie's desk and covered his face with trembling hands. There were no tears in him, just a great weariness, a feeling of hopelessness. He thought he had banished violence as savage as this from his life once and for all, but now it had searched him out again like an old enemy who refused a truce. Why Maggie? Who could have done this to her?

The police, summoned by a neighbour in the mews who was not quite brave enough to answer Steadman's call for help, but alarmed enough to call in the law, had burst into the investigator's house finding him cradling the dead body of his partner in his arms, his bare chest soaked in her blood. They had regarded him warily, listening gravely to his story, but ready to pounce at the slightest indication of aggression.

An ambulance had taken away the mutilated body and the hours that followed were filled with questions, questions,

questions. Who was the dead person? What had been her relationship to him? Had they quarrelled? Was the business going well? Were they lovers? Describe exactly what had happened. Again. Again. What had their quarrel been about? Had there *never* been disagreements in their partnership? What had their *latest* conflict been over? What cases were they currently working on? When was the last time he'd seen her before tonight? Describe again what had happened. What time had he woken? Why hadn't he phoned for the police? Was she alive when he had found her? Start at the beginning again.

His temper had flared then subsided. He was still in shock and the questions – the situation – seemed unreal. The small house appeared to be filled with moving figures, hostile, disbelieving faces. Their attitude towards him seemed to change imperceptibly as the hours wore on and answers he gave them matched answers he'd given earlier. They allowed him to shower and dress, then two detectives accompanied him to the agency in Gray's Inn Square where all three searched through recent files, looking for any clue in recent cases that might shed some light on the gruesome murder. One of the questions uppermost in their minds was why Maggie Wyeth's murderer should crucify her to her partner's front door. Could their agency have helped convict someone in the past, and now this lunatic was taking his revenge? Other policemen were going over Maggie's Highgate home with a fine-tooth comb at the same time, looking for such evidence, but they, like the two detectives with Steadman, found no leads.

Business hours were approaching when they finally left Steadman alone in Maggie's office, his mind weary with fatigue and his senses still dulled by shock. They asked him to come to New Scotland Yard to make a statement later on in the day, and warned him not to say too much to the Press at this stage of the investigation, who they felt sure would soon be on to him. And they warned him not to leave the city without telling them of his destination first.

Sue found him there when she arrived for work. The door to Maggie's office was open and, still in her coat and shaking the rain from her umbrella, Sue put her head around the door, expecting to see Maggie. She looked at Steadman's dishevelled figure in bewilderment.

'Oh, I thought it was Mrs Wyeth. Would you . . .'

'Come in, Sue.' Steadman cut off her words, barely glancing at the girl.

Sue was puzzled, then concerned, as she entered the room and drew nearer to the investigator. His eyes had an unfocused look to them.

'Are you all right, Mr Steadman? You look . . .'

'What case did Maggie have on last week, Sue?' His eyes now became clearer and fastened on the secretary's.

The question – and its intensity – surprised her. 'Er, it should be in her book. She was in court twice – er, Tuesday and Thursday, I think – and she investigated some suspected pilfering in the Myer's chain store. That was about it, I think. It's in the book.' She pointed towards the red diary lying on the desk in front of Steadman.

'Yes, I've been through it,' he said, picking up the diary and flicking through the pages again. 'Was there anything nasty going on with this pilfering business?'

'No. No, I don't think so. Mrs Wyeth had only just started on the investigation. But she should be in soon, she'll be able to tell . . .'

'Sue.' She stopped at his quiet tone. 'Mrs Wyeth won't be coming in.'

Sue stood in the centre of the room, the dripping umbrella still in her hand creating a pool of rainwater on the wood floor, her face suddenly pale. The look on Steadman's face told her she was about to hear something terrible, but she couldn't find the words to prompt him.

Steadman decided not to tell her until he'd learned as much as possible about Maggie's activities during the last week or so, for he knew the shock to his secretary would prevent further questioning. 'Try and think, Sue. Was Maggie involved in any-thing else while I was away?'

She shook her head, then froze. 'Well, there was another case, but . . .'

Steadman waited, but the girl seemed reluctant to go on. 'You've got to tell me, Sue. It could be important.'

'She wanted to tell you herself when you got back. She asked me not to say anything.'

'Please tell me, Sue.' There was frustration in Steadman's voice.

'The man . . . the man who came to see you last week. Mr Goldblatt? I think Mrs Wyeth was working on something for him.'

'Christ!' The girl jumped as Steadman's fist hit the desk. 'I told her I didn't want to handle that!' he shouted.

'She . . . she said we weren't busy, that we could easily fit it in. It was only tracing a missing person.' Sue felt un-comfortable for she felt a strong loyalty towards both her employers.

'I'm sure Mrs Wyeth will explain . . .'

'She won't though. She's dead!' The investigator regretted his anger immediately as Sue's face broke into lines of distress. He stood up and walked around the desk to her. 'I'm sorry, I shouldn't have told you like that.' He put two hands on her shoulders and guided her towards a chair.

'How did it happen?' she asked as she searched for a handkerchief in her pocket. 'She was fine on Thursday morning after court. There didn't seem to be anything wrong at all.'

'Was that the last time you saw her?' His voice was gentle now.

'Yes, Thursday morning.' She dabbed at her eyes with the handkerchief. 'She told me she would be out that afternoon and probably most of Friday. What happened, Mr Steadman? How did she die?'

Steadman hesitated, but realized the newspapers would carry the story even if the more grisly details were left out.

44

'She was murdered. Last night. That's why I have to know her movements last week.'

'Murdered? But who . . . ?'

'We don't know, Sue. The police will probably want to question you later today.'

Steadman tried to comfort the girl as her shoulders shook with sudden grief.

'When did Mrs Wyeth see Goldblatt?' he asked after her sobs had become more controlled.

'On the same day you did. She arranged to see him at his hotel that afternoon.'

'Which hotel, Sue? Have you got the name?'

She nodded. 'It's in my pad. I'll get it for you.' Sue rose from the chair, still holding the crumpled handkerchief to her nose.

'Who would do it, Mr Steadman? Who would murder her?'

Steadman could give her no answer. He doubted if he even wanted to find out. Somehow he knew it would lead to even more death.

The hotel was in North-West London, close to Belsize Park, a modern, motor motel, the kind favoured by businessmen who spent only a week or so in town, then moved on to other parts of the country. It was central to London and anonymous – ideal for members of organizations such as Mossad.

Steadman paid the cabbie and strode purposefully through the swing-doors into the hotel's reception area. He had left Sue in the capable hands of Sexton. The older detective had arrived with Steve just as Sue had been finding Goldblatt's address for him, and Steadman had explained to all three exactly what had happened to Maggie. There had been more hysterics from Sue and Steve had gone deathly white, but Sexton had taken it all in his stride. He had been stunned, of that there was no doubt, but experience and acceptance of the ills of the world had enabled him to cast emotion to one side for the moment, for he was needed to calm the others. The retired policeman had wanted to accompany Steadman to the Mossad agent's hotel, but his employer had insisted he stay behind and do his best, under the circumstances, to carry on the business as normal. His firmness would also be needed to keep the Press at bay. Sexton had accepted his role without argument.

The hotel receptionist eyed Steadman coolly. The investigator realized his appearance was unkempt, the stubble of an unshaven chin, the open-necked shirt, and the signs of a sleepless night apparent in his face, making him an unwelcome guest; but he was in no mood for offended hotel receptionists.

'You have a Mr Goldblatt staying here. What room is he in?'

The authority in Steadman's voice allowed no dissent from the man behind the desk. The receptionist quickly ran a finger down the guest list.

'Room 314, sir. Third floor. I'll give Mr Goldblatt a call and let him know you're here. What name shall I say?'

'Don't bother,' Steadman told him as he turned away and walked towards the lifts.

'Just a minute, sir,' the receptionist called out, but the lift doors were already opening, disgorging a group of businessmen, and Steadman had stepped in behind them. The receptionist hastily picked up the phone and dialled a number.

The lift reached the third floor and the doors opened smoothly. Steadman stepped into the carpeted corridor and looked for room numbers. A door further down opened and the Mossad agent's figure appeared. He raised an arm in surprise towards Steadman.

The detective walked towards him, his eyes fixed firmly on the Israeli's. The Mossad agent was still in shirt-sleeves and clearly had not expected a visitor so early in the morning.

'I'm pleased you have come, Mr . . .' His voice wavered as he recognized the look in Steadman's eyes. It reminded him of his old instructor's look when one of Goldblatt's companions had shot a fellow trainee in the throat with a machine-gun through carelessness; the veteran instructor had beaten his pupil to a pulp for wasting a badly needed Israeli life. That same cold look was now in Steadman's eyes.

He felt strangely powerless to prevent Steadman striking him, for the look held him rigid. The blow sent him reeling back into the room. He rolled over on his back and came to his knees, but Steadman's foot sent him over again. Goldblatt sprawled on his back then felt himself lifted by his shirt-front. 'Steadman, don't . . .' he cried out, but his words were cut off by a vicious slap in the face. His head shot to one side, then to the other, as Steadman brought his hand sharply back.

'You used her, you bastard!' Steadman shouted down into the agent's face. 'You used Lilla and you used me. Now you've killed Maggie, too!'

'Steadman, what are you saying?'

'Maggie!' Steadman screamed. 'You killed her!'

The Israeli agent was thrown to the floor again and Steadman raised his fist to bring it down into the upturned face.

'Enough, Steadman. Please do not move!' The command came from the bedroom doorway.

Steadman swung his head round and saw the woman standing there, a small but long-barrelled Beretta in her hand and aimed at his chest. He recognized her as the woman he had seen with Goldblatt in the car the week before.

'Please don't make me shoot you,' she pleaded, her eyes nervously glancing at Goldblatt. Steadman knew she meant it, for the gunfire would make little noise: it was Mossad's custom to use bullets carrying light powder loadings to reduce their blast. The only problem for them would be the disposal of his corpse, but with the help of others, that could be arranged without too much difficulty. He stepped away from the recumbent Mossad agent and towards the woman, ready to pounce at her slightest distraction.

Her long, black hair falling to her shoulders and dark skin, gave her a seductive attractiveness. The man's bathrobe she wore – obviously Goldblatt's – somehow heightened that attractiveness.

47

'It's all right, Hannah,' Goldblatt said hastily, wiping blood from the corner of his mouth. 'Don't shoot him. Yet.'

The Israeli staggered to his feet and went to the door, looking into the hallway before he closed it. No one had been disturbed. He walked back to Steadman, keeping behind him. He ran skilful, searching hands down the investigator's body, then straightened when satisfied there were no concealed weapons. He walked around to the woman called Hannah and took the gun from her hand, keeping it pointed at Steadman.

'Now, explain. Why did you do this?' he said.

'Don't you know what you've done?' Steadman asked angrily.

Goldblatt shook his head. 'Please explain.'

'You used my partner to find your missing agent, didn't you?'

'She came to us.'

'But I refused to work for you!'

'That was your choice, not hers. She wanted to take the job on. She said you could be persuaded once you saw it was just another routine commission.'

'Routine? With Mossad?' Steadman shook his head in disgust.

'What has happened to your partner, Mr Steadman?' It was the woman who spoke.

Steadman's eyes shifted to her. 'She was murdered last night. I found her nailed to my door. Her tongue had been torn out.' He said the words coldly, stifling the emotion he felt.

The woman closed her eyes and seemed to sway. Goldblatt reached out a hand to steady her, but he was too experienced to let the gun drift away from the investigator's direction.

'Why was this done to her?' he said to Steadman.

'You tell me,' came the bitter reply.

'But did they leave no message? Have they not contacted you?'

'They? Who would *they* be, Goldblatt?'

'It must have been Gant.'

'Why should he have done this to Maggie?'

'Perhaps she got too close, found out too much.'

'But why do that to her?'

'As a warning, Mr Steadman.'

'To me? But I wanted nothing to do with it!'

'Gant must know of your past association with Mossad.' The Israeli lowered his eyes briefly. 'Your partner must have told him.'

The realization hit Steadman hard. Maggie must have been frightened or tortured into disclosing that information. He clenched his fist and would have leapt at Goldblatt at that moment, gun or no gun, had not the woman suddenly burst into tears.

'That poor woman. Oh God, forgive us!' She slumped down on to one of the room's armchairs. Goldblatt lowered the gun.

'You see the evil of these people, Mr Steadman? You see what they will do to achieve their ends?'

'And what about you bastards? What do you do to achieve yours?'

'Not this. We do not make war on innocents.'

'But they get killed anyway.'

Goldblatt walked over to the room's other armchair and sat, no longer caring if the investigator attacked him again.

'Forgive us, Mr Steadman. We did not think they would harm a British citizen,' he said.

The anger had drained from Steadman. He had known people like these Mossad agents. They were mostly decent, dedicated people; their one common fault – to him – was their fanaticism towards Israel's cause.

He walked to the window and looked down on the busy street below. The drizzle had stopped and already fumes from the traffic were filling the air. 'Tell me exactly what happened when she contacted you,' he said quietly.

Goldblatt glanced at Hannah and an agreement seemed to pass between them. 'She came here to the hotel and we told her of Baruch's disappearance,' Goldblatt said. 'We were doubtful of using your agency after our meeting, Mr Steadman, but Mrs Wyeth convinced us you would see reason once the case was underway. And she thought perhaps you would not even have to know of it if Baruch could be found quickly. She said you were busy in the North.'

'But I'd have seen the books eventually,' said Steadman.

'By then – hopefully – it wouldn't have mattered.'

Goldblatt paused, but Steadman's expression urged him on. 'We told her of Baruch's contact with Edward Gant and how he had disappeared shortly after. She said she could start by making enquiries at Gant's London office to see if Baruch had visited him that day. A commissionaire, a receptionist – anyone in the building might recognize him if we could provide her with a photograph. It would be somewhere to start, anyway. She said she would check out the staff at the hotel where he had been staying. They might have seen something on that day and a few pound notes here and there would probably help them remember. She left after we had given her a thorough description of Baruch and an agenda of his activities since he'd been in this country. We told her as much as we could but, of course, not everything. Within twenty-four hours we had a photograph of Baruch – it was flown over from Israel – and this we gave to her on Wednesday. Since then, we have heard nothing.'

'Just how much did you tell her, Goldblatt?'

'We told her Baruch's mission was to make an arms deal with Gant.'

'And not that Gant is on your assassination list!'

'But he is not! We are merely investigating his dealings with terrorists.'

'My God,' Steadman scoffed, 'I could almost believe you.'

'Mr Steadman.' It was Hannah who spoke now. 'We did not realize the danger to your friend. We were desperate. It is not easy for our agents to operate in this country and we had used up all our resources to find Baruch. We thought her neutrality would protect her.'

'You were wrong!'

'Yes, we know that now. But doesn't this murder make you want to help us?'

'Help you?' Steadman shook his head in wonder. 'If – and I mean *if* – Maggie was killed by Gant, then the whole point of nailing her to my door was to serve as a warning for me to keep my nose out. And it worked!'

'But surely you will avenge her death?' Goldblatt was on his feet. 'Surely you will help us now?'

'Oh no. I've had my share of bloodletting in the name of revenge. Those days are over for me.'

The two Israeli agents stared at him in disbelief. 'You will let him get away with this murder?' Goldblatt said. 'What has happened to you, Steadman? How can a man be this way?'

'In this country we have a police force to find murderers,' Steadman told him evenly.

'You will tell the police of us?' The gun in Goldblatt's hand was raised towards the investigator again.

'I'll tell them everything I know.' Steadman saw the knuckles on the hand whiten.

'David. It would be wrong.' Hannah reached up and placed a gentle hand on Goldblatt's arm. After a few seconds' hesitation, the gun was lowered again.

'You are right,' Goldblatt said. 'Go then, Steadman. You are wrong about us, but we will never convince you of that now. I have pity for you.'

Steadman stood in silence, a tight smile on his face. It was ironic, he thought. A battle was going on inside him. These people didn't understand that he *wanted* to help them. Old fires had been rekindled, Maggie's death had stirred up feelings he had thought of as long buried; and now the struggle was to quench those fires, to remember the tragedies these feelings had led to in the past.

'You would do well not to mock us, Mr Steadman.' Goldblatt had mistaken the meaning behind the investigator's smile. His voice was menacing and his grip on the gun was rigid.

With a sigh, Steadman walked from the room. 'Go to hell,' he said mildly as he closed the door.

4

'It is becoming more and more obvious that a rift in public opinion is gradually widening, each individual going to the Right or Left as it suits them.'

'We shall have friends who will help us in all the enemy countries.'

ADOLF HITLER

Pope was waiting for Steadman when he returned to his house. The investigator had decided not to go back to the agency; he needed sleep and time to think.

He was surprised there were no reporters loitering as he pushed the key into the latch and twisted. A crucifixion in a London street was just the story to whet their ghoulish appetites. He went straight to the kitchen, poured himself a large vodka, and carried it through to the lounge. He had taken off his jacket and slumped into an armchair before he noticed the overcoated figure sitting on the sofa.

'Good morning, Mr Steadman. May I call you Harry?' The voice was gruff but contained a mixture of politeness and amusement. The man looked powerful, but in a gross

53

way – the muscles had long been covered by layers of fat.

'My name is Nigel Pope.' The big man leaned forward with effort and proffered an open wallet towards Steadman. 'British Intelligence,' he said, almost apologetically.

Steadman barely glanced at the perspex-covered identity card in its frame of leather, wondering how they had got on to Mossad so quickly.

The wallet was flicked shut and returned to an inside breast pocket of the man's suit. 'I let myself in, I hope you don't mind.'

Steadman settled resignedly back in his chair and sipped his vodka. 'What has my partner's death got to do with Security?'

Pope gave the investigator a reproving look. 'What has Israeli Intelligence got to do with Mrs Wyeth's death?'

'How did you find out about that?'

'Why didn't you tell the police about your agency's connections with Mossad?' Pope countered.

'We don't have any connections with them! I only found out this morning that Maggie had accepted a commission from Mossad! I was going to tell the police that.'

'A man named Goldblatt came to your office and saw you, in particular, a week ago. We know he is a Mossad agent.'

'He wanted me to trace a missing agent, Baruch Kanaan. I turned the job down.'

'Harry, let me tell you what we know of you. Perhaps that way we can avoid unnecessary time-wasting between us.' Pope rose and stood with his back to the mantel, closed his eyes for a few moments, and then proceeded as though giving a lecture. 'You were born in Chichester in 1940 and had a perfectly normal childhood until your father died when you were thirteen. Your mother took in another man a year later, whom she subsequently married. But you didn't like him and he didn't much like you. You left home at fifteen much to your mother's distress and, lying about your age, worked in restaurants around London. You joined the Army in 1956 – perhaps the Suez Crisis aroused the fighting man in you – as a Junior soldier, and were trained in The Junior Infantrymen's Company in Bassingbourn. You were soon transferred into a Junior Leader's Regiment when it was realized you had some potential as an NCO but, although you later reached the rank of captain, there was something of a – what shall I say – "rebel" would be too romantic, "oddball" not quite correct. Let's just say team spirit was not one of your finer points.' Pope smiled and wagged a finger at Steadman. 'Er, yes. Ironically enough, at the age of nineteen, you were diverted into the Corps of Royal Military Police – I believe the British Army enjoys ironies, don't you? – and you became more disciplined. You spent some time in Germany and Hong Kong and, while you were there, your mother died after a long illness.' He looked at the investigator as if for affirmation.

Steadman nodded, wondering how long it had taken the fat man to memorize all this.

'Let's see, that would be in 1959?'

'Sixty,' Steadman corrected him.

'Oh yes, you were twenty then. Four years of service behind you. In '62 you married a German girl, but that lasted barely two years. It seemed she didn't like army life. Fortunately, there were no children. In '65 you joined the Intelligence Corps and there, I think, you found your niche. Leastways, you seemed contented enough for a few years. You were loaned to Israeli Intelligence in 1970, more as a means of keeping an eye on their activities than anything else, I shouldn't wonder, and you were with them for quite some time.'

'Two years,' Steadman informed the fat man needlessly.

'Yes, two years. Just about. It was while you were there that you formed an attachment with one of their operatives, a young lady by the name of Lilla Kanaan – the sister of this missing Mossad agent, Baruch.'

Attachment? The word was hardly adequate for a relationship that had run as deep as theirs.

'Correct so far, eh?' Pope enquired, a smile of satisfaction on his broad face. There was no answer from the investigator and the fat man went on. 'Well, we know you were very close.

You more or less moved into her apartment in Tel Aviv, in fact. You spent a lot of time with her and her family, who lived in Anabta, and they became the family you had been denied. I think Israeli Intelligence probably tried to persuade you to leave British Intelligence long before you witnessed the mass- acre at Lod Airport.' He looked questioningly at Steadman, but still received no response. He shrugged his huge shoulders, then went on, 'You were on your way back to England, recalled to London. Whether or not it was already on your mind to re- turn to Israel I don't know, but it seems the incident at Lod was the turning point for you. Within a few months, you had bought yourself out of the army and were back in Israel as a member of Mossad, and in time to become part of the new "revenge squad" set up by Golda Meir at the encouragement of Major-General Zwi Zamir. The killing of their athletes at the Munich Olympics had set the final seal of approval on this new outward-going organization within Israeli Intelligence and they knew your background would help them in taking their war out- side the boundaries of their own country.

'You were not easily accepted by your Jewish colleagues, but your part in the attack on the Palestine Liberation Organiz- ation's quarters in Beirut in April '73 overcame their qualms, and you more than proved your physical abilities in the training camp at Caesarea.

'You and your friend, Lilla, became part of the squad known as Heth. Your role was to set up a cover in other countries which would help the rest of the group to operate as a whole. You set up communications, rented apartments, arranged hotel reservations, provided hire cars and supplied any information concerning the local area your group was to operate in. As an Englishman, your cover was ideal, and Lilla easily passed as a European. You worked together as man and wife.

'We're fairly certain of three killings you were involved in. Abdel Hamid Shibi and Abdel Hadi Nakaa, two known PLO ter- rorists who were living in Rome, were blown to pieces in their Mercedes. The same happened to Mohammad Boudia, a key organizer of Black September; he was blown up in his Renault in Paris.

'Oh, I don't say you actually carried out the killings yourself, but you and your woman friend certainly smoothed the way for Aleph, the assassins of your little liquidation group. There are other "incidents" we're not too sure of, but it seems it was a busy year for you.'

Pope sat down again, as though his bulk had suddenly become too heavy for his legs. He looked thoughtfully at Steadman, then continued: 'Apart from these missions, you were also involved in certain arms deals for the Israelis, working from Brussels and using your old army connections for contacts. You were, indeed, valuable to The Institute – as the Central Institute for Information and Espionage is known – and to the Israeli army itself. No wonder they were sad to see you go.'

Still Steadman was silent. He wasn't surprised that British Intelligence had this information – he was impressed more by Pope's memory than knowledge – but he was growing increasingly apprehensive as to the purpose of the fat man's visit.

'It was in August that, for you, tragedy struck. Mossad was suffering from a loss of morale due to the killing of an innocent man in Lillehammer, Norway, and the capture by the authorities there of the group involved. Lilla Kanaan and yourself were not part of that misguided mission. You were both exhausted by now and your nerve needed rest. The Israelis thought they had finally located the man behind the Munich massacre, Ali Hassan Salemeh, but in fact the man they killed turned out to be a harmless waiter. In a way, it was unfortunate you hadn't been included in the mission because you might have been safely tucked away in a Norwegian prison at that time. An explosion in your Brussels' apartment injured you and killed the girl.'

The memory no longer caused Steadman's hands to shake uncontrollably, but it still seemed to drain him of any strength.

Pope quickly went on: 'When you had recovered – your

health, that is – it seems you went on the rampage. At least, you appeared to be everywhere at once: Paris, Rome, Oslo, as well as Benghazi and Beirut, and in all these places, violence occurred prior to your departure. Even the Yom Kippur war in October of that year hardly seemed to contain your energies. But then, in January '74, it all stopped.'

Pope sat back in his chair and entwined his fingers across his huge paunch. He regarded Steadman quizzically. 'Why *did* you leave Mossad at that point, Harry?'

'I thought you knew all the answers,' came the reply.

'Not all, Harry. We have two conjectures: one, that you were suddenly sick of all the violence around you; two, that you didn't wash your hands of Mossad at all.'

Steadman raised his eyebrows.

'No, you see, we think perhaps it was meant to look that way, severing all ties with Israel, returning to England and joining Mrs Wyeth's enquiry agency. Perhaps it was all a new cover for you.'

'For nearly five years?' said Steadman incredulously.

'"Sleeper" agents are valuable assets to any espionage organization. Adopt a role, carry on as a normal member of a community for as long as five, ten, fifteen years even, until the occasion to be used comes along. It's far from rare in these uneasy times.'

Steadman laughed aloud, but he felt little humour in the situation. 'Why here? There's no hostilities between Britain and Israel,' he said.

'No, there's no open aggression. But Israel knows it has to spread its net, it has to fight its country's battles in other countries. With worldwide terrorism as it is now, the Israelis have to meet it on neutral territory. They can't afford to sit back and wait for it to hit their own country! Do you think I might have a cup of tea?'

Steadman was taken aback by the sudden innocuous request.

'Tea might do you some good too, Harry. It really is awfully early to be drinking vodka, you know,' Pope said reprovingly.

Steadman placed his glass on the carpet and rose from his seat. Bemused, he walked through to the kitchen.

'What use to Mossad would I be in this country?' he called back down the hallway as he waited for the kettle to boil. Pope's massive body appeared in the small hallway, almost blocking it completely. He leaned his bulk against a wall.

'Oh, keeping an eye on the scene,' he said casually. 'Maybe keeping an eye on the arms dealings, who's trading with whom, that sort of thing. Perhaps doing a little trading yourself.'

'Why would I need a cover for that?'

'Convenience? It's not unusual for a buyer to remain anonymous to the seller in such matters. You would be the link, the go-between.'

Steadman poured boiling water into the teapot and stirred it vigorously.

'Or maybe you were merely here to observe any terrorist activities,' Pope suggested. 'London, with its great foreign student population, makes a wonderful hive for such groups. Milk but no sugar for me, Harry. And do have one yourself. You look all in.'

Steadman poured two cups and carried them down the hallway. Pope backed into the lounge before him.

'It's awfully cold in here.' Pope took his seat again, shuddering inside his huge overcoat.

'I've been away,' Steadman said and added, 'as you probably know.' He went back into the kitchen and flicked down the switch that operated the central heating. 'It'll take a while to warm up,' he said, returning to the lounge. He sat facing the fat man once again. 'Do you really believe that?' he asked Pope. 'That I'm still with The Institute, I mean.'

Pope gulped his tea and watched Steadman over the rim of his cup. After a few moments' hesitation, he said, 'Actually, no, I don't. But that's just a personal judgment, neither here nor there. As a matter of fact, I rather admire the Israelis' cause, so it wouldn't matter that much to me anyway. However, we are not going to allow the wars of other nations to be fought in our country. We've kept a close eye on you, Harry, ever since your return to England and nothing you've done has given us grounds for suspicion of any sort. Until last week, that is.'

'Look, that was the first contact I've had with Mossad for nearly five years!'

'Drink your tea, Harry, it'll get cold.'

Steadman drank until the cup was empty, then he put it aside. 'Okay, Pope,' he said abruptly. 'My partner – who was also a close friend – has been murdered. I've been interrogated by the police for most of the night, I've had to organize the office, and now I'm beat. I just want to lie down and sleep. So let's get to the point. What do you want from me?'

'Why, Harry, you left out your visit to Mr Goldblatt this morning,' Pope said smoothly.

Steadman groaned aloud. 'I wanted to beat his brains in! For getting Maggie killed!'

'Of course, Harry.'

'I told him I wasn't interested last week. He hired Maggie in spite of that.'

'Yes, we know. I spoke to your staff this morning myself after you'd left. Your secretary told me you practically threw our Mr Goldblatt out of your office last week. It could have been an act, but I don't see that there would have been much point to it. I told you, Harry, I believe you – personally.'

'Then what the hell do you want?'

'Some help from you,' the big man said mildly.

'From me? How can I help you?'

'Well, you want to find your partner's murderer, don't you?'

'No, I bloody don't!'

Pope looked at Steadman in surprise. 'Dear me, Harry! You don't really mean that.'

'Listen to me, Pope. I've seen enough killing for revenge to last me a lifetime. I've had enough. It's all burned out of me. Can you understand that?'

'But Mrs Wyeth was an innocent bystander. Surely you can't let her death go unaccounted for?'

'Can't I?'

'I think you're trying to convince yourself you can. But it won't work, Harry, I can assure you. You've had five years to get over your last bout of bloodletting, five years for that passion inside you to simmer. It's still there, make no mistake.'

'You're wrong.'

Pope smiled coldly. 'It makes no difference. You're still going to help us.' Steadman shook his head, but the big man held up a hand. 'Just hear me out first,' he said to the investigator. 'You said Goldblatt only wanted you to find out what had happened to their missing agent, Baruch Kanaan. Correct?'

Steadman nodded.

'And did they tell you his mission in England?'

'He was to contact an arms dealer to place an order for weapons,' Steadman said tiredly.

'The arms dealer was Edward Gant.'

'Yes. How did you know?'

'Gant is a man we've been watching for a very long time now. Unfortunately, he's influential, and not a man to intimidate.'

'The Israelis think he's supplying weapons to terrorists, as well as training them.'

'Oh, he is. Has been for some years.'

'You know that? And you've done nothing about it?'

'Nothing we could do. Never been caught red-handed.'

'You couldn't have warned him not to?'

Pope scoffed. 'He would have laughed in our faces, Harry. He's a very unusual man, our Mr Gant. The outrage last night is a mark of his manic confidence.'

'You *know* he killed Maggie?'

'No proof. We've put the lid on this murder for now, Harry. You won't be bothered by police, or reporters for the moment.'

'But how . . .'

'It needed to be done – just for now. Publicity is the last

thing we want at the moment. Apart from finding the missing agent, did Goldblatt want you to do any other investigating?'

'He wanted me to dig up any evidence on Gant that I could.'

'What sort of evidence?'

'His dealings with terrorists.'

'Nothing else?'

Steadman shrugged his shoulders. 'Anything I could get on him, I suppose.'

Pope took a deep breath, then quickly let the air escape. 'I don't think our friend Goldblatt has been entirely honest with you, Harry,' he said. 'True, the Israelis would like to provide proof to the British Government of Gant's clandestine dealings, but their interest goes beyond that.' The big man paused and drained the last of his cold tea. He placed the cup and saucer at his feet and dabbed at his moist lips with a neatly folded handkerchief from his overcoat pocket.

'Are you aware of the growing revival of Nazism throughout the world, Harry? Perhaps not, because it goes under many different names and guises. You may imagine such fanaticism could never become a threat again after the last World War, but you'd be wrong. It's a cancer spreading throughout the world, a parasite feeding on political unrest, poverty – and terrorist activity. Do you know, for example, that an extreme right-wing group from Belgium known as the Flemish New Order are fighting with the UDA in Ireland? They are not alone. You'll find other right-wing groups encouraging wars and becoming involved in them in many countries, supplying money, *supplying arms.*'

Steadman looked sharply at Pope. 'Gant?'

'In this country, and in America, we have several such organizations, the National Front here and the National Socialist Party in America being the more obvious. But lurking beneath these, and well in the shadows, are the more sinister factions such as Column 88, and these Hitlerite movements are growing, many joining in the common cause. I hardly need tell you of these organizations' detestation for everything Jewish. We believe Gant is at the head of one of the most powerful, but shadowy, Nazi organizations, right here in Britain. The Thule Gesellschaft.'

'That's why Mossad are interested in Gant? Not because he deals with terrorists?'

'Oh no, no. Both. One goes with the other.'

'But why this story about Baruch?'

'Because it's true. They wanted to hire you to find him – anything else was incidental. But Baruch's purpose was not to find proof of Gant's dealings with Arab terrorists, but to find out more of this Thule Society, this Thule Gesellschaft. It would seem he found out too much.'

'As did Maggie.'

'Yes, we think so. Only this kind of fanaticism could breed such killers as these. She must have unearthed something they weren't prepared to let become common knowledge.'

The investigator's shoulders slumped. 'My God, in this day and age . . .' he said wearily.

'Especially in this day and age.'

'But why didn't Goldblatt tell me the whole story? Why would he let me walk into a set-up like that without warning?'

'I should imagine he thought it safer for you not to know. He wanted to hire you for a fairly routine investigation job, not to get you involved in this Hitlerite movement.'

'It didn't protect Maggie.'

'No, they underestimated the fanatical dedication of this group. I suppose they thought using her was even safer than your becoming involved. It's all very regrettable.'

'Regrettable? What do you intend to do about it?'

'What do you intend to do, Harry?'

'Me? You're Security. It's up to you to do something.'

'We will. With your help!'

'Sorry. I want nothing to do with it.'

'Did I offer you a choice, Harry?' Pope's tone was pleasant, but there was a sinister intent to the words. 'We could get you in so many ways. Suspicion of spying for Israel would do for a start. Coupled with suspicion of murder, of course.'

'Murder? You can't . . .'

'We can, Harry, and make no mistake – we will.' All hint of pleasantness was suddenly gone. 'We'd have to let you go eventually on those counts, of course, but then we'd ruin your business in this country for you, and in most other countries as well. Law forces of the world like to co-operate nowadays, Harry. It's in all our interests.'

'Bastard!'

With an effort, the fat man leaned forward, elbows on knees, and the pleasantness came back to his features. 'Look,' he said, his voice gentle, 'I know you're just stubborn enough to resist, even if you bankrupted yourself. But take a good look at yourself. Inside, I mean. You want your partner's killers to pay, don't you? You can't ignore that old feeling inside you. You've suppressed it for years, but you can never lose it. You fought for Israel because you didn't like the way it was being oppressed. You fought because you hated to see the innocent hurt. You'll help us not because we'll force you to, but because you'll want to. You haven't lost that aggressiveness, Harry, you've just kept it smothered for some time.'

And Steadman realized the fat man was right; the urge to strike back was still in him. He wanted this man Gant to pay for Maggie's death just as he had wanted the Arab terrorists to pay for Lilla's. Maybe Pope's blackmail played some part in it, but he realized the old anger in him was the deciding factor. 'But why me?' he asked. 'You must have plenty more qualified.'

'None of our chaps fit in as nicely as you, Harry. You're a link, you see. A link between Mossad, Edward Gant – and now us. It gives us an advantage.'

'How can I help anyway? Gant knows who I am,' he said.

Pope settled back in his chair once again. 'Yes, he knows who you are, but that doesn't matter. He'll play out the game.'

'Game? This is just a game?' Steadman said incredulously.

'To someone like Gant, everything is a game. He enjoys sub-terfuge, enjoys testing his cunning against others.'

'And what's to stop him giving me the same treatment as Maggie?'

'Nothing. Except we'll be keeping an eye on you.'

'That fills me with confidence.'

Pope gave a small laugh. 'Well, you see, if he does make a move against you, we'll have him for that, won't we?'

The fat man laughed once again at the expression on Stead-man's face, his stomach quivering with enjoyment. 'No, no Harry. I don't think even our Mr Gant can risk another murder so soon. Look, we need you because there's something in the wind. Something's about to happen and we don't know what. You'll be just a small part of this. Any information you come up with will just fit into a larger picture.'

'I feel like the sacrificial goat.'

'Nonsense. I told you, you'll be under surveillance all the time – we won't let any harm come to you. We want you to go back to your Mr Goldblatt and tell him you've changed your mind. You want Mrs Wyeth's murderers to be punished. He'll believe you because he needs you. You'll contact Gant on the grounds that you have a client who wishes to buy Gant's par-ticular kind of weapons.'

'And if he refuses to deal with me?'

'He won't. He's an arms dealer and it would be too unpro-fessional not to enter discussions at least with a prospective client. He'll be curious about you too; I told you he is an arro-gant man.

'Get close to him. He'll invite you to his private testing-grounds – it's his usual custom – and that's what we want to know about. Find out as much about the place as possible and what's going on there. That's all you need to do.'

'That's all?'

Pope pushed himself to his feet, his weight making the movement an effort. 'Yes,' he said. 'For the moment. Oh, you might find time to read this.' Pope reached for a green-covered file that had been lying unnoticed by Steadman on the side-board. He handed it to the investigator. 'Not much in there I'm afraid, mostly recent stuff. Something of a mystery, our Mr Gant, but the file will provide you with some information on the man, mainly his recent dealings with the Arabs. Don't lose it, will you?'

Steadman regarded him with suspicion. None of it made sense. It just didn't add up.

'I'll see myself out, Harry. You get some rest now,' Pope said, walking to the door. His parting questions gave the investigator even more cause for puzzlement.

'Just a small thing, Harry,' the big man said. 'Have you ever heard of the Heilige Lance?'

5

Steadman slouched low in the passenger seat of the Jaguar and flexed his shoulder muscles against its soft back. He let his head loll slightly to one side and gazed up into the clear blue sky. It was one of those bright winter days, the air crisp and cold, hinting at the chill months to come, but invigorating with its keen-edged freshness.

As the car sped through country roads and busy towns, he reflected on Pope's last words to him. He had shaken his head – no, he'd never heard of the Heilige Lance, but what had that got to do with this Gant affair? The big man told him not to worry about it, it was just that the arms dealer seemed to have an interest in the Heilige Lance, which was in fact, an ancient spearhead and he, Pope, had merely wondered if Steadman had any knowledge of the relic. With a wave of his hand as if to dismiss the subject, Pope had left Steadman with an even greater feeling of unease. Yet he felt a familiar excitement running through him, an old excitement that had been lying dormant for so many years. Now that he had no choice but to be involved, his reluctance had vanished, and increased adrenaline had sharpened his senses in the way it had years before when he had been a Mossad agent. Steadman appeared to be relaxed, but his thoughts and reflexes had become acute.

David Goldblatt and his companion, Hannah, had seemed relieved but not that surprised at his return, for it had been beyond their comprehension that he could walk away from the bizarre murder of his friend and business partner. The new Israelis no longer believed in turning the other cheek; in fact, they considered it cowardice and not humility to do so, and Steadman's past record showed him to be far from cowardly. His fire had been rekindled just as a cold blast would stir dying embers. His prior rejection of them had been due to shock and his passion had now overcome that shock. They understood. They needed him.

Peppercorn, a solicitor who had handled arms contracts for Steadman in the past, had arranged the meeting between him and Gant, and it was the solicitor's Jaguar in which they were travelling now. An arms exhibition was being held by the Ministry of Defence at their military range in Aldershot and Edward Gant, along with other private arms companies, would be present with his own weapons display. It was there that Gant and Steadman would meet.

'It was surprisingly smooth, you know,' Peppercorn's words broke into Steadman's thoughts. The investigator allowed his head to incline towards the solicitor.

'What was that?' he asked.

'Getting you the pass for the exhibition. Usually takes a while with these Ministry people, wanting to know who you are, what you've got your eye on, what country is it for? That sort of thing. They got you cleared in no time at all. Have you been pulling strings with your old military chums behind my back?'

'Old connections never die, Martin,' Steadman said. He guessed Pope had smoothed the way.

'Very opportune, really. Not an easy man to get hold of, this Gant. Better for you too, to meet him on neutral ground among his competitors. Should help your bargaining power psychologically.' He pulled out to overtake a heavy goods vehicle, then gently eased back into the stream of traffic. 'Why Gant's outfit in particular, Harry? Looking for something special?'

'Very special.' Steadman straightened from his slouched position knowing they would soon be at their destination.

'Well, Gant deals in specialities, all right. For Israel, is it?'

Steadman gave the solicitor a sharp look.

'Sorry, Harry. Shouldn't have asked at this stage,' Peppercorn grinned. 'I'll bet items like Swingfires and Blowpipes are on your shopping list though.'

It was an easy enough assumption for the solicitor to make, for not only did Gant deal specifically in these kinds of wire-controlled and hand-launched missiles, but Israel had suffered heavy losses when their tanks and jets had been attacked by such weapons in the 1973 conflict with the Egyptians. The Russian Strella shoulder-launched, infra-red-seeking anti-aircraft missile, for instance, had wreaked havoc on their air force, and if Steadman was representing the Israelis as Peppercorn more than suspected, then they would naturally regard such weapons as a priority for themselves.

'You'll know soon enough, Martin, when the deal is under way,' Steadman lied. The investigator hated to use his acquaintance in this way, but the deal had to look fairly legitimate so both parties could play out their deceptions without too much embarrassment. It was a game often utilized by politically opposite governments when superficial détente was not allowed to be harmed by private knowledge on both sides; undercurrents too dangerous to be acknowledged, but nevertheless secretly acted upon. He and Gant would play out the game until either one had reached the moment to strike. Steadman prayed the advantage would be his.

The car swung off the road and halted before tall, wire-mesh gates. An army sergeant stepped from an office built to one side of the gates and peered into the car. The two men showed their passes and the soldier gave a signal for the gates to be opened. The car swept through, making towards Long Valley where the solicitor knew they would find Gant.

Steadman mentally identified the various military vehicles they passed along the route: Chieftain and Scorpion tanks; Chieftain Bridge Layers; Spartan carriers; AT105 carriers; Fox armoured cars; Shorland SB301 troop carriers. Overhead, Gazelle helicopters hovered, occasionally swooping low. He was pleased he still had some knowledge of army hardware, but knew the progress made in other areas would leave him completely bemused. Computers were used to wage wars nowadays: microwave systems to detect the enemy, lasers to beam in on them, missiles to destroy. And the enemy had its own systems to counter every phase of an attack. The human brain could no longer react swiftly enough to cope in complex electronic warfare; computers had become the generals.

Muffled sounds of explosions came to their ears as they passed through a wooded area, which had warning signs of a quarry at intervals on their left.

'The Army showing off its Chobham armour, shouldn't wonder,' Peppercorn said.

Steadman nodded. The tank armour had been a British breakthrough which provided three times greater protection than conventional steel armour. It had regenerated the life of the tank throughout the world, for missiles had all but made the vulnerable vehicle obsolescent; the new armour, a honeycomb of materials such as steel, ceramics and aluminium, added little to the weight or the cost of the tank. He could imagine the smug smiles on the faces of the British in the deep quarry below, as their armour was blasted with rockets and mortar shells for the benefit of their prospective foreign buyers.

The car soon arrived at a huge area filled with exhibition

stands proudly displaying military hardware, ranging from laser rangefinders to barbed tape, from the multi-role MRCA combat aircraft to a set of webbing, from an AR18 rifle to pralidoxime mesylate counter-nerve gas tablets.

Peppercorn drove the Jaguar into the allocated parking area and the two men stepped out. The noon sun was high and harsh in the sky, feebly trying to warm the autumn air but succeeding only in stealing the dampness from it. The solicitor reached back inside the car and pulled out an overcoat which he quickly donned.

'Deceptive, this weather,' he muttered. 'Catch a cold without knowing it.'

Steadman smiled. If Peppercorn knew the true nature of the man they were about to meet, his blood would run even colder.

They trudged across the field and past a long stand where foreign officers, diplomats and civil servants sat on wooden chairs, observing the antics of Strikers, Spartans, Scimitars and Scorpions as they paraded before them. As they walked, Peppercorn asked, 'Tell me, Harry, why Gant in particular? There are plenty of other dealers who sell similar weapons and as far as I know, Gant has never dealt with the Israelis before.' He smiled at Steadman and added, 'Assuming your client is from Israel, of course. The contracts I've been involved in personally as far as Gant is concerned have been for Iran and some of the African states. To my knowledge, he's never been interested in selling to Israel.'

'Gant manufactures a wider range of more specialized items than most,' Steadman answered, 'from missiles to anti-terrorist devices. My client requires both and thinks he'll get a better deal by buying from the same source.' A little too pat, Steadman thought, but the solicitor seemed satisfied.

Peppercorn was too professional to press for the identity of Steadman's client any further, for that would soon be made clear the moment negotiations began; and besides, Steadman had virtually confirmed his suspicions in his last statement.

Who else would he be buying for – the Arabs? Hardly, with his past associations.

'Ah, there he is,' Peppercorn said, pointing ahead.

The investigator's gaze followed the pointing finger and he saw a group of men gathered around a green-uniformed figure demonstrating a shoulder rocket-launcher. The uniform was unfamiliar to Steadman and he assumed it was merely worn by Gant's demonstrators to give individuality to his company.

'Which one is Gant?' he asked Peppercorn.

'The tall one in the middle. The one talking to the girl.'

Steadman had not noticed the girl in his eagerness to catch sight of the arms dealer, but now he briefly wondered what connections she could possibly have with someone like Gant. His eyes quickly flicked to the man beside her.

Gant was tall, even taller than Steadman, towering over the assembled group, who must have been foreign buyers judging by their dark-skinned features. His body was thin and seemed stiff, as though having little flexibility. The assumption was wrong, for as Gant turned to answer a question from one of the group, his body swivelled with a controlled grace. It was a small movement, but Steadman was a professional observer and the action revealed the man's hidden suppleness. As they advanced, Gant's attention became focused on them. He stood without moving for several moments and Steadman could feel himself being scrutinized with cold efficiency. He returned the stare and suddenly a chill ran through him. It was inexplicable, but he felt as though he were being drawn into a spider's web; and the man before him was well aware of the thought.

The visual link was broken when Gant turned to his prospective clients and excused himself. He broke away from the group and came forward to meet Steadman and the solicitor. Their eyes locked again and Steadman was only vaguely aware of the man in military uniform who followed the arms dealer.

Gant stopped two yards away from them so they had to keep walking to meet him. Steadman saw his eyes were light grey and he thought he detected a mocking amusement in them. The tall man's face was long and angular, high cheek-bones and hollowed cheeks giving it a slightly cadaverous appearance; his nose was strong with a firm bridge, and his high forehead, with short, light-brown hair swept back from it, held few wrinkles. He seemed younger than his years and emanated a strength that belied his gaunt frame. Only his neck gave an indication of the ravage the years had taken. It was long, therefore not easy to disguise with collar and tie, and its hollowed and wrinkled flesh caused a faint revulsion in Steadman.

'Good morning, Peppercorn,' Gant said, his eyes not leaving Steadman's. 'And this is Mr Steadman?' He raised a hand towards the investigator and once again, Steadman noticed the amusement flicker in them.

Reluctantly, Steadman grasped the proffered hand and returned the hardness of Gant's grip. The investigator loosened his hold, but the arms dealer held it firm and he was forced to resume his own pressure. There were no secrets between them as they stood that way for several seconds. Gant seemed to see into him and mocked what he saw; Steadman returned the unspoken challenge and even allowed his own glint of amusement to show. He noticed there were many tiny scars around the arms dealer's cheeks and mouth, only visible at such close range, and he briefly wondered what kind of accident would cause such a proliferation.

His hand was abruptly released and the investigator was uncertain if he hadn't imagined the whole exchange.

'This is Major Brannigan,' Gant said, inclining his body towards the soldier who had followed him. The major leaned forward and gave a swift handshake to Steadman and Peppercorn. He was a few inches shorter than Gant, and Steadman judged him to be in his early forties. Whereas he had detected the mockery in the arms dealer's eyes, Brannigan's showed an unrelenting hardness.

'And this is Miss Holly Miles who is taking advantage of her distant relationship to my late wife,' Gant said, stepping aside to allow a view of the girl who had followed both men and had been hidden by their tall figures.

'Louise Gant and my mother were cousins – of sorts,' she smiled apologetically and Steadman was surprised to hear her American accent, but then he remembered Gant's wife had come from the United States. He nodded at her and she acknowledged with a broader smile, flicking her long yellow hair to one side and behind an ear with delicate fingers. He noticed the Pentax draped around her neck.

'Pictures? Here?' he said quizzically.

'I'm a freelance writer,' she explained with a grin. 'I'm doing a feature on arms dealers for one of the Sunday magazines.'

'She used her flimsy connections with my family to persuade the magazine to give her the commission,' Gant interrupted, but his mocking tones now had more amusement in them than malice. Nevertheless there was a disquieting quality to his voice, a rasping sibilance that was slight, but seemed to create unease in the people around him. 'Major Brannigan is keeping an eye on her, making sure she doesn't photograph the wrong things.'

Brannigan did not seem in the least amused.

'Now, Mr Steadman,' Gant said, his voice suddenly becoming brusque. 'Peppercorn tells me you have a client who is in the market for certain types of weapons which I have a reputation for producing rather well.'

'That's right,' Steadman answered, his attention now diverted back to the arms dealer.

'May we establish from the start who your client is?'

'I'm afraid that will have to wait until I'm satisfied you can meet all our requirements,' Steadman countered.

'Very well, that's not unusual. Can you tell me specifically what you are looking for?'

'There's quite a list. I have our broad order for you here.' Steadman produced an envelope containing a detailed list, compiled by himself and Goldblatt, of armaments and defensive equipment that Israel would logically need but were, at the moment, obtained from other sources. It had a bias towards the type of weapons produced in Gant's factories. He handed it to the arms dealer. 'I believe you manufacture most of these items.'

Gant scrutinized the list, nodding occasionally. 'Yes, most of these are in our range,' he said, and Steadman suddenly found it difficult to believe it was all a charade. The arms dealer appeared to be perfectly sincere. 'I have a few other items, in fact, that you might also be interested in. Our new laser sniper rifle, for example, accurate up to a distance of half-a-mile. Our submachine-gun, similar to the Ingram but far more accurate, made with many plastic components and very cheaply mass-produced.' The mockery seemed to return to Gant's eyes then, and he said, 'I also have certain kinds of missiles, small and convenient to launch, but with enough power to bring down a Jumbo jet.'

There seemed to be some special significance to the words, for Gant said them slowly and deliberately, his gaze fixed steadily on Steadman and throwing out some kind of challenge.

'Sounds interesting,' he said, and was suddenly aware that the exchange had not gone unnoticed among the other members of the small group. There was a tenseness in their silence. Even the girl had a puzzled expression on her face.

'You think your client could have a use for such a weapon?' Gant asked, raising his eyebrows.

'Possibly. It would depend on the price,' Steadman answered.

'Of course. Would you like to see it?'

'Yes, I would.'

'Difficult to demonstrate, of course.' Gant gave a small laugh and Steadman smiled back agreeably. 'But I think we can show you its range and power. Why don't you ring me at my office tomorrow and we'll fix something. Peppercorn has the number.'

'That would be fine.'

'In the meantime, I'll go through your list and work out some figures for you. I take it your client isn't too frightened of figures, is he?' Again the mocking tones.

'It takes more than that,' said Steadman, still smiling.

'Yes, I'm sure. You must excuse me now. I'm afraid our visitors from Latin America are rather demanding today,' he gestured towards the gathering he had just left, 'and I think they're in a buying mood. And you, too, Miss Miles, will have to forgive my rudeness. I'm afraid business transactions of this nature might embarrass your magazine. If not, perhaps our government, if they saw it in print. Why not take the time to tell Mr Steadman the nature of your article on armament sales and show him some of the nasty weapons you've discovered here today. He may have a view on the subject.'

With one last glance at Steadman, he turned and walked back to his group of impatient foreign buyers.

'Er, yes, I'm afraid I have certain duties to perform, too,' Major Brannigan suddenly said. 'I'll have to take your camera with me, though. I'm sure you've got enough shots for today, anyway.' He held a hand out and, with a shrug, the girl lifted the Pentax from her neck and gave it to the major. 'Thank you,' Brannigan said. 'I'll send it down to the sergeant on the gate and you can collect it when you leave.' With that, he strode briskly away.

'Well, that was short and sweet,' said Peppercorn turning to Steadman and the girl. 'I think Gant will show you some things that'll surprise you, Harry.'

'I don't doubt it,' the investigator said wryly.

'Now then, Miss Miles,' the solicitor said, turning on the charm. 'It's very rare to find such blue-denimed beauty at these functions. Makes a welcome change from khaki. Why don't we all wander down to the big top and have a little drink?'

The girl glanced at Steadman and he said, 'I could use one.'

'Okay, so could I. Lead on.'

Once inside the large tent, Peppercorn threw himself in quest of drinks into the crowd that pressed itself to the bar, leaving Steadman and the American journalist alone.

'Are you really a distant relative of Gant's?' Steadman asked her, finding her face an agreeable distraction from the tension before.

She laughed. 'Well, let's say my mother was a distant cousin to Mr Gant's late wife. I'm surprised he still allowed me to interview him, though. These arms dealers are usually shy people.'

'Yes, publicity is one thing they don't need. I'm surprised he did.'

'It took a long, long time, I can tell you. Then suddenly, last week, right out of the blue, he agreed.'

'What changed his mind?' Steadman asked, puzzled.

'I've no idea. Perhaps his wife's memory stirred his conscience; he had little enough to do with her relatives when she was alive.'

'Do you know what she died of.'

'Yes. She was killed in a car crash.'

'Have you found out much about him. He seems a very private man.'

'He is. But I've spent some days with him and he's let me photograph most of what I want. He suddenly seems to want to exploit his name – well maybe not quite his name, but the new weapons he's producing, at least.' She frowned and bit the nail on the small finger of her right hand. 'I don't know, it's as if he's suddenly emerging from his dark shell, and actively seeking publicity.'

The idea somehow worried Steadman. Why should a man like Edward Gant, whose business transactions had always been kept in the shadows, suddenly emerge into the public eye? It made little sense.

He decided to change the subject. 'How long have you been in England?' he asked.

'Oh, about six months now. I used to roam the world before that, writing stories, taking pictures to go with them. I used to work for a syndicate, but now I prefer to find my own commissions. It makes me feel more free to come and go as I like.'

Peppercorn returned at that moment, carrying a Campari for

the girl, vodka for Steadman and a gin drowned in tonic for himself, all precariously held in two hands.

'Look, Harry,' he said urgently. 'I've just bumped into a couple of people I know. It could lead to a nice little bit of business for me so I've rather selfishly arranged to have a spot of lunch with them. I hope you don't mind?'

Steadman shook his head, taking the Campari and vodka from his friend's outstretched fingers. 'Don't worry about it.'

'I could meet you back here afterwards and take you back to town?' the solicitor said anxiously.

'It's okay. I'll catch a train.'

'I could give you a lift,' said the girl.

'Ah, there you are, all settled.' Peppercorn grinned with satisfaction.

'Fine,' said Steadman, taking a swallow of his drink. The vodka scorched his throat, but it felt good.

'Right, must get back to them, Harry,' said the solicitor. 'I'll get my secretary to give you Gant's telephone number.' He was already moving away. 'Let me know how you get on and when you want me to do my bit. 'Bye for now, er, Miss Miles. Hope to see you again.'

The girl chuckled at the solicitor's retreating figure as it backed into a black-skinned dignatory who eyed him with wide-eyed alarm.

'Thanks for the lift,' Steadman said as her attention returned to him.

'I have to report back to the magazine, anyway. They'll want to know my progress.' She looked directly into Steadman's eyes. 'Tell me about yourself. Have you always been involved in the sale of weapons?'

'No, not always. I've spent a good portion of my life in the army.'

Holly raised her eyebrows. 'You don't look the military type,' she said.

Steadman grinned, presuming the girl meant it as a compliment.

78

'What made you leave?' she asked, sipping at the Campari.

'Oh, I decided I'd had enough of the British Army. There were other things to do.'

'Like buying and selling arms?'

'Among other things. I eventually joined an enquiry agency.'

'An enquiry agency? You're a gumshoe?'

Steadman laughed. 'It's a long time since I've been called that.'

Holly laughed with him. 'Sorry. You don't look like Sam Spade either.'

'Not many of us do. As a matter of fact, my partner . . .' He suddenly broke off and Holly saw the pain in his eyes.

'Is something wrong?' she asked.

Steadman took a large swallow of vodka, then answered, 'I was going to say my partner is a woman. She's dead now.'

'I'm sorry, Harry.'

He shrugged.

'Was it recent?' she asked, then was puzzled by the strange smile on his face and the hardness in his eyes.

'Very,' he replied. 'Let's drop it, eh? Tell me more about your article. Any startling discoveries about Gant?' The question was put lightly, but Holly sensed its seriousness.

'Oh, I haven't got that close. Everything I've seen, everything he's told me, all seems studied, as though he's only revealing a top layer. I get the feeling there's plenty more layers underneath. Usually, when you do this kind of in-depth study of a person, you find out certain things by accident – a slip of the tongue, or maybe they get carried away with their own reminiscences. But Edward Gant's information has been guarded all along. I just can't get under the surface.'

'You've been to his home?'

'The one near Guildford, yes. I spent two days there and he's invited me back again. It's a small mansion in about six or seven acres of grounds; very quiet, very private.'

'Does he have another place?'

'Well, it seems so. When I was there he seemed to have a

constant stream of visitors – some were important people, too – and I did hear them making arrangements for some kind of get-together in his home on the west coast. Gant was deliberately vague when I asked him about it though, but he did say it was a testing-ground for some of his more powerful weapons.'

'Do you know exactly where it is?'

'No. I asked directly, but he told me that in the arms business and especially with innovatory weapons, testing-sites were strictly private and their locations, as far as possible, kept secret. He clammed up after that.'

'These visitors. You said some were important.'

'You're kind of curious, aren't you? I guess that goes with the job, huh?'

'I guess it does,' Steadman said. 'Really, it's just that I want to know as much about Gant as possible so I can make sure I get a good deal for my clients. It might help to know his connections, that's all.'

'Okay. 'Nough said. A couple of them were politicians – minor ones, I may add. The others I recognized as industrialists and a few of your City guys. I can't put names to their faces, though.'

'Never mind. Would you like another?' Steadman pointed to the girl's empty glass.

'Er, no. I think I'd like to get back to town now. Are you ready to leave?'

Steadman drained his glass, then nodded. As he took Holly's arm and guided her through the crowded tent, the morning's displays over, the preliminary discussions having taken place, he caught sight of Major Brannigan listening politely to a foreign visitor. The major caught his eye, but gave no acknowledgment.

Steadman and the girl left the tent and the major's eyes followed them until they had disappeared from view.

Holly led the investigator towards her car, a bright yellow Mini. They climbed in and Holly snapped on her seat-belt. The car threaded its way through the other parked vehicles and turned into the gravelled roadway. It picked up speed and they left the display area with its business-like stands and array of sophisticated machinery of death.

'Tell me, Harry,' Holly said. 'Do you ever get a conscience about the weapons you buy?'

'Occasionally,' he replied, 'but greed generally manages to overcome it.'

She looked at him quickly, surprised at his rancour.

'I'm sorry,' she apologized. 'I didn't mean to sound high-minded.'

He studied her profile for a few moments, then said, 'I'm sorry, too. I didn't mean to snap. It's really a question of who you're buying for. There are certain countries and groups I would have nothing to do with, while there are others I have every sympathy for. Of course, dealers aren't supposed to have sympathy for any particular cause, it should be strictly business, but there are laws governing just who they can sell to.'

'And do you have a sympathy for the cause of the people you are negotiating for?'

'I used to,' was all he would say.

The road was winding through the wooded area now and the ground on either side was thick with fallen leaves. Steadman turned to the girl again and could not help glancing down at her body, her long legs bent to accommodate the slightly cramped space of the Mini. Her wrists were slender, yet handled the wheel firmly, and there was a quiet strength about her that had not been apparent on first sight. She suddenly turned her head towards him, feeling his gaze on her, and for a brief moment, something passed between them. Her attention went back to the road and he wondered if he had only imagined the under-standing in her look.

He, too, turned his head back towards the road, and it was at that moment that the tank roared from the trees on their left.

6

'Brutality is respected. *Brutality and physical strength. The plain man in the street respects nothing but brutal strength and ruthlessness – women, too, for that matter, women and children. The people need wholesome fear. They want to fear something. They want someone to frighten them and make them shudderingly submissive. Haven't you seen everywhere that after boxing-matches, the beaten ones are the first to join the party as new members? Why babble about brutality and be indignant about tortures? The masses want that. They need something that will give them a thrill of horror.'*

ADOLF HITLER

The girl saw the Chieftain emerging from the trees a fraction of a second later than Steadman. Instinctively, her foot jammed down on the accelerator and the little car surged forward in an effort to escape the fifty-two tons of crushing metal.

Steadman automatically pushed himself away from his side of the car, thankful that he wasn't restricted by a seat-belt, and taking care not to crowd the girl. Their lives depended on her reaction. The tank loomed larger in his window-framed vision until it filled the rectangular shape completely, and the investigator clenched his teeth against the anticipated impact. But the blackness left the window nearest to him and he knew there might just be a chance to squeeze by the cumbersome monster.

The Chieftain had been too close, though, and it smashed into the back of the Mini, slewing the car round, mercifully pushing rather than crushing. The screaming of tearing metal and shattered glass filled their ears as the girl fought to control the car's spin. It slid across the road and spun into a tree, almost facing the way they had just come.

Again it was Steadman's side which took the brunt of the crash, but he had steadied himself by pushing one hand against the dashboard and the other around the back of the driver's seat. His head snapped back with the impact, but the car's buckled metal failed to touch him.

He reached for the girl whose head hung low on her chest. She still clutched the steering-wheel, her seat-belt preventing her from being tossed around. He took her chin and her head came up and turned towards him. With relief, he saw she had not been hurt, but was stunned by the impact. Her eyes were wide and looked questioningly at him.

'Bloody fools!' Steadman shouted, the anger in him now rising over the shock. He looked through the windscreen at the green goliath completely blocking the road in front of them. 'Why didn't they check to see if the road was clear before they tried to cross!' He was about to push the passenger door of the Mini open when the tank began moving backwards, the pin-jointed links of its tracks spitting up gravel from the roadway. The movement puzzled Steadman into immobility for a moment, then he saw the tank stop. Its far-side track gripped the road and began to go forward once again, the near-side track rotating at a slower pace. The Chieftain was turning towards them.

'Holly, I think . . .' he began to say, but the tank's objective became frighteningly clear. 'He's going to ram us again!'

The girl's face was horror-struck and Steadman knew he

would never have time to release her from the seat-belt and get her out of the car before the tank crushed it to pieces.

'Drive!' he screamed at her. 'Into the trees!'

Fortunately, the engine was still running, for she had dipped the clutch as she had braked, and her feet still had both pedals pressed to the floor. Her eyes suddenly seemed to focus as she realized the further danger, and she reacted to Steadman's command. Pushing the gear-lever into first, she gunned the engine and the car leapt forward. Steadman prayed the back wheel hadn't been damaged in the crash, then once again clenched his teeth as the tank loomed up ahead of them.

It seemed there would be no escaping the mountain of metal this time as it rushed towards them, completely blocking their path, but Holly wrenched the wheel hard to her left and the Mini passed beneath the long 120mm gun of the Chieftain, scraping its side against the front of the tank's right-hand tracks. Metal clanged and buckled once more as the car was knocked to one side, but Holly managed to control the sideways deflection and the car skidded into the trees, its wheels tearing at the damp earth and leaves to maintain a grip. She turned the wheel to the right to avoid a tree which was directly in their path, but it was too late, and again Steadman's side of the car took a vicious blow against its metalwork.

The Mini stopped and Holly declutched to prevent the engine stalling. Steadman glanced back through the rear window and saw that the Chieftain was swiftly turning towards them.

'For Christ's sake, move it!' Steadman knew that even if the girl got clear, his door was jammed up against the side of the tree which would mean he'd have to try and scramble out on her side. The odds weren't promising.

The girl must have realized the same, and he was thankful for her courage in staying with him. The car moved forward a few inches, then sank back into the grooves it had dug for itself. Once again, the tank completely filled Steadman's view from the rear window and seemed poised to overwhelm them.

Then the car lurched forward, the wheels spinning but gaining a small grip, enough to draw them from the crushing belly of the Chieftain. It gathered speed as the wheels found firmer ground and Steadman saw the tank hit the tree they had skidded into, tilting it as though it were on a swivel, then coming on, chasing them as an armadillo would chase a millipede.

The car's speed was limited, for Holly had to steer a careful path through the trees and undergrowth, whereas the tank had only to avoid the stoutest trees, the other less firm trees and undergrowth easily succumbing to its massive weight. Steadman urged the girl on, his eyes constantly switching from the path ahead to the tank behind. He was shocked at the audacity of the attack, at Gant's – it *had* to be Gant behind it – arrogant confidence that he could get away with two outrageous murders within just a few days. First Maggie, now him. And the girl. Three murders.

Holly's eyes were narrowed in concentration as she struggled to keep the car under control on the slippery surface of leaves, and he saw that although there was fear in her there was no panic.

The Mini suddenly bumped over a fallen branch hidden by leaves and it rose into the air, throwing the passengers forward and up. Holly's seat-belt and her grip on the wheel checked her movement, but Steadman was tossed towards the windscreen. His arm struck the window first and fortunately the glass held. His head hit the roof of the car and he was thrown back into his seat, dazed but still conscious.

The car spun round as it landed and this time Holly lost control completely. It bounced off a tree and came to rest sideways on to the advancing tank. Steadman saw that the ground sloped down into a dip on his side of the car. The engine had stalled and for a few valuable seconds, Holly was too numbed by the sudden jolt to move. Steadman shook the haze from his head and looked at the girl. Beyond her profile, he saw the Chieftain looming larger and larger. Holly quickly looked to her right and saw that the tank was only a few yards from them and she desperately reached forward for the keys in the ignition. She twisted them viciously and depressed the accelerator to the floor. The engine roared and the car lurched forward and stalled again; in her haste she had left it still in gear. The tank was only a yard away.

Steadman knew they wouldn't make it and was reaching for the release on the girl's seat-belt in a vain attempt to pull her from the car on his side, when the Chieftain tank ploughed into them.

The noise of crunching metal, the rumbling of the tank's engines, and Holly's scream combined into a terrifying sound. The car on her side rose into the air and Steadman was thrown back against the passenger door. The world outside the small windows spun round crazily as the car was pushed completely over, first on to its side, then on to its back. The trees and the sky began to spin even faster as the Mini rolled over the brink of the dip it had come to rest on. Steadman threw one arm around the back of his seat and pushed the other against the dashboard in an attempt to wedge himself as the car rolled over and over down the slope. The dip had saved their lives for that moment, for if the car hadn't plunged into it, then it would have been crushed completely under the massive bulk of the tank.

For those few nauseating seconds as the car rolled down, Steadman lost his senses. He still managed to keep his grip on the seat and the dashboard through sheer reaction, only losing that hold when the car crashed to a halt on its back. He found himself lying bundled on the upturned roof of the car when he opened his eyes. He wasn't sure if he had blacked out or his mind had just gone blank for a few moments, but instinct told him he had no time to lose. From his curled-up position inside the overturned Mini, he could see back up the slope, and the tank poised at the top, a huge metallic predator making ready to plunge for the kill.

He pulled himself around on the buckled metal and saw Holly hanging upside down, her head and shoulders against the roof, her lower body still trapped by the seat-belt. Her eyes were closed, but when he called her name, they opened and looked towards him.

'Jesus Christ!' she said.

He scrambled into a better position to reach her, barely registering the fact that no sudden pain bespoke broken bones. He pressed the button to release her, taking her weight with his arm. She slid to the roof which was now the floor.

'We've got to get out!' he told her urgently. 'The tank'll be coming down after us.' He reached past her and tried to push open the driver's door. It opened two inches then jammed solidly into the hard earth.

He quickly turned around and tried the door on his side and it opened easily. He pushed it wide and to his horror saw the Chieftain had begun its descent. This time, the Mini would be squashed flat under the impact. Steadman reached back for the girl and yanked her towards him, heedless of any harm she might have suffered in the crash. She gasped at his roughness, but threw herself forward, realizing their danger. They scrambled from the car together and the tank towered above them, its speed increased by the angle of the slope.

Holly tried to scramble to one side, but Steadman knew it was already too late. The sheer width of the tank allowed them no room for escape – they would be crushed by either of its two-foot-wide set of tracks. He grabbed her arm and threw her upwards towards the onrushing monster. She screamed in fright, not understanding his motives. He pushed her down hard into the earth, throwing a protective arm over her head, holding her there, trying to make them both as flat as possible.

Everything went black as the Chieftain rumbled over them, and Steadman pressed his face close to Holly's, exerting pressure on her with his arm to make sure she didn't try to rise in panic. The underbelly of the tank was only inches from their bodies and the smell of diesel fumes and oil was overpowering. The investigator prayed that the angle of the slope would not alter before the vehicle had passed completely over them, for if it did, the tank's rear end would become lower as the main body righted its angle, and their bodies would be scraped into the earth.

They felt the tank shudder as it ploughed into the Mini, and the screech of grinding metal threw fresh terror into them.

'Try to move upwards!' he screamed at her over the noise. 'Keep moving up, but keep low!'

They inched forward as the tank sped over them, for any distance they gained could save their lives. He saw the rectangle of daylight ahead and realized the angle was narrowing; the juddering tank was beginning to level. He closed his eyes and stopped moving forward, knowing there was nothing they could do to save themselves now. He pressed himself close to Holly, holding her head against his, his lips against her cheek.

The noise of the car being crushed rose to a crescendo and suddenly he felt all movement around them judder to a halt. The tank's engine still roared on, but the clanking links of its tracks had ceased to move. The small car's tough little body had halted the tank's progress momentarily and Steadman realized they had been granted a few seconds' grace.

'Quick, move!' he yelled at the girl, and began to pull her up with him. With relief, he felt her body begin to worm its way up; she hadn't frozen.

The Chieftain's engine began to whine and suddenly it lurched forward again, demolishing the yellow car completely. But they were clear. Steadman reached safety first, then dragged the girl after him just as the tank's rear dropped and almost brushed the soil of the slope.

Holly fell against him and they stood drawing in deep breaths, their bodies heaving. Steadman looked back at the tank and could see nothing of the flattened Mini. The Chieftain was motionless and, irrationally, Steadman had the feeling the battle vehicle was a living thing, a mechanical beast that had somehow come to life to destroy them. It seemed to be watching them.

The tracks began to clank into life once again, but this time they had changed direction. The tank was coming back for them.

'Run!' he shouted, pushing the girl forward but keeping a grip on her arm in case she should fall. The slope would have been too treacherous to have attempted to climb, so they ran along the side of it, stumbling once and rolling down into the gully created by the dip. Steadman pulled the girl to her feet and looked into her face anxiously and again he felt an understanding pass between them. The Chieftain had turned its huge bulk towards them and now it made its destructive way along the gully, picking up speed as it came. They fled from it.

Leafless branches tore at their clothes and skin as they stumbled through the undergrowth, their throats raw with the effort of breathing. The gully took on a gentle slope and soon they were free of the dip, running towards an area of dense bracken and bramble. Steadman glanced back over his shoulder and saw they were out of the tank's vision.

'In there,' he gasped, pointing at the thick canopy, and they plunged into the bracken, wading deep, ignoring the stings of resisting bramble. They heard the rumbling of the tank behind them as it cleared the rise, and Steadman pulled the girl to the ground, the foliage closing around them. He lost sight of the tank but could still hear its engine. They tried to control their breathing as though the mechanical dinosaur might hear and seek them out.

'Why?' Holly whispered, desperation in her voice. 'Why are they trying to kill us?'

Steadman put a finger to her lips and shook his head. The Chieftain's engine seemed to be getting louder and they could hear the crashing of broken undergrowth. The investigator raised his head slightly to catch sight of the approaching vehicle and nearly cried out when he saw it was heading straight towards them. It was as if it could sense their presence.

They ran again, away from their relentless pursuer, lost in the woodland, not knowing in which direction lay the road. Bursting free of the bracken they discovered the ground was rising slightly, but they couldn't see what lay beyond the incline. Their muscles were aching now, their bodies bruised.

Steadman dragged the girl forward, knowing she could not carry on much further. Her legs were dragging and she leaned heavily against him. They heard a muffled explosion and something vaguely registered in Steadman's head.

He put one arm around Holly's waist and helped her up, pulling her towards the incline. The tank, now relatively unimpeded by trees, was gaining on them. They staggered on and finally reached the top of the gentle slope. The ground dropped away dramatically into a vast quarry.

'It's the explosives' testing-ground,' said Steadman, realizing now why the muffled explosion moments earlier had registered in his mind. Deep below, they could see the long slabs of concrete, shelters for observers in the man-made valley, as they witnessed the damage caused by rockets, mortars and shellfire. Battered skeletal frames of army vehicles lay scattered around the grey plain, victims of weapons turned against them to demonstrate their destroyers' deadliness. As they watched, they saw a rocket leave the muzzle of a launcher held on a soldier's shoulder, and strike what must have been a sheet of Chobham armour three hundred yards away; the rocket exploded on impact but the metal sheet appeared to remain undented.

'We're trapped!' the girl cried and seemed to be about to sink to her knees in despair.

Steadman held her steady and pointed towards a clump of gorse that ran along the rim of the huge pit. 'In there!' he yelled at her. 'We may be able to hide from them!'

They stumbled towards the gorse patch and threw themselves into it, keeping as far away from the cliff edge as possible. They buried themselves in the waist-high spiky bushes, but Steadman forced them on, crawling on hands and knees until they were in the centre of the patch. They lay there panting and the investigator put an arm around the frightened girl's shoulders, pulling her towards him. He felt her trembling against his chest and tightened his grip on her. Her confusion was adding to her fear.

He decided he had to risk seeing if the men – or man – in the tank had observed their desperate run for cover. The rumble of the Chieftain was close and their position too vulnerable if their location was known.

He raised his head above the gorse and was dismayed when he saw the close proximity of the armoured vehicle. And it was headed straight towards them, increasing speed as it came, knowing where they were as if by instinct. He dragged the girl up and she screamed when she saw the approaching tank. She began to move away but he held her tight, to prevent her from backing towards the quarry's edge. He pulled her through the gorse, running to their left in a desperate attempt to dodge their uncanny and unerring pursuer; but a stout root, hidden from his view, tripped him and they both went down in a heap, the winter foliage cruelly ripping at their faces and hands. Holly lay slumped against him, unwilling or unable to move any more, giving in to their relentless hunter, too exhausted, too despairing to go on.

The tank was above them, the long phallic muzzle of its gun barrel passing over their heads like an antenna sensing their presence. In one last hopeless gesture of defiance, Steadman picked up the girl bodily, and with all the strength he could gather, leapt to one side, afraid to go under the tank again in case it stopped above them to grind its tracks backwards and forwards until their bodies had been crushed into the ground.

He almost made it, but the right-hand track caught his shoulder and he went down. The girl was clear, thrown forward by his rush, and she saw his body fall beneath the tank's wheels. Fortunately for Steadman, he had fallen into the angled space between the upper and lower wheels of the Chieftain, and it was enough to save the investigator from being dragged beneath the vehicle: he kept rolling, pushing himself away from the deadly moving links. He was inches clear, then suddenly found his movement checked. The back of his jacket was caught beneath the grinding track. He tried desperately to prevent his weight being pulled back under and his hands reached out to clutch roots – anything to hold on to.

Holly clamped her hands around his wrists and pulled with all her strength, her eyes tightly closed against the effort. Steadman felt his jacket tear, then suddenly he was free and moving forward into her arms. They clutched at each other as the tank lumbered by.

Steadman twisted his head, ready to pull the girl up and begin running again.

His eyes widened when he saw the Chieftain had not decreased its speed, but was trundling onwards towards the quarry's edge only feet away. The tracks spun in free air and screeched when the huge vehicle tilted forward, the edge of the cliff breaking away under its weight. The tank gave Steadman a view of its metal underbelly before sliding forward, the bare tracks now spinning in the air. Then it was gone, careering down towards the grey plain two hundred feet below.

Steadman scrambled forward, carefully avoiding the freshly broken earth at the cliff's edge, and was in time to see the Chieftain bounce off the limestone wall of the cliff and turn over, its gun pointing towards the sky. It bounced again, and again, then the tank seemed to disintegrate. Its tracks tore loose, and ran as streamers behind the main body; its gun caught against the rock-face as the tank turned over, and the turret was ripped from the hull. The fuel tank must have been punctured, for suddenly a bright flame flowered from the body and the blast of the explosion swept back up against the cliff face and hot air seared Steadman's face. A large, more powerful explosion joined the first almost immediately, and he realized the Chieftain had been carrying live ammunition.

The Chieftain reached the bottom of the quarry in many separate pieces.

Steadman blinked his eyes, moistening them against the scorching heat of the blast, and he saw figures emerging from behind concrete shelters. They were too far away for him to see their expressions, their faces just white blobs, but their shock was apparent in their stance.

He pushed himself away from the edge and scrambled back through the rough gorse towards the sobbing girl.

7

'*But then it is the curse of the great to have to walk over corpses.*'

HEINRICH HIMMLER

'*Terrorism is absolutely indispensable in every case of the founding of new power.*'

ADOLF HITLER

Steadman drew back the covers of the bed and gazed down at Holly's golden body. The tips of her breasts were pink and alive, protruding from their soft mounds, erect and excited. His eyes followed the curve of her waist and reached the rise of her hip, then travelled inwards along the triangle that dipped into her smooth thighs. Her stomach was flat and had a firmness that told of muscles developed just beneath the skin; her whole body had that firmness to it, soft to look at and to touch, but conditioned to a surprising toughness.

'Please,' she said, looking up at him, 'just hold me.'

He was aware of his hardness as her eyes searched his body too, and he slid in beside her, pulling the sheets up to their shoulders, encircling an arm around her waist, drawing her to him. They stayed that way, their bodies pressed together, enjoying each other's warmth, relaxing into one another.

The girl had surprised Steadman earlier that day. Army vehicles had arrived at the top of the quarry within seconds of the tank's descent and questions had been fired at them mercilessly. Holly had recovered from her tear-shedding and remained calm at the barrage, whereas Steadman had soon lost his temper and flayed the curious officers with his tongue. They had been taken into the Aldershot HQ and the questioning had continued. Why had they wandered off the road towards the quarry? Hadn't they seen the warning signs? Why should a Chieftain chase them? Hadn't they just driven into the woods into the path of the tank? What had made the Chieftain plunge into the quarry? Had they spoken to the crew at any time?

All through the interrogation, the girl had answered quietly and firmly, showing no sign of the ordeal she had been through, apart from the physical aspect – her clothes were torn in places and scratches showed on her hands and face. Then she had turned the interview about, demanding to know why there was not stronger security on the site, and why they were being treated like offenders when it was *they* who would be suing the British Army.

The Lieutenant-Colonel in charge of the questioning was taken aback by the sudden onslaught and Steadman had smiled at his confusion. The arrival of Major Brannigan, who vouched for their identities, had brought the hasty inquisition to a close. Reserved apologies and assurances were given that the matter would be fully investigated – the fully implying that they were most definitely still under suspicion.

Major Brannigan had organized a limousine to take them back into London and, after they had picked up Holly's Pentax from the Long Valley guard post, Steadman suggested she return with him to his house for a nerve-steadying drink and to clean herself up after her ordeal. She readily agreed for, at the moment, she was living and working out of an address in North

London and felt she could not face the trip across the busy town just yet.

She was quiet on the trip back to London, and the moment of closeness their mutual danger had brought about seemed to have been lost. But when he had settled her in an armchair in his lounge, and before she had even sipped the brandy he had offered her, the tears broke through and she had buried her head into his shoulder. He'd held her and tried to soothe her, knowing it was merely the relief of having survived the nightmare, the fear having gone.

After a while, her trembling had stopped and again, he forced the brandy on her, urging her to drink. He saw the tension begin to drain away. He drank with her, for she was not alone in having been shaken by the experience. The worst moment for him had been when the tracks of the Chieftain had tried to drag him back by his jacket and crush him. He remembered her hands clutching his wrists, her closed eyes and the effort on her face as she had struggled to pull him towards her. The brandy warmed them both, their senses acute and vulnerable after the shock, and as they looked into each other's eyes, the understanding – the intangible closeness – returned.

Steadman wasn't surprised when she asked him to take her to bed and, somehow, both knew the prime purpose was not to make love, but to share physically this closeness they were both feeling. For Steadman it was a feeling he hadn't experienced for a long, long time; not since Lilla. Strangely, the memory of her gave him no sense of guilt. He had felt it and rejected it when he had made love to other women – even Maggie – but now, when his emotions were beginning to run deep, the guilt hadn't even appeared. Who was she, this Holly Miles? And why were they reacting so strangely towards each other?

He led her upstairs and watched her undress. She had showered and reappeared, her hair now darkly wet and clinging. Her legs were long and the curve of her calves graceful, her thighs swelling just enough to give them shape. Her shoulders were wide for a girl, but only noticeably so when they were compared to her slim hips. Her breasts were full, and firm with youth.

She had climbed into bed, water from her hair dampening the pillow and, resting on one elbow, had watched him undress. His body was still lean and well-muscled enough to be pleasing; he felt no self-consciousness under her gaze. He caught her look of concern when she saw the old scars scattered across his back, but she made no comment. He showered, then returned to the bedroom, finding a peacefulness in her he wanted to share.

Now he held her close and, for a fleeting second as her eyes opened, he thought he glimpsed something. Not fear, not confusion, but anguish. It was gone in a moment, yet he knew it wasn't imagined.

'Why did they try to kill us, Harry?' she asked, drawing slightly away so she could see more of his face. 'Why would the men in the tank want to do that?'

'I don't know, Holly,' he lied. 'You make enemies in this business. Maybe someone was trying to get at me. We don't know that there was a complete crew in the tank.'

'Hijack a tank just to kill you?'

Steadman shrugged. 'Like I said: you make enemies.'

'Unless whoever it was was trying to kill me.'

Steadman looked at her sharply. 'Kill you? Why should anyone want to do that?'

'I don't know. I just felt the menace there. Didn't you feel it? It was somehow – evil. As if the tank were a living thing.'

She had experienced it too. It had been uncanny.

Her body shivered and he drew her close again.

'Put it out of your mind for now,' he told her. 'They'll find the bodies – or body – in the tank and maybe their identities will tell us why they were trying to kill us.'

She pressed against him. 'There's more isn't there? You're not telling me everything.'

He suddenly felt the overwhelming desire to tell her all – about Maggie, Mossad, British Intelligence, this man Edward

Gant. He wanted to confide. After all these years of introversion, he now felt the need to talk to someone, maybe not to share in the problems he faced, but at least to know of them. But something held him back.

Was it years of discretion as a private detective, as a Mossad agent, as a member of Military Intelligence? Had years of never trusting anyone been ingrained into his character? He felt he knew the girl so well, yet common sense told him she was still a stranger. Maybe it was that which held him back.

'Yes,' he said to her, 'there is more, but it's better that you're not involved.'

She was silent for a while, then said, 'Who are you really, Harry? Why are you involved in weapons? Can't you tell me that?'

'I've told you who I am.'

'You've told me what you are.'

He grinned at her. 'What I am is who I am.'

She shook her head. 'No, that's too easy. It doesn't explain anything. Why do you deal in armaments, Harry?'

'If it wasn't me, it'd be somebody else,' came the stock reply.

'You're still evading.'

His hand touched her cheek. 'Give it time, Holly,' he said quietly. 'We've been thrown together by mutual danger. Tomorrow, our feelings could be different. So let's be patient, eh?'

She nodded and silently reached behind his neck to touch his damp hair. 'You feel it too, then?' she asked.

He smiled back, then kissed her softly. 'I feel it,' he said.

'Then let it happen.'

She kissed him fiercely and quietened nerves became alive again, this time responding to a far different sensation than fear. His hand swept down her back and found her buttocks. Pulling her tight against him, he grew erect once more against the softness of her stomach.

He heard her sigh as their bodies filled each other's, their skin joining, its coolness turning to heat. His fingers fondled the sensitive base of her spine, and her long fingers reached down to touch him in the same place, then travelled further to the back of his legs. He could feel her stretching against him and suddenly her legs parted and his thigh filled the gap. He ran his hand down the smoothness of her skin and pulled her leg up slightly so that it rested over his own; then he caressed the back of her leg from the top to the sensitive area behind her knee.

Holly reached up again, laying her hand flatly against his back, exerting pressure so that his lips bore down hard against hers. The softness of her mouth aroused him further and her teeth bit down gently on his probing tongue. He felt her hand reach around to his chest and their bodies parted slightly to give it access. She touched him easily at first, then squeezed the firm skin of his chest hard, not to hurt, but to excite. Her fingers slid down towards his stomach and the muscles there quivered at her touch. He pushed himself towards her searching hand, demanding to be touched at his most sensitive area. Her fingers ignored his demands and passed that point, reaching below and encircling his testicles. She squeezed them and he groaned aloud at the warmth of the touch.

His own hand swept back upwards, never losing contact with her body, heightening her sensations as it journeyed towards her breasts. He covered a breast with his hand and moved his fingers gently to find her nipple, stroking it delicately, controlling the passion he felt.

They paused in their movements for a moment and kissed softly, both afraid to talk of love for it was too soon, but allowing their kiss to express feelings that ran deep, feelings that surprised them both. Only then did they allow their passions to rise uncontrolled.

He reached down, still keeping his fingers against her skin, tantalizing her with the direction his hand was taking. Over her stomach, staying there briefly to explore and awaken, then down into her hair, stroking and kneading, firm enough to reach deeper nerve cells, but soft enough to excite rather than fulfil. She could wait no longer and grabbed his wrist, forcing his hand lower, down between her thighs, into the aroused wetness there.

Her moan of pleasure mingled with his, for the sensation of probing her sweet dampness was almost as great as the exhilaration she felt at his touch. His fingers entered her, careful not to hurt, but she pushed against him and her wildness incited him further. His touch was hard now and her motion was rapid. Her whole body squirmed as she reached for his penis, reluctant to lose the excitement of his hand, but eager for something more fulfilling, more satisfying.

She turned on to her back and he rose above her, kissing her face and neck, her closed eyes. Her smile was inward, but she suddenly put an arm around his neck to pull his cheek against hers, to let him know she was sharing their pleasure, not retreating into her own. Her other hand was gently insistent, drawing him into her. He paused, then advanced slowly so there would be no pain, no sharpness; he sank further, pausing again when she gasped. But pain meant little to her now and she urged him on, pushing upwards with her hips to help him complete his journey.

His weight bore down on her and their mutual desire became exquisitely intolerable. It was no time to linger, no time to tease; that could come later when they were used to each other. Now they needed to climb and reach their peak, to find release for screaming sensations. He thrust into her and she met and countered his movements with equal force, her fingers crooked and pressing into his skin, her knees raised slightly, her thighs squeezing against him.

She surprised him by reaching down between their bodies, her hand desperately feeling underneath him, finding the area between his legs and pulling upwards as though to force him further into her. His passion grew even more and he felt the nerve-tingling tension begin its ascent, all the senses in his body drawn to that one region as though through a vortex. The same was happening to Holly. Her mouth was open, lips drawn back from her teeth. Her eyes were tightly shut and short gasps escaped her as she twisted her head against the pillow. Her muscles stiffened and juices inside her began to flow as though being squeezed through tiny apertures, faster, faster, until they burst through and flowed freely.

And Steadman's juices flowed to mingle with Holly's at the same time.

Even as the sensations subsided they still murmured their delight, Steadman resting against her, unwilling to relinquish the physical closeness. Holly kissed his neck, slowly stroking his back with gentle fingertips, happy at what had passed, but confused at the strength of her feelings for him. She was giving too much too soon.

She was unaware that the same confusion was running through Steadman. When he finally withdrew and lay by her side, they regarded each other with curious eyes.

'What's happening to us?' she asked, and she seemed nervous.

He put a finger to her lips. 'It's too uncertain to say.'

Holly seemed about to speak again, then changed her mind. She pulled her head away, but not before Steadman had seen the troubled look on her face. He turned her head back towards him and kissed her lips. 'Don't worry about it, eh?'

Her eyes were misted and damp as she pulled his head down and kissed his lips.

'I don't want to be involved with you,' she said.

'What are you afraid of, Holly? Are you really that scared of giving yourself to someone?'

'You don't understand . . .'

Her words were cut off by the insistent ringing of the telephone downstairs. She suddenly felt Steadman's whole body go rigid and a distant look came into his eyes.

'Harry, what's wrong?'

There was no recognition when he looked at her; his mind had travelled back to another time, in another country. The phone had rung there too, in their apartment in Brussels, when he and Lilla had just finished making love. It was to be the last time for them.

Lilla had urged him to ignore the ringing, had clung to him, demanding more, more love. Laughing, he'd smothered her face with a pillow, telling her the call might be important, perhaps a new mission. He was becoming too used to the inactivity, getting to like it. All the more reason to let it ring, she had called after him as he leapt away from her and went through to the lounge.

The pillow had sailed through the air after him and struck the side of the open door, her pretended anger making him smile as he headed towards the phone. As he picked up the receiver he saw she had followed him and was standing in the doorway, a mischievous grin on her face, one hand cupping her breast, the other reaching between her legs, as if to say if he wouldn't stay to please her, she would amuse herself.

He turned his eyes away from the provocative sight and said hello into the mouthpiece.

A voice, in French, asked if it was Monsieur Clement speaking, and he had answered yes – Clement was the name he used at that time.

He knew immediately what the high-pitched whine from the earpiece meant, for the Israelis had used the same device against the Chief PLO representative in France, Dr Mahmoud Hamshari. The sound was an electronic signal transmitted through the telephone, to trigger off a bomb hidden somewhere in the apartment, probably near the phone itself.

As he dived towards Lilla he knew he was already too late.

The sudden searing flash which lit up the horror on her face told him there was no escape.

Not for Lilla. But he had survived.

They told him later it must have been the angle of his body as he had dived for Lilla. Shrapnel had imbedded itself in his feet and legs, but the rest of his body had been spared from the worst of the blast. A miracle they had called it, but for him there was no mercy in his salvation. He had no desire to live if Lilla was to die.

It had taken her three days to do so, this young, once vivacious, Israeli, her face torn away and her body lacerated and burnt. Three hideously pain-filled days. Never fully conscious, but her shredded lips constantly moving in her agony.

Steadman had prayed for her death, had begged the doctors to end the torture for her; but their job was to preserve life no matter how shattered or painful, and they paid no mind to his entreaties, finally sedating him against his own pain and anguish.

When he had finally recovered and she was long dead, there had been a blackness in him that had taken many other deaths to purge.

Now, in circumstances so similar to that time before, the telephone was ringing, calling to him, reminding him, telling him the past was always present.

'Harry?' Her hand shook his shoulder. 'What is it? You look so pale.'

His eyes snapped back into focus and he looked down into the anxious face of Holly.

'Aren't you going to answer it? It keeps ringing,' she said.

He eased himself from the bed without a word, and picked up a bathrobe lying over the back of a chair. He moved as though automated, but the concern in Holly's voice finally sank through.

'Stay there,' he ordered, and she saw the somnambulic quality of his movements change to one of alertness. He shrugged on the robe and disappeared through the doorway. She heard his footsteps padding lightly down the stairs.

Steadman reached the lounge and quickly glanced around, ignoring the shrilling phone for the moment. Nothing seemed out of place, but he quickly checked on the few places where a bomb could have been concealed, carefully lifting the settee and armchair to check beneath, peering behind the books on their shelves, examining the back of the television to see if it had been tampered with. Reasonably satisfied that everything was in order, he turned his attention to the telephone itself, the caller's persistence arousing his suspicions even more. There was nothing underneath the small coffee-table it rested on, but he knew the telephone itself could contain a bomb. He picked it up to feel its weight: it seemed normal enough. He took the gamble and lifted the receiver to his ear.

'Steadman, is that you?'

With a sigh of relief, he recognized Pope's voice.

'For Christ's sake, Steadman, answer!'

'It's me,' he said quietly.

There was a pause at the other end, then Pope said gruffly, 'It took you long enough to answer.'

'How did you know I was here?' Steadman countered.

'It's my business to know,' came the curt reply. The tone changed as the fat man relaxed. 'I heard what happened to you down at Long Valley. Tell me your end of it.'

Steadman told him flatly, without emotion, as though making a report to a client. He mentioned the invitation from Gant to arrange a further meeting.

'Good,' said Pope. 'Do so. Who's this girl, this, er, Holly Miles?'

'She's a writer – freelance. She's doing an article on the arms trade for one of the Sundays.'

'And Gant's obliging her?'

'It seems so.'

'Hm. Peculiar. Not like him to want publicity.'

'Maybe he wants to come out of the shadows.' Steadman whirled as he felt a presence in the room. Holly stood in the doorway, his shirt covering her small body seductively. She smiled at him and he relaxed. Pope's voice drew his attention back to their conversation.

'You say this tank was definitely chasing you,' he was saying.

'Yes, it was trying to ram us.'

'You're sure it wasn't just a runaway?'

'Look, we've been through all this with the military. The

bloody thing wrecked the car, then tried to squash us flat when we ran for it! It chased us for at least five minutes.'

'Yes, yes. Very strange.'

Steadman's impatience grew. 'Is that all you can say? We know it was strange, but you and I . . .' He cut off his words, remembering Holly was still in the doorway. 'Look, who was in the tank? Were they working for him?' He was careful not to mention Gant's name.

There was a long silence on the other end of the line.

'Pope? Did you hear me?'

'Er, yes, dear boy,' came the reply eventually. 'The tank was a complete wreck, of course, by the time it reached the bottom of the quarry. Its fuel tank exploded, you know, then its ammo.'

'I know that. Were the bodies badly burnt?'

'That's just it, Harry.' Again, Pope paused, as though considering his words. 'There were no bodies. The tank was empty.'

'But that's impossible! They must have escaped or been destroyed completely.' There was alarm in Steadman's voice and a chilling sensation in the pit of his stomach.

'No chance of escape. And there would have been some trace of human bodies, no matter how bad the damage. No, Harry. The tank was empty. There was no one driving it.'

Steadman stared at the receiver, unable to believe the words. Then he turned towards Holly and she saw the confusion in his eyes.

8

'*The eternal life granted by the grail is only for the truly pure and noble.*'

ADOLF HITLER

'*And many of them that sleep in the dust of the earth shall awake, some to everlasting life, and some to shame and everlasting contempt.*'

DANIEL 12:2 (RSV)

Smith shivered and tightened his scarf, silently cursing the coldness of the night. It was morbid too, sitting in the churchyard in the dark, ancient gravestones scattered around, black and weathered, some tilting at odd angles suggesting their occupants had become restless. He wondered briefly if he should risk lighting a cigarette, but decided against it. Although the bench on which he sat was well-hidden in the darkness, there was just a chance that the cigarette's glow would be seen from the small road opposite. It wouldn't do to have any passer-by getting curious about someone sitting in a graveyard in the dead of night smoking a fag. Not that there *were* any passers-by at this time of bloody night!

He glanced at his watch, the luminous dial telling him he still had two hours to go before he came off shift. Two more hours in this stinking burial ground, he grumbled to himself. Two more hours of watching the stinking house opposite! And for what? They wouldn't be stupid enough to try anything like the other night. God, what kind of bastards would nail a woman to a door? He wondered if there were any other eyes watching the house. The police, maybe? It was strange they hadn't made more of the business, it wasn't the normal everyday kind of murder. And they'd managed to keep it out of the news, too. That must have taken some doing. Probably didn't want to encourage any similar types of crime. Unusual murders were always followed by other unusual murders. All the nuts around read about the first, got a kick out of it, and tried it out themselves. Same with bomb freaks.

What kind of man was this Steadman? He'd heard the detective was reluctant to help them at first, but the killing of his partner had persuaded him. Goldblatt had been furious at the investigator's previous refusal, even though he, Smith, had told the Mossad chief it would probably be so. He had kept an eye on Steadman over the years, it was part of his job as a 'sleeper' in this country, and he had seen how the agency had begun to flourish, how Steadman had settled down to live a relatively peaceful existence in England. The man had left wars and violence behind. Why should he become involved again? The brutal murder of Mrs Wyeth was the answer to that!

How *he* would like to be free of the organization. Joseph Solomon Smith, aged fifty-eight, jeweller in Walthamstow. Known as Solly to his friends. *Schmuck* to his wife, Sadie. Solly had fled to England along with thousands of other Jewish refugees just before the outbreak of the last World War, when Hitler's purge of Germany's and Austria's Jewish population was in full swing. It had been either flee or be interned in those days, not many realizing it was actually flee or die. The mass name-changing that had taken place, as the refugees had arrived in England and gone through the far from friendly formalities of entering the country, had been almost comical. The group in front of him had told the official their family name was Harris, for they had heard the people in front of them use the name. It sounded English. If the officials receiving the immigrants had been surprised at the amount of Harrises, Kanes and Golds among the arrivals, they'd given no indication of it. Perhaps they understood the stigma attached to names ending with 'berg', or 'stein', or 'baum', the danger such names threatened in the world at that terrible time. Perhaps they couldn't have cared less; there were too many to check.

He had chosen Smith because he knew it was indisputably British and he'd heard one of the customs officers call his companion by that name. It was a safe name. In fact, he'd nearly wet himself at the official's suspicious look and feared he'd been too blatant with his choice. However, the moment had passed and with a resigned smile, the man had cleared him.

Many of his compatriots had reclaimed their original names when the threat had died years later, but he had found no need to go to that trouble. Smith suited him fine.

He had escaped from Germany alone, his parents, two brothers and one sister having been rounded up by Hitler's thugs on the very eve of their departure from the country. He would have been taken with them, but he was young, and young men, when about to leave a place forever, often have bittersweet goodbyes to say, undying love to pledge. His farewell had taken most of the night and the girl had used his body as though there would never be any others for her.

He watched in horror from the shadows as the SS dragged his screaming family from their house, and he shrank back deeper into those shadows. He'd wept at his own cowardice then, and had wept with that same shame for many years after. Even the sight of his father falling into the gutter, his white beard now black in the moonlight – black because it was matted with blood – and the old man's screams as the rifle butts battered his frail body into unconsciousness, had not overcome his own terror. The brutality had only increased it. He had sunk to a squatting position, pressing himself hard against the rough wall, afraid to run lest the Gestapo hear his footsteps, stifling sobs with both hands against his mouth, unable to look away from the dreadful scene and unable to help his family. Even when his younger brother had been kicked senseless when he tried to go to the aid of his aged father. Even when his mother had been dragged by her hair into the waiting van. Even when his sister's young body had been bared and pawed by the uniformed thugs. Even when his older brother had been shot through the throat as he'd tried to escape. The terror had only been compounded.

The nightmares had finally ceased twenty years later, the horror gradually diminishing through repetition. The shame, too, had become numbed, for his spirit had grown weary of it and now kept it contained in a remote part of him. But the memory remained. And two faces burned within that memory: the faces of those who had caused the holocaust, the evil countenances of the two men responsible for the genocide, the decimation of his race, the murder of his family. Adolf Hitler and his henchman, Heinrich Himmler!

Their faces haunted him still because they were the cause of his terror, the source of his shame. And because he was aware their evil could so easily rise again.

After the war, when he learned the rest of his family had died in Auschwitz, he had tried to join the remnants of his race in Palestine, desperate to atone for his cowardice, yearning to take part in the rebirth of his nation. But the new Israelis now had a different way of thinking. For them, the centuries of oppression were over. They had returned to their home country and there they would either be free or perish fighting for that freedom. No longer would they accept persecution.

Defiance had to be tempered with cunning if they were to survive. They were a small nation in a small country; the world stood outside their boundaries, a giant wolf outside the door. The Israelis would never trust another nation again: they would work with them, they would trade with them, they would even encourage social intercourse. But they would never trust another race, another country.

Because they were surrounded by enemies on all sides, their strength would have to reach beyond their own boundaries so they would always be forewarned of enemy action against them, enabling them to strike from behind when necessary.

They had persuaded Smith to remain in England, to build an identity there, to become British. And to be ready.

He had worked in a small jewellers in the Hatton Garden area of London at first, for that had been the family business, a trade he had been taught by his father. His claim against the German government for the restoration of his family's wealth had taken years to materialize, for there were many others like him claiming compensation for losses they had suffered under the Nazi regime, and each claim had to be carefully checked. Very few received compensation from the then impoverished country, but Smith was lucky enough to receive a small settlement. This, plus the marriage to Sadie which brought in some extra capital, enabled him to set up his own shop in Walthamstow.

Another source of income which Sadie never knew about were the regular amounts of money he received from the Shin Beth. The payments were small, but the work he carried out for his country was minimal and irregular. When he was younger, he had become impatient with the menial tasks they asked of him, but they had begged him to wait, to stay calm and serve his nation in the way they asked. His day would come.

It hadn't though, and gradually the fires in him dimmed and almost burnt out. He carried out the minor tasks asked of him with a sense of resigned duty and no passion. One of his 'duties' had been to keep an eye on the man Harry Steadman when he had returned to England from Israel and joined an enquiry agency. Smith had done this by employing the agency to check on the background of his one and only employee, an innocent little countryman of his, whom he knew to be completely trustworthy, but who provided a good excuse for making contact with the investigator. The ex-policeman, Blake, had carried out the investigation, providing Smith with a clean bill of health for his shop assistant, but complimenting the jeweller on his wisdom in checking out his staff. One could never be too careful where goods of such value were involved. Smith had cultivated a friendship with the ex-policeman and engaged him privately in other concocted matters to do with his business. In that way, he was able to hear of the agency's progress and catch odd bits of information relating to Harry Steadman without becoming directly involved himself. He had skilfully avoided his curiosity about the investigator from becoming overt in any way, and most of the information had been volunteered by Blake without direct questioning. After all, they were good friends, they and their wives sometimes dined out together or visited the theatre. Hadn't he, Smith, introduced his friend into his own golf club at Chingford? If the very-British ex-policeman ever wondered about the beginnings of his friendship with the very-Jewish dealer in precious stones, then he would put it down to an obvious desire for the jeweller to have some connections with the law.

Smith blew on his hands to try and warm them, then pushed them deep into the pockets of his overcoat. I'm becoming too old for this sort of thing, he told himself. Surveillance in this kind of weather was no good for a man of his health. His heart wasn't as strong as it used to be, his constitution no longer robust. It seemed a waste of time anyway. Surely Steadman wouldn't be touched in his own home? Why was he so important to Israeli Intelligence? Smith cursed the secrecy his employers maintained. Why couldn't their own people be informed of what was going on? And what do I tell Sadie who knows nothing of Mossad and my little jobs for them, when she asks what kind of business deals keep me out till the early hours of the morning? The woman is becoming tiresome. Becoming? She always was. You got a loose woman, she'll tell me. Chance would be a fine thing, I'll tell her. You got . . . His body stiffened as something caught his eye.

Did I see something? he asked himself. Or was it my imagination? The street lighting is bad there over the road. Was it something moving?

Smith peered into the darkness, his eyes narrowed and his breath held. There it was again, a movement among the shadows!

He rose to his feet, his limbs stiff with cold, and bent his body forward as though it would help him see more clearly. He thought he saw movement again, but it somehow seemed unreal, his imagination playing tricks on him. The air around him was still, no wind to cause the stirring of tree branches which might create mysteriously moving shadows.

He moved forward, careful to make no sound, his breathing now thin and uneven. He had a number to call if anything suspicious occurred, but the nearest phone-box was two streets away. How stupid of them! If anything were to happen it would all be over by the time he reached the phone-box and they got here. But then, he had been told nothing had been expected to happen; he was only being used as an extra precaution.

He silently cursed the men who employed him, the silly little Jewish boys playing at cloak-and-dagger. Then he forced himself to relax. It's probably nothing at all. I've been in the dark too long – and in creepy surroundings at that. My eyes are tired and small wonder! My God, what time is it now? The luminous dial told him it was 1.35 a.m.

The jeweller stood and stared at the terraced house for a few seconds more and was about to return to his bench when he noticed something odd. His mind couldn't register just what that oddness was for a few moments, and then he focused his vision on the door of the house. There was a long, dark shadow at one side. It may just have been a shadow cast by the half-moon against the door's frame, but then he realized the moon was on the other side; the shadow – if there had been one caused by the frame on that side – should have been cast on the left and not the right. He moved forward for a closer look, keeping to the hard earth and grass of the churchyard so his footsteps would not be heard. He pushed his way through the sparse shrubbery at the perimeter and peered over the iron fence. Only then did he see that the front door to Steadman's house was partially open.

What to do now? Phone his contact or investigate further? If Steadman were sleeping – and he undoubtedly was – he could be in serious danger. But what could he, an old man, do to help the detective? Warn him, at least.

Perhaps it was the memory of having done nothing so many years before, or perhaps it was just the thought of it being a false alarm and his looking foolish in the eyes of the young Israelis who employed him. He decided to investigate further before calling in help.

He reached the gateless exit to the churchyard and stealthily crossed the road, welcoming the concealing shadows on that side. The jeweller, one hand on the wall as if to steady himself, moved along towards Steadman's house. He reached the open door and hesitated.

All the muscles in his ageing body had become tense, making his movements awkward and stiff. He felt a strange fear, as though someone – something – was waiting for him inside that house. Something that compelled him to enter.

He tried to break the spell, tried to tell himself he was being a foolish old man. He should try to get away, now, while there was still time. But there was something in there he had to see. Something there waiting just for him.

He pushed the door open further, his fingers trembling. His breathing had become heavier and he tried to suppress small whimpers escaping from his throat. Even then, he tried to turn and run, but his body – or was it his mind? – refused to obey. The door swung open and the hallway was a black, ominous tunnel.

Smith stepped over the threshold and felt his way along the passage, his eyes becoming more accustomed to the darkness. He stopped when he thought he heard breathing. Breathing that wasn't his own. But no other sounds came as he listened, although he felt that the beating of his own heart would surely drown out any other noise. He moved on and suddenly stumbled against the base of the stairway.

His hands took his weight, holding on to the high stairs for support, one knee resting on a lower step, and he grunted with the sudden jarring. Then he felt its presence.

His gaze travelled up the stairway, step by step, until it reached the bend. It was darker just there, a black hole in the general gloom, but there was someone – something – lurking in that pool of darkness. His whole body began to shake now, for he felt its evil; it seemed to emanate from that dark area, to flow down the stairs in a vaporous cloud, sweeping over him and chilling his mind.

A movement. A shape began to descend the stairs.

Smith moaned and tried to break away, but his limbs were locked rigid, paralysed by a fear that was even greater than the night of his family's abduction in Berlin. His eyes widened as the dark shape emerged from the total blackness of the bend in the stairs, and his mouth opened to form a scream as the figure became more discernible. And yet, the image still wasn't clear. It was just a black shape against the overall darkness of the hallway; but his mind saw more than his eyes. It came closer and stopped just before him. He tried to pull his hands away, for they were almost touching the shadow, but he found they would not obey him. The smell of decay pervaded the air, assailing his nostrils and almost causing him to vomit. He slowly looked up, searching the length of the figure towering over him and when he reached its head, a face came floating down at him as though the shape was bending.

'Oh, dear God.' Smith's moan rose to a wail. 'You! Oh God, it can't be!'

It was then he screamed.

The scream hadn't roused Steadman, for he'd been awake minutes before. He had lain there in the dark, unsure of what had dragged him from his deep slumber. He listened for any noises, and none came. He had become aware of the iciness of the room. It was a still coldness, penetrating the blankets of his bed, and not the normal chill of autumn. It was as though the temperature of the room had taken an abrupt downward plunge. He was aware of being very much alone.

Steadman had taken Holly home to her flat earlier that evening, both of them shaken by the revelation that the Chieftain tank which had tried to crush them that day had been empty. They were halfway to Holly's flat when the thought struck Steadman of how it could have been managed, and he had difficulty in keeping his sudden theory from the girl. There was no point in involving her, it would have meant telling her everything, better it remain a mystery to her.

He ran the idea through his mind as he drove and it seemed to fit; at least, there were no *other* possible explanations. Gant dealt in sophisticated armaments, the advanced technology of his weapons renowned and respected. It would not have been impossible for him to rig up remote-controlled operating machinery inside the tank, a mechanical driver which would obey instructions from afar. But from where? The operator had to be able to see them to send the Chieftain on their track. He had to be in close visual proximity. Weight was added to his theory when he realized how: helicopters had been buzzing over the testing-grounds all morning. They had been too busy trying to escape the tank to be aware of any helicopter hovering above them, but that must have been the answer! How else could their hiding places have been found so easily? The searching eyes had been above them! For a moment his theory floundered: whoever had been guiding the tank from the helicopter must have seen the quarry and would have taken avoiding action. But then he had been close to the quarry's edge; maybe the controller had not been quick enough to change the Chieftain's direction, maybe his eagerness to crush the detective had distracted his judgment. It had to be the answer! Steadman relaxed a little: he liked his mysteries to have some solution.

He had kissed Holly goodbye in his car when they reached her home, neither invited inside nor wanting to be. They were both curious about each other, both disturbed by the strength of their feelings; but both had had enough for one day. It was time for them to be alone, to lick their wounds and digest the events of the day. An unease showed in her eyes as she promised to see him soon. Then she was gone.

Steadman had driven to the agency, luckily catching Sexton and their young trainee, Steve, before they left for the night. He briefed them on two specific jobs they were to carry out during the following few days – current assignments would have to be slotted in somehow even if it meant spreading their load on to another agency. After warning them their investigations would require the utmost caution, he returned to his home in the back streets of Knightsbridge.

He made coffee, then settled down to reread the file on Edward Gant. Five cigarettes and three cups of coffee later he lay the document down by his feet, rubbing his eyes in weariness, his mind buzzing with unformed thoughts. There was still a smell about the whole business he didn't like. Why should British Intelligence, with all their resources, use him to get at Gant? Pope's explanation that he was a link with all the parties concerned didn't quite ring true. He was even more certain he was being set up as the sacrificial goat, the bait to draw out the tiger. Mossad's use of him seemed more genuine, but just as ruthless. Their resources in England were limited and he was in a good position to find their missing agent. But was that all there was to it? They had admitted they wanted to nail Gant, but then why not just eliminate him? They'd done so with their enemies in the past, so why balk at it this time? There was much more to it than either intelligence organizations were letting on and that was why he was taking out extra insurance. Sexton's task was to find out more about Gant, hearsay matters that might not be entered in official documents; young Steve's task was to keep an eye on the hotel near Belsize Park, to follow the movements of Goldblatt and Hannah. Steadman had decided not to tell the two men any more than they would need to know, but he warned them there would be danger involved. Steve's eyes had lit up at the idea and Sexton had accepted it with a weary grin. If it had something to do with Mrs Wyeth's death, then they were only too pleased to put in as many extra hours as it would take to help find the murderer or murderers. And that *was* what it was all about, wasn't it?

He had nodded and both men had resisted asking further questions. Before Steadman left the office, Sexton had promised to begin his investigation of the arms dealer the following morning when he had sorted out their current jobs, and Steve was already on the phone to Goldblatt's hotel, booking a room for an indefinite period beginning the following day. It would work out expensive for the agency, but Steadman was determined to recoup any losses from both Mossad and British Intelligence, whatever the outcome. He prayed he would still be around to forward the bills himself.

He had prepared a simple meal for himself, then phoned Holly, dialling the number she had given him earlier. He had been disappointed when there was no reply. She hadn't relaxed even after their lovemaking that afternoon, and who could blame her after what she'd been through? He replaced the receiver with a shrug. Perhaps she was in a dead sleep. Or visiting friends. What did he really know about her anyway? He had climbed the stairs, thrown off his clothes, and slumped wearily into bed. But first he had made sure all the doors were locked.

He lay there listening, his breath held. The coldness of the room made him shudder. What had made him wake so abruptly? Light from the street filtered through the open curtains, but was no match for the room's darker shadows and gave little comfort. No sounds came to his ears, yet the tension inside him mounted. His impulse was to leap from the bed and draw out the revolver he kept in the top of his wardrobe, but something held his body in check. Somehow he knew there was someone downstairs. The atmosphere seemed heavy with menace and he trusted his instincts too much to ignore the feeling. Then he sensed that the stairs leading to the bedroom were being mounted. The approach was slow, deliberate, its only physical warning a breathing sound, a sound which grew louder and more urgent as it drew nearer. The smell drifted under the door then. It was vile, choking, the smell of defecation and . . . he struggled to remember where he had experienced it before. It came to him. Years ago, when one of Israel's border towns had been heavily mortared by their enemy, he had helped clear the rubble and search for bodies. A family had hidden in the cellar of their house, a cellar specially dug for such emergencies, and the building had collapsed around them, burying them alive. It had taken days to find them, and when they had, the flesh had decomposed. This was the same smell, only far stronger, more putrid: the stink of long-rotted flesh.

Steadman forced himself to sit upright, using every ounce of willpower he had. He felt his strength was being inexplicably drained away, drawn from his body, leaving him lifeless. He had to reach the gun. He moved as though deep beneath the ocean, pressure all around him, his breathing harsh and quickened. He staggered and fell to the side of the bed, forcing himself up again, moving towards the wardrobe, his naked body bent, walking like an arthritic old man. His eyes never left the door to the bedroom even though he was moving towards the wardrobe. He was afraid to look away. He thanked God it was locked. But then he had locked the front door downstairs.

A sudden bump stopped him. The sound had come from outside. Everything had become still.

He thought he heard a moan, then words, but he couldn't understand them. The scream snapped him into action.

It was as though a spell had been broken; the heaviness was gone, the fear overcome for the moment. Steadman jerked open the wardrobe door, reached up for the metal case containing his .38, pulled open the lid and snatched the gun out. He was thankful his old habit of always keeping it loaded was still with him. He leapt towards the bedroom door and fumbled with the key, the screams from downstairs still ringing in his ears.

The sounds stopped as he pulled open the door.

He jumped into the bend of the stairs, sure of his footing even in the dark, the gun held before him, the hammer ready to cock. He saw a dark shape lying at the bottom of the stairs and for a moment he thought he saw another shape moving away from it along the hallway, towards the open door. It could have been a trick of light, though, or imagination, for it seemed to have no form and was gone in an instant.

Steadman descended the stairs, moving cautiously, his senses alive and jumping. In the darkness, he could just make out the shape of a man lying at the foot of the stairs, his eyes white and staring. He leapt over the figure and ran to the open front door, quickly looking into the street beyond, oblivious of his own nakedness. The street was empty, although it would have been easy for someone to disappear into the churchyard opposite.

He slammed the door shut and flicked on the hall light all in one movement. Still keeping the gun poised before him, he quickly checked the lounge and then the kitchen, ignoring for the moment, the still figure on the floor. Only when all the downstairs lights were on and he was sure no one was lurking in any of the rooms did he return to the collapsed body.

The man's eyes stared at the ceiling, the eyelids pulled back revealing their whites, the pupils dilating under the sudden glare. His lips were moving, but Steadman could hardly hear the words; they were soft and rambling. Spittle bubbled at the side of the man's mouth. His body was stiff and the investigator could see he was in a catatonic state. He had the look of someone who had seen a creature from hell.

9

Steadman brought his car to a halt outside the large wrought-iron gates and waited for the guard to step from his hut on the other side. The two Alsatians accompanying the guard looked menacingly towards him.

'Mr Steadman?' the guard called out and the investigator nodded.

'Identification?' There was neither belief nor disbelief in the guard's voice; it was all a matter of routine.

Steadman was forced to leave the car and walk over to the gate, pulling his licence from his wallet as he did so.

The guard, dressed in green tunic-like overalls, took the

licence from him and said, 'Won't keep you a moment, sir.' He disappeared into the tiny hut, leaving the dogs glaring through the bars at the investigator. Steadman glared back but decided he couldn't outstare them. He walked back to his car and leaned on the bonnet, hands in his pockets. He wondered if the Mossad agent had come out of shock yet.

As he'd crouched over the trembling form the night before, he had been puzzled by the absolute terror on the man's face. What had put that look there? And why had he broken into his house? Steadman had tried to shake the man into awareness, but the eyes never lost their glaze and the lips never stopped their burbling. He had tried to catch the words, but they were incoherent. He quickly searched the shaking body and found no weapons. His driving licence revealed the man to be Joseph Solomon Smith and it was then that Steadman remembered him; Smith's features had altered so drastically in his horrified state that the investigator hadn't been able to recognize him, but the name had jolted his memory. Smith had come to the agency some time ago and had become one of their smaller clients. He was – what was it? – a jeweller. That's right, he'd wanted the background of one of his staff checked, a job Sexton had handled. There had been a few minor assignments for him over the last couple of years, but Steadman had had no call to see the jeweller again after the initial visit. It was only his particular ability to remember names, places and events, that helped him place the man at all. The obvious connection soon hit him. Smith, despite his English-sounding surname, was Jewish. It didn't take much to realize he was a hireling – or perhaps even an agent – of Mossad. Steadman shook his head in disgust. That was why the little jeweller had come to the agency in the first place, to keep an eye on him for The Institute. Sexton had been Smith's contact. How much had the ex-policeman told the jeweller over the years? There wasn't much to tell anyway, and Steadman was confident that his employee would have committed no serious indiscretions. But to use an old man like this, even for just a routine and periodic check! Look at him now. If the little Jew's heart didn't give way under the strain, then he would be fortunate.

It was the sudden draught rather than any sound which had caused Steadman to throw himself against the wall and point the .38 towards the slowly opening front door. Whoever was entering had silently used a key and was now stealthily pushing the door to one side. It suddenly opened all the way, still quietly, but very swiftly. Two men stood on either side in crouched positions, their bodies partially hidden, and two revolvers were levelled at Steadman's naked figure.

'Don't shoot, Steadman!' a voice commanded, and the investigator's finger froze on the trigger. 'MI5,' the voice came again, low but urgent. An open wallet was tossed down the hallway coming to a halt against the head of the prostrate jeweller. Without taking his eyes off the two men, Steadman reached forward for the wallet. He quickly checked the credentials framed inside the wallet and then stood up, waving for the two men to enter.

They did, the second man closing the door quietly behind them.

'What the hell's been going on?' the first asked, staring down at Smith.

'Let me get something on,' said Steadman, suddenly aware of his nakedness.

'Leave the gun,' the first man ordered as the detective turned to climb the stairs.

'Go fuck yourself,' Steadman said over his shoulder as he climbed.

The two MI5 agents looked at each other and the second shrugged his shoulders.

When Steadman returned, his heavy gun tucked into the deep pocket of his bathrobe, the two men were kneeling over the little Jew.

'What's been going on, Steadman?' the first man asked again, rising. 'What's happened to him?' There seemed to be some disgust in his tone as he pointed down at the figure lying on the floor.

'You tell me,' Steadman replied, irritated by the agent's abrupt manner. 'I heard a noise, then a scream. I came down to find him lying at the bottom of the stairs.' Had he heard a noise at first? He was already casting aside the unreasoning fear he had felt while lying in his bed.

'Did you see anyone? Did anyone get out the back way?' the second agent asked as he searched through Smith's pockets.

'No, it's still locked. I thought I saw someone going out of the front door though. It was just a shadow, I couldn't make much out in the dark.'

The two agents regarded him with puzzled expressions. 'No one came out, we'd have seen 'em,' the first said.

'But I'm sure . . .' Steadman's voice trailed off.

'He's an old man,' the MI5 agent said. 'He's been sitting out there in the cold, in the churchyard over the road for hours. Maybe it was too much for him. He came over to see you and collapsed on the stairs.'

'How do you know he was over there? And why should he come over to see me at this time of night?'

'He was there watching you. And we were watching him. Your Mossad friends seem to want to keep an eye on you. They must be bloody desperate to use old men like him, though.'

'But why were you there?' Steadman asked.

'To keep an eye on you, of course. Compliments of Mr Pope. As to why the old man came over – who knows? Maybe he thought he saw something.'

'How did he get in? The door was locked.'

'Same way as us, Mr Steadman.' The agent held a Yale key aloft. 'I'm afraid we had it made during your absence. It was for your own protection,' he added by way of an apology, then looked back at the figure huddled on the floor. 'He's probably got a key on him somewhere or maybe he picked the lock. We'll find out later.'

Steadman shook his head resignedly. 'What do we do about
him?' he said, kneeling once again by the old man whose body
was still shaking. 'He needs to go to hospital.'

'We'll get him to one. Don't mention any of this to your
Mossad friends or they'll want to know how MI5 got involved.
They've got to think you're working on your own.'

'Aren't I?' Steadman asked caustically.

The two agents ignored the question. 'As far as you're concerned, you never saw this man tonight. Let them worry about
his disappearance.'

They had carried the old man out, assuring Steadman that
one of them would maintain the vigil outside the house through
the night. Steadman made sure the door was locked, then
poured himself a stiff drink. He spent the rest of the night doz-
ing fitfully in an armchair, the .38 near at hand on a coffee table.
The next morning, after shaving, showering, and eating, he had
rung Holly. Again, there had been no answer but, although a
little concerned, he told himself she was a working girl and was
probably at the magazine which had commissioned her current
feature. Besides, she had nothing to do with this business, so
why should she be in any danger? Yesterday's incident with the
tank was because of him and nothing to do with any involvement on her part. Later, he had rung Edward Gant's company,
using the number supplied by Peppercorn, and had been told
the arms dealer would like him to visit his home that day where
their business might be better dealt with. With some trepidation, Steadman had agreed and had been given instructions on
how to get there. He had rung Pope immediately after and the
fat man had been delighted with the invitation. 'Do be careful,
dear boy,' had been his only hint at the risk Steadman was running. They had briefly discussed the incident of the night before
and Pope had questioned the investigator on exactly what he
had seen. Steadman detected a keen interest in the large man's
voice and had almost told him of his own uncanny feelings
towards the incident, but in the cold light of day, it all seemed
very much a part of his own imagination.

After a quick call to his office and checking with Sue that everything was in order as far as their clients were concerned, he set out in his car towards Guildford, a nervousness in him and yet, an excitement. Maybe Pope was right: he had only smothered the flames inside him, the fire not completely put out.

The guard came back to the gate and held Steadman's licence through the bars. The investigator took it and climbed back into his car.

The gates were opened and he drove through, the Alsatians silent, but their eyes never leaving him. The gravel road curved through a small cluster of trees, then the house loomed up before him. It was a large house but by no means as grand as Steadman had expected, for Gant was, reportedly, a wealthy man. He remembered that this was not the arms dealer's only property: hadn't Holly mentioned a place on the West Coast?

The grounds appeared to be perfectly normal for an English country house, and showed little evidence of the nature of the man's business. But surely there must be a testing-range somewhere on the estate, otherwise why would Gant have invited him there? Why indeed? he asked himself. There were several other cars parked outside the house and a BMW was just pulling away. The two men inside glanced around at Steadman, then quickly turned their heads, the passenger looking through the window on his side so only the back of his head was visible. But in the brief instant before, Steadman had recognized him: he was a Tory MP, well-known for his right-wing views and the brilliant but incitative speeches he made in support of those views. He seemed appropriate company for Gant, Steadman thought wryly, as he parked beside a silver Mercedes. His door was already being pulled open by a man wearing a dark suit, as he turned off the ignition.

'Mr Gant is in the house waiting for you, sir,' the man said. 'Can I take your briefcase?'

'I don't have one,' said Steadman, climbing from the car.

'Follow me then, sir.' The man's voice and movements were brisk, and his words were more like an order than an invitation. Steadman followed him.

'Won't keep you a moment, sir,' the dark-suited man said, leaving him standing in a wide, gloomy hallway, and disappearing into one of the high-doored rooms leading off from it. Steadman began to wander down the hallway, studying the gilt-framed portraits hanging on either side, portraits of men he'd never heard of, but all dressed military style, when the door opened again and Gant stepped into the hall.

'Ah, Mr Steadman. Glad you could come,' the arms dealer said, smiling.

Steadman's eyes widened in shock, but he quickly recovered and strode towards Gant. The arms dealer did not offer his hand and his eyes glittered with some inner amusement.

'Did I . . . surprise you?' he said. 'It is a shock at first, but you'll soon get used to it.'

Steadman found it hard to take his eyes away from the large, square sticking-plaster, punctured by two small holes, which covered the area where Gant's nose had been only the day before. He cleared his throat and said, 'Sorry, I didn't mean to . . .'

'No need for apologies,' Gant raised a hand as if to ward off the sentiment. 'This happened many years ago. Fortunately my nasal passages function quite normally. It is unsightly at first, I know, but it's very uncomfortable wearing an artificial nose all the time. When I'm at home, I like to dispense with such vanities. Now do come in, there are some people I'd like you to meet.'

The room was large, the ceiling high, the furniture tastefully traditional. The four people in the room, two seated, two standing, looked towards Steadman as he entered and their conversations stopped. He was surprised to see that one of the men was Major Brannigan, this time out of uniform but still looking very much the military type, open hostility on his face. The other faces showed interest – perhaps curiosity would have been more accurate. Steadman felt uncomfortable under their gaze.

One of the seated occupants was a woman and Steadman found his eyes drawn towards her, to be held by her own deep gaze. She had extraordinary beauty: her hair was dark and lush, cascading down to her shoulders, her skin smooth and sallow in an exotic way; her nose was strong but well-formed and her lips full, half-smiling, slightly arrogant. It was her eyes that mesmerized him though, for they were dark, almost black from this distance, and seemed to draw him into her. And there was a shining expectancy about them that puzzled yet attracted him.

'Let me introduce everybody.' Gant's words broke the contact and Steadman swiftly took in the other two members of the group. The man seated next to the woman was aged and wizened, his skin full of deep creases and his eyes set back in shadows cast by a prominent forehead and brows. His wispy white hair was long, straggling over his ears, and his body seemed frail, ready to crumble at the slightest pressure. He held a thin, black cane before him, his gnarled yellow hands resting on its metal top.

The other man was much younger, probably in his early thirties. His short hair was sleeked back, cut in old-fashioned style, his face pale and unblemished, the sneer on his lips part of his features rather than an assumed expression. He wore a suit of darkest grey, elegantly cut and accentuating the slimness of his body. His eyes, though showing curiosity, were heavy-lidded, giving that curiosity a disdainful insolence.

'Kristina, this is Harry Steadman,' Gant said, presenting the investigator to the seated woman. Her lips widened into a full smile as she rose and walked towards him, a hand outstretched.

He took the hand and was surprised at its firmness.

'I'm very pleased to see you, Harry.' Her voice had a sensual huskiness to it. She was tall, at least five-nine, and wore a deep green velvet suit, the jacket thrust open by high breasts be-

neath a beige blouse. He recognized the same amusement in
her look that he had noticed in Gant's the day before, and his
feeling of taking part in a charade heightened. He smiled back,
the hardness in his eyes causing her a brief moment of unease.

'Dr Franz Scheuer,' said Gant, indicating towards the old
man still seated. Steadman nodded, making no attempt to go
over. There was no reaction from the old man.

'Felix Köhner,' Gant looked towards the slim, young man
who raised a hand in acknowledgment, 'and of course, you've
already met Major Brannigan.'

The soldier glared at Steadman.

Nice to be among friends, the investigator told himself, and
the thought helped him keep the amused defiance in his own
eyes.

'Mr Steadman is here for preliminary discussions in arranging an arms contract for an overseas client,' Gant said, leading
the detective towards an armchair and indicating that he should
sit. 'Would you like a drink, Mr Steadman? Sherry? Martini?
Something stronger for a man like you, I suspect.' That same
mocking tone to his voice.

Steadman noticed that the man who had ushered him into
the house was poised at a large cabinet containing an array of
drinks.

'Vodka would be fine,' he said. Steadman was aware he
was under scrutiny while other glasses around the room were
being replenished. The old man leaned forward and whispered
something to the woman and she hid a smile behind her
hand.

'Now then, Mr Steadman,' said Gant, placing himself with
his back towards the huge fireplace, 'can you tell us who this
mysterious client of yours is, yet? Or must I make wild
guesses?'

'No need to,' Steadman replied. 'I'm working for the
Israelis.'

If Gant was surprised at the investigator's frankness, he hid
it well. 'I see. You know I've never made any arrangements

with the Jews before, don't you?' The word 'Jews' seemed to carry all kinds of insinuations.

'I was aware of it. I wondered why?'

'Because they've never approached me before,' Gant said, and laughed aloud. 'Until a few weeks ago, that is.'

Steadman raised his eyebrows in surprise.

'Yes, a young Jew approached me with a request for arms. I told him I was sure something could be arranged, but unfortunately . . .' he smiled down at Steadman '. . . he never returned. I wonder why he suddenly lost interest?'

Bastard, Steadman thought, tired of the cat-and-mouse game. 'I wouldn't know, Mr Gant. What was his name, this . . . Israeli?'

'Oh, Kanaan, something like that. Something very Jewish. It's not important now, is it?' His voice taunting.

Steadman grinned, wanting to smash the glass in the arms dealer's disfigured face. 'Not to me,' he said. 'I'd like to inspect some of your weapons.'

'Naturally. I've studied your list and I think I can accommodate you on all counts. Felix will show you the more moderate weapons we keep here, then perhaps you would like to visit our other testing-grounds for further demonstrations of our more powerful weapons.'

'And where is that?' Steadman asked mildly.

Gant chuckled. 'All in good time, Mr Steadman. Our Wewelsburg is not for your eyes yet.'

Heads turned sharply towards Gant, and Steadman saw the surprise – or alarm – in their eyes.

'I'm sorry. Your . . . ?' he prompted.

But Gant only laughed again. 'Never mind, Mr Steadman. All in good time. Felix, will you go through the list and tell our guest of the weapons we can provide his clients with? These are weapons developed only by my company, Mr Steadman, weapons far superior to any of those of our competitors – government or otherwise.'

For the next hour, he was lectured by the man called Felix

Köhner, who, as his name implied, was a German, while the
others silently looked on as though studying him, only Gant
sometimes expounding on the merits of certain weapons mentioned. Steadman felt his every movement was being watched,
his every question analysed and filed in their minds. It was un-
nerving, yet the sense of challenge appealed to him. He felt a
brooding malevolence emanating from the group, almost a
force, and the old man with the shadowed eyes was at its
centre.

Even Kristina's beauty seemed to conceal something corrupt, yet he found it difficult to keep his eyes from straying in
her direction. She returned his looks with meaningful smiles
and twice he caught a look of annoyance on Brannigan's face at
those smiles. Was there something between them? What was
a major in the British Army doing in such company anyway?
What were his ties with Gant? Come to that, what had a Member of Parliament to do with the arms dealer? He had been told
Gant had influential friends, but he had not realized they were
in government.

Later, he was taken by Köhner and Brannigan through to
the rear of the house where he was surprised to find a firing
range and a long, brick building in which many kinds of
weapons and their machinery were housed. A Gazelle helicopter rested lifelessly on a circular launching pad a hundred
yards from the house, and Steadman wondered if the same
machine had been used to guide the Chieftain the day before.
Thoughts of danger were cast aside for the moment when
he became absorbed in the new weapons demonstrated to
him by green-uniformed teams. Most of the demonstrations
were in principle only – it was hardly practical for the effects
to be shown, but the effects *could* be shown on film and in
the next two hours, the lethality of the weapons was pro-
jected on screen for his benefit.

It was early evening by the time the demonstrations were
completed and Steadman was weary of the deadly machinery,
the sharpness of Köhner's voice, and the open hostility of

Major Brannigan. They returned to the house to find Gant waiting for them, the usual mocking smile on his face.

'Do you like what you've seen, Mr Steadman? Will your
friends be interested?' he asked.

'Yes, I think so,' said Steadman, playing the game. 'But it's
all pretty soft stuff so far. There are bigger items on my list.
When do I get to see them in action?'

'We have, as I've already mentioned, more suitable testing-
grounds for the weapons you have in mind. Today we wanted
to whet your appetite. We've done that, haven't we?'

'Yes, you've done that. Where are these testing-grounds?'

Gant laughed aloud and turned to the woman, Kristina.
'*Unser Parsifal ist neugierig – und ungeduldig.*'

She gave the arms dealer a sharp look and quickly covered
it with a smile at Steadman. 'Would you like to see some other
demonstrations, Harry?'

He was puzzled. Gant's relish in the game he was playing
was obviously not shared by his companions. That had been
the second remark of Gant's that had made them nervous. Why
had he spoken in German? And why had he called him Parsifal?
'Yes, I'd like to see more,' he answered.

'And so you shall,' said Gant taking him by the shoulder. 'Instantly. Please come with me, Mr Steadman.' The flattened
face made his grin seem all the more sinister.

'Edward! Is this the way?'

All eyes turned towards the old man who was now on his
feet, his cane supporting him. His voice was thickly accented,
and had a strength which belied his feeble frame.

Gant's eyes were cold as he appraised Dr Scheuer. '*Bezwei-
felst du jetzt die Wörter des Propheten? Alles be wahrheitet sich
doch?*'

The old man returned the cold stare. '*Dazu zwingen Sie es,*'
he said with suppressed anger.

Now Steadman knew the game was drawing to a close, the
pretence coming to an end. And he had achieved nothing apart
from putting his head inside the lion's mouth. He tensed, wait-

ing for the right moment to make a break. The advantage was all theirs, but he felt disinclined to wait for them to make their final move. The arms dealer's grip on his shoulder tightened.

'Please come with me, Mr Steadman.' All humour had gone from his eyes as they bore into Steadman's. 'I promise you what I have to show you will be of great interest.'

The moment, for the investigator, had gone. Curiosity had replaced resistance. It could also be a chance to buy more time. He nodded and followed the arms dealer from the room, Major Brannigan and Köhner falling in close behind as an undisguised escort.

Gant led the way into the hall and up a broad staircase. They turned into a long corridor and marched its length to a room at the far end. Gant pushed open the door and motioned Steadman to go through. With some trepidation, he did so.

The sight confronting him wrenched at his gut, dragging it down and his spirits with it. The two slumped figures tied to chairs in the centre of the room were barely recognizable, their faces distorted by swelling and covered in blood. He went to them, knowing instinctively who they were, but lifting the sagging heads to make sure. The woman first, then the man.

David Goldblatt and Hannah.

10

'*Follow Hitler! He will dance, but it is I who have called the tune!*

'*I have initiated him into the "Secret Doctrine", opened his centres in vision and given him the means to communicate with the Powers.*

'*Do not mourn for me: I shall have influenced history more than any other German.*'

DIETRICH ECKART

'*Thule members were the people to whom Hitler first turned and who first allied themselves with Hitler.*'

RUDOLF VON SEBOTTENDORFF

'*The legend of Thule is as old as the Germanic race.*'

LOUIS PAUWELS AND JACQUES BERGIER

'What should we do, Mr Blake? Shall we follow them or go in?' Steve looked towards the ex-policeman, trying to discern his features in the darkness of the Cortina's interior.

Sexton shivered, wanting to be on the move, but his training curbed his impatience. 'No, boy. We'll just wait a bit longer and see what happens.'

The car was parked off the road and invisible in the darkness to anyone emerging from the gates further down. Steve had spent half the day within sight of the entrance to the house and his boredom was hard to contain. His only break had been his hasty dash to the nearest phone-box to contact Sexton and let him know what had happened and why he was there. The older man had arrived shortly after dusk and found Steve lurking in the undergrowth not far from the spot where they were now parked. He'd had to drive slowly along the quiet stretch of road twice before the apprentice detective had emerged from the trees; he had felt pleased the boy was so cautious.

'Do you think Mr Steadman's all right?' Steve asked, blowing into his hands to create some warmth. 'Maybe he was in one of those cars that left.'

'I dunno, Steve. There's something very funny going on. I just wish Harry had taken me into his confidence.' Very funny indeed, Sexton thought. All starting with Mrs Wyeth's terrible murder. Was this man Gant connected with that? Sexton had spent the best part of the day probing the few old friends he still had in Special Branch, but they couldn't tell him much about Gant. A bit of an enigma all round, it seemed. Quietly supplying arms to governments abroad – and our own – for years, then suddenly coming to the fore, becoming one of the most import-ant dealers in the country. His dubious association with the Arabs had worried them at first and they'd taken great pains to investigate his background, only to find he was vouched for by men of considerable power and influence. There were certain details they could give Sexton, but nothing that would reveal any deeper insight into the man. The phone call from Steve had sent him racing through town and down into the country where the boy had explained his reason for being there in greater detail.

Steve had taken a room as instructed in the same hotel as Goldblatt and his woman friend. Unable to get a room on the

same floor as the two Israelis, he had spent most of his time in
the reception area reading newspapers and magazines, situated
close to the lifts and stairway so that neither Goldblatt nor the
woman would be able to leave without his seeing them. It was
a busy hotel and people – mostly businessmen, it seemed – were
coming and going all day. But Steve had had trouble keeping
the newspaper he was holding from shaking violently when the
lift doors had opened and the two Israelis had emerged with
three men pressed close to their sides, hemming them in, forming a tight group. He had seen the other three enter the lobby
fifteen minutes earlier and disregarded them as they had waited
for the lift; they looked like normal businessmen to him. But
now, because of the nervousness on the faces of the two
Israelis, the woman in particular looking quite agitated, and the
rigidity of the tightly packed group, they took on an altogether
more sinister aspect. He watched them walk to the reception
desk, one of the men breaking off from the group, leading the
woman with a hand on her arm towards the swing-doors. With
the other two on either side of him, the Israeli asked for his
bill, informing the clerk he was checking out and that his lug-
gage would be collected later that day.

Steve was both nervous and excited. To him, this was real
detective work, the kind he had read about. There was obviously something dangerous going on – you didn't have to be a
super-sleuth to see that – but what to do about it? He didn't
have time to ring the office or Steadman at his home, for the
men would soon be leaving the hotel and he might lose them.
He had to move fast. His Mini was parked in the hotel's underground garage; if he were to follow them, he had better be
ready. He folded the newspaper with trembling hands, making
a great effort to look outwardly calm. Then he strolled non-
chalantly towards the swing-doors and out into the open. He
saw the man who had left first with the woman, sitting in a car
opposite, a grey Daimler and he gulped anxiously; he hoped his
Mini would be able to keep up with it. When he was out of sight
of the vehicle, he dashed down the ramp leading to the under-

ground parking area and jumped into his little car. He dropped the keys once and then tried to use his front-door key in the ignition by mistake before he finally gunned the engine into life, and he emerged just in time to see the other three men climbing into the Daimler. Hands were taken from pockets and he realized that the two strangers must have been holding guns inside their overcoats. His bowels felt loose at the thought.

The car moved slowly out of the forecourt and nosed its way into the stream of main-road traffic, Steve following and checking his mileage indicator before he, too, eased into the flow. He would have to charge for mileage, of course, and Sexton insisted on accurate figures and no rounding off. The Daimler was easy to follow through London, but once they were past the busy roads of the southern suburbs, the pace increased, and Steve broke into a sweat trying to keep the fast-moving car in sight. He managed to, though, more than once due to opportune traffic lights halting the Daimler's progress, and it was with relief that he saw the car turn off the road to stop outside a pair of ornate wrought-iron gates. He drove by slowly, glancing quickly to his right as he drew level with the opening gates, and just having time to see the guard and two vicious-looking Alsatian dogs. He parked his car further down the road and round a bend where it couldn't be seen from the gates, then he crept back through the trees on that side of the road. A high wall enclosed the property, the only break being the iron gate itself. He settled down behind a tree when he was opposite the gate and wondered what his next course of action should be. The words of his tutor came to him. 'When in doubt,' old Sexton would say, 'sit and wait for something to happen. Remember, you're an observer, not a partaker in the action.'

So he settled down to wait, checking the time and making a note of the morning's events in his notebook. He felt pleased with himself, but soon the cold dampness in the air and the increasing boredom of the observation began to depress him. He had just made up his mind to find a pub and have a beer and a sandwich – after all, he was entitled to have lunch – when a

familiar car slowed down and pulled over into the gate's entrance. It was Harry Steadman's grey Celica! He almost called
out, but ducked down when he saw the guard emerge from his
wooden hut on the other side of the gates. Steve watched as
the detective left his car and walked over to the guard, passing
something through the bars. The temptation again to call out
when Steadman strolled back and rested against the bonnet of
the Celica was overpowering and he had a hand cupped to his
mouth ready to shout when the guard was back at the gate. He
stilled his voice and swore under his breath. There was nothing
he could do.

Dismally, he watched the car drive into the grounds and disappear down a road leading into a clump of trees. Only a few
moments later, a BMW emerged from the drive and stopped
before the gates for them to be swung open. He thought he
recognized the passenger as the car swept into the road, but
he couldn't quite place the face. Steve waited another twenty
minutes before he made up his mind. He would have to get in
touch with Sexton – he would know what to do.

He found the phone-box a few miles further down the road
and fortunately the ex-policeman was still at the agency. Steve
returned to his lonely vigil, happy in the knowledge that Sexton
would soon join him and glowing with the praise that had been
bestowed upon him. An hour or so later, Sexton's Cortina had
slowly driven by, but he had waited until he was sure it really
was the ex-policeman, before he'd run further down through
the undergrowth and stood by the roadside waiting for the car
to pass again.

'Do you think Mr Steadman's in trouble?' he asked Sexton
for the third time. 'He's been in there a long time.'

The old man pondered over the question again. Finally, he
said, 'Let's give it another hour. Then we'll go and find out.'

'Have you heard of the Thule Gesellschaft, Mr Steadman?'
Gant stood over the investigator, his hands tucked neatly into
his jacket pockets, his body straight, the smile on his face now
arrogant rather than mocking.

Steadman tried to clear his thoughts. He wasn't tied, but the
.38 Webley, pressed into his neck by Major Brannigan, bound
him to the chair more securely than any ropes. He saw the
hate in Goldblatt's eyes as the Israeli glared at the arms dealer.
Hannah's body was still slumped, held to the chair by restraining ropes. Goldblatt had recovered consciousness minutes before and had groaned aloud when he saw Steadman,
utter despair filling his face. He had tried to speak, but a vicious
slap from Köhner had quickly silenced him.

Flickering shadows, cast by a blazing fire, played on the
room's high ceiling, creating sinister patterns which were
never still. The room itself was large and lit only by the red
flames and a single corner lamp. The only furniture was the
straight-back chairs on which Steadman, the woman and the
old man and the two Israelis sat, and a long table at the far end.
Gant, Brannigan and Köhner stood over them all; their very
stance seemed threatening.

'The Thule Gesellschaft, Mr Steadman. The Thule Society.
Surely, in your years in Military Intelligence and with the
Israelis you learned something of our organization?'

Steadman tried to clear the clouding fear from his mind.
There was a coldness around him: a coldness that shouldn't
have been, for the fire was fierce, its flames high. The chill
made his limbs tremble and he consciously fought to keep them
still. He vaguely remembered mention of the Thules in the
many lectures on the Second World War he'd had to attend as
part of his training in Intelligence. They were some kind of
occult society which had come into prominence just before the
war, but had faded since.

'Ah, I see you have heard of us.' There was some satisfaction in Gant's voice. 'But obviously, our part in the events leading to the last war has not been emphasized to you enough.'

He looked around at the assembled group. 'It seems our knight needs some education if he is to know his enemy.'

Köhner, standing over the Mossad agent, chuckled and looked at Steadman with contempt. 'I think our *knight* will soon shit himself,' he said.

Gant joined in the laughter but the remark, if anything, helped steady the investigator's nerves. His fear gave way to anger and Steadman had learned a long time ago to control that anger and channel it into a single-minded strength. And curiosity helped too. Why had they referred to him as a knight? Just what *was* his part in this whole bizarre affair?

'I'm sure you've heard, read – perhaps studied – the allegations that Adolf Hitler was involved in Black Magic, Satanic Rites and such like, in his rise to power, haven't you, Mr Steadman?' Gant raised his eyebrows and waited for a reply, his flat face even more repulsive now that it was bathed in a red glow from the fire, almost shadowless because of the absence of any prominent feature.

'I've heard the theories,' Steadman answered, 'but nothing's ever been proved conclusively.'

'Not proved? Hah! The refusal of men to accept such things is astounding! Keep such things away in the shadows, don't examine them too closely, don't bring them into the light. We might find it's true; then what? We might decide we like the joys such worship brings.' His sarcasm bit through the air. 'And that might mean the rejection of everything we've achieved since the Dark Ages. And look at those achievements: poverty, starvation, continual wars! What has happened to our spiritual quest? We believe we are advancing, mankind, aided by science, moving further away from his primitive beginnings; but just the reverse is happening, Mr Steadman. We are moving further away from our spiritual – our ethereal – beginnings! That was our sin, don't you see! Our Original Sin! Mankind's bestiality! His lust for the physical. And Hitler's great crime against mankind – in the eyes of mankind – was trying to lead us away from that evolvement, back to the spiritual. That's why he was rejected, that's why he had to die. *They killed your Christ for the same reason!'*

Steadman shuddered at the madness in Gant's eyes. He had seen that same madness in the eyes of fanatics all over the world – that same blind reasoning, that same passion for a belief that was based on perverted logic. And he knew the hypnotic effect it had on others, men who looked to a leader because of their own inadequacies, who yearned for someone to give a greater meaning to their own existence. He looked around the room and saw that yearning on their faces, their eyes shining with the emotion that the words had instilled. Only Goldblatt's eyes were filled with loathing.

'Hitler tried to purify his race from the breeds that had infiltrated it, mingled and brought it down to their own animal level, away from its natural Germanic heritage. That he failed meant a step backwards in man's national evolution – I might say reversion, for Thulists believe we need to *return* to our beginnings, not progress away from it. Hitler's plans for the Master Race were based on *völkish occultism*, and it was there the Thulists were able to help and guide him, for we were the roots of National Socialism! Even in those early days, our arms was the swastika with a curved sword and a wreath. A Thulist even designed the Nazi flag for Hitler! A swastika on a white circle against a red background, a symbol of the movement's ideology: the white its nationalism, the red its social ideal – and the swastika, itself, the struggle for victory of Aryan man.' Gant turned away from the group, his hands tucked deep into his jacket pockets, and walked towards the huge fireplace. He gazed into the flames for a few moments then spun round to face them again. 'Do you know the meaning of the swastika, Mr Steadman?' he said harshly.

With the blaze behind him, Gant's body was thrown into silhouette, the outline tinged red. Without waiting for a reply he said, 'It's a symbol of the sun, light, life itself; and for thousands of years, among many races, it's been used as such. The Buddhists believe it to be an accumulation of luck signs possessing ten thousand virtues. For the Thulists – and for Hitler – it was a symbolic link with our own esoteric prehistory, when we were not as we are now, but energy patterns existing on the lost island of Thule. Ethereal shadows, Mr Steadman. You might call them spirits.'

Steadman shivered again. The temperature of the room had dropped even more – or was it only his imagination? The air seemed charged and the arms dealer's silhouette had grown more dense, blacker.

'Signs, symbols, rituals – all are used by occultists to evoke power, just as the Eucharist and the Mass are used in the Church to evoke power. Whether that power is used for good or bad is up to whoever calls on it. Think of how the Catholic Church has abused its use over recent centuries, the crimes committed in God's name. But there is a direct way to tap evil forces and Hitler was advanced spiritually enough to know the Christian Good was evil, the Christian Evil was good! His reading of Nietzsche, the man who claimed God was dead, had convinced him of this. Hitler sought to draw from those evil powers and to do this he used the knowledge he had been given by men like Dietrich Eckart, the Thule propagandist, a dedicated satanist; Karl Haushofer, the astrologist, who later persuaded Hess to defect to England; Heilscher, the spiritual teacher to many of the Nazis. Even Wagner played his part in Hitler's spiritual ascension. Men like the Englishman, Houston Stewart Chamberlain, who had written the *Foundations of the Nineteenth Century*, the inspiration of the Third Reich, while possessed by demons. And Friedrich Nietzsche, who had announced that the time was right for the Übermensch – the Superman, the Élite of the Race. They had helped form Hitler's ideologies. But it was the magicians who initiated him into the practices that would enable him to draw on the forces he needed to reach total power.

'And one of those practices was the reversal of magic symbols. As the Black Mass is a reversal of the Holy Mass in order to evoke powers of evil – the ceremony performed by an unfrocked priest, feasting rather than fasting takes place as a preparation, lust replaces chastity, the altar is the body of a naked woman, preferably a prostitute, the Crucifix is reversed and broken, and the Host becomes a black turnip which is consecrated in the whore's vagina – so symbols are reversed to do the same. The swastika, as a solar symbol, spins clockwise to attract the Powers of Light, the trailing arms indicating the direction of the spin. Hitler ordered that *his* swastika be reversed, to spin anti-clockwise, to attract the Powers of Darkness! And the whole world was witness to his meteoric rise!'

Gant was still speaking in low tones, but the words were hissed, sibilant, as they carried round the room. His audience was rapt and Steadman considered tackling Brannigan, who stood behind him, but the pressure from the gun on his neck never ceased for a moment. He glanced over at Goldblatt and flinched at the desperation on the man's face.

'But Hitler rejected all occult societies, didn't he?' he suddenly shouted at the arms dealer. 'He banned them from the Party.'

All heads swung towards Steadman as though he had suddenly roused them from a dream. A thin laugh came from Gant as he moved away from the fire and approached the investigator, his steps slow and deliberate. He stopped before Steadman, hands still inside his jacket pockets. One hand suddenly snaked out and grabbed the investigator's hair, forcing his head back, and he brought his own forward so that his flat face was only inches away.

'He did not reject *us*, Mr Steadman,' he said, his voice tight. 'In the end, *we* rejected *him*.' He pulled Steadman's head forward again, released it, then slapped him viciously. The investigator tried to heave himself from the chair, but the restraining arm of Brannigan encircled his neck and the gun pressed even deeper into his skin.

'I wouldn't do that, Steadman,' the major warned. 'Just sit quietly, will you?'

Steadman allowed himself to relax back into the chair and his neck was released. Gant smiled, then turned away, returning to the fireplace as though it were a stage for his oratory.

'When Adolf Hitler's ideals were still unformed – perhaps that is a bad word – "unchannelled" might be better, the Thule Society and the German Order Walvater of the Holy Grail were practising Nordic freemasonry, to counter the orthodox Jewish freemasonry which was slowly strangling the German economy in the years after the First World War. We were strongly opposed to the Republican government in Berlin at that time because of their sinister alliance with the rabble of the land: Jews, Slavs, Marxists. These – these degenerates – were gradually seizing control of the state and industry, crippling the country with their demands and their greedy conniving ways, and had created a situation that is not too unlike the situation in Britain today. You would agree with the similarity, wouldn't you Mr Steadman?'

Gant waited for a reply, but when none was forthcoming his voice suddenly shrieked through the stillness of the room. '*You would agree?*'

'The comparison's a little extreme,' Steadman said blandly.

'You think so, do you?' There was malicious sarcasm in Gant's voice now. 'You think the elected government still rules this country? You think management still runs industry? You think the pure Anglo-Saxon still owns the country? Look around you, Mr Steadman, with your eyes open. Not just at this country, but throughout the world. It's happening everywhere, just as it happened in Germany so many years ago: *the upsurgence of the lower races*! The African states, the Arabs – look how fast they're growing. Latin America. China. Japan. *Russia!* And, of course, Israel.

'The comparison is too extreme, you say. Let me assure you: today, the threat is even greater!'

Steadman knew there was no point in arguing. Men like Gant were too obsessed with their own bigotry to see reason.

'The Aryan people needed a strong leader then, just as they need one now. Hitler knew this and he saw we could help him be that leader. We were already creating the climate of feeling against the Jewish-Bolshevik infiltration. We, the Thules, and the members of the German Order Walvater, had already formed a new party within our own – the Deutsche Arbeiter-partei, later to become known as the National Socialist German Workers Party. The Nazi Party.'

Gant paused as if for effect, and Steadman wondered if his audience was going to break into applause. They didn't, but there was a lustre in both Köhner's and Kristina's eyes. The old man sat rock-like, unmoving, his eyes hidden beneath deep shadows. Steadman's attention was drawn back to the arms dealer as he went on.

'Hitler, who was still in the army at that time, had been selected by his commanding officer for a course in political in-struction and one of his duties was to attend meetings such as ours. It wasn't too long before he had joined us in our cause! And it was with us that men like Eckart and Guthbertlet in-itiated him into the study of Teutonic mysticism. It was with us he found his destiny.

'After years of struggle, after persecution and bloodshed, we conquered the enemy within our own country. In 1933, Hitler was made Chancellor of Germany – a great day for the Thules! And a tragic day for Hitler. For it was then he turned against us. He endeavoured to purge Germany of all mystical societies, and on the surface, we suffered with the rest. To the world it appeared he had rejected such cults, but in fact he had found a new source of power. A symbol. A weapon that had been wielded by glorious conquerors of the past! And he set in motion his plans to obtain it.'

11

'*This modern (British) Empire shows all the marks of decay and inexorable breakdown because there is nowhere in it the courage of firm leadership. If you no longer have the strength to give orders to rule by means of force, and are too humane to give orders, then it's time to resign. Britain will yet regret her softness. It will cost her her Empire.*'

'*For England, the First World War was a Pyrrhic victory.*'

'*To maintain their empire, they need a strong continental power at their side. Only Germany can be this power.*'

ADOLF HITLER

'*One thing is certain – Hitler has the spirit of the prophet.*'

HERMANN RAUSCHNING

'Hitler did not reject occultism, as you seem to believe, Mr Steadman. Even the historians who dismiss such ideas as cheap fantasy cannot explain the many indications of Hitler's deep faith in all things occult. The Russians, when they finally over-ran Berlin, found a thousand corpses of Tibetan monks, all wearing the Nazi uniform – but without any insignia. Every one had committed suicide. Why would Hitler have such men drafted into his army and why should they have finally killed themselves? Why the bizarre experiments carried out on the degenerates of his concentration camps? The deep-freezing of living bodies; the scattering of the ashes from the gas ovens across the land; the thousands of severed skulls the Allies found when they invaded. Hitler held up experiments on the V2 rocket – the weapon that could have won the war for Germany – because he believed they might disintegrate an etheric structure he believed encircled the earth. Were these the acts of a man who had rejected occultism? The SS symbol of the Schutzstaffeln was derived from the ancient Sig rune; the black uniform itself, with its black cap and necromantic death's head insignia – would a man who no longer believed in the Black Arts place such importance on regalia of this kind? Even British Intelligence made use of an occult department as a counter-measure to the Nazi Occult Bureau.'

Although Gant's face was in darkness, Steadman could feel his eyes boring into him. 'You said Hitler had found a source of power. Some kind of symbol.' He remembered Pope's mention of an ancient spearhead. 'Would it have been the Heilige Lance?'

'Why yes, Mr Steadman.' There was a malicious satisfaction in Gant's smile. 'The spear that was believed to be the weapon that pierced the side of Christ as he died on the cross. The Spear of Longinus the Centurion. Adolf Hitler found the spearhead in Vienna's Hofburg Museum when he was little more than a vagrant in the city and made an extensive search into its history. Even at that time his head was filled with the past glories of the German people – and the glories yet to come. He also had visions of other battles, those fought in another dimension, mystical wars between the forces of God and the forces of the Devil.

'Richard Wagner portrayed these conflicts in many of his finest works and Hitler believed Wagner was the true prophet of his race! It was in *Parsifal,* Wagner's last and most inspired opera, that Hitler discovered the true significance of the Holy Grail, the search for mankind's spiritual fulfilment. The kings, the emperors – the tyrants – who had claimed the holy relic throughout the centuries also knew its secret. It had caused Christ's blood to flow into the ground, to replenish, regenerate the very earth. Its spiritual powers were regarded as the symbolic manifestation of the constant cosmic struggle. It was a symbol of the conflicting powers and only the bearer could choose which it represented. Hitler's knowledge of both history and mysticism made him realize that he had found the link between earthly and spiritual forces. That link, in its material form, was the Spear of Longinus, for it was the weapon, in the hands of a Roman soldier, that had spilled Christ's very spirit into the ground. Hitler vowed he would one day possess the weapon. That day came when he annexed Austria!

'Churchill himself ordered the true facts to be kept secret from the public. The Nuremberg Trials did not even try to explain why such "atrocities" took place. The world had been frightened enough without bringing demonic significance to its attention. Oh no, Mr Steadman, the Führer did not give up his beliefs; far from it. He banned such secret societies because he believed them to be a threat to his own occult power. But the Thule Group continued. We had already become integrated into the SS thanks to the vision of another man, a man far greater than the failure who deigned to be Führer! The man who never gave up even when his beloved country had been betrayed by Hitler. I mean, of course, the Reichsführer, Heinrich Himmler!'

Steadman almost laughed aloud, but he knew Gant was deadly serious. The arms dealer's hands were held clasped together before him, almost in a gesture of prayer.

'Himmler knew the power of the Spear. He had pleaded with his Führer to allow him to take it from Vienna to his Wewelsburg, his shrine of the new Holy Order. But Hitler refused. He had other plans for the sacred relic. The Spear, along with all the other regalia of the Hofburg Treasure House, would be removed legally – not plundered – and taken to St Katherine's Church, Nuremberg, where it would remain until he had attained world dominance. *He failed because he ignored Himmler.*'

Gant was silent now, his shoulders heaving slightly as though he were finding it difficult to breathe. Vapour escaped from his mouth and Steadman realized just how cold the room had become. Unnaturally cold. The fire roared behind the arms dealer, yet no heat seemed to come from it. Gant would never have been able to stand so close otherwise. The arms dealer approached Steadman once again and the investigator tensed, knowing he would not accept another slap without some resistance. But Gant returned his hands to his pockets and stood over Steadman, his attitude menacing.

'But that is the past, Mr Steadman,' he said. 'Let us concern ourselves with the present. As you see – ' he nodded towards Goldblatt and Hannah ' – your two colleagues are of no use to you now. But we would like to know more about you, about your feeble plans to destroy our organization. I'm afraid your friends are not very good talkers. I wonder if your other Mossad associate is?'

'My other associate?' Steadman was perplexed. 'Wait. You mean Baruch Kanaan. You have him . . .'

'No, Mr Steadman.' Gant spat out the words. 'I mean your colleague, Holly Miles.'

'Holly? No, you've got it wrong! She's got nothing to do with Mossad.'

'Really? I must say, she had a perfect cover. Even her credentials checked out. It seems she really is some distant relative of my late wife. But then Mossad is known for its thoroughness. As for the other one – this Baruch – I think he regrets the day he ever visited my Wewelsburg.'

'He's alive?'

Gant grinned maliciously. 'Almost,' he said.

Steadman wondered what 'almost' meant. 'Look, the girl –

Holly – she has nothing to do with all this. She really is a journalist.'

'Of course.'

'No, I mean it. I don't belong to Mossad either. I finished with The Institute years ago. They hired me for a job, that's all, to find their missing agent, Baruch Kanaan.'

'I haven't got time for all this, Mr Steadman,' Gant said with an air of weariness. 'Köhner will find out all we need to know from you when we're gone. We have more important things to attend to, you see. I'll give your love to Miss Miles. I shall enjoy speaking to her.'

'Where is she, Gant? What have you done with her?' Steadman began to rise, but Brannigan pressed a heavy hand down on his shoulder. 'For Christ's sake, Brannigan, why are you involved with this madman? You're in the bloody British Army!'

Gant's hand cracked across his face again, snapping it to one side and drawing blood from the corner of his mouth.

'Please don't be so impolite, Mr Steadman,' Gant said quietly. 'I am not mad. It's the leaders of this country who are mad, allowing it to sink to these depths.'

'But your sympathies were with the Germans, weren't they,' Steadman said through his clenched teeth. 'You kept saying we – we helped Hitler, we, the Thules.'

'I am a German, Mr Steadman. And a loyal friend to Heinrich Himmler. But we never hated the British. We wanted them as allies. We even admired the British aristocracy, for their views were much in line with ours. Unfortunately, your country chose to condemn us. The ironic part is that many see their error now – not just in this country but in others, too. They've witnessed the rise of the lower races and are suffering because of it! It isn't too late, though. Powerful men are behind us now that the climate is right for the counter-revolution. It will be slow at first, but various "happenings" will cause its escalation. And these "happenings" will be engineered by us, the Thule Gesellschaft. Our first major strike will be tomorrow, which is why we have to leave you in the hands of Mr Köhner. He rather enjoys gathering information from people, you know. He especially enjoyed his conversation with your partner, Mrs Wyeth.'

Steadman ignored the restraining hand on his shoulder and the gun at his neck. His hands found Gant's throat and he began to squeeze with all his strength, the blind fury in him overcoming any fear. His head spun wildly as the gun barrel glanced off his skull, but still he clung to the arms dealer, still he tried to choke the life from him. Gant's fingers clenched around Steadman's wrists and tried to pull his hands away, but incredibly strong though the arms dealer's grip was, Steadman's hate was stronger. Only another blow from the gun-barrel weakened his hold. The weapon struck yet again and he slowly sank to his knees, grasping at his victim's body as he went down. Gant's knee sent him keeling over on to the floor. He tried to rise, dazed and hurt, succeeding only in getting his knees under him, his hands flat against the floor. Brannigan stepped forward and kicked his ribs viciously, sending him rolling over on to his back. He tried to clear his head and open his eyes. Through the spinning haze, he saw the withered face of the old man peering down at him, the eyes still hidden inside the two dark caverns. A shriek made him twist his head and though the room tilted and turned, he could see it was Goldblatt who was screaming, straining at his ropes, his hands tied to the arms of the chair, like claws, pointing towards the tall figure of Gant as though wanting to tear him to shreds.

'You bastards,' he was screaming. 'You're still Gestapo filth! You're still the animals you always were. Assassins. You were called the Society of Assassins! And that's all you are!'

Everything took on a dream-like quality as his vision slowly began to fade. He saw Köhner draw something from his inside pocket, saw it gleam redly in the light from the fire, saw Gant slowly nod his head, saw Goldblatt's head pulled back by the hair, saw the knife's blade sweep across the exposed neck as if in slow motion, saw the blood spurt out in a great flood, turning the Israeli's shirt a deep crimson, soaking the floor at his feet. He saw the body stiffen then go into a spasmodic twitching dance.

And he felt the terrible coldness enveloping him as he lost consciousness.

12

'A great deal of potentially useful information can be extracted from suspects. Even if suspicion of their treasonable activities proves to be unfounded they can often be persuaded to give the SD information that will lead to other suspects. Such information is usually given under duress, threat, or promise of release.'

HEINRICH HIMMLER

'Bloody hell, a helicopter!' Steve looked anxiously at the older detective, then ducked his head towards the windscreen so he could see the red tail-light of the helicopter as it rose above the treetops and into the air. 'It's come from the house, I'm sure!'

Blake squinted into the night. 'It must be Gant's own private helicopter. Now I wonder where he's off to?'

'If he's in it. I can't see it too well in the dark, but it looks big enough to carry four or five people. D'you think Mr Steadman's there?'

'God knows. It doesn't make me feel any easier, though. I think we're going to have to do something soon.'

Steve nodded in agreement. He was cold, tired and bored. Cramped, too. Sexton hadn't let him leave the car to exercise his stiff limbs. 'What do we do? Drive up to the gate and demand to see him? Or shall we get the police?'

'Get the police? What for? As far as we know, everything's in order. The governor's doing a bit of business with the arms merchant. What could we tell the police?'

'Sorry. Just feeling a bit twitchy, that's all.'

'All right, son, I feel the same. Harry's been in there a long time. I think the first thing we'll do is get nearer the gates, see if anything . . .'

'Hold it!' Steve's hand closed over his arm in the dark. 'Something's happening. Look, headlights!'

Bright beams of light swung into view, shining through the gates and lighting up the dense forest opposite. Their movement stopped for a few seconds, the vehicle presumably waiting for the gates to be opened. Then they were in motion again, swinging away from the two hidden men, moving off down the road towards the west. They had just made out the shape of a large truck before it had turned fully away from them. They watched the tail-lights disappear down the road and were aware of the helicopter's drone fading into the distance.

'Looks like an exodus,' mused Sexton.

'What, Mr Blake?'

'Nothing. Come on, let's have a closer look.'

They left the Cortina and crept as quietly as possible through the undergrowth towards the entrance to the grounds. When they were opposite and still well-hidden, they waited, shivering against the chill night air.

Steadman brought a hand up to the back of his head, wincing at the sudden sharp pain. He was still lying on the floor where he had fallen, the hazy red shadows dancing on the ceiling confusing him for a few seconds. His head began to clear slowly, but when he tried to raise himself on one elbow, the room spun crazily and he sank back, both hands covering his eyes. Hearing movements, he lowered his hands again and blinked. Still not rising, he swung his head round, careful not to move too fast. He saw the hunched figure of a man – the same man who had shown him into the house that afternoon – dragging something along the floor, something that left a dark, liquid trail behind. It hit him suddenly, the memory tearing into his numbed brain. He tried to rise again, turning himself over on to his side, pushing against the floor with his hands, and this time he was partially successful. He was able to support himself with an elbow and get a clear view of the room. Dimly, in the background of his awareness, he heard the fading sounds of what could only have been a helicopter.

'You bastard!' he yelled, seeing Köhner at the far end of the room standing by the long table. He tried to stagger to his feet, but it was too soon and he fell to the floor again.

'Ah, Steadman. So glad you are awake again.' Köhner walked towards him, hands behind his back, a pleasant smile on his face. The man who had been dragging Goldblatt's bloodied body along the floor continued his journey after a curious glance at Steadman. When he reached a far corner of the room, he bundled the body up and pushed it as close to the wall as possible until it was just a black shape in the shadows. Köhner stopped just before Steadman and the investigator stared at the immaculately polished shoes, their highlights hued red in the glow from the fire. The room was no longer so cold, but now Steadman shivered with the rage building up inside him. What kind of man would kill as cold-bloodedly as this one had?

'We are just a small group now, Steadman. You and me, Craven – ' he indicated towards the small man who was now wiping blood from his hands with a handkerchief ' – and a few guards. The others have all gone to the Wewelsburg. A big day tomorrow, you know. Many preparations to make.' A shoe playfully tapped Steadman in the ribs. 'So, for tonight, you're all mine.' Still smiling, Köhner raised his foot to Steadman's shoulder and pushed him down on to his back again. Then he walked away.

Questions crowded the detective's mind. What was the 'Wewelsburg' and why had Gant and the others gone there? What was going to happen tomorrow? Was Gant completely mad, with all his talk of Hitler and this spear? If he was, it was a dangerous madness. But just how dangerous? Were they just a small group of fanatics or were they widespread? Pope had said Gant had influential friends, powerful men. My God – the man he'd seen drive away in the BMW that afternoon, the MP. Was he one of them? And Holly. Why had they taken her? Did they really believe she was a Mossad agent? What would they do to her? Why had they left him with this murderer, Köhner?

His mind stopped churning when he saw his captor standing behind Hannah, his hands resting on her shoulders, fingers kneading the flesh. She was still tied to the chair, but she was conscious. Her eyes were staring at the bundle lying in the corner.

'Come along now, Steadman,' Köhner said, the smile, so pleasant, so sinister, still on his face. 'Come and join us here.' He picked up the empty chair next to Hannah, the chair which had been occupied by Goldblatt, and moved it to a position facing her, a little distance away. 'Bring him over, Craven.'

The small man ran forward, drawing a gun from inside his jacket. Without a word, he grabbed Steadman just above the elbow and yanked him to his feet. With a hard push, he sent the investigator staggering down the room towards the empty chair. Steadman stumbled and fell, but a prod in his back from Craven's gun encouraged him to rise again. He stood in front of the chair, swaying slightly and was roughly pulled down into it. He looked across at Hannah and there was sadness in her eyes. Regret.

'I'm so sorry . . .' she began to say, but Köhner lashed out with his hand, stopping her words abruptly.

'Shut up, you Jew bitch! You'll talk, but you'll talk to me – not him!'

'Let her be, Köhner,' Steadman said wearily. 'She's only a woman, she . . .'

Köhner's hand lashed out and again it was the woman he struck. She cried out this time and the regret in her eyes was replaced by fear.

Köhner smiled sweetly at Steadman. 'You see, she is the one to be hurt, not you. You are going to tell me what we need to know because if you don't, it will be the woman who will suffer.' He pulled Hannah's jacket apart, then ripped open her blouse. 'It's incredible how sensitive certain areas of the body are, you know, the erogenous zones, in particular. Ironic, isn't it, how parts that can give so much pleasure can also give so much pain.' He reached inside his jacket and once again withdrew the wicked-looking blade from a sheaf worn like a shoulder holster. Steadman saw the knife was double-edged and still bore the bloodstains of its previous victim. He prepared to launch himself forward as the blade descended towards Hannah's exposed stomach, but Köhner glanced towards him and hesitated.

'Better tie him, I think, Craven,' he said. 'This may be too much for the poor man.'

The cold metal of the gun barrel was placed against Steadman's temple and Craven's rough hand grabbed his shirt and jacket collar, sharp fingernails raking the back of his neck. 'Don't worry, sir, he won't move while I've got him like this.'

Satisfied, Köhner knelt before Hannah and once again directed the knife towards her bare flesh. His other hand reached for the waistband of her skirt and tugged at the material, inserting the blade into the gap, then ripping, tearing the skirt down its middle until the two sides flapped open and hung loosely by her sides. He repeated the process with her panties and tights, then snipped open her bra as he rose again. Now her body was completely exposed to him.

Steadman averted his eyes, feeling her shame, wanting to strike out, but forcing himself to wait for the right moment.

There were tears in Hannah's eyes and she closed them so she would not have to see the three faces before her. Their cause was lost now: David had been murdered and Baruch was

159

probably dead too. Steadman would be killed even though he was an innocent in the whole affair. But they'd had no choice; *they'd had to use him.*

Köhner left them and walked to the end of the room towards the table. He picked up something and as he returned, Steadman was puzzled at the object's familiar appearance. 'A simple hairdryer, Steadman. It doesn't take sophisticated instruments to hurt someone – anything handy will do. This is one of my specialities, actually.' He plugged it into a socket by the door, unwinding the long lead as he rose. Köhner flicked the switch with a thumb and the machine whirred into life. He switched it off again, satisfied, and took up a position behind Hannah.

He grabbed her under the chin and held her head against his body in a vice-like grip. 'The ears, first, I think. It'll do terrible damage to her eardrums. Bad enough when it's cold air, but when it really warms up . . .'

'There's nothing to tell, Köhner. For God's sake! They hired me to find their missing agent and that was it! That's all I can tell you!' Steadman's hands gripped the sides of the chair, his knuckles white. The hold on his collar tightened.

'Oh, come now,' Köhner said, shaking his head. The dryer was switched on again and air was sucked into its fan and thrown out in a quickly heated stream. 'You can't expect me to believe that, Steadman. You're much more involved. Mr Gant expects quick answers, that's why he left you to me. Pity he was too busy to watch: I think he'd have enjoyed my skill. He has in the past.' He tested the heat by blowing air against his own cheek. 'Ah, yes. Nicely warming up. It's of the more powerful variety, of course – the type used by hairdressers – so it gets a little hotter than usual. Although that isn't really necessary. An ordinary hairdryer is just as good – it takes a little longer, that's all. Let me see, the breasts after the ears. No, perhaps not. I think she'll be too far gone by that time to feel anything there. Maybe the eyes. Yes, the eyes will be good, even with the lids closed.'

'Köhner!'

'And finally, the vagina. That will kill her, of course, Steadman.' The whining machine was pushed against Hannah's ear
and she tried to struggle away from it. She screamed as the
hot air blasted its way down her ear canal and reached the ear-
drum.

'Please, stop! I'll tell you everything I know!' Steadman
pleaded.

Köhner looked disappointed. He took the dryer away from
Hannah's ear but left the motor running. She moaned and tried
to twist her head from his grasp, but he was too strong for her.
'Well?' he said.

'It's true what I said about being hired by Mossad to find
Baruch Kanaan. I did belong to Israeli Intelligence, but that was
years ago. I'd left them.'

'Why would you do that?'

'I – I was sick of the bloodshed. The Arabs killed someone
. . . someone close to me. I went on the rampage after, killing,
killing – until I was sick of it!'

'How traumatic.'

'It's true, fuck you! I'd had too much of it! Too much killing.
Too much revenge.'

'And you left them.'

'Yes. I wanted nothing to do with them any more. But they
had someone watching me all the time, an old man who'd lived
in this country since the war.'

'The jeweller.'

'Yes.' Steadman stared at Köhner. 'Yes, how did you know?'

'It doesn't matter how I know. The old man's dead now – he
didn't survive his visit to you last night.' Then he added with a
grin, 'Something frightened him to death.'

There was so much happening that Steadman didn't understand. He shook his head and went on: 'They came to me a
couple of weeks ago, Goldblatt and this woman, Hannah. I refused to help them find their missing agent, but my partner
agreed to without my knowing.'

'Yes, Mrs Wyeth. I had an interesting chat with her. Unfortunately – for her – she couldn't really tell me much. Mr Gant was right: she really didn't know anything.'

'You . . . you were the one . . .'

'Keep talking, Steadman. No questions, just answers, please.'

Craven made the gun's presence known even more strongly when he felt the investigator tense again. Steadman was nearing breaking point he told himself. Perhaps they should have tied him after all. Pity he was talking so soon, though; he'd have liked to have seen the woman squirm more. She had a beautifully ripe body, the cut clothes accentuating its sensuality; it would be good to see it writhe, see those smooth thighs open wider with agony. Pity to kill her. Maybe Köhner would let him use her first. If he didn't . . . well, he would be the one who had to dispose of the body. Plenty of time then . . .

The dryer was moving towards Hannah's head again and Steadman quickly resumed talking. 'After Mag . . . my partner . . . was killed, a man named Pope came to see me. He was from British Intelligence and knew Mossad were operating here. He's also investigating Edward Gant.'

Hannah stopped twisting her head and stared across at the investigator, her eyes wide. 'Steadman, don't . . .'

Köhner clamped his hand over her mouth and snarled, 'Don't interrupt, you Jew whore. It's getting very interesting. Go on, Steadman.'

Köhner suddenly yelped in pain as Hannah bit deep into his hand, her teeth drawing blood. He dropped the dryer and reached for the knife again, all in one reaction.

Steadman screamed 'No!' as the blade plunged deep into the flesh of Hannah's stomach, and Craven, whose eyes had been watching the exposed parts of her body, froze at the suddenness of it all. The knife, still embedded, was travelling upwards in a straight line towards her chin when Steadman grabbed the gun-barrel and pushed it aside.

The investigator was on his feet, the hand at his neck having no effect on his enraged strength, the chair crashing over be-hind him. He still held on to the gun and realized the little man hadn't even released the safety-clip. Twisting his body, he brought his leg up and Craven was lifted into the air, his scream piercing the air.

Steadman whirled, forgetting about the injured man for the moment, knowing his agony would keep him out of action for a while. He flew at Köhner, hands outstretched, grabbing for the knife that was now raised against him, its blade red with blood. He was lucky enough to find the knuckles clasped around the knife's handle and he pushed the weapon away as both men went over, dragging the chair holding Hannah with them. They went down in a heap, Steadman pushing the knife-hand to the floor, while Köhner kicked and struggled beneath him, grabbing at the investigator's hair and trying to pull his head back. Hannah, still tied securely to the chair, rolled on to her side, the blood flowing from the long rent stretching from her lower stomach to her breast-bone, creating a dark viscous puddle on the wood floor.

As Köhner pulled at his assailant's hair, he managed to bring a knee up and bring it hard against Steadman's hip, the blow sending the investigator to one side, Köhner rolling with him. The knife came up from the floor and he almost managed to wrench himself from the investigator's grip. But Steadman knew if the knife-hand got free again, Köhner had the speed and experience to kill him easily. Both men were on their sides and Köhner used his strength to carry his body through with the roll so that he gained the advantage of having Steadman beneath him. He let go of the investigator's hair to add strength to the hand pressing the knife towards Steadman. The pointed tip pushed against Steadman's cheek, pressing the skin inward until the flesh broke and a trickle of blood emerged. Steadman had both his hands around Köhner's and he tried to hold the straining blade away, but he felt it slowly sinking into his cheek, millimetre by millimetre, eager to burst through into the cavern of his mouth. Köhner's eyes were above him, staring down, a gleam of triumph and blood-lust in them. He felt no pain; only the relentless force of the cold metal.

He slowly turned his head, feeling the skin tear as the steel blade sliced a shallow red-lined path across his cheek.

He used his whole body to try and squirm away from Köhner and felt his opponent moving with him, endeavouring to keep him pinned. The knife edge was grating against bone now and he knew his head would move no further; metal and bone were locked together. With a roar he changed his direction and heaved upwards, using all his strength against the other man's weight. Köhner resisted but the movement was too sudden; he was forced backwards. When he knew he had reached the point of overbalance and the knife had been pushed clear of Steadman's cheek, he allowed himself to be carried with the momentum, skilfully using his weight and strength to his own advantage. His intention was to continue the roll, using pressure only when the movement would put him on top again. But Steadman still retained enough cunning in hand-to-hand combat to break away at the right moment. He hadn't wanted to release the hands holding the knife, but he had guessed Köhner's reason for withdrawing the pressure. He twisted away from his surprised antagonist and kept rolling, knowing the weapon would be following, striking towards his exposed back.

He felt rather than heard it thud into the floor behind, and swiftly rose to a crouching position while the knife was tugged free. He turned to face his antagonist, hands held poised before him.

Köhner had also risen and both men were silent as they watched one another, each waiting for the other to make the first move. Steadman stared into Köhner's eyes, the blade still in the periphery of his vision but not in focus, the eyes would tell him what the man would do. He could hear Craven groaning and writhing on the floor to his left and he knew he would have to move fast if he were to avoid having two opponents again: Köhner was enough on his own. Köhner's eyes widened slightly before he lunged, but it was enough to give the investigator warning. He threw himself to one side, ducking low, and the blade went on past his shoulder. Their bodies made contact and Köhner staggered, spinning round, but managing to control his movements so that he was balanced and ready to lunge again. Steadman wasn't there though; he was racing towards the black object lying in the centre of the room. Köhner followed, confident that the knife would be deeply embedded in the investigator's back before he had time to use the gun.

Steadman realized the same. He stooped and reached for the back of the overturned chair he'd been held captive in only minutes before and, hearing the footsteps behind, he swung his body round, bringing the chair up as he did so. It crashed against Köhner's shoulder causing him to stumble to one side, and before he could recover fully, the chair was on its return journey, this time aimed at his head. He ducked instinctively and Steadman was momentarily thrown off balance. He recovered quickly enough to swing the chair up again, this time as a shield against Köhner's oncoming rush. It struck Köhner's body and Steadman pushed, the knife waving in the air in a vain attempt to reach him. Steadman exerted all his force and kept pushing, moving the other man backwards. Köhner resisted, hopelessly caught up between the legs of the chair, unable to thrust it aside. He took the only course available: he dropped to the floor pulling the chair with him but lifting it so it sailed over his head. It still left him at a disadvantage, for he was flat on his back, and he struck out at Steadman's legs with the knife as he lay there.

The investigator drew in his breath as the knife's razor-sharp edge slid along his shin-bone, only its angle preventing it from cutting deeply. He tried to leap clear of the thrashing blade as he staggered over Köhner's recumbent figure and fell heavily against the chair which had crashed into the floor just beyond the fallen man's head.

Steadman found himself lying on his stomach, the chair leaning against him and, for the briefest second, he looked into the face of Hannah still trapped in her chair in the centre of the big room. Her eyes were pleading and her lips moved as her life oozed from her. She was looking directly at him. He staggered to his feet, bringing the chair up so it cracked against the advancing Köhner's chin, sending the German reeling back. Köhner raised a hand, reaching for his eyes as if to wipe the dizziness from them. Steadman was on him, relishing his sudden advantage, reaching for the arm clutching the weapon with both hands and bringing it down sharply against his rising knee in an effort to break it. He didn't succeed, but at least the knife flew from Köhner's grasp, clattering uselessly against the bare floorboards.

The investigator used his elbow against the other man's ribs, still holding the now limp arm outstretched with one hand. Steadman heard Köhner gasp, but his satisfaction was short-lived as his opponent twisted and managed to encircle the investigator's neck with his other arm, squeezing hard to cut off his air. Steadman leaned forward and jerked Köhner off the floor, bending almost double so the other man tumbled over his shoulders on to the floor before him.

Lithe as a cat, Köhner was up again and turning to face him. But Steadman's rage at this creature who could destroy lives without remorse, and with an ease that said he was a master of it, drove him on relentlessly. He plunged into the murderer, his fists striking the man's face, sending him staggering back towards the low-burning fire. Fear began to show in Köhner's eyes as Steadman bore down on him. He knew the investigator's rage had made him unstoppable; only a weapon would have any effect. He looked around, desperate for a means of escape or a weapon within reach and saw there was nothing. The knife had disappeared into the shadows, Craven's gun was on the other side of the room. But Craven was beginning to rise now. He was on his knees, his shoulders hunched, his hands still pressed between his legs. But he was beginning to rise! If he would only reach for the gun!

Köhner was about to call out to the kneeling man when another blow sent him reeling. 'Wait, I can help you! Don't . . .'

Steadman paid no heed to the words. The same hatred he had felt when Lilla had been so mercilessly killed had once again taken over.

Köhner recognized the hate and put up his hands to ward Steadman off, but they were easily knocked aside. He backed away until he could feel the heat behind him. The fire! Oh God, he was backing into the fire! He tried to make a break to one side, but Steadman grabbed his collar and struck him again, a hard, stinging blow that covered his vision with a blinding light. He fell, his arms flailing, instinctively trying to grab the sides of the fire surround. His hands made no contact and he screamed as he fell into the small, dancing flames. As the heat burnt his coat and scorched his body, he pleaded with the investigator to pull him out.

Steadman raised a foot and planted it squarely on the burning man's chest, holding him there, his loathing rejecting any mercy. Köhner screamed again and again, twisting his body, trying to wriggle free while Steadman held him, no expression on his face. It was only when Köhner's hair began to burn that the investigator reached forward, grabbing him by the lapels of his jacket, and pulled him clear. Köhner's screams echoed round the room as Steadman tore the jacket from him, much of the shirt coming away with it, and threw it towards the fireplace. The investigator beat out the smaller flames on the man's clothing with his hands, not even wincing at the sight of the scorched flesh. Köhner's singed hair hung in blackened clumps on the back of his head and his teeth chattered as though he was freezing.

Craven's cry of alarm warned Steadman and he turned just in time to see the little man crawling rapidly towards the gun lying on the floor. The investigator sprang forward, racing towards the scrambling man, who looked up in fear at the sound of his approach. It was that moment of hesitation that lost Craven his chance. He was half up, no longer crawling, reaching down for the gun, when it was kicked from under his grasp. He saw it scudding away into the shadows and felt terror as a hand fell on to his exposed neck. Another hand grabbed the back of his trousers, and then he was being propelled forward, his own rush towards the gun now working against him. He was powerless in the grip that held him and the floorboards sped beneath his feet as he tried to keep his balance. They were gathering momentum, heading towards the table at the far end of the room, towards the twisting body of Köhner. He tried to sink to the floor when he realized Steadman's intention, but the grip was too strong, the pace too fast. He felt himself lifted, skidding across the table's surface – and then beyond.

He felt the glass break around him, yet did not hear the sound. The ground rushed towards him and, mercifully, he felt nothing as his head broke open against it.

Steadman stood with his hands resting against the table-top, breathing in deep lungfuls of the cold night air as it gushed through the shattered window, his shoulders heaving with the exertion. The fury was still in him, hardly dissipated by the violence he had just committed; but it was a cold fury now, his mind working almost dispassionately. He knew the disgust for himself would come later, would torment with the knowledge that he was little better than the men he had acted against. For the moment, though, those feelings would be held in abeyance – there was so much more to do.

He pushed himself away from the table and crossed the room, ignoring Köhner, who lay on his stomach, moaning softly, parts of his clothing still smouldering. Steadman knelt beside Hannah and grimaced at the sight of the terrible wound the knife had inflicted. The floor around her was awash with blood and he turned his eyes away from the long gash when he saw glistening organs beginning to protrude from the opening. He thought she was dead, but as he began to untie her bonds, her eyelids fluttered, then opened. Her lips moved as she tried to speak.

'Don't talk,' he told her. 'I'm going to get you to a hospital.' He knew the words were without meaning, for there was no chance she would live.

168

Hannah knew it too. 'Steadman,' she said, her voice faint, as though she were calling back to him from a distance as her life seeped away. He leaned down towards her, putting his ear close to her mouth to listen. It was difficult to make out the words, but she kept repeating them as though making sure he understood. 'The . . . Spear . . . for . . . Israel, Steadman . . . you must . . . for Israel . . . get . . .'

Her voice trailed off as Hannah sank into her death. Steadman drew away from her, closing her eyes with his fingers and arranging her clothing to cover her nakedness and the awful gaping wound. He touched a hand to her cheek, then rose to his feet. He looked towards Köhner, his eyes cold.

The burnt man was on his hands and knees, moving towards the door. He turned his head at the sound of Steadman's approach and his eyes widened in fear when he saw the expression on the investigator's face.

Steadman pulled him to his feet, and pushed him on to the table. Köhner screaming as his scorched back made contact with the table-top.

'You're going to tell me some things, Köhner,' Steadman said, shaking him by his shoulders. 'You're going to tell me what will happen tomorrow.' He brought Köhner's face close to his own and said, 'You're going to tell me where Holly Miles and Baruch Kanaan are being held.'

Köhner tried to pull himself away, but his injuries – and his fright – had weakened him. 'I can't tell you anything, Steadman. Please, you've got to get me to hospital.'

'Not until you've told me all I want to know, Köhner.'

'No, they'll kill me!'

'*I'll* kill you.'

'Please, listen. There's nothing you . . .'

'Where has Gant gone to?'

'I can't tell you!'

Steadman slammed him back down on to the table. He placed his elbow under Köhner's chin, pushing it up, ignoring his feeble efforts to pull away. He grabbed the German's right hand

and held it by the wrist with one hand, then with the other he took hold of one of the fingers. The smallest. He pulled it back swiftly and it snapped.

He closed his mind to Köhner's scream and fought his own revulsion. He had to fight them on their own level, evil for evil. For Holly's sake. For Baruch's. He would not let them be taken as Lilla had been taken.

'Tell me, Köhner. Where have they gone? Where are they holding the girl?'

Tears ran down the sides of Köhner's face and Steadman was afraid the man might pass out. It said much for his toughness that he hadn't.

'The Wewelsburg! They've gone there! Please don't!'

The Wewelsburg. That name again. Steadman took hold of another finger. 'What *is* the Wewelsburg, Köhner?' he asked, beginning to apply pressure again.

'Don't! It's a house – an estate. It belongs to Gant.'

'Where?'

'On the coast. North Devon. Please don't hurt me again . . .'

'Where exactly?'

'Near a place called Hartlands. Further on!' Köhner tried to squirm away and the investigator pressed down harder with his elbow. 'The girl is there, Steadman. She's all right, she's alive!' The words were meant to appease him.

The West Coast. Holly had said Gant had a place on the West Coast. Was that his Wewelsburg? 'Okay. Now tell me what Gant is up to? What's happening tomorrow?'

'I can't. I can't tell you.'

It was only footsteps on the stairs that prevented another of Köhner's fingers from being broken.

13

'We must interpret "Parsifal" in a totally different way to the general conception . . . It is not the Christian-Schopenhaurerist religion of compassion that is acclaimed, but pure, noble blood, in the protection and glorification of whose purity the brotherhood of the initiated have come together.'

ADOLF HITLER

The two guards, both armed with a general-purpose machine-gun and rifle similar to the NATO FN, but of Gant's own manufacture and considerably lighter because of it, raced up the stairs to the room where the prisoner was being held. They were veteran mercenaries who had finally found a binding allegiance – as had all the soldiers in Edward Gant's private army. It was a small army, no more than fifty carefully chosen soldiers, a Guard really – a *corps d'élite*. Some were mercenaries who fought battles for others, their loyalty only bought with money; others were taken from the crack SAS regiments, chosen because of their special skills and aptitudes by Major Brannigan and steered into Gant's organization. Their common bond was their extreme right-wing views and a dislike for the world in general. They admired strength and craved strong

171

leadership: Gant provided them with that leadership. Officially, they were merely employees of Gant's weapons' factory, testing the weapons in practical ways and acting as security for the plant. They wore dark green overalls which somehow succeeded in having a military air without actually being uniforms. There were no insignia, no badges of rank; but each man knew his position and who his superiors were. They enjoyed their secret military ceremonies which took place only on the arms dealer's vast North Devon estate, even grateful for the harsh discipline imposed on them there, and disliked their dealings with the various factions who visited the estate to learn how to use the many weapons they were buying from Gant. They sneered at the groups of Arabs, Africans, Japanese and Irish they had to teach, *wanting to turn the weapons on them*, but patiently went through the exercises, demonstrating, explaining, because they knew it helped the cause of world disunity. These groups of fanatics would help create the world unrest which would succour their own movement. They had learned to obey their orders without question, the fate of their comrades who had failed to do so ever-present in their minds. Hanging may have been abolished in England, but Edward Gant worked to his own laws. They had no title, but sometimes, when they were very drunk and only when they were safely inside the estate's boundaries, they laughingly gave themselves a name. They called themselves the Soldiers of the Fourth Reich.

These two, McGough and Blair, had been left behind with the guard on the gate, the three others of their unit returning to the estate by lorry that night. The rumour was that a special op was planned for the next day, but as yet no briefing had been given and speculation on their part was strictly forbidden. They had regretted being left behind, though did not question it. Nor did they question Gant's particular instructions.

They rounded the bend in the wide stairs and stopped abruptly, aiming their guns at the two figures that had appeared on the landing above them. One of the figures was Köhner, his face contorted with pain and his blackened shirt hanging loosely around him; the other man standing immediately behind Köhner was the prisoner, the private investigator who had been shown through the weapons store at the back of the house that afternoon.

'Don't move!' Blair commanded and resumed his ascent of the stairs, McGough following close behind.

Steadman did not hesitate. There was no time to search for the fallen gun in the room he and Köhner had just left, so he used the nearest thing at hand to stop the progress of the two men below: Felix Köhner. He shoved the injured man hard, sending him careering down the stairs, his arms flailing wildly. Köhner's body struck McGough and Blair with a force that sent all three tumbling backwards until they landed in a tangled heap at the bend. Steadman descended the stairs three at a time and was able to kick the gun from one of the soldier's hands before it could be aimed at him. The other man was scrambling towards his gun which had clattered further down the stairs, and Steadman hooked a foot beneath him, sending the soldier well beyond the fallen weapon.

The investigator lifted the dazed Köhner to his feet and said, 'Come on, I still need you.' He pushed him forward and turned to the soldier who was beginning to rise. Steadman's knee hit him full in the face and the soldier slammed back against the wall, then slid to the floor. The investigator pulled Köhner away from the banister and raced him down the stairs past the disorientated second man lying at the bottom. He dragged Köhner down the hall towards the doorway, knowing only speed would prevent a bullet in his back. If he had tried for one of the guns himself, the men would have been on him before he'd had a chance even to aim it; past experience told him, when outnumbered, keep on the move. He reached the front door and yanked it open, pushing Köhner ahead of him into the night.

On the stairs, McGough had reached his weapon and was automatically sighting it on Steadman's back below, when he caught sight of Blair's upturned face. It was white and the lips were clenched, but it shook hastily. McGough lowered the gun and stared regretfully at the front door as it slammed shut.

Steadman was relieved to find no guards outside and his car still waiting. He hurried the dazed Köhner over to it and yanked open the passenger door, pushing the injured man into the seat. He ran round the front of the car, reaching in his trouser-pocket for the keys, then jumped into the driver's seat, hauling the weakened Köhner back as he tried to scramble out.

'I told you I need you, Köhner. You're going to get me through the gate.'

He gunned the engine, expecting the door of the house to be flung open at any moment and the two guards to run out, machine-guns blazing. But his luck held: there was no movement from the house. They still must have been stunned. The Celica spewed up gravel as it roared away from the building towards the main gate. Steadman switched on full-beam to blind the guard and his dogs, knowing he would have to be through those gates within seconds, for the two soldiers would soon ring the hut from the house – if they hadn't already done so.

As the car sped round the curve in the long drive, the guard, standing before the solid gate with the menacing Alsatians, was frozen in the headlights. The investigator brought the car to a halt ten yards away from him and the guard raised an arm up to his brow to cut out the blinding glare. The dogs strained at their leash.

'Who's there?' the guard called out. 'Turn those bloody lights out so I can see you.'

'Tell him to let us through, Köhner,' Steadman said quietly.

Köhner shook his head, his injured hand clasped to his stomach. His smoke-dirtied face was streaked with tears. 'Go to hell,' he managed to gasp.

The guard began advancing on the car, a hand reaching inside his tunic for a gun he kept hidden away from usual visitors to the house. The dogs were excited, instinctively catching the mood of the situation. The guard's arm was at full-stretch as he tried to hold them back and he had to dig his heels into the gravel to prevent himself being dragged forward too fast. The growls of the dogs became barks and then howls as they struggled to break free.

Steadman moved fast. He reached across the injured man and hooked his finger around the door-catch, pushing the door open. Then he shoved Köhner out of the car.

Köhner rolled on to his back, screamed and tried to rise. It was too much for the Alsatians. They broke away from the guard and pounded towards the rising man. They leapt upon him, teeth slashing, sensing their victim was injured and easy prey.

The confused guard was hurrying forward, his gun aimed at the frenzied group, the car's lights still dazzling his vision. Steadman depressed the accelerator and the car shot forward, striking the guard, knocking him over the bonnet and into the gravel. Hitting the brakes immediately, Steadman leapt from the car, snatched the revolver from the stunned guard's grasp and reached for the key to the gate which hung on a chain from the man's belt. It was a huge key and Steadman's shaking hands fumbled at the clasp securing it to the chain for several precious seconds before it was free. He could hear Köhner's screams and the blood-chilling snarls of the dogs on the other side of the car as he fumbled. The guard, whose legs felt numb and lifeless from the blow they had received, raised himself on to his elbows and tried to grab at the gun. Steadman pushed the man's head back on to the driveway with a force that put him completely out of action.

The investigator finally yanked the key free and ran to the gate, keeping a wary eye over his shoulder in the direction of the dogs who, by now, were wild with bloodlust. He inserted the key and twisted, then swung the gates wide. As he returned to the car, holding a hand up against the headlights' glare, he knew he could not just leave Köhner to the mercy of the Alsatians. He stepped out of the beam of light, the gun raised before him, and blinked his eyes rapidly to get them used to the sudden darkness again. The screams had stopped and the snarls were less wild as the dogs pulled and tugged at the inert body. One of the Alsatians sensed his approach and turned its eyes towards him. Its growl was deep-throated and full of warning. The other looked up too, its mouth bloody and drooling pink foam. Steadman saw their muscles tense as they readied themselves to spring at him. He raised the gun and fired two rounds into each body as they leapt, taking a step back as one of the dogs slumped against his legs.

He quickly glanced at the unmoving body of Köhner, then walked around to the other side of the car and climbed in. He drove through the open gateway on to the main road.

Steadman was forced to jam on his brakes once again as he began his turn. Two figures had emerged from the woodland on the opposite side of the road and were frantically waving their arms at him.

'Sexton! Steve! What the hell are you doing here?' Steadman wound down his window and looked at his two employees with amazement.

Sexton jerked a thumb at his companion. 'Goldblatt and a woman were picked up by three men. Steve followed 'em here. Are you all right, Harry?' he asked, suddenly noticing the fresh blood on Steadman's cheek.

The investigator ignored the question. 'I've got to get to a phone.'

'There's one about a mile-and-a-half down the road, Mr Steadman,' Steve said, excited by the action.

'Okay. Jump in, both of you. There'll be men coming from the house any minute.'

The two men hurried around to the passenger side of the car, Steve nimbly climbing past the front seat into the back and Sexton slumping his cold-stiffened frame beside Steadman.

'It's back that way, Mr Steadman.' Steve pointed. The investigator quickly reversed, the rear of the car almost entering the grounds again, then spun the wheel to the right as it screeched forward. Sexton just had time to see a dark figure sitting in

the driveway rubbing the back of his head. He turned to face
Steadman as the car gathered speed along the road.

'What's been happening, Harry? We were a bit worried.'

'It's Gant. He's a madman. He had Goldblatt and the woman
killed. And Maggie.' There was a weariness in Steadman's
voice.

'Christ! What do we do? Get the police?'

'Not yet. I'm going to call a man named Pope. He works for
Intelligence – MI5. He'll have to sort it out.'

'But what about this Gant? He'll get away.'

'Already gone,' Steadman replied grimly.

'The helicopter. We saw a helicopter leave and a truck drove
out shortly after.'

Steadman dimly remembered the sound of rotor blades as
he'd recovered consciousness back in the house. 'Yes, that
would be it. I saw one earlier in the afternoon. He's gone to
somewhere he calls his "Wewelsburg". Somewhere in North
Devon.'

'He's got an estate there where he tests weapons,' Sexton
said. 'I found that out this morning. A lot of the country around
that area is used by the Military for testing.'

Steadman nodded. 'He's got something planned for tomorrow – I've no idea what. It sounds important to him and his
crazy organization, though.'

'What's he up to?'

'He imagines himself as the new Hitler – only stronger. I told
you – he's completely mad. Where's this bloody phone, Steve?'
There were street lights now, and houses lined the roadside.

'Not far. Just up here a bit on the left.'

'What happened back at the house, Harry?' Sexton asked.
'How did you get away?'

'Gant left me behind – with his special inquisitor. Fortunately
for me, neither he nor the few remaining guards were too ef-
ficient. I had a lot of luck on my side, though.' He pulled over
to the telephone box. 'Wait here,' he told the two men as he
left the car, its engine still running. 'Keep an eye on the way

we've come. They may decide to look for me.' Sexton and Steve turned their attention to the rear window.

The pips indicating someone had lifted the receiver at the other end began almost as soon as Steadman had finished dialling the memorized number, and he pushed the coin into its slot. A voice said, 'Pope,' and the investigator breathed a sigh of relief.

'Pope,' he said. 'Thank God you're there.'

'Steadman? I've been waiting for your call. Been rather anxious, actually. Now, have you found out any more on Gant?'

There was a hint of relief in Pope's voice, but it was hardly comforting to Steadman. 'I found out plenty, but it's all so incredible. You were right. Gant is the head of an organization called the Thule Gesellschaft.' Steadman quickly told him what had happened at the house and Pope listened patiently, occasionally interrupting with a pertinent question. 'But why did he leave you in the hands of this man, Köhner?' he asked when Steadman explained Gant's departure from the house.

'To get information from me, to find out what I knew and who else was involved. Gant has a big operation to mount and he had no time personally to waste on me.'

'Operation? What sort of operation?' Pope's voice had a keen edge to it.

'I don't know. He's gone to his North Devon estate – somewhere near Hartlands – to carry it out. Do you know anything that's going to happen some time tomorrow, Pope? Anything in that area?'

There was a long silence at the other end then Pope said, 'There is something, but . . .' Another silence. 'No, it can't be that, it's nothing to do with that area. Unless . . . Oh God, he wouldn't try to do anything like that.'

'What, Pope? Remember, he's a madman. He'd do anything to further his crazy cause.'

'Not over the phone, Harry – I'll tell you later. We'll have to move in. We know this estate – a large part of his weapons-testing takes place there, so it's usually under some sort of surveillance by us.'

'There's another thing. He's got the girl there. Holly Miles. He thinks she's working for Mossad.'

'The journalist? *Is* she working for Mossad?'

'I was going to ask you the same question.'

'I've no idea, dear boy. Rather confusing, isn't it?'

'What about Major Brannigan and the MP I saw down here? What will you do about them?'

'They'll be hauled in when we have Gant. It's all very delicate, though.'

'The murders of Maggie, Goldblatt and Hannah – and maybe Baruch Kanaan – are all very *indelicate*, Pope,' Steadman said angrily.

'Of course, Harry. They'll be accounted for, don't worry. Now listen, can you get to Hartlands?'

'Are you crazy? Why the hell should I go there? It's up to you now.'

Pips began, informing them that their allocated time was up, and Steadman fiercely pushed another coin into the slot.

'Harry, are you still there?'

'I'm here.'

'I need you to go there, Harry. You know Special Branch has to make the arrests – I haven't that power as MI5. You're the only man who knows the full story, and if I order a large force into the estate, I need some verification. Your personal evidence will save a lot of unnecessary official wrangles. Please believe me, I need you there if only to convince my superiors.'

'Why can't I just come over to your HQ now?'

'It's easier this way. It's pointless for you to come back to London when you're already on the way to the west. I want you on the spot, Harry. Do you feel up to it?'

'I'll manage.'

'Good man. There's a town called Bideford not far from Hartlands. Find yourself a hotel and book in. We'll find you there easily enough by checking round.'

'Will you involve the local police?'

'They'll be informed but not involved. Too many people in high places involved for this to be made public, I'm afraid.'

'Listen, Pope, if you're going to protect . . .'

'Please, Harry, there's no time for discussion now. I've got a lot to do and you have a long journey ahead of you. I'll have to have any calls from Gant's estate in Guildford intercepted for a start. If any of those guards warn Gant before I can get a squad down . . .'

'Christ, Pope . . .'

'Please, Harry. There's no time. Remember the girl's in danger. I'll see you tomorrow.'

The receiver at the other end was put down and Steadman stared blankly at the burring earpiece. He slammed down the phone and left the booth.

His two companions looked at him anxiously as he threw himself back into the driver's seat. He ran his hands over his face as though to wipe away the fatigue.

'What now, Harry?' Sexton prompted gently.

'I'll take you back to your cars, then I've got a trip to make. To Devon.'

'Are we coming with you, Mr Steadman?' Steve asked eagerly.

'No, I don't want either of you involved in this thing.'

'We work for you, Harry,' said Sexton. 'If you're involved, we're involved. Besides, we thought a lot of Mrs Wyeth.'

Steadman smiled at them. 'There's one thing you can do, but I'll tell you what on the way back to your cars. Tell me though: have either of you heard of something or someone called "Parsifal". When I was in the house, Gant said something in German to his friends. He said: "Our Parsifal is inquisitive and impatient." He was referring to me and obviously didn't know I understand a little German thanks to my ex-wife. Have either of you heard the name before?'

Sexton shook his head, but Steve leaned forward towards the front seats, his eyes gleaming.

'There is a Parsi*val*, Mr Steadman. He was one of the Teutonic Knights. Wagner wrote an opera about him, but he changed the spelling to "Parsifal" for some reason. It was all about the Holy Grail and the sacred Spear that was stolen from the king, Amfortas, the Keeper of the Grail.'

The two men twisted their bodies to stare at his excited face, lit by a nearby street light.

'A sacred Spear?' Steadman said quietly.

Steve suddenly became embarrassed under their scrutiny. 'I'm a bit of an opera freak – that's how I know the story. I think *Parsifal* was one of Wagner's greatest. He was . . .'

Steadman interrupted him. 'You say this Spear was stolen?'

'Yes, by Klingsor, the evil magician. It was Parsifal who had to get it back . . .'

'What's all this got to do with Gant, Harry?' Sexton asked impatiently. 'Aren't we wasting time?'

Steadman silenced him with a raised hand. 'Tell me the whole story of this *Parsifal*, Steve,' he said. 'Try to remember every detail. It could be the key to this whole bloody business.'

Steve looked in bewilderment at the investigator, took a deep breath, then began.

14

'But are we to allow the masses to go their way, or should we stop them? Shall we form simply a select company of the really initiated? An Order, the brotherhood of Templars round the holy grail of pure blood?'

ADOLF HITLER

Steadman relaxed on to the bed and reached for the cigarettes on the small side-table. He lit one and drew in a deep breath, watching the smoke swirl in the air as he exhaled. He felt rested now and his mind was beginning to think more clearly. He winced when he crossed his ankles, then drew up a trouser-leg to examine the knife wound inflicted by Köhner the previous night. It wasn't deep, but it was irritatingly painful. Fortunately the hotel receptionist hadn't noticed the torn trousers from behind the desk. After reading the investigator's London address as he filled in the card, she had merely accepted Steadman's somewhat dishevelled appearance as a result of his long drive. In fact, Steadman had broken his journey.

It was just outside Andover that events had caught up with him. He had been forced to stop the car as tiredness overwhelmed him, and a feeling of remorse had had a lot to do with that tiredness. Even the thought of the danger Holly – and Baruch, if he really was still alive – was in could not spur him on. In his present condition, he knew he could not help anyone. Slumping against the steering wheel, he cursed himself for having become involved with such violence, for having broken his vow to himself and Lilla that never again would he become part of such things. It wasn't his fault, he knew. He'd been reluctantly drawn into it; yet he'd used their own kind of violence against them. And it had been perpetrated with a coldness that now disturbed him. Pope had been right at their first meeting. His aggressiveness *had* only been smothered; it was still there waiting to be unleashed.

He felt no pity for Köhner or the little man, Craven – they had deserved to die – but he felt concern for his own actions. He had recovered enough energy after a while to find a motel and there he'd spent the night, surprisingly falling into a deep and dreamless sleep. The following morning, after a shower, then a half-eaten breakfast, and covering the gash in his cheek with a Band-aid obtained from the curious but sympathetic motel receptionist, he had resumed his journey, feeling better for the rest, his mind clear again. The guilt was still there but, he thought cynically, he would wallow in it when matters had been put right. The remainder of his journey had been more relaxed and it had given him time to sort out his thoughts. By the time he reached Bideford he had a new resolve. Before, his purpose had been to protect Holly, to let Pope deal with Gant and whatever he was up to; but now he had decided to take care of the arms dealer himself. After all, wasn't that the reason for his involvement in the whole bizarre affair – the final confrontation between himself and Edward Gant?

The blood on the knife-wound had hardened, forming a natural healing seal. He slid his trouser-leg back down and rested the injured limb; he could bandage it later. He looked at his watch, impatient for Pope's call. Had he missed him because of his unplanned late arrival at the hotel? No, Pope would keep checking all the hotels until he showed. What was keeping him though?

It was strange how it all made a crazy kind of sense: Hitler, the Spear of Longinus, Gant's referring to him, Steadman, as Parsifal. But what was the Wewelsburg? More symbolism, ancient beliefs? Steve had told him about Wagner's opera, and the significance had begun to sink into Steadman's confused brain. It was the reason for his involvement, why it had to be played out to the end. It was the fulfilment of the legend, but this time with a different ending, and that ending would be the omen of their success.

The ringing of the bedside phone startled him from his thoughts. He picked up the receiver.

'Oh, Mr Steadman? Two gentlemen in reception to see you. A Mr Griggs and a Mr Booth. Acquaintances of a Mr Pope.'

'I'll be right down,' he replied and put down the phone.

He stubbed out the cigarette in an ashtray and swung his legs off the bed, groaning at the stiffness of his bruised ribs and limbs, then donned his jacket and left the room.

Mr Griggs and Mr Booth were sitting in the lounge area, a small coffee table between them, an empty chair awaiting his arrival. He recognized them as the MI5 agents who had taken the collapsed jeweller from his house two nights before. They jumped up at his approach and one said, 'Glad you made it okay, Mr Steadman. I'm Griggs, by the way.'

Steadman nodded and took the provided easy-chair. 'Where's Pope?' he said bluntly.

'Up at the estate. We moved in early this morning without much trouble.' Steadman could not be bothered to register surprise.

'Is the girl all right?'

The second man, Booth, spoke up. 'Fine, sir, a bit confused though.' He grinned at the investigator.

'And you've got Gant?' Steadman didn't grin back.

'Yes, Mr Pope's still interrogating him,' said Griggs. 'He's

185

refusing to say anything even though he knows the game's up. I think the sight of you should unsettle him, though.'

'What about Major Brannigan and the others?'

'Quiet as mice. The whole operation was extremely smooth. Hardly any resistance at all.'

'Have you found out what they had planned for today?'

'Not yet,' said Booth, 'but we think we know already.'

'Can you tell me?' Steadman looked directly at Griggs, who seemed to be the senior of the two.

'Afraid not, Mr Steadman. Not yet, anyway. I'm sure Mr Pope will fill you in on the details, though. In fact, er, I think they're rather anxious to see you out there. Special Branch have co-operated rather well, but they'll be relieved to have some hard evidence to substantiate the allegations against Gant. What we've found is highly suspicious, but not enough to warrant any arrests to be made. It's your evidence that will hang Gant and his friends.'

'But what about the dead bodies of the two Mossad agents at Guildford? That's pretty damning evidence.'

'He denies any knowledge of them.'

Steadman laughed humourlessly. 'They died in his house,' he said. 'Does he deny that.'

'He says he left Guildford early yesterday evening, and you were still there at that time!'

'And I probably killed them.'

'And Köhner. When we told him the man called Köhner was dead he said you must have been responsible.'

Steadman shook his head, a thin smile on his face.

'We'll soon break him, Mr Steadman. We've got too much against him and his organization now. But they do need your help at the estate. The SB boys are hopping up and down with frustration and demanding to see you personally.'

'Okay, let's go then,' the investigator said, rising to his feet. 'I'd like to make a phone call first.'

'Oh, you can do that from the house,' Griggs said as the two men rose with him. 'It really is important that you get there right away. Booth and I just have to check in with the local police to put them in the picture – it's all a bit much for country coppers – so I'll tell you how to get to Gant's estate and you can go on ahead. Mr Pope will be waiting for you.'

And so the game continues, Steadman thought grimly.

Ten minutes later, he was in the Celica driving along the A39 towards Hartlands. It was a cold day, the clouds hanging dark and heavy against the horizon, but Steadman kept his side-window open, wanting to feel the cool air on his face. His mind was clear and resolute.

He turned right when he reached Hartlands, and the banks of the narrow roadway rose up sharply on either side, blocking the view to the surrounding fields. Then the road swung to the left, suddenly widening, and an ancient church confronted him. It was a grey stone building with a high, square-shaped tower that must have offered a fine view over the surrounding countryside. A grotesquely twisted tree stood beside the low, stone wall which enclosed the churchyard, reaching towards the building like a withered and gnarled claw. Then it was gone, the road dipping suddenly, and he saw the sea less than a mile ahead. The road levelled once more, and again the steep banks of undergrowth restricted his vision.

There was no sign at the entrance to the estate, but Stead-man knew from the directions he had been given that this was the right place. He stopped before the open gates, feeling very much alone.

His hesitation was brief. He pushed the gear-stick into first and sped through the wide opening, changing up and gathering speed, as though his pace would override too many doubts. The road was well-laid and straight, and he saw the huge white mansion in the distance, surrounded by open fields fringed with deeply wooded areas. The brooding metal-grey sea lay beyond the house, a dark backdrop that seemed to threaten him as ominously as the building he was approaching. The stillness of it all added to his unease. There were many cars parked in the forecourt of the mansion, but no people anywhere. He slowed the car, delaying his arrival at the house, his resolve giving way to trepidation. He could turn back now, swing the car round and race back to the gates before they had a chance to lock them. But where would that leave Holly? And Baruch? He was their only chance.

A rainspot came through the open window and touched his cheek as the threatened drizzle began to soak the ground. His speed was less than ten mph now, and the huge house loomed up before him, giving him the feeling that the black windows were eyes staring. Watching. Waiting for him.

He saw the main door open and a rotund figure step out on to the low terrace that ran the length of the house. A hand was raised in salutation, but Steadman failed to respond to Pope's greeting. He stopped the car, switched off the engine, took a deep breath, and climbed out.

15

'One day ceremonies of thanksgiving will be sung to Fascism and National Socialism for having preserved Europe from a repetition of the triumph of the Underworld.'

'That's a danger that especially threatens England. The Conservatives would face a terrible ordeal if the proletarian masses were to seize power.'

'Fanaticism is a matter of climate.'

ADOLF HITLER

The interior of the huge house was clinically clean: it resembled an expensive sanatorium. Pope had stepped aside wordlessly, indicating that Steadman should go ahead of him through the polished wood doors. Once inside, Pope closed the doors almost ceremoniously, then turned to face the investigator.

'I'm glad you arrived safely,' he said. 'We were rather concerned this morning when we couldn't locate you at any of the hotels in town. It was a relief when we went through the list again later on.'

'I broke my journey,' Steadman replied, then added by way of explanation, 'Events kind of caught up with me.'

The hallway they stood in was wide and long, almost a room in itself. An occasional gilt-framed picture broke up the blinding whiteness of the walls.

'It's very quiet,' Steadman commented.

Pope smiled, two cheeks suddenly blooming like rosy apples at each end of the smile. 'Everything's under control, Harry. Things have worked out rather well.'

'No trouble?'

'None at all.'

'And the operation? Did you find out what it was?'

'Oh yes. Come along with me and you'll hear all about it.' The large man took Steadman's elbow and gently propelled him towards one of the doors leading off from the main hallway. He knocked, pushed open the door, and once again invited the investigator to enter before him.

Steadman stopped just inside the room and stared into Edward Gant's mocking eyes, too weary of the game to fake surprise.

'It's good to see you again, Mr Steadman. Unbelievably good.' Gant's artificial but perfectly natural-looking nose was back in its place, disguising his disfigurement. He looked around the room and the sight of Major Brannigan, Kristina, and the old man, Dr Scheuer, gave him a feeling of *déjà vu*; it was like their first meeting in Guildford all over again. But there were some new faces present this time: new, yet familiar. All eyes were on him, and all eyes revealed a strange curiosity, a discerning interest in him.

He swung round as he heard the door close behind him and looked straight into the face of the still-smiling Pope. The Intelligence man was leaning against the door, both hands behind his broad back and clasped around the handle, as though his huge bulk was an extra barrier for the investigator to break through should he decide to run. The smile wavered slightly under Steadman's steady gaze and Pope was relieved when the investigator turned back to face Gant.

'So he's in it with you,' he said to Gant, not having to point at the fat man behind him.

'Yes, Mr Steadman, Mr Pope has been enormously helpful to the cause – as you have.'

'Me? I've done nothing to help you, Gant – or your crackpot organization.'

'Ah, but you have.' Gant walked to a high-backed easy-chair and sat facing Steadman, his hands curling round the arms of the chair like talons. 'We have many men like Pope among the Thulists, men in positions of power who see the hopeless plight this nation is in – indeed, the world is in. Make no mistake, Mr Steadman, we are not a tiny "crackpot" organization existing in this country alone. Our society has a network spread throughout the world, the United States providing us with some extremely powerful members, one of whom will join us later tonight. We have money, influence, and most important, an ideal.'

'An ideal to conquer the world?'

'No, Mr Steadman. To govern it. Look at the men in this room,' Gant said, his arm sweeping outwards. 'I'm sure you recognize most of them. Ian Talgholm, financial adviser to the Chancellor himself – some call him the inner Cabinet's secret member; Morgan Henry and Sir James Oakes – industrialists well-known for their nationalistic pride, envied and feared by the Jewish money-grabbers because of their wealth and power; General Calderwood, a soldier who will eventually govern all the Armed Forces of this country – he is but a representative of many other high-ranking military men who support our Society; and last, but hardly least, Lord Ewing, fast becoming the most vital and powerful man in today's media.

'And these are just a few of our Order, Mr Steadman. The rest will be joining us later today and this evening. Our special council of thirteen, I, myself, being the thirteenth and principal member.'

'Just who are the others, Gant?'

'Ah, you're really interested. Excellent. Well you, of all people, have the right to know. After all, without you, the omens would not have been in our favour.' Gant chuckled, but it was obvious that not everyone in the room shared his humour. Steadman saw several members of the 'Order' give the arms dealer uncertain looks. One of them – Talgholm, the financier – spoke up.

'Look, Edward, do you think this is necessary?' he said, irritation in his voice. 'We've gone along with you on most of this, but he could have been highly dangerous to the whole project. Why tell him any more?'

'Because,' Gant snapped back, 'my dear Ian, because he has played a key part. Because there is no danger from him, nor has there ever been.'

'But the risk last night, letting him go free . . .'

'There was no risk, everything was planned. But he had to come here of his own initiative. *It had to be his choice!*'

The financier looked around at his companions as though appealing for support, but they avoided his eyes. He shrugged his shoulders and said, 'Very well, there's nothing he can do now, anyway.'

'Thank you, Ian,' Gant said icily, then proceeded to list the names of the absent members of the Order, one of whom was the racialist Member of Parliament Steadman had seen leaving the arms dealer's estate at Guildford, the day before; the others were important men in their fields – and their fields were greatly diversified.

'We are but the nucleus,' Gant explained, 'the governing body, so to speak. We make quite a powerful group, wouldn't you agree?'

Steadman nodded, but his mind was concentrated on making a quick count of the names. 'You said there were thirteen in the Order and you've mentioned, including yourself, only twelve. Who is the thirteenth member, Dr Scheuer or Major Brannigan?'

'Why, neither, Mr Steadman. They, although extremely important, are only tools. Men like our Major Brannigan and the unfortunate and unstable Mr Köhner – it was his unreliability, by the way, that prompted us to leave you in his hands: a calculated test for you, if you like – these men merely implement our plans. As for the esteemed Dr Scheuer,' he smiled benignly at the wrinkled old man, 'he is our medium, the one who brings our thirteenth member to us. He is the physical voice of our Leader.'

Even as Gant said the name, Steadman knew who the thirteenth member of the Order – the Teutonic Order of the Holy Knights – was. They had rejected Hitler because he'd failed them and switched their allegiance to the SS Reichsführer, founder of the Nazi Occult Bureau, who had encouraged and sustained the Thule Group.

Gant was smiling as he spoke, his eyes radiating a passion felt by everyone in the room. 'He will be with us tonight. Dr Scheuer will bring him to us. And you will meet him, Mr Steadman. You will meet our Führer, Heinrich Himmler, before you die.'

Gant spoke to the investigator for over an hour, laying out his plans for the new Order before him, treating him almost as a confidant; or perhaps a guest to be dazzled by his host's genius. The others had added their own comments, reluctant at first, then swept along by the arms dealer's fervour, realizing Steadman could do them no harm, for he was already a dead man. They needed an outsider they could boast to, impress with the magnitude of their schemes. And Steadman listened, sometimes goading, sometimes visibly astonished at their thoroughness, at the far-reaching effects their fanatical plans would make on the governance of the country. By intricate and brilliantly devious routes, it all arrived at one simple but major conflict: Right against Left. It would be the only choice for the people of Britain. No in-betweens, no fence-sitting. The public would be forced to choose. Civil war would be balanced in favour of the Right, for the majority would be the wealthy, those whose sympathy lay towards nationalistic pride; and the middle classes who had suffered so much between the élite of the country and the working classes, would choose to join them rather than be ruled by the economy-wrecking socialists. The choice would be made easy for them. New leaders would emerge and their ideals would be uncompromising, just as Hitler's had been in the 1930s. Edward Gant had been in the shadows for many years weaving his sinister power behind the scenes. Now he was emerging from those shadows, a new figure to the public, but already powerful enough to repel any attacks from those already in power. Steadman saw how their inner Cabinet – their Order – had been carefully chosen, comprising men already in key positions, all waiting for the right moment to throw off their disguises and unite publicly, and so unite the masses to them. Timing was of the essence, and events to further their cause were manipulated at *exactly* the right time.

Steadman prodded and they eagerly reacted. He drew information from them in a way that made them feel they were merely obliging a doomed man's last wishes to know the reason for his impending death; and their fanaticism, calm though it was, made them try to convert him to their cause and accept his sacrificial role. And all the while, the woman smiled, and the old man gazed at him from shadowed pits.

The Thule Society's next move was imminent. Other actions had already been implemented over the past years, insignificant in themselves, but creating a pattern vital to their cause, subconsciously affecting the climate of the free world's feelings. The worldwide terrorist attacks, the emergence of the neurotic African nations, the ever-present threat of Russia, détente merely used as a cover while they took a further step towards controlling the Western world, the gradual breaking-down of the world's economic structure, the Middle-Eastern countries' sudden strength and bold demands because of their ownership of two-thirds of the world's oil: all these shifts in the world's power balance were creating fear and mistrust on a universal scale which could be easily exploited by those who sought to create a new regime where only the pure-blooded races would rule. Thulists in many countries had contributed to the unrest, working behind the scenes, encouraging, advising, building the strength of their own enemies to the point where other nations would be forced to take action to break that strength lest its greedy eyes look towards them.

Gant, and many like him, secretly sold arms to terrorists not just for profit, but to encourage them on their road to self-destruction. The more outrages they committed, the more they were reviled and feared. And fear was the perfect tool for the new Reich, for fear created revolution.

A strategic move was to be made in the early hours of the following morning – 1.55 p.m. to be exact – when the American Secretary of State would be flying to Britain for talks with the Prime Minister and Foreign Secretary before journeying on to a neutral country in a new bid for peace – reconciliations between the Arab countries and Israel. The world knew that this was the culminative peace-talk, all others – particularly Egypt's, which had begun the fresh moves towards peace in '77 – having led up to this point, both frustrated nations poised for a war that would decide the ultimate victory for either side. But the American statesman's jet would never touch down in England, for the Thulists wanted no such peace between Arab and Jew. The aircraft would be blown to pieces while still over the Atlantic.

No one would know just who had been to blame, although the suspicions and accusations would lean more towards the Arabs than the Israelis, for the PFLP and the PLO had the worst reputation for such atrocities. The responsibility would hardly matter though: civilized countries had had enough. The two opposing nations would be allowed to attempt mutual an-nihilation, the world would stand by and watch. Of course, cer-tain evidence would be 'discovered' amongst the floating wreckage of the aircraft which would suggest it had been destroyed by a missile of probable Russian make. It was well-known that the Russians supplied their Middle-East friends with such weapons.

The fact that the missile had been produced by Edward Gant's munitions factory and launched from the shores of North Devon would never be discovered; anti-radar devices would ensure its flight path was not traced. Ironically, the RAF had a Radar Tracking Station not far away at Hartland Point, but they would never suspect the missile had been launched from their own area.

At that point, Steadman's probing had been brought to an abrupt halt, for there had been new arrivals at the estate – other members of the Order, Steadman assumed – and details of the operation had to be discussed with them. The assassination of the American Secretary of State was just one of a series of major catastrophes, Gant had explained to the investigator; there were more to follow in rapid succession, each escalating to the next, until world hysteria reached breaking-point. Anarchy by the left-wing had to be nurtured until it could be smashed, terrorism encouraged, until it could no longer be tolerated by the masses.

The door was opened for Steadman and he found the two bogus MI5 men who had come to the hotel in Bideford waiting outside. Neither of them spoke as they led him away, and Steadman felt little inclined to acknowledge their previous meeting; his mind was too busy absorbing all he had learned.

They took him upstairs and along a stark, white corridor, then pushed him into a room, locking the door behind him.

Holly was sitting on a bed facing him, her face white as the walls around them.

'Harry?' she said, not believing what she saw. Then she was on her feet and rushing towards him. 'What's happening, Harry? Why are they keeping me here?'

She raised a hand towards his injured cheek, concern in her eyes, but he held her at arm's length, looking down into her frightened face, unsure, not believing in anything any more. She smiled up at him, her pleasure at seeing him undisguised. It faded as she looked into his cold eyes, and suddenly her mouth quivered as though the toughness had finally been knocked out of her.

'Harry, you're not with them . . . ?'

'Do you work for The Institute?' he asked harshly.

'The Institute?'

'Come on, Holly, don't lie to me. You're a Mossad agent. You've been playing me along, like all the others.'

'No, Harry.' She pulled away from him, angry now and defiance beginning to show through the tears. 'They've been asking me the same thing. What the hell's going on, Harry? Why do you all think I'm working with the Israelis?'

Her anger seemed genuine and he wavered for a moment. Could he trust anyone? They hadn't reached the end yet; the Final Act had not been played out. Was Holly part of that?

'Okay,' he said softly, placing his hands on her upper arms. 'Okay. Just tell me what's happened to you, nice and slow. And tell me who you really are, Holly, it's important that I know.'

He led her back to the bed and gently pushed her down, then sat by her side.

She looked at him, hurt and confusion showing on her face. But was it all an act? 'You know who and what I am, Harry. I told you, I'm a freelance writer and photographer. I came here to do a feature on Edward Gant, using my family connections with his late wife. That's all there is to it, why should I lie to you?'

He ignored the question. 'And you've never heard of David Goldblatt and Hannah Rosen? You've never heard of Baruch Kanaan? You're not a member of Israeli Intelligence?' She shook her head vehemently, and then another thought struck him. 'Or British Intelligence?'

'No, for God's sake, no! What have I got into, Harry? What have *you* got to do with all this? The other day at Long Valley, the tank – why were they trying to kill you? Who are they and who are you?'

He told her then, not because he believed her, but because if she was with Mossad, then she already knew most of it, and if she wasn't . . . Well, what did it matter? But he didn't tell her everything. Just in case.

When he informed her of the plan to assassinate the US Secretary of State at one fifty-five that coming morning, she just sat there, a stunned expression on her face. Then she said, 'So that was why they locked me up.'

He looked at her quizzically.

'The missile launcher,' she said. 'I found it. They caught me taking photographs of it. I thought it was just another part of Gant's testing-ground – the whole estate's riddled with testing-ranges.' She flicked her blonde hair away from her face. 'No wonder they got so mad.' She almost managed a smile.

'Where was it, Holly? Where did you find it?'

'Oh, it's towards the shoreline,' she pointed vaguely in the direction of the sea. 'I'd slipped my guard – Gant wouldn't allow me to wander around free, naturally enough, even though he was anxious I do this article on him – and I pretended I was going to take a nap. It was late afternoon and we'd been trudging around most of the day, so I guess my guide believed me when I told him I was tired. Anyway, he escorted me up here, then disappeared for a while. I sneaked out and started exploring the areas he'd taken care to keep me away from. This is a strange house, Harry. Did you know the back half is completely different from the front, as though the section we're in now is just a façade?'

He shook his head but remained silent.

'Well, I'd been taken in completely opposite directions before, towards the weapons plant about half-a-mile away, but this time I headed round the back. I was surprised it was so easy, but I guess with Gant away they'd all relaxed a little. Anyway, I got to the back of the house and took a peek in some rear windows on the way. The interior's like a castle back there, very old, dark wood and heraldic symbols, you know? There was no way in, though, all the doors were locked. I heard guards coming – did you know he's got his own private army here? – so I took off away from the house, towards the cliff-tops.

'I hid behind an old outhouse for a while, waiting for the guards to disappear. It was a little way off from the main house, but was locked and the windows boarded up, so I didn't get a look inside to see what it was used for. When the coast was clear, I took off again, staying away from the road leading to the beach, not looking for anything in particular, but curious enough to keep a look-out for something peculiar. Well, I found something peculiar, all right, but I found it by accident. I'd ducked into some undergrowth about fifty yards or so from the cliff-edge because one of their patrol Range Rovers was heading in my direction – they keep regular patrols all over the estate – and I nearly fell into a huge hole the undergrowth had been disguising. It was about twenty feet wide and had camouflage netting spread over it. I could see through the netting, and the hole looked natural enough except the sides had been smoothed with concrete all the way down, and there was a circular staircase running round the edge. I looked into it and saw it was about forty feet deep and light was coming in from one side below. It was the shaft of a cave, you see, the cave leading up I assume, at an angle from the beach – I could hear the sea down there. The tide wouldn't get into it because the bottom of the well was much higher than the beach. And there, at the bottom of the shaft, was the missile mounted on its launching pad. It wasn't very big, but it looked kind of lethal.'

'They must keep the shaft camouflaged because of all the low-flying military aircraft around these parts,' said Steadman.

'I guess so. Anyway, it was too good to miss. I started clicking away with the Pentax and I became too engrossed in what I was doing. Two guards snuck up on me and all but threw me into the hole. They brought me back here and confiscated my camera. Then the grilling began.'

She put a tentative hand out towards him and rested it on his arm, unsure of his reaction. He let it stay there. 'They asked me about you, Harry: what I knew about you, who you were working for, were we working together. Then they started in on me about Mossad. I told them the same as I told you: I'm a freelance journalist trying to make some bread. *They* didn't believe me, either.'

She stared earnestly into Steadman's eyes. 'Didn't the other day mean anything to you? Weren't your feelings the same as mine?'

He looked away from her, confused.

'God, you're like a stranger,' she said, anger returning.

'Holly,' he began, trying to come to terms with his doubts, wanting to believe in her. 'So much has happened in the last few days, I swear to God I don't know who I can trust. Those men downstairs with Gant – Christ, they're high-level people. And Pope. He's with British Intelligence! Even one of my own clients has been spying on me since I left Mossad. How can I trust anybody?'

She drew his hand towards her and at that point he wanted to give in, to hold her, to believe. But another part of him held back.

'Okay, Harry,' she said, no longer angry. 'Don't trust me, be as suspicious as hell. But what it all boils down to is that we – just you, if you like – are in big trouble and have to get out. Now, does anyone else know you're here?'

He shook his head, still doubting.

'That's kind of dumb, but okay, we're on our own. So, let's think of a way.' She tried to smile. 'Like the movies, huh?'

'Some movie,' he said, extricating his hand and moving away from the bed and towards the curtainless window. She watched him peering down into the grounds below.

'There's a guard out there all the time,' she said, 'and the window can't be opened – I've tried. You'd break a leg jumping, anyway, and the guard would put a bullet through you before you even reached the ground.'

The guard was looking up at him, face expressionless, but his pose menacing. Steadman looked back at Holly. She seemed calm enough now. Did she have reason to be or was it just a natural facet of her character?

'Any ideas?' she asked, conscious of his gaze.

'We wait,' he said. 'Gant wants me to meet someone later tonight.'

He grinned without humour at her surprise and suddenly felt she had been telling the truth. But still he remained withdrawn. He could be wrong.

Major Brannigan's face was flushed with a brooding sulkiness as he tapped lightly on the door. He wanted to rap hard at the wood with his fist, for he knew she would be laughing inwardly at his mood. He wanted to throw open the door and slap away the smirk she would have on her face. He held his anger in check, however, for he was both afraid and in desperate need of her.

Kristina's voice came to him from inside the room: 'Who is it?'

'It's me – Andrew,' he said, leaning close to the wood, his voice already losing its rancour. 'May I come in?'

'It's open, Andrew.'

He entered and closed the door quickly behind him. He hesitated before approaching, the mere sight of her filling him with the usual desire – *and shame for being in bondage to such a creature.*

She was sitting before a mirror, deftly tucking strands of damp hair beneath a towel worn around her head. The long, white bathrobe she wore was parted around one thigh, and he could not help but stare at the smooth skin, wanting to touch its softness, stroke it, to reach for her and hold her close.

She knew his look, and knew his desire; and laughed at him.

He looked down at her, resisting the temptation to reach out for her elegant neck, the neck he had caressed with his lips so many times, wanting to choke the life from it now, but knowing his hands would never have the strength. They would squeeze until the knuckles were white, until her eyes showed panic, fear, laughter, gone from them; then his grip would loosen and his hands would reach down, across the smooth flesh, down until they cupped her hard-nippled breasts – for her very fear would have aroused her, made her want him as much as he wanted her. That was the kind of perverse creature Kristina was. And her fear would have aroused him – *that was the kind of perverse creature he was*. He would sink to his knees and beg forgiveness, his hands still clutching her breasts as though afraid to let go. And Kristina would sink down beside him and they would make love in their unnatural way.

'No, Andrew,' she said, reading his mind. She turned from him and resumed tucking away the damp strands of hair, watching the reflection of his clenched fists in the mirror, smiling at the conflict of desires he was going through.

'Please, Kristina, I . . .' He fell to his knees and pushed his cheek against the roughness of the bathrobe, a hand resting on her exposed thigh, fingers spreading and moving inwards towards the even softer flesh on the inside of her leg.

She snatched his hand away and drew the bathrobe over her nakedness. 'You know what has to be done later,' she said scornfully. 'We've no time for this.'

'Why?' Brannigan said, almost wearily. 'Why does it have to be you?'

Her eyes flashed angrily. 'You know why. He has to be debased.'

'As I was? As I am now?'

'This is different, Andrew. It's nothing to do . . .' She stopped abruptly, but he completed the sentence for her.

'Blackmail? No need to blackmail him as you did me?'

'It began as blackmail, Andrew. But you believe in our cause now, don't you? You've told me so many times that you do, and you've done so much for us.'

'Of course. But why Steadman? For God's sake, Kristina . . .'

'God? What has He got to do with this?'

Brannigan was silent.

'Dr Scheuer says the legend has to be refuted,' Kristina said impatiently.

'And Gant believes all this nonsense.'

'Nonsense? You can say that after all you've seen?'

'I . . . I don't understand all of it, Kristina. I don't understand how these . . . things happen.' His voice was pleading. 'You said you loved me. Was that also just for the cause?'

She dropped a hand to the back of his head and stroked his hair. Her voice softened. 'Of course not. You know how much I think of you.' The major could not see her smile at her own reflection in the mirror. 'I have to do this, Andrew. Our Parsifal has to be – ' her smile was filled with malice ' – corrupted.'

Without force, she pushed Brannigan away, then tilted his head up so she could look into his eyes. 'Now go away and check that everything's secure for tonight. This is the beginning, Andrew, and nothing must go wrong.' Kristina kissed his lips, holding herself back from his passion, restraining him with a gentle hand. 'I must rest,' she said. 'Tonight is important to us all.'

Major Brannigan rose clumsily and, with a last penetrating look at Kristina, left the room. He walked towards the right wing of the house and entered a room next door to the one in which Steadman and Holly Miles were being held. A green-uniformed man wearing headphones, seated next to a tape-recorder, looked up and acknowledged him with a respectful nod.

'Anything?' Brannigan asked.

The man shook his head. 'They've been quiet for some time now. He asked her direct if she worked for Mossad when he first went in and she denied it. Looks like she really is clean.'

'Unless she suspects the room is bugged. What else did Steadman have to say?'

'He told her quite a bit – about Mr Gant and the organization, about tonight's op – but he doesn't know the whole story himself.'

Brannigan nodded briskly and turned to leave. 'Keep listening till he's taken out of there. I still don't think that woman is what she seems. If anything does slip out, let me know immediately.'

'Very good, sir.' The eavesdropper saluted and Brannigan left the room, making his way towards the main stairway and the front entrance. A check on the guards, posted at various spots around the estate's boundaries, then a visit to the missile site to make sure everything was set for tonight's – or more accurately, tomorrow morning's – launching. Things would be moving at last and they'd begin to see some fruition of their dream. The Society had remained in the shadows for so many years, but the time was coming for the strong leaders to emerge. *They* would rule and the military would no longer be the puppets of weak men. No longer would the country's defences be whittled away by the weaklings in government. No longer would the leftists be allowed to dominate. That kind of destructive freedom was to end in England. It had to if the nation was to survive. Of course, the identity of their true leader would never be revealed, for it would be abhorrent to the people who had so misguidedly fought against his great ideals in the last World War. And they would never allow themselves to be ruled by someone they thought had perished so many years before.

Dusk fell and the white house was silent. The drizzle had ceased, but it seemed all life, animal and human, was still sheltering from its dampness. Only the roar from the ocean could be heard, the sound of cruel Atlantic waves breaking on the rocky beaches, their thunderous crashes drifting up the cliff-faces and rolling over the grassy slopes.

The night slowly closed in around the house and its whiteness turned grey, the windows black and impenetrable. A cold wind stirred the grass in spreading ripples and disturbed the tree branches, dislodging the final stubborn leaves.

The darkness became solid and a heaviness, despite the just-fallen rain, seemed to hang in the air. It was as if the very night was waiting, and time was a creeping thing.

16

'But the day will come when we shall make a pact with these new men in England, France, America. We shall make it when they fall in line with the vast process of the re-ordering of the world, and voluntarily play their part in it. There will not be much left then of the clichés of nationalism, and precious little among us Germans. Instead there will be an understanding between the various language elements of the one good ruling race.'

ADOLF HITLER

'Come along, Harry, separate rooms for you two, dear boy.'

Pope's gross figure stood in the doorway, a grin on his face and a gun in his hand. When he saw the investigator was a safe distance away from him and not lurking near the door he returned the gun to his jacket pocket. He always felt ridiculous holding the 'Baby' Parabellum .25 in his immense hand anyway, but it was a convenient and unobtrusive size for his pocket.

Steadman swung his legs off the bed, his hand squeezing Holly's as he stood, his eyes warning her to keep quiet.

'Where are you taking me?' he asked Pope.

'Mr Gant felt that now you've been assured of Miss Miles' well-being, you should be kept apart just in case you should get up to any mischief.' Griggs and Booth leered from their position behind the fat man.

Steadman walked towards the trio crowded in the doorway and Pope stood aside to let him through.

'Harry, don't go with them!' Holly suddenly shouted, leaping from the bed.

Pope turned his huge bulk towards her and held up a hand to keep her at bay. 'He has no choice in the matter, my dear. Now go back to where you were *and keep quiet!*'

Holly glared at him defiantly. 'What are you bastards going to do with him?'

'Nothing, dear lady, absolutely nothing.' The smoothness had returned to Pope's voice. 'Until midnight, that is. In fact, it should be rather pleasant for him until then.' One of the men in the doorway chuckled aloud, but there was no amusement in the fat man's eyes. 'Now, move!' he ordered Steadman.

With a last backwards glance at Holly, the investigator stepped into the hallway and began to follow Griggs and Booth with Pope close behind.

She looked scared, Steadman mused. Genuinely scared for him. Was she really innocent in all this or was it merely an elaborate ploy to get him to talk to her, to make sure he knew only what *they* wanted him to know? And to make sure he was completely alone?

He was led up a flight of stairs on to the next floor, taken along another corridor and finally shown into a room that was infinitely more comfortable than the one he had just left. The decor was still stark, but a fire blazed in the grate, throwing a warm glow around the walls. A small lamp gave the room an intimate atmosphere and a long pin-buttoned couch stood at right-angles to the fire. A four-poster bed dominated half the large room and its soft, inviting quilt reminded Steadman how tired he was. It had been a day full of tension. He fought against the tiredness that suddenly dragged him down.

Turning to the big man, he said bitterly, 'Why, Pope? Why did someone like you get involved in all this?'

The fat man laughed hollowly, then motioned his two henchmen to leave the room. When he and Steadman were alone, he said, 'I've always been *involved*, Harry. The British Secret Service was never much *before* the last war, and after . . . just a shambles, a complete bloody shambles.'

Pope crossed the room and gazed into the fire, one pudgy hand resting on the mantelshelf above. 'You were in Military Intelligence,' he said, his face lit by the flames, 'so you must have been aware of the general incompetence that was rife throughout the whole of the British Secret Service.'

Steadman nodded unconsciously, remembering the frustration he had felt over the apparent idiocy of many of his superiors. At the time, he had forgiven their seemingly senseless directives on the assumption that there was some deeply hidden motive behind them, and when he had often later discovered the motive was just as senseless as the directive, he'd almost given up in despair. That was why the Shin Beth had been so attractive to him. Israeli Intelligence had been, and probably still was, the most respected intelligence organization in the world, the British equivalent paling in comparison. However, some sense of loyalty forced the investigator to refute Pope's damning statement.

'But it's changed now – the dross has been cleared out, the "old school tie" network doesn't work any more.'

'Hah!' Pope faced him, amusement and scorn turning him into a jovial gargoyle. 'I *am* part of the "old school tie" network, dear boy. Only *I* do not choose to socialize – ideologically, of course – with my peers at the Ministry. Even after the outrageous attempts by the SIS to protect traitors like Philby in the sixties, the "old boy" network was allowed to go on ruling the roost. Even when Burgess and Maclean defected and it was evident Kim Philby had tipped them off, they went on protecting him – *and were allowed to*. God, it was no wonder the CIA lost all confidence in us after that débâcle – after all, they suffered as much as us through our incompetence. Co-operation between our two organizations has been slight, to say the least, after the sixties. The exposé of spy rings such as Lonsdale's, and the internment of men like Vassal, far from gaining our security service glory has, in fact, cast serious doubts on our reliability in matters of State secrecy. And these are only our publicized defections! You'd be amazed at the disasters that have been swept under the carpet in the interest of national confidence in the department! You can't blame the bloody Americans for not collaborating with us any more!'

Steadman sank down on to the couch. Before he could speak, Pope had continued his tirade against his own organization. 'And when the change comes in this country, dear boy, I'll be directing the new broom as far as my own department is concerned. No more kid-glove treatment for suspect aliens, no more foreign trawlers in our waters. Family connections will mean nothing in the organization. Chinless wonders and nancy boys will be flushed out. Our "grey" people will be made to earn their keep.'

'You're as insane as Gant,' Steadman said quietly.

'Insane? Am I ranting, Harry? Am I raving? Do I really sound as though I'm mad?'

Steadman had to admit, he didn't. 'But what you're talking about – what you're all talking about – is revolution. That's impossible in England.'

'What we're talking about is *counter*-revolution. The revolution is already taking place. We intend to oppose it.'

'What's to stop your kind of power from becoming corrupt?'

'Our one ideal, Harry. Don't you see, we are a Holy Order? The thirteen men who will ultimately control the country will not be ordinary men. We'll use the corruption around us, we'll fight fire with fire . . .'

'And not get burnt yourselves?'

'Our spiritual leader will see we don't.'

'Himmler? A man who's been dead for over thirty years? How can a corpse help you, Pope?'

The fat man merely smiled. 'You must rest now, tonight will not be an easy one for you.' He walked to a large oak bureau to one side of the room, on which stood a tray containing a dark bottle and one glass. He brought the tray over to Steadman and placed it at his feet. 'Brandy,' he announced. 'I'm sure you need it.' He straightened his huge frame, grunting at the effort. 'Compliments of Mr Gant. Now, would you like some food, Harry? I'm sure you must be starving.'

Steadman shook his head. The hollowness in his stomach couldn't be filled by food. The brandy might help, though.

'I'll leave you to rest.' Pope walked to the door and for a brief moment, the investigator considered attacking him, smashing the brandy bottle over that obese head. His muscles tensed and he reached down for the neck of the bottle.

'I shouldn't, dear boy,' Pope warned with a pleasant smile. 'Griggs and Booth are just outside; you wouldn't get very far. There is no escape for you, don't you see? You've almost served your purpose, so why not relax and enjoy your final hours?' Before the fat man disappeared through the door he gave Steadman a meaningful look. 'Thank you, Harry, thank you for all your co-operation.' Then, with a deep-throated chuckle, he was gone.

Steadman stared at the closed door for some time before he picked up the brandy. He uncorked the bottle and poured the dark brown liquid into the glass. He raised the glass to his lips and just before he sipped, he wondered if the drink could be drugged. But what would be the point? He was captive here, no chance of escape. Would they need him in a drugged state for whatever was to happen later that night? He doubted it; they had enough strongarm men to keep him passive. He took the tiniest of sips and rolled the fiery liquid around his mouth. He longed to swallow, knowing the brandy would do him good, but the faintest bitter taste held his throat muscles in check. Was it only his imagination or was there really a strange taint to the drink? Because of his danger his senses were acute; but was their sensitivity exaggerating the ordinary bitterness of the spirits?

He spat the liquid into the fire and the sudden flare-up made him jump back. The interior of his mouth burned with the thin coating of brandy left there, and he ran his tongue round it to dilute its strength. He looked longingly at the remaining contents of the glass and asked himself what they would try to drug him with – *if* they were trying to drug him – and his mind ran through the legend, the mythical story of the Holy Grail which had inspired Wagner's *Parsifal*. The mystical opera he insisted be performed only at Bayreuth, the spiritual capital of the Germanic peoples. The opera Hitler had believed was the divine ideology of the Aryan Race!

Young Steve had told Steadman the basic story of the opera, which was a dramatization of the thirteenth-century poet's Grail Romance, and the investigator had begun to understand why Gant – perverse though it was – had referred to him as 'his Parsifal'. The central theme of the opera was the struggle between the Grail Knights and their adversaries, over the possession of the Holy Spear – *the Spear of Longinus which had pierced the side of Christ.*

The Spear had been stolen from them by Klingsor, a castrated evil magician who embodied Paganism, and in so doing, had dealt Amfortas, the leader of the Knights, a wound with the Spear that would never heal. In the hands of Klingsor, the Spear had become an evocator of black powers which only a completely guileless knight could overcome.

In Gant's devious – or was it desperate – reasoning, he had seen himself as Klingsor, for Gant believed more in the powers of evil than in good, despising – as had Hitler – the Christian rituals connected with the myth, and in the arms dealer's strange mind, Steadman had become his Parsifal, the 'guileless' knight who would have to be thwarted if the legend's meaning was to be revoked. Parsifal had become a battle-weary soldier, a man whose mother had died grief-stricken when he had left her while still a boy. Although Steadman had always believed in the cause he had fought for, he would hardly have ascribed any deeply noble instincts to his own character, yet Gant had cast him in the romantic role of defender of the Good. Was it desperation on the arms dealer's part, a need to create an omen where none existed, a megalomaniac's desire to symbolize his own destiny? Perhaps Gant felt time was running out for him, the moment to launch his offensive was at hand, and someone was needed quickly to re-enact the final scene of Good against Evil, with the outcome this time heavily weighted on the side of Evil. A charade, a false ceremony for the benefit of the New Order! Steadman found it difficult to smile at the foolishness of it all. This was why he had been drawn into the elaborate game. Unwittingly, David Goldblatt had provided them with their symbolic knight, a single man to be foiled, then destroyed as an omen of their future success. Gant must have been filled with elation when Maggie, under torture, had revealed she had been sent by Mossad, but only as second choice to her partner, Steadman, an ex-soldier, an ex-Mossad agent. An untainted Englishman.

It would have been easy for Pope to have gained access to the file kept by Military Intelligence on his, Steadman's, past activities, and they had probably gloated on how his background could be compared – albeit loosely – to the mythical Parsifal's. From then on, it had just been a matter of drawing him in. Maggie's vile murder had been committed in order to tear him from the state of passivity he had built up over the last few years; the visit from Pope when he had declined to go against them despite his partner's cruel death; the meeting with Gant at the armaments exhibition to assess his worth as an opponent; and the subsequent test when the tank had tried to crush him (had Holly's life been as expendable as Köhner's, or was this real proof of her innocence in the deadly game?); the revelations at Guildford to ensure his further involvement, and the next test of his worth against the sadistic Köhner, knowing if he escaped, he would contact Pope who would send him off on the last part of the charade without risk to their plans; and his luring to Gant's North Devon estate, the '*Wewelsburg*'.

And now the Final Act was drawing near and one last test remained; but they wanted him to fail this one, so that his degradation would refute the outcome of the original legend. In the thirteenth-century *minnesinger*'s poem adapted by Wagner for his opera, a woman, Kundry by name, had tried to seduce Parsifal and degrade him as she had so many other knights. How these ancient standards of honour and chastity could compare with today's, Steadman was at a loss to know, but nothing was sane in this whole bizarre plot. Gant and his followers would derive their own meaning from his sexual 'downfall'. Anger boiled up in him and he threw the contents of the glass into the fire, enjoying the searing throwback of heat as the fire flared greedily, almost as though it were an emanation of his own rage. But they had made one small mistake in their elaborate scheme: Köhner had known about the Israeli agent, Smith; he had told Steadman the man had died. How could he have known unless he had been told by the bogus MI5 agents, Griggs and Booth? And that implicated Pope. It was enough for Steadman to have taken precautions before allowing himself to be drawn finally and irrevocably into the spider's web. But had those precautions been enough? He looked at his watch and cursed. Where were they? What the hell were they waiting for? Were *they* part of the game too?

He leapt up and strode briskly to the window. It, too, was locked, and he looked out into the dark night, seeing little but his own reflection in the glass. He had lost track of time standing there, when the sound of a key turning in the lock made him look towards the door. The handle turned and the door opened slowly.

He was almost relieved when she slipped into the room; relieved it wasn't Holly.

17

Holly decided it was time to make her move. She knew her people would be reluctant to close in, but her absence would force them to do so. That might be too late, though.

She had been genuinely astounded when she had 'stumbled' on the hidden missile site. She was aware that Gant and his lunatic followers had some pretty twisted plans in mind, but had not realized those plans could involve such overt armed aggression. Even though it was known to her organization that Gant encouraged terrorist activities and supplied these various factions with arms – for a price – it was thought his own methods of undermining world peace were more subtle, more insidious. She had been stupid to get caught taking 'snaps' of the site, but they were still unsure of her. After all, if she *was* a freelance journalist and photographer as she claimed, then it would be perfectly natural for her curiosity to be aroused at such a discovery. Many journalists had been anxious to write a feature on 'Edward Gant, Twentieth Century Arms Dealer', over the past decade, so it was not unnatural that she had been so persistent. The fact that Gant had now begun to seek publicity and that her story of connection with his late wife's family in the States had checked out, had led to her privileged position. Some privileged position, she reflected wryly.

Gant had invited her to his closely guarded estate the day before, promising her an 'exclusive' that would be the envy of the journalistic world. A car had arrived at Holly's flat in the early hours of the morning with the arms dealer's message, and had whisked her away before she had time to inform her own people. She was sure they were keeping tabs on her, though.

When she learned from Harry the purpose of the missile, she had been astounded at the flagrant cunning of Gant's plan. There would be no tracing those who launched the rocket, though both Israelis and the Arabs would obviously be suspected. But the Israelis would *know* the Arabs were the perpetrators, and the Arabs would *know* the Israelis were the perpetrators. It would unsettle all the negotiations for peace between the two nations, and lead to another full-scale war which, in all likelihood, the Israelis would not win this time.

Holly had guessed the room was bugged – why else would they send Harry in to her? – and had had to deny any knowledge of Gant's secret organization. However, she hadn't lied about Mossad. She had wanted to hold him, tell him he wasn't alone in all this, that others knew of the arms dealer's intent. Harry had looked so grim, his mistrust undisguised, and she had wanted to blurt out the truth, to tell him of her government's suspicions and anxiety over this, the most powerful Hitlerite group since the war. They knew its tentacles spread into high places, British Intelligence not the least of those places, and that they had to tread carefully and secretively in this country where the actual nest existed and thrived, for it was not just a threat to Britain, but to world equilibrium in general.

The investigator's sudden appearance on the scene had mystified them at first and Holly still hadn't figured out why he was so important to Gant. Her brief, though unexpectedly emotional, acquaintance with Harry had revealed nothing of any significance apart from the fact he had once been a Mossad agent. So why was he so important to Gant and why had he been allowed to get so close? And why, Holly asked herself, had he become so important to her?

Holly rose from the one easy-chair in the room and moved towards the door. She pressed her ear against the wood and listened: no sound came from the other side. Even if they thought she wasn't involved, Holly doubted that they would leave her unwatched. She tried the door handle, twisting it to and fro.

'Leave it, lady,' a voice commanded from the other side. 'You're not going anywhere.' Holly looked around the room, searching for an idea more than an object. But it was the object that gave her the idea.

Kristina closed the door and smiled across the room at Steadman.

He had to admit she was beautiful, her long, dark hair framing her pale face like a black sea flowing around an ice drift. The deep red of her full lips could have been an imprint of blood on the snow, a curving stain that was as cold as the ice around. Only her eyes were alien in the frozen landscape of her face, for they were alive, deep and glowing as though containing some inner amusement. Yet, there was an excitement in them too, and he felt it was to do with desire.

Her skirt was of the darkest umber, velvet in texture, and ending well below the knee where high and slim-heeled boots clung to her calves and ankles, flowing with the shape of her lower legs as the skirt flowed with the shape of her thighs. A brown shirt, two tones lighter than the skirt, open to a point below the cleft of her breasts, completed the picture of aggressive sexuality and, despite himself, he felt the opening pangs of desire. He caught the sudden flick of her eyes towards the brandy bottle and his passion was immediately stemmed.

'I wanted to see you, Harry,' Kristina said, before advancing on him.

'Why?' he asked bluntly.

She stopped before him. 'To talk to you. Perhaps to help you escape.'

For a moment he was too stunned to speak. 'You'd help me escape from here?'

'I'd help you escape from the fate Edward Gant has in store for you.'

The sudden hope drained from Steadman and he asked, 'How?'

'By persuading Edward to let you live, by convincing him you could be useful to us.' She was close to him now, having imperceptibly drawn nearer as they spoke. He looked down at her, interest more than contempt in his eyes.

'How could I be useful to your Thulists?' he asked.

'You're a resourceful man; you've done well to survive so far. You know much about Israeli Intelligence, a natural enemy to our movement, and any information you could give us would be invaluable. Your past record shows you are a ruthless man, and ruthlessness is something this country will need in the years ahead.'

'But wouldn't I have to believe in Nazism?' Steadman asked scornfully.

'You'd come to believe in time. Not all our members are convinced of our ideals, we're aware of that. They seek power for power's sake, not for race advancement, but for personal gain. Eventually, they'll see it our way.'

'And you think Gant would trust me?'

'You'd have to convince him you could be trusted. I could help you do that.'

'How?'

'If I trusted you I could influence his judgment. I have in

218

the past.' She placed a hand on his shoulder and, inexplicably, a shudder ran through him.

'But why should you believe in me?' he said.

'If we were lovers . . .' he almost laughed aloud as she said the words. '. . . I'd know.'

'And Major Brannigan. Isn't he your lover?'

She smiled indulgently at Steadman. 'You're very observant. Andrew is a weak man. He doesn't have your qualities, your strength.'

'But I bet you helped draw him into all this.'

'It's not important now, Harry.' She closed the gap between them and pressed her body against his. The contact was at once strongly repulsive yet intoxicating. Had the tiny amount of tampered-with brandy he'd allowed into his mouth begun to have some effect? Or was it her eyes? They had a peculiar mesmeric quality and he felt a tiredness overcoming him. He tried to flood any other thoughts from his mind, filling his head with the Parsifal legend, reminding himself of Gant's malignity. Yet when he looked down at the beautiful face before him, it was difficult to imagine any reasonable motive behind the seduction. It would hardly be humiliating to succumb to such a woman, and he had certainly not taken any knightly vows of celibacy. Her dark eyes gazed back at him, unblinking, drawing him down, his head bending towards her, his lips reaching. It was almost as though he was being hypnotized, she exerting a stronger will over his . . .

It was then he realized exactly what was happening: she was drawing his strength, sapping his will. Her power was not in her body, but in her mind. It drank in his will, drew him into a mental whirlpool, her deep eyes sucking him in, drowning him. Her hand took his and placed it on her breast, holding it there, making him feel her firmness, the nipple hard and thrusting. Their thighs pressed close, his body stirring, no longer unwilling, oblivious to the legend, subject now only to physical need. Their lips were almost touching, only minimal resistance preventing him from crushing his against hers. But it was the physical stirring in her that suddenly froze his movement, that tore through the overwhelming net of carnality she had cast over him. For her own desire had manifested itself against his lower body, a protuberance that pushed against her clothes, and deemed to match his.

With a cry of rage he pushed her away, driving his fist hard into her face. She screamed with the shock and sudden pain, falling to the floor, and he knew why they'd sent *her* to seduce him. Why he would have been humbled before them, and more importantly, himself, if he had succumbed. The door flew open and Pope stood there, others behind him with guns drawn. There was anger in Pope's eyes as he looked at Steadman then down at Kristina who lay propped up with one hand against the floor, the other clutching an already-swelling face.

Kristina spat at Steadman. 'You bastard!' she screamed, and her voice had become guttural. 'You lousy bastard!'

Disgustedly, and before Pope's muscle-men could rush him, Steadman took a step forward and aimed a vicious kick at the hermaphrodite lying prone on the floor.

It took two minutes for Pope's men to knock him senseless, but as Steadman sank into unconsciousness, he took relish in the sobs of pain coming from the creature lying only a few feet from him.

Holly Miles stood on the bed and reached up towards the light bulb, a pillowcase cover draped over one hand to prevent her fingers being burnt by the calescent glass. With a deft twist, the light bulb was free of its socket and the room plunged into darkness. She stood still for a few seconds, allowing her eyes to adjust to dense blackness, the hand clutching the light bulb becoming warm with the heat. The full moon outside suddenly broke free from smothering clouds and she was grateful for the increased visibility, although it might work against her in a few moments. She stepped off the bed and moved silently towards the thin bar of light that shone beneath the door from the hallway. Once again, Holly listened with her ear pressed against the woodwork, praying she would not hear sounds of muffled conversation indicating there was more than one guard outside; she didn't think she could tackle two of them. Reasonably satisfied, she tapped lightly on the door with her fingernails.

'Hey,' she called softly. 'Open up. I want to see Gant.'

There was no reply and this time she rapped harder, using her knuckles.

'Hey, you! I've got something to tell Gant. It's important.'

Still no answer, and she began to wonder if there *was* still someone out there. 'Can you hear me?' she demanded to know, thumping the door angrily.

'Keep it down, lady,' came the surly reply.

'Ah, the zombie speaks,' she said, loud enough for the guard to hear. 'Listen to me, I've got to see Gant.'

'Mr Gant's busy.'

'No, look, I've got information for him. I warn you, it's important.'

'Go fuck yourself,' came the lazy reply.

'Cretin!' she said, and gave the door a powerful kick.

'Cut it out, lady, I'm telling you!' There was menace in his voice now.

She kicked it again.

'I'm warning you, I've got orders to keep you quiet,' Holly heard the disembodied voice say, and she smiled grimly. She kicked at the door again.

'You'd better let me see him, moron. You'll regret it if you don't.'

There was a brief silence as though the guard was pondering, then his voice came through the woodwork again. 'What have you got to tell Mr Gant?'

'That's between me and him.'

'Oh no. There's a meeting going on tonight and I'm not interrupting it just for you.'

'Then let me see whoever's in charge of you – your commanding officer.' She used the description of rank scornfully, refusing to accept that these mercenaries were genuine soldiers. Perhaps if he went to find his superior she would have a chance to work on the door. It was a slim chance, but slim was better than one at all.

'Major Brannigan's busy.'

Yes, probably supervising the missile launch, Holly told herself. 'Okay, your captain or sergeant, or whatever,' she shouted back.

'Leave it out, lady. There's enough going on tonight without you causing problems.'

She swore furiously and began to pummel at the door. My God, what if she really *had* some vital information for Gant? This cluck would still carry out his orders and keep her imprisoned here, no matter what.

'Cut it out!' the guard shouted. 'I'm telling you, I'll come in there and sort you out!'

She nodded to herself and increased the rain of blows on the door.

'Right!' she heard him say. 'You've asked for it!'

The rattle of a key entering the lock was music to her ears. She flew across the room, diving on the bed and rolling over it on to the floor beyond. She crouched there, praying for a cloud to snuff out the moon's brightness. The door opened, slamming back against the wall, the guard's way of ensuring she wasn't lurking behind it. Light flooded in from the hallway and she heard him curse and the light-switch being flicked.

Holly knew if he was professional he would immediately step back into the hallway and to one side, to make his silhouette less vulnerable, so she had to act first.

Without showing herself, she hurled the still-warm light bulb into the corner of the room to the left of the guard. The glass popped and shattered, the noise resembling the blast of a small firearm. The guard whirled towards the sound, his single-hand submachine-gun aimed at the corner.

Holly was like a banshee streaking from the shadows and it was already too late for the guard as he turned to meet her rush. She hurled herself at him, twisting her body as she leapt, so that her back and one shoulder struck him just below chest level. He cried out in alarm, falling backwards, striking the door frame as he went down, the shock of the blow causing him to lose his grip on the submachine-gun. They sprawled halfway out into the hall and Holly, lithe as a cat, rolled to a crouching position, her eyes already searching the long corridor for other guards. With relief, she realized it was empty.

The guard's gun was lying back through the door, bathed in light from the hall, and she scrambled towards it. A hand grabbed her ankle and tripped her, sending her flat.

The guard, still stunned and wincing at the numbing pain between his shoulder-blades, had seen her intent and was quick enough to snatch at her leg. He pulled her towards him and that was his second mistake.

His first had been to underestimate her because she was a woman. His second was to clutch at one lethal appendage while allowing the other to remain free. Her other foot shot out and struck him just below the chin, snapping his head back so it struck the hard wood of the door frame once more. The foot struck again with deadly skill as his head bounced back, smashing his nose and hastening his already speedy flight into unconsciousness.

Holly sprang to her feet, the guard's hand falling limply away from her ankles. She cleared the curtain of blonde hair that screened her vision with a toss of her head and peeped back into the hallway, listening for the sound of approaching footsteps. Satisfied that their struggles had not aroused anybody's attention, she reached down for the unconscious guard's ankles and dragged him away from the doorway and further into the room. Flicking his eyelids up, she was careful to avoid the blood flowing from his broken nose, and guessed he would be out for quite some time. Nevertheless, she decided to bind him with bedsheets just to be safe. Within minutes it was done, and his inert body lay beneath the bed out of sight of anyone who should casually check on the room. It was probably an unnecessary precaution, for she knew her mere absence and the sight of the unguarded hallway would set off alarms throughout the estate, but she was a firm believer that in her business, every little detail could sometimes help. Her one concession to the man's condition was to leave him ungagged; with his nose and throat clogged with blood, she knew he could easily choke if air from his mouth was cut off. She even positioned him on his side to help the flow of blood run on to the carpet rather than down his throat, feeling slightly foolish and knowing her past instructors would have cursed her vehemently for her unprofessionalism. But she was prepared to take the small risk of his coming to his senses and calling for help rather than let him die in such a defenceless manner.

Holly straightened, running her hands down her jeans, trying to wipe the bloody stickiness from them. She walked over to the submachine-gun still lying near the doorway, light bouncing off its oily, black surfaces, and noted it was similar to an Ingram. Small and compact, inaccurate over any great distance, but deadly effective at close quarters. She wondered if it had the same firing power of twelve hundred rounds a minute as the Ingram. A small stock was hinged to the main body, providing a recoil buffer when pulled back and held against the upper arm. She picked it up, surprised because it was even lighter than the Ingram: Gant's private army was privileged with the finest equipment.

Once again she checked the hallway, listening for sounds, her senses keened to the atmosphere. All was quiet.

She closed the door, locking it with the key still protruding beneath the handle, and crept stealthily down the long corridor, keeping close to the wall, prepared to use the recessed doorways as cover should anyone suddenly appear. Holly made her way towards the back of the house, away from the main stairway, and towards the curiously castle-like older part.

The wind howled around the ancient church tower, the breeze cold, sweeping over the land from the sea, biting and tangy with salt. As the moonlight struggled through the thick, rolling clouds once again, a group of men was revealed crouching for shelter behind the parapet at the top of the tower. At all times, however, one man remained kneeling, his elbows resting against the cleft in the fort-like wall, night-sighted binoculars held to his eyes, watching the dim white house in the dip of the land almost a mile away.

'Still no movement, sir,' he muttered, ducking his head below the parapet so his words were not whisked away by the wind. 'Reckon they've settled down for the night.'

The man he was speaking to half-covered his watch with a hand so that the luminous dial could function. 'Nearly half-eleven,' he said to no one in particular. 'The last helicopter arrived about ten, didn't it?'

Sexton, crouched next to him, nodded and said, 'Yes, about that time. Look, it must have been the last of 'em. Can't we move in now?'

'Sorry, we can't go in until we've been given the order from the Commissioner.' Detective Chief Inspector Burnett sympathized with the retired police officer, Blake, but there were bigger things at stake here than the safety of one man. He was acting under the directions of the Commissioner *and* the Home Secretary. They were running the show – so if his orders were to wait, then wait he would.

'But what are you hanging on for?' Blake persisted. 'For fuck's sake, he could be dead by now.'

The chief inspector turned to him and said patiently, 'Look, Mr Blake, I can appreciate your concern, but this Steadman went in there of his own free will . . .'

'He said he had to. He had to play it out the way Gant wanted. He was worried about the girl, he didn't know if she was involved or not, whether she was safe or . . .'

'Holly Miles. Yes,' Burnett said wearily, 'we know all about her now.'

'Why weren't we informed about her before, governor?' a voice came from close by.

'Mistrust, Andy. They played everything close to their chests. Christ, who would have thought Pope was dodgy?'

The detective sergeant shook his head in the dark. 'How long have they known about him?'

'God knows. You can bet that's why the CIA were in on it, though – nobody knew who could really be trusted in MI5. If someone with Pope's rank could be part of Gant's group, then who else – upstairs *or* downstairs – could be involved. Aah,' he waved a hand disgustedly, 'makes you sick to think of it.'

Sexton rose to his feet, his cramped position making his bones ache. The wind hit him instantly and he pulled the lapels of his overcoat up around his neck, tucking one point beneath the other to protect his chest. He looked over the edge and could clearly make out the ugly, twisted tree that stood by the roadside at the base of the old church. On the other side of the ancient stone building, groups of cars and Special Branch Land-Rovers lay hidden from the road, all filled with cold, bored men, impatient for the action to start.

It had been a frustrating twenty-four hours for Sexton and with every passing minute his concern for Steadman's safety grew. They had done what Harry had told them, he and Steve, continuing their vigil on the house at Guildford, waiting for the police to arrive, trying to keep awake through the night. All that had happened was that the guards had come and locked the gates, seemingly unconcerned with thoughts of escaping, gathering up the bodies of the man and the two dogs, loading them into a truck, and driving back up to the house. He and Steve waited beyond that time because Harry had said to wait a few hours, give this man Pope the chance to act – give him the benefit of the doubt.

Nothing had happened though, and in the early hours of the morning, Sexton had felt sure nothing was going to happen. He had left poor Steve there – the boy had really acted well throughout all this – and driven back to town, straight to New

Scotland Yard. It was fortunate he still had good contacts there, otherwise he would have had a difficult time convincing them his story was true. It sounded unlikely even to him as he related it, but eventually the police had been persuaded to make a few enquiries, strictly as a favour – and there were a few of them there who owed him a favour or two – about Pope. Special Branch had been contacted to see if they knew anything of the matter, then the whole thing had taken on a new pace.

When questions are asked by Scotland Yard about a member of MI5, the reaction is swift and tight. Sexton had soon found himself being interviewed by several obviously senior people, one of whom was an American. He told them all he knew, which wasn't much; but it seemed to be enough for them. Events took on a new impetus and a clampdown on internal security was immediate; only a select few seemed to know exactly what was going on.

Steve was brought in and a discreet guard placed around the Guildford house. The house was still under observation, untouched and unwarned. The men inside were probably feeling very smug.

There was much Sexton didn't understand and it was obvious the Special Branch officers he was now with were not fully in the picture either. But one thing was certain: the authorities – those at the very top – were aware something was afoot, otherwise action on such a grand scale would never have happened so promptly. It was as though Harry Steadman was the trigger that had set it off. And the American who had interviewed him earlier that day – did that mean the CIA were involved too? It seemed Harry had uncovered a hornet's nest.

He crouched down again, out of the stinging wind, cursing softly under his breath.

'We can't just sit here!' he shouted at no one in particular.

Burnett placed a hand on Sexton's arm and moved his head closer. 'We've got to wait, Mr Blake. It won't be much longer, I promise. The Commissioner's coming down himself to direct operations. That's how important it is.'

'Then why isn't he here now?' Sexton said angrily. 'Why is he keeping us bloody waiting?'

'I don't know for sure. I think he's got to make arrangements at the other end. The word is that it's not just a bunch of terrorist fanatics we're bringing in, but some very high-placed bastards, men as rich and powerful as Gant himself, maybe even more so. If you ask me, the Commissioner's consulting the PM himself on just how to handle the whole affair.'

'It's wasting so much bloody time, though!'

'We'll be in there in a matter of minutes once we get the word. We're having a force of Marine Commandos flown up from their base in Plymouth by RNAF helicopters. We know Gant's got his own private army, so if he resists there's going to be some bloody battle. Now I'm just as keen to get it over with as you – waiting makes me nervous – but there's nothing we can do until we get the order. So be patient and try not to worry about this Steadman. He hasn't done too bad so far, has he?'

Sexton turned his head away in frustration. No, Harry hadn't done bad so far. But how much longer would his luck last?

18

'He clipped him in such a way that he can never more give pleasure to any woman. But that meant suffering for many people.'

WOLFRAM VON ESCHENBACH

'We are more valuable than the others who now, and always will, surpass us in numbers. We are more valuable because our blood enables us to invent more than others, to lead our people better than others. Let us clearly realize, the next decades signify a struggle leading to the extermination of the sub-human opponents in the whole world who fight Germany, the basic people of the Northern race, bearer of the culture of mankind.'

HEINRICH HIMMLER

Steadman's eyes slowly began to focus on the moving floor beneath him. His head still rang with the blows it had received.

He realized he was being hauled along a corridor, hands gripping him by the armpits and his feet dragging behind on the dark wood floor. He twisted his head to see where he was and recognized the voice that spoke; it belonged to Griggs.

'He's awake. Let him walk the rest of the way.'

The investigator was hoisted to his feet and the sombre face of Pope glared at him.

'I'm very glad you've rejoined us, Harry, though I think you'll wish you never had.'

'Go screw yourself, Pope,' Steadman replied, trying to shake the dizziness from his head. Griggs and Booth on either side prevented him from falling again.

'Ah, still the same arrogance. I could admire it if you weren't such a fool.'

'You're the fool, Pope, to think all this is actually going to happen.' Steadman managed to steady himself, but rough hands still gripped his upper arms.

A deep scoffing sound came from the fat man's throat. 'Look at it this way, Harry,' he said without smiling. 'What's the alternative?'

He turned away, motioning his two men to bring the investigator along. Steadman was propelled forward and felt too groggy to resist. His curiosity was aroused by the long corridor's decorations. It was like being in a medieval castle, for the walls were dark-grey stone, tapestries hanging in the spaces between doorways. The doors themselves were of intricately carved oak, the handles elaborately shaped wrought-iron. His examination of the carving on the doors was perfunctory, but they seemed to be individual coats-of-arms, with an inscription or a title worked into each, and embellished with metal and what looked like precious stones.

They soon reached a point where the corridor opened out on one side and he realized they were now on a balcony overlooking a large, darkened hall. They stopped at the head of a broad stone stairway and Steadman's eyes widened in new alarm at the sight below him.

The huge room was decorated in the style of an ancient banqueting hall, with deep rich carpets, heavily brocaded curtains flanking the high windows; more tapestries adorned the walls. High, thick candles were placed symmetrically around the room, their colour black, providing the only light apart from the fire that raged in the deep, man-sized cavity behind what appeared to be a dais. The design theme throughout was that of a golden spear.

In the centre of the vast floor stood a huge round table, made as far as Steadman could tell, from solid oak, and around it were placed wooden high-backed chairs. He could see from those facing away from him that each had an inscribed silver plate on the back. Every chair – save for two – had an occupant; and the face of each occupant was turned towards him.

'Welcome to our Wewelsburg.' It was Edward Gant's voice and Steadman's eyes darted around the table to trace the source. A figure began to rise and he saw it was Gant in a central position, his back to the curious dais. 'Bring him down!' There was anger in the command.

Steadman was shoved brutally from behind, causing him to lose his balance and reach out for the stout banister to one side of the stairway. It prevented the fall from being too serious, but still he tumbled down, losing his grip and rolling to the bottom. Footsteps behind, then he was again hauled to his feet. He shook the clutching hands off, forcing himself to stand alone.

'It would appear Kristina has failed in her task.' Gant's voice was cold, the familiar mocking tones absent now.

'Did you really believe I could be corrupted by that . . . thing?' Steadman said harshly.

'Her power is in her mind, Mr Steadman. Yes, I am surprised you resisted that. It seems she still has much to learn from her mystagogue, Dr Scheuer.' Gant made a motion with his hand, and a chair was brought from the shadows of the room to be placed three feet away from the round table. Steadman was shoved into it. A gap had opened up between the seated figures, offering him an unrestricted view of the arms dealer opposite. He had time to notice several uniformed guards situated at strategic points around the room, submachine-guns held across their chests, before looking into the mad, glaring eyes of Edward Gant. The artificial nose was still affixed to the arms dealer's disfigured face, making him at least look human. He was dressed in a charcoal-grey suit, his shirt white, though it looked yellowish in the suffused light, and his tie was black. The investigator was surprised Gant and his cohorts were not clad in robes or medieval costumes, such was the atmosphere in the dark baronial hall. Around the table, neatly placed before each member of the group, was a short ceremonial dagger and he noticed that those whose hands were placed on the table's surface wore curiously designed signet rings. The guests he had met earlier that day were among those seated, and others were familiar to him through the media. Dr Scheuer was there, looking even older and more frail; Steadman felt his eyes boring into him even though he could not see them in their dark caverns. He was distracted as the vast bulk of Pope filled one of the unoccupied chairs.

'You are an honoured person, Mr Steadman,' Gant's voice echoed around the stone walls, increasing its sibilance.

'Honoured? To be part of this?'

'To be one of the few outsiders to visit the Wewelsburg.'

'I'm overwhelmed.'

'Don't mock us, Mr Steadman!' Gant warned, his hand toying with the dagger before him. 'Your death will be painful enough, but it can be made excruciating. The honour bestowed upon you is to see this, almost an exact replica of the Reichsführer's fortress which he had built in Westphalia. A shrine devoted to the Teutonic Knights. Only a select few, twelve in all, were allowed to visit Himmler's domain, all SS officers. There they meditated, remembered their Nordic origins. Each had his own room and that room was dedicated to great kings and emperors such as Otto the Great, Henry the Lion, Frederick Hohenstauffen, Philip of Swabia and Conrad IV. The Reichsführer's own room was in honour of Henry I. Adolf Hitler's belonged to Frederick Barbarossa. But Hitler refused to visit the Wewelsburg! He turned his back on the forces that brought him to power. He would not even allow Himmler to bring the Spear to its natural resting-place! That is why the Führer failed, you see. Because at the end, he no longer possessed the Holy Spear – Heinrich Himmler had taken it for himself!'

Gant twisted in his chair and pointed towards the altar-like dais. 'And we have possessed it ever since!'

Steadman saw the leather case resting on top of the dais and guessed at the object lying inside. So the Heilige Lance was here!

The arms dealer turned back to face Steadman across the table, but his eyes flicked upwards to the balcony above.

'Come, Kristina, join us. You have failed, but then so did the original Kundra. It matters little now; the final achievement will be ours.'

Steadman heard the footsteps on the stone stairway behind him and the man/woman came into view. Her face was swollen and bruised where he had struck her, and her beauty now seemed obscene. She scurried around the table, avoiding all the eyes that were on her, and sat in a chair placed behind Dr Scheuer. The old man ignored her, still looking directly at Steadman.

The figure of Major Brannigan emerged from the shadows then, pure hatred in his eyes. He strode towards Steadman, a hand reaching for the revolver strapped to his side.

'Major!'

Brannigan halted at Gant's harsh command. 'Wait outside for our latecomer, Major Brannigan, and take your guards with you. We have no need for them here.'

'But what about Steadman? You know he's dangerous.' The Major's voice was resentful.

'I'm sure Griggs and Booth are capable of taking care of Mr Steadman should he become . . . restless. Now go and wait by the helicopter pad. Our visitor should be here at any minute and I want him brought straight in.'

Brannigan whirled and called for the soldiers around the room to fall in after him. They marched out, boots heavy on the solid floor.

'Forgive the Major, Mr Steadman,' Gant said. 'He's insanely

jealous over Kristina. Rather pathetic, don't you think, to be so concerned over such an aberration?'

The hermaphrodite's head snapped up and she looked balefully at Gant.

'Unfortunately,' the arms dealer went on smoothly, 'she is of the utmost importance to our cause. She will eventually take over from Dr Scheuer, you see. Our poor doctor's health is failing and I'm afraid he has not much longer for this world. Somehow, I think he will prefer the next.' Gant smiled warmly at the old man.

'Don't you think we should get on with the ceremony, Edward?' Sir James Oakes, the industrialist Steadman had been introduced to earlier that day, said from the far side of the table.

'I agree.' It was Talgholm who spoke, and a few others murmured their approval. 'Time's running out, Edward. The missile will soon be launched.'

'Gentlemen, there is ample time. Our ally from overseas expressed a specific desire to be present tonight and we shall abide by his wish. You all know how necessary he is to us.' Gant held up a hand, warding off any further protests, but when the voices still persisted he banged his fist down hard on the table. 'Enough!' he shouted. 'Have you forgotten what is to happen tonight? The atmosphere must not be disturbed for Dr Scheuer!'

Their protests faded into silence and Gant smiled grimly. 'There is too much tension in the air,' he said by way of explanation to Steadman. 'Our members are – shall we say – on edge?'

'They're as crazy as you, Gant,' Steadman said evenly.

'Yes. And you are the only sane one here tonight.' The mockery was back in the arms dealer's eyes. 'I wonder if you will still be sane before you die?'

Steadman's brain was racing. What had happened to Sexton and Steve? Had they failed to convince the authorities? Were they *still* trying to? Or worse – had they been taken by Gant's men at Guildford? They were his only chance, but now it looked a very poor one.

'Okay, Gant,' he said. 'I'd like to hear more about your organization. You say you're Thulists, but I thought such societies in Germany were wiped out after the last war.'

'Only people are "wiped out" in wars, not ideals. Some of us survived to further those ideals.'

'You were in Germany during the war?'

'Oh yes.' Gant chuckled, enjoying the puzzlement on the investigator's face. 'I was not a common soldier, but I served the Reich in a more meaningful way. I've already told you how Hitler rejected us and how, because of the Führer's final foolishness, the power passed on to Reichsführer Heinrich Himmler. Thanks to plans carefully laid out long before the end of the war, Herr Himmler and I managed to escape the clutches of the Allies . . .'

The four men hurried single-file across the field, their feet sinking inches into the mud at each step, their breathing – particularly the third man's – laboured and sharp. It was quiet in this part of the country, for the rumble of guns had been left far behind. But still they hurried, knowing they were near to freedom, near to Kiel where a boat would be waiting.

They had successfully evaded the clutches of the US Ninth Army, abandoning their armour-plated Mercedes early on in their hazardous journey for a less-conspicuous grey Volkswagen. The little car had taken them a great distance and they had kept to the smaller roads and away from the jammed autobahns, travelling only when it appeared safe to do so, hiding the vehicle in wooded areas off the road when not. But now they were on foot for, in their haste, they had neglected to bring along extra cans of petrol. It may have been for the best though: the roads were too dangerous and SS Colonel von Köhner felt they had pushed their luck far enough in that respect.

The third man in line suddenly stumbled and went down on one knee in the mud. Von Köhner took him by the elbow and gently helped him back to his feet, asking if he might carry the faded leather case for the Reichsführer. Himmler shook his head and they continued their traverse of the field, eyes wary for any other signs of life.

Heinrich Himmler held the leather case containing the ancient spearhead tightly against his chest, refusing to let anyone else take possession, unwilling to let it out of his grasp, even for one second. The others – Reichskriminaldirektor Mueller, Erik Gantzer, and SS Colonel von Köhner – could carry the money and the valuables that would buy their escape and ensure their freedom. And of course, the secret files, his beloved files kept through the years: documents concerning not only the devious activities of his fellow countrymen, but men, influential men, of other countries. Regretfully, they had taken only the most important, those which could be used again at another time; they would have needed ten trucks to bring all the others along. His three loyal followers would manage those between them but he, alone, would bear the holy relic.

All four wore civilian clothing, Himmler, Mueller, and Köhner having discarded their uniforms at the beginning of the journey, Erik Gantzer a civilian anyway. A strange and powerful man, this Gantzer, Himmler reflected, studying the tall figure ahead of him. His grandfather, Otto Gantzer, had been apprenticed to the Royal Prussian Arms Factory in Spandau, near Berlin, working there as a master gunsmith for many years until he left to establish his own business in the port of Rostok, which his son Ernst, also a master gunsmith, had continued. The business had prospered after the old man's death, Ernst developing and diversifying the range of weapons he produced. His son, Erik Gantzer, after graduating from high school, was apprenticed to the arms factories in Suhl and Zella-Mehlis, following the family tradition, and eventually took over the whole Gantzer industry when the father died. Spared from service in the army because of his immense contribution to the war effort, Erik Gantzer had played a great part in introducing the Führer himself into the Thule Gesellschaft, the society in which Gantzer had become a key member. He had proved to be extremely useful, a brilliant young man with no conscience, who fought only for the future of the Aryan race. A man whose eventual disenchantment with the madman, Hitler, had led him to switch his allegiance to the Reichsführer himself. And now, even though their beloved country had been crushed, he would still serve him. It was his con- nections that would see they survived, his genius that would ensure the furtherance of the cause! It was he who had devised the escape, planned the route, made the contacts, long before it was inevitable that Germany would lose. He had ignored the normal Nazi escape routes, had dissuaded Himmler from making deals with the Allies, had insisted all was not finished, that the new beginning would be better planned, more guile, more subterfuge, would be used. Nothing was lost; only the moment delayed.

From Kiel, the boat would take them through the Kieler Bucht, travelling by night till they reached the rough waters of the Store Baelt, then on to Ebeltoft in Denmark, where they would journey overland to a small landing-strip owned by a contact of Gantzer's. From there they would fly to Iceland and eventually, when world affairs had moved on to more important matters than the hunting down of elusive Nazis, they would go to Canada, then down into America, and finally, the ironic twist – back across the ocean to England. A bitter smile contorted Himmler's lips at the thought and, if he had had the breath, he would have laughed aloud. No South America for Heinrich Himmler! Let the Bormanns and the Mengeles go there!

He suddenly doubled over as pain wrenched at his gut and, once again, Colonel Köhner was there to support him. Himmler waved him away, grateful for his concern but indicating he would be all right in a short while. Franz von Köhner: another good man! A true German, prepared to leave his wife and young baby son – as he, himself, had left his own family, not to mention sweet Hedwig, his mistress – for the good of the cause! It was von Köhner who had secretly replaced the real Heilige Lance with a

237

skilfully made replica which Himmler, himself, had had made even before the annexation of Austria. The fool Hitler had never realized he possessed only a forgery painstakingly reproduced with metal almost as ancient as the Spear itself! He, Himmler, kept the original spearhead in the Wewelsburg, his mighty fortress in Paperdorn, Westphalia, dedicated to the Teutonic Knights: it was the natural resting-place for the legendary relic.

Despite the pain, Himmler smiled grimly. Von Köhner had served him well. And so had Heinz Hintzinger, the corporal in the Feldpolizei who looked so incredibly like him! When it had become an indisputable fact that Germany would lose the war, the hunt for doubles had almost become a game among the Nazi generals and officials, so many of them unwilling to face the wrath of the Allies. Cowards, all of them! For Himmler, it was different. It was his duty to survive! Now that the Führer had lost his mind, someone had to carry on, to rise like the Phoenix when the ashes had settled. He was that man.

Von Köhner had found many who resembled Himmler, but all had been rejected for Hintzinger; this man was prepared to die for his Reichsführer. His zeal for the Nazi cause amounted to fanaticism and the Schutzstaffeln knew how to use fanatics. He had been sent out under an escort who believed him to be their real leader, thinly disguised, and ready to admit he was no less than Heinrich Himmler himself when caught. And ready to crush the cyanide capsule between his teeth when he was sure the officials believed his statement.

Himmler again sank to his knees. He had to rest, just for a little while. The other three gathered round him, but he waved them on. See if it was safe on the other side of the field. Von Köhner could stay with him, help him on when the pain in his belly had subsided.

Mueller and Gantzer turned away, concern on their faces. They began to trot towards the screening hedge at the far side of the field.

Von Köhner squatted beside the Reichsführer and waited patiently.

He had been present when Himmler had received the message from Hitler's successor, Admiral Dönitz, dismissing the SS Reichsführer from the service of the Reich. How could they humble such a great man in that manner, a man who was prepared to fight on when others had given up? He had never looked impressive, this middle-aged man with his paunch, his narrow shoulders and curved back – too many hours hunched over paper-work – but what vision! What stature! The generals – traitors like SS General Wolf – already falling over each other to make deals with the enemy, to save their own necks, were not fit to lick his boots! The untermenschen *would never defeat this man!*

He wished the mystical masseur, Kerston, was here to ease his master's pain with those strange deft fingers that gave the Reichsführer such instant release. He wished he could provide a glass samovar containing a hot mixture of gentian and dandelion tea, for he knew how it soothed the Reichsführer's stomach pains . . .

The explosion shook the ground beneath their feet and mud and stones spattered their clothing. They looked in horror across the field to where two bodies lay, one still, the other writhing and screaming in agony.

They raced towards the two bodies, wondering which one was dead – Gantzer or Mueller? One of them must have trodden on a landmine or disturbed a concealed unexploded bomb; whoever had made the contact would be the dead one.

They reached the twisting body and realized only by the clothing that it was Erik Gantzer. His knees were hugged to his chest, his hands between them, clutching at his lower body. Von Köhner resisted the urge to vomit as he looked at the arms manufacturer's face – or lack of it. Blood spurted from a red hole in the centre of his face, a loose piece of flesh hanging by a thin tendril, the remnants of his nose.

Himmler's stomach was not as strong as the SS Colonel's. He paled and bent over as the contents of his stomach spilled on to the muddy earth. As he looked down, he caught something that made him close his eyes tightly and wheel his body away. Two feet that must have been Mueller's, one still inside a boot, lay on the ground before him. The one in the boot was standing upright, the bloody stump facing up at him, splintered bone showing whitely against the red flesh. His vomit had covered it before he twisted away.

Himmler dropped the leather case containing the Spear and fell to his hands and knees and retched, his whole body shuddering with the effort. He crawled, trying to get away from the grotesque sight of Mueller's dismembered feet, and when he finally found the strength to look up, he saw von Köhner's figure kneeling beside the twitching body of Gantzer, a Luger pointed at the injured man's temple.

Himmler staggered to his feet. Gantzer must not be shot. If there was a chance that he might live, no matter what pain he was in, he must be saved!

He pulled von Köhner's arm away just as the SS Colonel's finger began to squeeze the trigger. The gun never fired, but when Himmler stared down at Erik Gantzer's body and the mass of blood that covered his face and groin area, he wondered if he, the Reichsführer, should not have been more merciful . . .

'But Himmler was captured. He was identified before he committed suicide.'

Gant laughed and the sound echoed hollowly around the hall. 'That was another man, a double. A good German, prepared to die for his Reichsführer. Of course, his family would have suffered if his courage had failed him at the last moment. Fortunately, that was not necessary.'

'But he was examined, surely? They'd have had to be sure.'

'Can you imagine the confusion that was taking place in Germany at that time, Mr Steadman, with thousands – millions – fleeing? Have you any idea how many Germans the Allies caught trying to escape and whom they thought to be Himmler, Goebbels, Göring or Bormann? Or even Hitler himself? When they found one who confessed to being a Nazi leader and looked exactly like him with his disguise removed, do you really think they questioned the matter in any great detail? And when the chaos began finally to take on some order, it was too late; the body of the Reichsführer had been long buried in an unmarked grave. I promise you, the aftermath of such a war, with each nation fighting over territories like wolves over a dead carcass, is infinitely more complex than the planning of an enemy's defeat. With the removal of the obvious enemy, the allied nations became enemies to each other. It was not difficult for mistakes to be made.'

'But where could a man like Himmler go? Surely he would have been recognized?'

'You forget just how insignificant our great leader looked. I mean this as no disrespect, for this was the wonderful dichotomy of the man. He was one of Germany's greatest heroes, yet his appearance was that of an ordinary man.'

'I've read that he looked like a typical filing clerk,' said Steadman pointedly.

'Exactly, Mr Steadman,' said Gant as though the slight had been a compliment. 'A filing clerk with true Nordic blood.'

'So his very insignificance allowed his escape?'

'It allowed him to exist in another country.'

'Might I ask where? I take it that South America, the obvious place, was out of the question.'

'Of course. We could have fled there, lived among the Nazi colony; but we would have been impotent. No, we needed a country where we could build again, not a place where we could sit in the sun and reminisce over the past glories of the Fatherland.'

'So where, Gant? Where did you choose?'

'Why, England, of course. What better place?'

Steadman looked incredulously at the smiling faces around him. 'But that would have been impossible!'

'At the time, yes,' said Gant. 'Although we had many friends in Great Britain, even then – several were Thulists – many had been interned for the duration of the war because of their sympathies, and were never entirely trusted after.

'No, our first stop was Denmark. It hadn't been our intention, but we stayed hidden there for many months. I had been severely injured, you see. It was the Reichsführer who saved my life.'

The arms dealer paused as though the memory was a precious thing. 'We left Flensburg on 10 May 1945; Reichsführer Himmler, Colonel Franz von Köhner – the father of the inept fool you disposed of last night, Reichskriminaldirektor Ernest Mueller, and myself. Unfortunately, after making good progress towards Kiel, a bomb killed Mueller and almost killed me. It was only the Reichsführer's intervention that prevented von Köhner from putting a bullet through my brain. Herr Himmler insisted that I should be carried to our rendezvous point where my wounds could be treated. He even sacrificed his sacred files for my life. They were buried, along with Mueller, in that very same field. Colonel von Köhner carried me, and the Reichsführer carried our valuables and our talisman, the one object he refused to leave behind: the Heilige Lance!

'I was almost dead by the time we reached our contact near Kiel, but again Herr Himmler refused to allow me to die. They treated my wounds as best they could and then we went on by sea to Ebeltoft in Denmark. The journey was an extraordinary nightmare for me, Mr Steadman, and I pleaded with the Reichsführer a hundred times to put me to death; he would not allow it, though. He saw that some day, I would be the new leader, the Grand Master, in his place. His vision was far beyond human limitations.

'We stayed in an area far inland from Ebeltoft until I had recovered from my injuries; not fully, you understand, but enough to travel on. From there we were flown to Iceland and, a few years later, to Canada. Seven years passed before we dared enter the United States of America. Our contacts, both in America and England, had been renewed long before, and our movement was already beginning to thrive. We kept under-

cover, for obvious reasons, allowing the more vulgar nationalistic organizations to take all attention from us. Subterfuge
and progressive infiltration has been our policy since the
setback.'

'You call the last World War a setback?'

'Yes, Mr Steadman. Nothing more than that!' There was
silence around the table as though each member was defying the
investigator to refute Gant's statement. Steadman shrugged.

'So Himmler was alive all that time,' he said.

Gant nodded solemnly. 'Yes. Colonel von Köhner died in '51
while we were still in Canada. A stroke. Before he died he
made us promise to find the young son he'd left behind in Germany, and to indoctrinate him into our cause. We readily
agreed. The offspring of a man like Franz von Köhner would
indeed be valuable to the Society. Perhaps it was fortunate for
the Colonel that he never knew the incompetent his son was
to become. The youth, Felix, readily joined us, for in Germany
he had nothing. Von Köhner's wife had died shortly after the
war and the boy was being raised by relatives. They allowed
him to come to us, for they were poor, the war having stripped
many such families of their wealth. Felix joined us in England
when he was twenty-one.'

'When . . . when did you . . . and Himmler come to this
country?'

Gant smiled and the smile made Steadman shudder. 'In 1963,
Mr Steadman. An historic date.'

The others around the table voiced their agreement. 'He was
very ill by then. The stomach pains that had plagued him most
of his life had finally broken his health, but even at that time,
we did not realize how serious his condition was . . .'

Steadman was so stunned at the idea of the infamous mass-
murderer living in England that he missed the arms dealer's
next few words. When he had recovered enough to listen
again, Gant was talking of his marriage in America.

'Louise was an extremely rich American, from the Deep
South. Our ideals matched, for the Southerners' intolerance

towards race impurity was almost on a par with the Nazi's. She never really knew the true strength of our ambitions, and the real identity of our permanent, reclusive house-guest was kept a secret from her. She suspected he was an ex-Nazi, I'm sure, for she knew I was, but I don't think it ever occurred to her she was housing one of the world's most "notorious" men. She was an extraordinary woman who shared our ideals and demanded nothing physically from me. She lived only for the day when our ideals would find fruition, and I cannot tell you how much her wealth and contacts furthered our cause. It was tragic that a road accident should have taken her from us so early in our rising.'

The whir of helicopter blades suddenly drew everyone's attention. 'Ah, that sounds like the arrival of our twelfth member,' Gant said.

'It's about time!' said Lord Ewing, the news magnate.

'The General has had a long journey,' Gant reproached, and the man fell silent.

Astonished by the arms dealer's authority over such powerful men, Steadman looked around the table at each one in turn, then said, 'How can you follow a man like this? An ex-Nazi, a man who helped one of the most evil men in history, a man who fought against us in the war. How can you betray your country for someone like that?'

'Betray? You're the one who's a traitor, Steadman,' said Talgholm. 'You claim to be British, but you'd sit by while the country sinks. What kind of loyalty is that?'

'Look . . .' Steadman began.

'Shut up!' It was Ewing who shouted across the table, his face red, his eyes bulbous with rage. 'We're sick of do-gooders like you. Live and let live, that's what you believe, don't you? Do you think *they'll* let us live once they've taken over? Your kind are almost as bad as them!'

'Let's get rid of him now, Edward,' came another cry.

'Yes, we don't need him,' Talgholm agreed. 'The legend will still be fulfilled.'

'Not yet!' Gant's voice was stern. 'You know how it's to be done.'

'We're running short . . .'

'There is time.' The pronouncement was made quietly, but the assembled group became silent again.

'Tell me more, Gant,' Steadman said with a calm he hardly felt. 'How . . . where did Himmler live in this country.'

'Always in this area, Mr Steadman. He was fascinated by the Arthurian legends. King Arthur's Knights were based on the Teutonic Order, and their activities took place mainly in this part of the country. He was so overjoyed when I had the Wewelsburg built here for him.

'The Thule Gesellschaft was a wealthy organization by then. The arms industry I had set up, aided substantially by the money my dear, late wife had left me, was thriving, and donations from our secret members were flooding in. We had recovered the files von Köhner had buried so many years before and they opened many . . .' he smiled and looked at the faces around the table '. . . so many doors for us.'

Steadman began to realize how blackmail had played such an important part in the rebuilding of their movement.

'The Reichsführer, despite the pain he was in, was very happy in his final days,' the arms dealer said softly. 'He knew this time we would win.'

'He died here?' Steadman asked, somehow – inexplicably – expecting a denial of the Reichsführer's death, for his presence felt so real.

'Yes, Mr Steadman. In a sense. He was sixty-seven when cancer took his life. But even though his body failed him, his spirit did not. Almost a year after his death he sent someone to us.' Gant turned to Dr Scheuer seated next to him. 'Dr Scheuer was a spiritualist living in Austria. The Reichsführer chose the Herr Doktor to be his intermediary.'

At that point, approaching footsteps were heard outside the

hall. A door set back in the shadows against the wall, opened, and a broad-shouldered figure strode in briskly followed by Major Brannigan.

'Good evening, gentlemen.' The voice was unmistakably American, and when the man drew closer to the light, Steadman groaned inwardly as he recognized him. The assembly stood in deference as he took his place in the empty chair beside Dr Scheuer.

'Is this the man?' He glowered across at Steadman.

'Yes, General, this is our Parsifal,' Gant said smoothly. 'Mr Steadman, I'm sure you recognize Major-General Cutbush, the US Forces Deputy Commander.'

They weren't crazy at all, Steadman realized. They really had the power and influence to dominate a nation's thinking. Over the years, by bribery, blackmail, or sheer mutual agreement on racial ideals, they'd built up an incredible force, a force strong enough to direct public motivation wavering between the two extremes towards their own aims. It was just the worship of the dead Himmler and all it entailed that was their madness, and he was puzzled at the necrophiliac devotion displayed by such men. What could instigate such an insanity? Suddenly, he was terrified.

'Okay, Edward, I said I'd go along with all this because *he* wanted it this way.' The American's burly figure and grizzled features looked strange to Steadman, for he had been used to seeing pictures and film of him in full military uniform. 'But I don't like it one bit. It's too . . .' he searched for the word '. . . theatrical.'

'I understand your feelings, General, but it would be unwise not to comply with *his* wishes now,' said Gant.

'Mebbe,' the General said gruffly, 'but I still don't like it. Brannigan!' The British major flinched to attention. 'Shouldn't you be at the launching site?'

'We were just waiting for your arrival, sir. I'm on my way now.' Brannigan marched from the room, his back stiff and his stride determined.

'Goddamn fag,' Cutbush muttered to no one in particular when the door closed. 'Okay, let's get on.'

Gant stood and made to move away from the table towards the dais, but Steadman's shout stopped him.

'For God's sake, General, you're a veteran of the Second World War. You fought against men like him!' The investigator's finger was pointing at Gant and the two guards on either side had stepped forward and clamped their hands on his shoulders to prevent him rising from the chair.

The General looked across at him and his eyes narrowed. 'Now you . . . shut . . . your . . . mouth, mister. Sure, I fought against him and his kind. That was my mistake. I was with Patton throughout the damn war and I saw how his ass was kicked around by the so-called free-thinking leaders of our country. We had long chats, the old war-horse and me, and I know the kind of man he was. He saw the Russian threat while everyone else was still messing with the Germans. He wanted to march right through Germany and straight on into Moscow itself! It was he who told me the legend of the Spear – even though he was a pragmatist, he had a deep belief in such things – an' I was with him in a Nuremberg bunker when he thought he'd found it. We didn't know it then, but there'd been a switch. "Blood and Guts" never could figure out why nothing had happened for him. Himmler had already vamoosed with it!

'Now I don't mind admitting it: General Patton was my God, an' if he said there was something in the legend, there sure as hell was! I saw what they did to Patton when they no longer needed him. You think the car smash that killed him after the war was an accident? And I see what they're trying to do to me because they think I'm not needed. Old "Blood and Guts"' aggression became an embarrassment to them, and they feel the same about my hard-line views. But unlike the General, I started making plans a long, long time ago and it was our good fortune . . .' he waved his hand around the table '. . . that Edward Gant brought us together. We all believe in the same thing, sonny, and we don't need any crap about who we were fightin' in the last fuckin' war!'

Steadman relaxed back into his chair and managed to stare insolently at Cutbush. 'So they were putting you out to pasture.'

'You fuckin' crud. I'll break . . .' Gant checked the General's rising figure with a hand on his shoulder. The General sat but glowered at the investigator. 'I'm goin' to enjoy the next few minutes, jerk,' he said.

Steadman returned the glare.

Gant nodded at Griggs and Booth, and Steadman felt his arms gripped tightly.

'The time has come, Parsifal,' Gant said, walking towards the dais. He reached inside the leather case and turned with a long dark object in his hands. Steadman saw it was the spearhead, the holy relic whose legendary powers had caused the bloodshed of millions and the glory of a chosen few. There was no shine to the ancient black metal, only a dull glow from the section of gold, but the blade still tapered to a menacing point. Gant placed it on the table, its flattened blade pointed towards the investigator.

Steadman looked at the ancient relic and began to tremble inwardly. It was strange, but it felt as if a force were emanating from the cold metal, a force that was already piercing his heart. And then, he knew what was to be his fate: he was to die from a spear thrust. Gant would refute the Parsifal legend by using the weapon itself to kill his adversary.

He closed his eyes, but the image was still there in his mind: the evil tapering blade, the nail driven into an aperture in the blade, the small crosses engraved in the dark metal. He tried to force it from his thoughts but it stayed, a cold, dark object, a dead thing that somehow thrummed with energy. In his mind's eye he saw it was bloodstained.

'Can you feel its power, Parsifal?'

Steadman opened his eyes and now he saw the spearhead only as an aged piece of metal, lifeless and cold. He tore his eyes away and looked into the face of Gant who was leaning forward over the spear.

'Do you know Wolfram von Eschenbach's legend of Parsifal?' The arms dealer's eyes seemed to glow in the darkness of the room. 'The legend which inspired Wagner's mystical opera. Parsifal served the dying king, Amfortas, and sought to regain the Spear of Longinus, the holy symbol, for his master. As you sought to regain it for your masters – the Jews!'

'That's not true!' The hands on Steadman's arms tightened their grip. 'They wanted me to find their missing agent, Baruch Kanaan. You know that!'

'Lies, Parsifal. Their agent came for the Spear and when he failed, they sent you.'

Why hadn't Goldblatt told him of the Spear? Why hadn't he levelled with him from the start? The woman, Hannah, when she lay dying in his arms, had told him to find the Spear. But why hadn't they told him at the very beginning? Did they assume that finding Baruch would lead them to the ancient weapon? Resentment rose up in Steadman. They had used him just as the Thulists were using him. He'd been manipulated by both sides, one side using him as a tool, a lever to uncover a viper's nest, the other using him as a player in a symbolic ritual.

'You were to kill me, just as the knight, Parsifal, killed Klingsor, who held the Spear at his castle. Klingsor, the evil magician whose manhood was cut away by the fool king – as mine was taken from me. A sword took Klingsor's testicles from his body – an explosion took mine. The Reichsführer saved my life and when he saw the damage that was done to me, *he knew* I was Klingsor reincarnated! He knew I would be the future bearer of the Spear of Longinus.'

Gant's shoulders were heaving with the mental stress he was going through. To Steadman, it seemed as though the man was possessed. Abruptly, the tone of the arms dealer's voice changed, and he spoke as if he were revealing a long-kept secret to friends.

'The legend, you see, was neither a myth, nor a prophecy.

It was a warning. Von Eschenbach was our guide from the thirteenth century. He was warning us of the disaster that could come if we allowed it. And he warned us again at the appropriate time in this century through Richard Wagner!'

'It's fantasy, Gant. Can't any of you see that?' There was desperation in Steadman's voice now. 'You're just twisting everything to make it seem as if the story is coming true. I'm not your Parsifal and he's not your Klingsor. The Spear has no power. It's all in *his* mind!'

A rough hand was cupped over his mouth and his head jerked back. He tried to twist away, but Griggs held him firmly.

'No, it's not all in *my* mind, Mr Steadman,' Gant said calmly. 'We are led by another. Someone who knows you now. Someone who sent a tank against you as a test. Someone who visited you at your home just two nights ago, but who was disturbed by the meddling old Jew. Someone who wishes to meet you again.' Gant chuckled. 'As it were, face to face.'

There was silence in the vast room, the shadows flickering and weaving with the dancing candle-flames. Gant sat and the thirteen around the table put their hands on its rough surface as though a signal had been given. Their fingers touched and Steadman could see that their eyes had closed and each man's face was creased in concentration. Nothing happened for a while, then suddenly he felt his muscles weakening as if all strength was being drained from them. His head was released and he felt, rather than saw, the two MI5 men step back from their position directly behind. He tried to rise but found he couldn't; an invisible force seemed to be holding him there. He opened his mouth to speak but no sound came. The sudden oppression in the room had become an increasing pressure, weighing down on him like a physical force. He saw that several members of the circle were sagging in their seats, their heads lolling forward as though their energy was being sapped. Dr Scheuer's head was resting almost on his chest.

A stillness had crept into the room. The candle-flames seemed to be frozen solid, their light dimmed. It became cold.

A terrible, cloying coldness that closed in and gripped the skin. An odour pervaded the air and the room became even darker, the chill more intense.

Steadman stared hard into the shadows behind Gant and Dr Scheuer, for he thought he had seen something move, a dark shape against a black backcloth. From the balcony overlooking the hall, he had noticed steps set to one side of the room lead-ing down to a door, the top half only, level with the floor. The black shape had seemed to emerge from that point. But now it had disappeared and he wondered if it had been merely a trick of the fading light.

A humming vibration reached his ears and his attention was drawn to the table's surface. Some of the Thulists' heads were sagging, almost resting on the table, but still their fingers touched, trembling and greyish in the poor light. His eyes came to rest on the dark object lying opposite, and somehow he knew that was the source of the vibration. The ancient weapon lay unmoving, yet it seemed to throb with some inner life. He shook his head and the effort seemed almost too much; he felt giddy with fatigue. He knew the humming vibration was only in his own head, yet it seemed to come so definitely from the talisman. He became weaker and for a moment his eyes rolled in his head; he had to fight consciously to control them. He found himself looking across the table at the bowed head of the old man, Dr Scheuer, the scant white hair hanging loosely around his hidden face.

Steadman stared, for it seemed all the energy in the room had been drawn into the old man. The others, those who could, were watching him too, their bodies swaying slightly. The in-vestigator fought against the weariness, trying to build a wall in his mind against the will-devouring force. But he could not tear away his eyes from the bowed head of Dr Scheuer.

As he looked, the white-haired figure began to straighten. The head came up, slowly, smoothly, taking long, long seconds for the eyes to meet Steadman's. And when they finally looked deep and penetratingly into his, the investigator's blood seemed to stop flowing, and the hair on his neck rose as though a cold hand had swept it upwards, for he found himself staring at the hate-filled image of SS Reichsführer Heinrich Himmler.

19

'*Though he had the mind of an ordinary clerk or schoolmaster he was dominated by another Himmler whose imagination was controlled by such phrases as "The preservation of the Germanic race justifies cruelty", or, "Unqualified obedience to the Führer". This other Himmler entered realms which transcended the merely human and entered in to another world.*'

FELIX KERSTON

'*For us the end of this war will mean an open road to the East, the creation of the Germanic Reich in this way or that . . .*'

HEINRICH HIMMLER

Holly crept stealthily down the corridor using only the balls of her feet, measuring each step and gently easing her weight on to the solid floorboards. There was a tension in the house that had nothing to do with her own nervousness. The air was heavy with it.

She wondered about the strange building, half-house, half-castle. What was the purpose of such a place? She had found her way towards the back of the house, heading for the baronial-type rooms she had seen only from the outside. There had been only a blank wall at the end of the corridor leading from her room – it was too short to have run the length of the house – and she had been forced to retrace her steps to the staircase near the front of the house.

Guessing it might be a mistake to descend – bound to be more guards around – she had decided to go up on to the next level and make her way back from there. There had to be another way of getting to the rear of the house on the second floor. She moved silently up the stairs, holding the miniature machine-gun ahead of her, wishing she had taken time to search the unconscious guard for the silencer that went with the deadly weapon. She knew that the Ingram MAC II, on which this weapon's design had been based, could be fitted with a lightweight sound suppressor which cut out even the light 'plopping' noise silenced guns usually made. She would have to take her chances without it – if someone discovered her, she would shoot to kill and to hell with the noise.

She reached the top of the stairs and paused: the house was deadly silent.

The long corridor running down the building's centre lay ahead of her, two minor corridors ran to the left and right from her position at the top of the stairs. She had just begun her long walk down the central corridor when a door ahead opened.

Her reaction was fast. She ducked back into the left-hand corridor, prepared to run its length if the footsteps came her way. They didn't; she heard the footsteps receding into the distance. She stole a quick look around the corridor's corner and caught sight of the woman, the one they called Kristina. She was holding the side of her face as though she had been hurt and Holly caught a glimpse of her leaning against the wall momentarily for support. Holly held her breath, waiting for the footsteps to fade away. She was a strange one, this woman, Holly felt intuitively. She couldn't quite understand why, but was distinctly uneasy in her presence when Gant had introduced her. Not that she'd felt at home with the arms dealer himself.

She took another look and saw that the woman had vanished. Good. She'd definitely walked the length of the corridor, so maybe she was headed for the back of the house. There had to be a way through. Holly stole down the passageway.

There was a T-junction at the end and Holly debated with herself which way to go. She chose the right and at the end of it found a solid-looking oak door, its intricate carving suggesting it wasn't just the door to the broom-cupboard. She tried the wrought-iron handle and discovered it was locked. Okay, the left-hand turn might have a similar door. It did, and this one was open.

It was like stepping into another world: the walls on either side of the dim passageway were of heavy grey stone and the doors along its length again were of delicately carved oak. The lights overhead were deliberately dim so their brightness would not jar against the medieval atmosphere. Holly moved forward, carefully closing the door leading from the new to the fake-old behind her. If anything, the tension was even more acute in this part of the unusual house.

She crept forward, remembering to breathe again. Fainting from lack of oxygen wasn't going to help her any.

Holly stopped at one of the doors on her left and listened: no sounds came from within. She noticed a name was inscribed in the carving of the door and tried to decipher it in the poor light. It looked like Philip of . . . somewhere or other . . . Swabia? That was it. Where the hell was Swabia? She moved on to the next door which was even more difficult to read. Frederick Hohen . . . oh, what difference? She listened again, but still heard nothing. She gently tried the handle and found the door was unlocked. Pushing it open slowly and pointing the gun into the widening crack, she peered into the dark room. Deciding it really was empty, she pushed the door wide and was provided with a soft light from the hallway.

The room was furnished with antiques and smelled musty, unused. A four-poster bed dominated the floor-space and a portrait of someone in ceremonial – or at least, ancient – garb hung over the mantel. Maybe that was Fred what's-his-name. Holly closed the door and went on to the next room. She was able to make out Henry I on this one and sheer instinct told her that this time the room was not empty. The question was: to look in or not to look in? Well, she decided ruefully, I'm not going to find Harry by not looking for him. She turned the handle as softly as she could.

The odour hit her nostrils immediately, vile and unclean; it was as if a malevolent spirit was rushing past her, fleeing through the opening she had created. It was a smell of dust, human sweat – and something else. Rank meat? No, it was indefinable. She pushed the door open further.

Holly saw the rows of books lining the walls first, then, as she cautiously stepped into the room, its other contents were revealed to her. It was a larger room than the one she had just peeked into, containing a long, solid-looking desk, two high-backed chairs, a carpet of richly woven design, the shelves running around the walls on three sides, holding volumes of books. In a break between the shelves to her left, hung a picture – it looked like a portrait in the dim light – and again, the subject seemed to be wearing the clothing of centuries before. Old Henry, presumably. Opposite, on the wall to her right, another picture hung between two bookshelves, its enclosure almost shrine-like. It was a portrait also, but this time the clothing was not as ancient. The man in the picture wore a uniform. A black uniform.

She guessed the identity of the subject: the modern-day Nazis still worshipped their old heroes.

A sudden sound drew her attention towards the desk. Something had moved there, she was sure. She raised the machine-gun, her hand trembling slightly. Above the desk, between the heavy drapes concealing the room's two high windows, hung their symbol – the white circle on a red background, the circle containing the evil black swastika. She felt exposed under its glare and suddenly sensed that the two portraits on either side

were watching her. She quickly shrugged off the uncanny feeling.

Again she heard the noise, a slivering sound as if something
had dragged along the floor. It came from behind the desk.

She wondered if she should turn and run, but quickly dismissed the thought. If someone was hiding from her, someone
who'd seen she had a gun, they would raise the alarm as soon
as she left the room. Whoever it was had to be temporarily put
out of action. The decision made, she crept towards the desk.

It was a wide-top desk and its base was solid, a panel covering the centre leg-space. It was a pity, for Holly could not duck
down to see if anyone was lurking behind. The smell seemed
to hit her in waves now, but it was human staleness that dominated the general rancidity of the room.

The natural course of action would have been to move
around the desk, rapidly but cautiously, ready to spring away
from anybody crouched behind it; Holly believed in unpre-
dictability, though. She smoothly swung her hip on to the desk
and slid herself across its surface, ready to poke the machine-
gun into any enquiring face. As she peered over the edge she
realized she had been mistaken: the noise hadn't come from
beneath it, but beyond it.

What looked like a bundle of rags lay on the floor against the
wall and, even in the gloomy light from the hallway, she could
see two frightened eyes staring at her. The bedraggled figure
seemed to be pushing itself away, trying to sink into the wall
itself. That had been the sounds she had heard: the slivering
of bare feet on the floor, as the figure had tried hopelessly to
get away from whoever had entered the room.

Holly slid off the desk and knelt beside the quivering bundle
and it was then she realized the figure was that of a man and
that he was cruelly tied, a noose-like rope around his neck,
biting into the flesh, making it raw; the rope stretched down
behind his back to bound wrists and ankles. A shirt hung loosely
round him, the front completely open and exposing a chest
which bore the marks of severe beatings. His trousers were

filthy and stiff with stains as though the man had soiled himself many times. He lay on his side, his neck craned round to see her, and she noticed his wrists and ankles were caked in dry blood caused by the tightness of the ropes. Fresh blood was seeping around the ropes binding his ankles, probably caused by his struggle to get away from her. His hair was completely white, yet, as she looked into his frightened eyes, she realized he was not an old man. His face was lined with strain, heavy dark circles surrounding his eyes, the lips cracked and sore. But even through that, and through the bruises and dried blood that marred his features, she could see he was young. His face had aged not because of years but because of shock. She'd seen the same kind of ageing in released Nam prisoners – the ones who had been returned to their own country, but would probably never return to their own homes. Their minds had deteriorated beyond repair.

'Who are you?' she whispered.

The eyes only watched her in terror.

'Can't you speak? Can't you tell me who you are?'

Still the eyes watched her, but now a wariness had crept into them.

'Look, I'm a friend,' Holly tried to reassure him. 'I'm not with these people, I'm against them. Something's going to happen here tonight that I've got to prevent and time's running out. You've got to tell me who you are.'

She reached forward to touch his shoulder and the figure tried desperately to move away. The sudden movement jerked the noose around his neck tighter and a gurgling noise came from his throat as he began to choke.

'Hey, take it easy,' Holly whispered in alarm. She grabbed his wrists and pulled them upwards to ease the pressure on the noose. He stopped twisting and kept his body still. Holly wondered if his mind was functioning normally again or sheer animal instinct had made him stop moving.

'Look, I'm going to untie these ropes, but before I do, I want you to realize I'm not with the people who did this to you. I'm a friend, okay?' Holly placed the machine-gun on the floor and reached for the ropes binding his wrists. The knots were difficult, obviously pulled tighter by the man's own efforts to free himself. She looked around for something sharp to cut them with. Rising, she scanned the desk-top and found what she had been searching for. The paper-knife had a long point to it and could be pushed between the twists of rope to loosen the knots. She knelt beside the tensed figure again, placing her free hand on his upper arm. This time, he did not flinch.

'I'm going to get you free with this, so just try and relax. If you pull against the ropes they'll only get tighter.'

Holly tossed her hair back over her shoulder and set to work on the knots.

It took several minutes, but eventually she pulled with her fingers, using the knife as a lever, and then his wrists were free, one length of rope hanging loose from his neck, the other from his still bound ankles.

Holly breathed a sigh of relief and relaxed on to her haunches. She examined her broken fingernails and shrugged. 'I hate long nails, any . . .' The man pushed her back with a strength that belied his appearance. He grabbed the gun lying on the floor and pointed it at her, using two hands to hold the light weapon steady.

'Do not move,' he hissed fiercely. The three words were thickly accented.

'Hey, I'm trying to help you,' said Holly from her prone position. 'We're on the same side – I think.' She bit her lip when she saw him flick the safety-catch off. 'I was trying to help you,' she said desperately.

'Who are you?' His eyes were burning, all fear from them now gone. 'Why are you here?'

'My name's Holly Miles. I'm a freelance writer.' Better to tell him that, she thought. Better to find out more about him first. 'I was doing a feature on Edward Gant as an arms dealer until I found out he was into something more sinister.'

His eyes darted around the room, wild again.

'Can't you tell me your name?' she pleaded. 'I promise you I've nothing to do with Gant.'

His eyes came to rest on her again. 'How do I know that?'

'I set you free, didn't I?'

He sagged back against the wall as though the sudden effort had drained him of any strength he had left. His bound feet slid out from beneath him and came to rest against Holly's denimed legs. He motioned at her with the gun and murmured, 'Untie them.'

She began to work at the knots again with the paper-knife.

'Why would a journalist carry a gun like this?' he asked, indicating he still had his wits about him even in his weakened state.

Holly threw caution to the wind and told him everything, realizing she had to move fast, had to trust the man. She thought he showed some reaction when she mentioned Harry Steadman's name and that he was also being held a prisoner in the house, but he sat up in alarm when she told him of the proposed plan for the US Secretary of State's jet.

'The missile site – where is it?' he asked, his feet free now. He tried to rise, but the circulation was still not flowing freely.

'At the back of the house, towards the cliffs.' Holly moved closer to him and he waved her back with the gun's barrel.

'You've got to trust me,' she cried out in frustration. 'Someone might come along at any moment!'

He ran a hand across his face, wincing in pain as it touched the bruises. 'I . . . I don't know. They've done so much to me. I cannot think.'

'How long have they kept you here?'

'Years . . . years. No, it cannot be. I do not know.'

'Let me help you,' she said softly.

'They used me. They used my strength!' The man rolled his head in despair. 'They left me in this room so *he* could take my strength.'

'Who?' Holly urged. 'Who took your strength?'

'Him . . . him . . .' He pointed the machine-gun at the picture on the wall behind them. She saw his finger tighten on the trigger and for a moment she thought he would fire at the portrait.

'No, don't,' she said quickly. 'You'll bring the whole house down on us.'

The hand holding the weapon dropped limply to his side and she exhaled in relief. 'How did they take your strength?' she asked him.

'They . . . beat . . . me. Kept me tied . . . in here. That is how . . . he survives. He draws . . . power . . . from others. Used me.'

Holly shook her head, not understanding. She glanced down at her wristwatch. Twelve thirty-five. 'Look, we have to get moving. You must trust me.'

He nodded, knowing there was no choice. Some of his strength was returning, but he didn't know how long it would last. They had barely fed him, just given him enough to keep him alive. Had it been years? Or was it really only weeks? Time had become meaningless to him. He had been able to stand the beatings – for a while, anyway. It was the other things that had defeated him. The humiliation. The abuse of his body by the freak human, the one that was both man and woman. The base things they had made him do with the creature, taking away his manhood, shaming him . . . Tears clouded his vision and his shaking hand wiped them from his eyes.

He had told them everything they wanted to know, for eventually they had reduced him to an animal state. The man, Köhner, how well he knew the most vulnerable parts of the body, where to apply pressure, where to insert a blade. Even worse were the nights alone in this room where *he* had visited him – the jew-hater – mocking him and existing parasitically on his spirit. Had it all been in his own mind? Had they finally driven him mad with their torture?

But even more terrible than that were the times they had taken him to the strange room below, beneath the great hall. To the room they called the crypt.

It was there that all previous horrors had been surpassed.

He felt the girl shaking him and he opened his eyes to look into her concerned face. He had to trust her; there was nothing else he could do.

'Will you help me?' she was saying. He nodded his head and she gently took the light machine-gun from his loose grip.

'Tell me, then,' she said. 'Who are you? Tell me your name.'

'Baruch Kanaan,' he said. 'My name is Baruch Kanaan.'

The Commissioner looked around the ring of tense faces. Operational HQ had become the interior of the church over-looking the Gant estate. The vicar, who had been roused from his peaceful evening by the fireside in his nearby house earlier that evening, was busy organizing relays of coffee for the bit-terly cold men, and had even allowed the ancient church's heat-ing system to be switched on to combat the icy cold. It was no match for the wind that had collected its chill from the ocean and sought to invade any opening in the old masonry it could find.

The Commissioner knew his men were impatient for action; this was always the worst time for them, waiting and praying they'd come out of it all right. It bothered him too; he liked to get things over with. However, the years had taught him to be patient. So much harm could be done by rushing in at the wrong time. Sir Robert had been a great advocate of patience and the Commissioner had learned well from him.

He caught sight of the man called Blake, the retired police-man who worked for Steadman's agency. Blake's face was anxious and he was looking at the Commissioner as though deciding whether to approach him or not. The police chief beckoned him over and Blake bounded forward like a puppy to its master.

'We'll be going in at any moment, Mr Blake, so please try not to worry.'

'I'm sorry, sir. I don't mean to be an old woman, but Mr Steadman has been in there for quite some time.'

The Commissioner nodded sympathetically. 'I know that, but if we move in now we could upset some carefully laid plans.'

'I don't understand, sir,' said Sexton, puzzled.

'We're waiting for one last guest to arrive. The others – those we know about – have already been accounted for. Their movements have been watched for weeks and we're sure they're all down there with Edward Gant. They make a power-ful group and we can't just barge in and arrest them purely on grounds of conspiracy. They have to be taken away and broken separately. I've spent most of the day with our American col-leagues in Central Intelligence persuading the Prime Minister to let us do so.'

Sexton caught his breath. This really was the big one.

'We've got a fair amount of evidence on this group, but much of it is circumstantial,' the Commissioner went on. 'We need to catch them red-handed and then, as I say, break down their stories individually. Thanks to your employer, Harry Stead-man, I don't think that will be too difficult. He seems to have triggered off quite a bit of action.'

'But did you know what Harry – I mean Mr Steadman – was getting into all this time? Did you know about this man Pope?'

The Commissioner raised a hand as if to ward off Sexton's questions.

'We've known about Nigel Pope for some time; his intoler-ance towards his superiors and his own colleagues could hardly go unnoticed. But he was part of the pattern and we couldn't remove him without destroying the whole framework. It had to be allowed to fester so it could be lanced once and for all – at the right time. Harry Steadman is the instrument we are using for drawing the poison.'

'You could have warned him . . .'

'No, Mr Blake. We didn't know his part in the whole business. He appeared out of the blue. For all we knew, he was one of them.'

'But Mrs Wyeth!'

The Commissioner had the good grace to look down at his shoes. 'I'm afraid we weren't aware of any involvement from your agency at that time. It was most unfortunate.' He looked up again and gazed steadily into Sexton's eyes. 'We were only really sure of Steadman's good intent when he sent us the warning through you last night.'

Sexton shook his head wearily. 'I don't pretend to understand all this, Commissioner, but it seems to me no one was really bothered about Harry getting himself killed. He was getting kicked from all sides.'

'Not at all, Mr Blake,' said the American who had just returned from the vicar's house where he had been using the telephone. 'We just allowed him to wander around loose for a while until we could be sure of him.'

'And even if he was straight, he might stir something up anyway. Is that right?'

The American smiled, his chubby face friendly but his eyes steely. 'You got it, Mr Blake. Let me say, though, we had someone watching out for him some of the time.' He suddenly turned to the Commissioner, his manner now brusque. 'We got the word from your man outside on the radio, Commissioner; I said I'd let you know. The last helicopter just landed. The General's in.'

'Right. I'll give the order to move in immediately.'

'Also, there's activity around the estate's perimeter. Gant's private army is keeping the area tightly sealed, I guess.' The American frowned and looked at his watch. 'I'd be happier if we really knew if this meeting tonight has anything to do with the Secretary of State's arrival in the country.'

'They'll be able to tell us that themselves.'

'I wouldn't count on it.'

The Commissioner did not bother to reply. Instead he began issuing orders to the Special Branch officers around him. When his men were moving he turned back to the American. 'I'll be going in immediately after the first assault. Will you be with me?'

'Sure,' the American said, smiling pleasantly. 'I wouldn't miss it.'

'You'll have to stay here I'm afraid, Mr Blake,' the Commissioner said, then he was gone, his officers jumping from his path. He disappeared through the church doorway. The American tucked his hands into his overcoat pockets and headed after the Commissioner. Sexton caught his arm.

'You said someone was looking out for him some of the time. Who was it?'

The American grinned. 'One of our agents. Girl by the name of Holly Miles. We poached her from our Domestic Operations Division when we discovered she was a distant relation of Edward Gant's late wife. She's in there with Steadman now.'

Blake was left standing alone in the empty church.

20

'I witnessed for the first time some of the rather strange practices resorted to by Himmler through his inclination towards mysticism. He assembled twelve of his most trusted SS leaders in a room next to the one in which von Fritsch was being questioned and ordered them all to concentrate their minds on exerting a suggestive influence over the general that would induce him to tell the truth. I happened to come into the room by accident, and to see these twelve SS leaders, all sunk in deep and silent contemplation, was indeed a remarkable sight.'

WALTHER SCHELLENBERG

'The Beast does not look what he is. He may even have a comic moustache.'

SOLOVIEV: *The Anti-Christ*

Steadman's muscles were locked rigid.

His mind tried desperately to deny the vision his eyes saw so clearly. Heinrich Himmler was dead! Even if he had not killed himself at the end of the war as the world believed, the arms dealer had said the Reichsführer had died of cancer at sixty-seven. Yet he was here in this room, his eyes burning with life!

Hypnosis, Steadman rationalized. It had to be hypnosis of some kind. It couldn't really be happening.

'Ist das der lebendige Parsifal?' It was a thin, piping voice, completely different to that of Dr Scheuer's, and came from the apparition that had somehow superimposed itself over the old man's features.

'Ja, mein Reichsführer, der ist unser Feind.' It was Gant who spoke, his face shining in a strange ecstasy.

The men around the table were staring at the vision, some rapturously, others in fear. They all appeared unsteady, as though their energy had been drawn. One or two could barely lift their heads off the table. The figure of Kristina lay inert in her chair.

Gant spoke again, a deferential tone to his voice. *'Herr Reichsführer, darf ich ergebenst darum bitten, dass wir uns auf Englisch unterhalten? Viele Mitglieder unseres Ordens verstehen nicht unsere eigene Sprache.'*

'Er versteht sie.' The words were hissed and the apparition glowered at the investigator.

Steadman flinched. The vision was so real: the pudgy white face and small pig-like eyes; the clipped moustache and hair cropped to a point well above the ears; the finely formed lips marred by a weak chin receding into a flabby neck. Was it just a dream? Would he wake soon?

The figure began to rise and it was stooped, still in the shape of Dr Scheuer; its eyes never left Steadman's. It smiled evilly. 'Do you feel weak, Parsifal?' The words were spoken in English. A snigger from the apparition rang round the room. 'They feel it too. But they give me their strength willingly, while you resist.'

The investigator tried to move his arms and found it impossible. It was all he could do to hold his head up. He tried to speak, to shout, to scream, but only a rasping sound came from his throat.

'It's useless to struggle,' said Edward Gant as the macabre creature beside him chuckled. 'You cannot resist his will. This is how the Reichsführer still lives, you see. He draws etheric energies from the living, and feeds upon it. Adolf Hitler could do this when he lived. Heinrich Himmler learned the art, with the help of Dr Scheuer, when he was dead.'

'*Adolf. Ja, der liebe Adolf. Wo ist er doch jetzt? Nicht mit uns.*' The figure swayed and a hand rested against the table-top. The head sank for a moment and the image of Himmler's face seemed to waver, become less distinct. Then the moment was gone and the head rose again, the small eyes piercing into Steadman's, transfixing him.

'It is time, Herr Gantzer. He must die now. His death will signify our beginning.'

'Yes, Reichsführer. It has finally come.' Gant reached forward for the ancient relic lying on the table's rough surface. 'The Spear that protects the Holy Grail, Reichsführer. Take it now and feel its potency. Let its force flow through you. *Use its power!*'

The figure took the Spear of Longinus from Gant and held it in both hands. The weapon quivered in the apparition's hands and Steadman sensed or saw – it was all the same now – the light emanating from it. A blueness seemed to glow from the worn metal and the light stretched and grew, travelling over the gnarled hands that were still those of the old man, up along the arms, spreading and enveloping the frail body.

The figure began to straighten and Steadman could hear a screaming sound tearing around the hall, screeching from corner to corner, an inhuman cry that told of unseen demons. The coldness of the room deepened, becoming so intense that Steadman felt ice stiffening against his skin. His limbs were trembling uncontrollably, his hands a shaking blur. He wanted to cry out against the screaming cacophony of the unseen things, but only frosty air escaped his lips. The sounds tore from wall to wall like birds trapped in a dark room, screeching across the round table, sometimes beneath it, the seated men shying away as though their flesh had been touched by something unholy. The strident pitch grew louder, higher, reaching a crescendo.

Steadman saw the figure was no longer stooped and frail; it stood erect, powerfully vibrant. The etheric glow encompassed the whole body and the Spear was held in arms stretched rigid at chest level. The face of Himmler was directed towards the ceiling, the eyes closed but movement beneath the eyelids showed that the pupils were active. The lids began to open slowly and Steadman could just see the slits of white between them. Then the head began to lower and the screaming became even more shrill. The investigator pushed himself against the chair, trying to break free of the invisible bonds that held his body and mind. It was no use, his strength was no longer there.

He could not tear his eyes from the face of Himmler even though he managed to twist his head; no matter in which direction he turned, his eyes remained locked on the creature before him.

The face was directed at him, watching his vain struggle with a grin made vile both by its intent and the shiny wetness of the lips. The eyes were watching him, but the fully opened lids revealed only blank whiteness; the pupils were still turned inside the head. The figure laughed aloud and the laughter mingled with the undulating screams. Suddenly the pupils dropped into place and Steadman tried to close his own eyes against their glare.

He had to make himself move! He had to will himself to run!

The figure began to move, the Spear held before it. Around the table it came, moving nearer to the investigator, the wicked point aimed low, ready to strike at his heart.

Gant was on his feet, his face covered with a sheen of excitement. This was the time! This was the time for Parsifal to die, not by the hands of Klingsor, but by the true Master – *the Antichrist*! And the Spear of Longinus would pierce the side of their adversary just as it had pierced the side of the Nazarene two thousand years before!

The figure raised the Spear higher, but the point was still aimed at Steadman's heart. It was drawing near to him now, still walking slowly around the huge table, the eyes always on him, holding him there. And then the figure was looming over him, the blackened spearhead held in two hands, raised above the head, ready to strike deep into his heart.

He was aware that the screaming had reached fever pitch, and the air was being violently disturbed by the frenzied, unseen things. He was aware that he was going to die by the hand of this unclean, drooling demon who bore the features of a man the world had despised. And he was aware there was nothing he could do to save himself.

But as the ancient weapon quivered at its zenith, ready to plunge into his unprotected chest, the table's surface erupted in an explosion of flying splinters. The bullets imbedded themselves in the old wood, then spattered into the soft body of the creature bearing the Spear of Longinus.

21

'*We shall never capitulate – no, never. We may be destroyed, but if we are, we shall drag a world with us – a world in flames.*'

ADOLF HITLER

'*I am a strong believer that, in the end, only good blood can achieve the greatest, most enduring things in the world.*'

HEINRICH HIMMLER

Jagged splinters from the oak table flew into Steadman's face and the shock galvanized him into action. His strength had returned and with it, old instincts. He threw himself to the floor and lay still, stunned by the piercing sounds around him: the screams of those hit by the deadly rain of bullets; the noise of the bullets themselves, thudding into the table, into bodies, ricocheting off stonework; the agonized gurgling of the old man, Dr Scheuer, as his body was shredded, blood vomiting from his mouth in an explosive stream.

Steadman saw the old man still held the Spear aloft in one hand, but it suddenly skidded from sight as his wrist was shattered. Dr Scheuer fell to his knees, then slowly toppled forward, his head striking the floor inches from the investigator.

For the first time, Steadman was able to see the old man's eyes, as they stared into his, wide but with no disturbing force emanating from them; just the inanimate stare of the dead, even though the body twitched and seemed alive.

The hail of bullets continued, spraying the hall at random, a lethal, indiscriminate strafing. Steadman twisted his head and felt a flicker of recognition when he saw the man with the gun on the balcony above. But it couldn't be; it was an old man up there, his hair white, his hate-filled face lined and aged. His mouth was open and he seemed to be shouting, but the investigator could not hear him over the barrage of sound. A figure appeared next to the dishevelled man and Steadman called out her name as he realized it was Holly. He saw her try to snatch the light machine-gun, but the white-haired man held her off with one hand, continuing his vengeful onslaught.

He saw her quickly scan the room, fear in her face, and when their eyes met, he knew that fear was for him. Her lips formed his name.

A wild bullet suddenly stung the side of his hand, close enough to burn, but not enough to tear the skin. Pushing himself forward with toes and knees, he dived beneath the heavy table, drawing his legs after him. There were other bodies crouched there.

He watched the carnage around the hall from his place of safety, saw the running legs, the overturned chairs that tangled and tripped them, the bodies that suddenly slumped into view as they were hit. Booth was crawling towards the table, gun in hand, but staring straight ahead. He almost made it.

As he reached the shadow of the table his head suddenly jerked up, a look of astonishment on his face. A line of bullets had raked across his back, snapping his spine. He tried to turn and fire back, but his body collapsed and he rolled over, the gun pointing at the ceiling, his finger curling around the trigger guard and squeezing it uselessly. He lay there looking into the blackness overhead and waited for the pain to begin.

Steadman began to crawl towards the other side of the table

and saw there were at least three others crouched in the darkness. It was the hugeness of the shape before him that told
him the identity of one of the cowering men.

There was just enough light for Pope to see it was Steadman
moving towards him. The fat man wasn't afraid, only angry that
everything had gone so terribly wrong. He had just had time to
see it was their prisoner, the Israeli agent, who was causing such
havoc, before he dived for cover. They should have killed him as
soon as they had captured him. He cursed Gant for his sadism,
the sadism he disguised as ritualistic symbolism. Major-General
Cutbush was dead – Pope had seen him rise then fall across the
table, arms outstretched – and so were many of the others.
Talgholm, Ewing, Oakes – he'd seen them go down. Others he
could see writhing around the floor, curling themselves into tight
balls to avoid being struck again. Griggs had been one of the first
to be killed and Booth had not made it to cover, so he, Pope, was
on his own. These others – those not dead or wounded – were
not fighting men, didn't even carry arms. Where was Gant? What
had happened to him? It was only seconds since the firing had begun, but every fragment of time stretched into a bloody eternity.
They had been foolish not to have kept some guards in the room.
It was Gant who refused to allow them full knowledge of the
Order. Now they were paying the price.

Pope reached inside his jacket pocket for the small gun, his
hand fumbling in its haste. There would at least be some
revenge.

Steadman accelerated his movements when he saw the big
man reaching for the weapon. Unfortunately, he was too restricted and, as Pope drew the gun and aimed it at his head,
Steadman realized he wasn't going to make it. It was at that
moment that another body hurled itself into the table's shelter
and staggered between Steadman and the MI5 man. Pope's
gun went off and the body in front of Steadman twitched violently but remained poised on hands and knees; the power of
the small firearm was not enough to topple its victim even at
that close range.

The investigator went barging on, keeping the injured man between himself and Pope. His shoulder hit the man just below his ribs and Steadman shoved hard, pushing him against Pope. Pope pumped bullets into his dying fellow-member, wanting him prone so he could get a clear aim at the investigator. It was no use; the body was pushed into him knocking him backwards.

He struggled to prevent himself from being ejected from the table's protective cover and, as the body finally fell to the floor, he grinned with relief, aiming the gun once more. Steadman had abruptly changed his tactics. As soon as the body he had been pushing had slumped to the floor, he had swivelled his body around in order to strike out with his feet. He lay with his back against the stone floor and kicked with all his strength.

Pope, despite his great weight, went tumbling out into the open, rolling once with the force of the thrust. There was a lull in the shooting from above and the big man had a moment to reach his knees and aim the gun at the figure beneath the table.

The firing began almost at once and bullets flew off the stone around Pope. He whirled, this time aiming upwards at the balcony, but bullets tore into him before he even had a chance to pull the trigger. He keeled over backwards and tiny explosions ripped his obese body.

It was then that Steadman saw the shadowy figure emerge from behind the altar-like structure which shielded the room's blazing fire. The movement was fleeting, and whoever it was had ducked into the shadows of the hall. Steadman realized that the machine-gun fire was now in short bursts rather than the continuous onslaught of before. The shape appeared again, then plunged down into the stair-well that led to the door set in the room's wall. Before it disappeared completely, Steadman had time to recognize the hawk-like features of Edward Gant.

He pushed himself from the protective cover and ran, leaping over Pope's recumbent form, tripping once but rolling with the fall, jumping into the stair-well and crashing through the open doorway below.

Holly screeched Steadman's name and tried to grab the machine-gun at the same time.

The Mossad agent seemed to realize who it was below and his finger suddenly released the trigger and he swayed backwards. Only the screams and moans of the dying filled the air now, but the atmosphere was heavy with the smell of death.

Baruch stiffened as though recovering his senses and once again, he aimed the machine-gun at the twisting bodies below.

'No,' Holly implored. 'Leave them – please!'

He stared at her with uncomprehending eyes.

'We've got to stop the missile from being launched.' Holly held his head between her hands to keep him looking directly at her, desperately wanting him to understand. 'The missile will be launched soon. We've got to stop them.'

A sadness swept over the Israeli. He tore his head from her grasp and surveyed the carnage he had created. When he turned to look at her once again, there was a hardness in his eyes and she knew the sorrow had not been for those he had just killed.

'How . . . long . . .'

She guessed his meaning and glanced down at her watch. She groaned. 'We're too late. There's only four minutes left.'

He gripped her arm. 'Where . . . is the site? Where is it?' His grip tightened.

'Near the cliffs. It's too late, though; we'd never make it.'

'Helicopter. All day . . . I have heard . . . a helicopter landing and . . . taking off. If we can find it . . .'

'Can you fly helicopters?' she asked, hope rising in her.

He nodded, then clung to the balcony for support. 'Get me to it, quickly,' he whispered.

Holly gripped him around his back, her shoulder beneath him. 'Give me the gun,' she said, and he handed it to her without any reluctance.

They staggered down the stairs, almost stumbling once but Holly's determined effort saving them. She averted her eyes from the terrible scene below and prayed that those still alive would not try to stop them. She hated to kill.

Once again Holly called out Steadman's name, but there was no answer. She had seen him leap into the stair-well at the side of the hall and knew he had been chasing somebody – why else would he have broken cover? She longed to go after him, but the stair-well would only lead to the lower level of the house, and not to the outside. Her priority was to prevent the US Secretary of State's jet from being blown to pieces. She said a silent prayer for the investigator and ignored the awful wrenching feeling inside her.

'This way,' she said to the Israeli, pointing the gun into the shadows. 'I think there's a door over there. It's in the right direction, anyway.'

The pilot and the two guards who had been patrolling the exterior of the house glanced nervously at each other. They had heard gunfire inside and were making towards the back entrance when a different sound, much further away, had attracted their attention.

'What's that?' one asked, skidding to a halt with the others. Instead of going on towards the back door, they rushed to the corner of the house and peered inland, towards the estate's easterly perimeter. They were filled with dismay at what they saw.

'Oh, fucking hell,' one said in a low voice.

Four helicopters, powerful light beams descending from them, hovered in the distance. They began to fly along the estate's boundaries where Edward Gant's private army was deployed and dropping what looked like small bombs on to the soldiers below. The three men realized they were gas canisters as white vapour erupted from the ground. Lights suddenly appeared on the road leading down to the estate as vehicles began moving in.

'It's the bloody Army!' the pilot exclaimed. 'We're under attack from the bloody Army!'

Even as he spoke, one machine broke away from the action and came racing towards the house. The others began to settle on the ground and the three men saw figures begin to pour from them. Above the whirring of rotor blades they heard the crackle of gunfire.

'I'm getting out!' the pilot suddenly announced, whirling round and racing back to the Gazelle.

The two soldiers glanced at each other, their faces white in the moonlight. Without a word, they turned and chased after the pilot. 'Wait for us,' one of them called out, 'we're coming with you!'

The pilot was already in his seat and had set the chopper's blades in motion, thankful that the aircraft's engine was still warm from its previous flight. The two soldiers had almost reached him when the door of the house behind them opened and Holly Miles and Baruch Kanaan staggered through.

The brightness of the moon gave Holly a clear picture of the two running soldiers and the small four-seater helicopter they were headed for. She and Baruch had the advantage; the men had their backs to them and the pilot was too busy with his controls to notice them.

She freed herself from the Israeli and raised the light machine-gun.

'Hold it!' she shouted and the running soldiers halted dead in their tracks. They turned and one went down on his knee aiming his standard machine-gun at the two figures in the doorway.

Regretfully, she squeezed the trigger and the fast-firing machine-gun spewed its lethal dosage at the soldier. As he fell, his companion threw down his own gun and ran to the right, screaming back at Holly not to shoot. She let him go.

The pilot inside his cabin was frantically increasing his engine's power to give him lift and the machine was trembling around him. Holly shouted, ordering him to cut his motors, but he didn't hear her over the noise of the whirring blades. She bit her lip and said, 'Shit,' then raised the gun in both hands and sighted it at arm's length. Only when she was sure of her aim did she squeeze the trigger; she did not want to damage any of the Gazelle's machinery.

The pilot toppled from his aircraft, the short burst killing him instantly. He hit the hard landing pad with a dull thud.

Holly stole a quick look at her wristwatch, but the moon suddenly vanished behind a heavy black cloud and she failed to see its hands.

'Come on,' she said to Baruch and pulled him towards her. 'We don't have much longer.'

Baruch took a deep breath, then pushed himself away from her and stood erect. 'I will be all right.' The words were spoken singularly, but there was a certain strength behind them. He began to move towards the helicopter, his legs stiff, as though he were consciously willing them to bear his weight.

Holly caught up and the wind tore at their bodies as if to hold them back; she held on to his arm to keep him steady. The moon suddenly burst through again and she took advantage of the light to have another look at her watch.

She swore silently. They would never make it. There were only thirty seconds to go.

22

Darkness enveloped Steadman like black liquid. He had fallen through the doorway at the bottom of the stair-well and continued his descent, for there were more stairs on the other side.

The stone steps had scraped painfully at his limbs as he had tried in vain to halt his tumbling fall. He reached the bottom with stunning force and lay there, gasping to fill his lungs with air again.

He managed to push himself to a sitting position, groaning softly at the effort. He blinked and tried to see into the blackness ahead, but the only light was coming from the doorway above and behind him, and that was very faint. He reached out and felt nothing before him, then waved his hand from side to side. It came in contact with a wall to his left.

The wall was damp and he could feel the velvety smoothness

of moss. He rose to one knee, leaning against the wall for support, and drew in a deep breath. Jesus, it was freezing. Cold like a tomb.

He stood, cautious of broken limbs. The plunge had numbed him and he could not be sure he hadn't damaged himself badly. His legs supported him and he could move his arms around, so all he had suffered was some nasty bruising.

Keeping one hand against the wall, he moved out at right angles to it and stretched his other hand outwards. The fingertips touched another smooth surface and he guessed he was in a fairly narrow passageway. He knew what lay behind him, so the only way to go was forward. Dropping his right arm, he inched forward, using his left to feel his way. It was an eerie sensation; at any moment he expected his hand to come in contact with human flesh, Gant lurking there, waiting for him in the dark.

The only sound he heard was his own harsh breathing and he briefly wondered what was happening above.

His hand came in contact with a wall running across the one he was following. He ran his fingers along it and felt it dip forward again. He touched a rough surface; there was a door in front of him. Holding his breath, he felt around for a handle, hesitated, then gave it a twist.

The handle was stiff, rusted by the dampness of the underground passage, but with extra pressure, it gave. Steadman pushed the door open slightly, listening for any sounds before he entered. Then he opened it fully and stood to one side.

A wave of icy air hit him and he shivered against it. It had been cold enough in the narrow passageway, but it was even colder ahead. A faint aroma reached his nostrils and it was familiar to him. Just a waft of – what? Oil, spices? It was too slight to be certain.

There was a diffused light coming from a point in the blackness ahead and the investigator narrowed his eyes to make out some shape or form. The light was too soft though; it was just a dull hue against a black backdrop. For some reason, Steadman felt it was beckoning, inviting him to come closer. He fought down the inclination to go back the way he had come; he had to find Edward Gant. And kill him.

He stepped through the doorway and crept stealthily towards the light source, each step measured and slow. He stretched out his hands on both sides as he walked and neither made any contact with the walls. He was either in a wider passage or in a room of some kind, perhaps an antechamber. He drew nearer to the hazy light and realized it was being diffused by something and, when he was close enough to touch, he reached out, his fingers brushing against coarse material. It was a curtain and the light shone through the tiny apertures in its rough texture. Once again, he stood and listened, controlling his breathing, but unable to still the pounding in his chest. A small voice inside told him not to look, to turn away and run from whatever lay in wait on the other side of that curtain, that some things were better left unseen. The voice persisted, but he succumbed to the compelling fascination that had taken hold of him. It was as if there were no choice; he dreaded what might be there, but there was no denying its lure. Steadman ran his fingers over the rough, mildewed material, searching for an opening.

He found it slightly to his right and manoeuvred himself so his eyes would be directly before it when he parted the curtains. He drew them open and looked into the strange chamber beyond, his pupils shrinking against the unimpeded light.

It was a circular room, the walls of stone shiny with damp. Recesses containing small, black crucibles in which green flames glowed were placed at regular intervals around the room's perimeter. It was these tiny green flames that gave the room its peculiar light, and the colour suggested that chemicals or herbs of some kind were being burnt. It explained the aroma that drifted along the passageway. A stone platform ran around the wall's edges and another door lay directly opposite to where Steadman was standing, steps leading down from it to the chamber's lower level.

The floor area was large even though the ceiling was comparatively low and, because of its shape and the higher-level walk around the sides, it had the appearance of a miniature arena. Twelve four-feet-high pedestals stood around the circumference at well-ordered points like stone sentinels gazing silently towards the room's centre. And there, at the centre stood a solitary, high-backed chair.

It was facing away from Steadman so he could not see whether it was occupied, but kneeling six or seven feet from it was the shadowy form of a woman. The long, black flowing hair identified her as Kristina and Steadman could see she was clutching something rising from between her thighs, like a huge phallus. As he watched, she crawled forward holding the object before her, and placed it on the stone floor two feet away from the high-backed chair. She crawled back to her original position and began to sway on her knees, her arms stiff by her sides.

Steadman knew by its shape it was the Spear of Longinus she had put down before the chair and, as he prepared himself to enter the chamber, a fresh feeling of unease swept through him. Sounds came from the hermaphrodite's lips, but they were unintelligible, a wailing incantation. He closed his mind to his misgivings, forcing himself to ignore his frenzied imagination, and began to slip through the curtain.

It was then he became aware that he wasn't alone in the antechamber.

A sound from behind. A rustle of material? A scraping of a foot against the floor? He couldn't be sure. But as he turned, his back now to the curtain, he heard breathing. It came in jerky rasping sighs, as though whoever it was could no longer control its rhythm; and as he listened, it became even more agitated, louder, the air sucked in greedily and exhaled in short gasps.

Steadman felt momentarily paralysed, wanting to move away from the curtain, knowing the dim light shining through must show his body in rough silhouette. The rasping grew louder and he peered into the darkness, trying desperately to discern a shape. It was no use, he could see nothing. But he could feel the warm breath on his face; and the cold fingertips that reached out to touch his cheek.

He staggered back from sheer reaction and hardly felt the knife-blade slice across his stomach, the tip barely penetrating the skin through his shirt. He went through the curtain and his assailant came after him, the ritual dagger slashing at the air between them. The investigator fell but kept his body moving, twisting to his right, aware there was a drop on to the chamber's floor behind him. The tall figure of Edward Gant lunged and missed again, overbalancing and falling to one knee.

They both crouched, facing each other, Gant's eyes wild with malice and Steadman's cold with hate.

'I still have you, Parsifal. I can still destroy you,' Gant hissed.

'You can try, you crazy bastard,' Steadman replied, rising immediately and aiming a foot at the arms dealer's face.

Gant avoided the blow and rose more slowly, the silver dagger pointing at the investigator's stomach. He inched forward, his manner even more menacing because of its deliberation. Steadman backed away.

'Stay, Parsifal. You can't run from fate.' Gant smiled, his face evil in the soft green hue. 'My soldiers will take care of the Jew and the slut. They won't get far.'

'It's all over, Gant, don't you understand?' Steadman's attention was directed more at keeping the blade at a safe distance than his own words. 'There's too many dead up there. Important men. How will you explain their disappearance?'

'Why should I have to?' The familiar mocking look had returned to Gant's eyes. 'No one knows they were here. Our associations have been quite discreet.'

'But you've lost the power behind your organization.'

Gant sneered. 'They were only the nucleus; there are others equally revered only too eager to take their place. All we have suffered is a setback.'

'Another setback, Gant? Like the war?' The mockery now in the investigator's attitude had the desired effect. Gant screamed with rage and leapt at his quarry, just as Steadman reached for the burning crucible in the recess he had been trying to reach. His hand encircled the hot metal and brought it from its resting-place in one swoop, smashing it into the side of Gant's face as he advanced. The arms dealer screamed again, this time in pain, as the hot, burning oil poured into his face and down his neck. The dagger imbedded itself in Steadman's arm and was jerked free again when the arms dealer staggered away.

Steadman cried out with the sudden tearing pain, but he had the satisfaction of knowing his assailant's wound was far greater. Gant had dropped the dagger and was slapping at his face, trying to dislodge the fiery oil that was sizzling into his skin. Small dots of fire were spattered over his jacket and shirt, but he ignored them for the greater pain in his face. Steadman saw oil had splashed on to Gant's nose and it was melting like wax, a pink stream flowing over his tortured lips. The investigator flinched as the naked bone and gristle beneath the artificial organ was exposed, but he felt no pity for the injured man.

Even in his agonized state, the arms dealer's virulent hatred for the investigator and the force he symbolized rose to the surface like a bubbling volcano. He had known great pain before, and had learned to keep one part of his mind secure from its distracting influence. With one eye only, the other seared by the oil, he searched for the fallen dagger. It was lying close to his left foot and he quickly stooped, screeching against the intense heat in his flesh.

Steadman saw his intention and stepped forward, his right arm outstretched, reaching for the weapon.

Gant was faster. He picked up the silver dagger and began to bring it up, the wicked point aimed at the stooped investigator's chest. Steadman grabbed at the wrist holding the knife and deflected its direction, using his own strength to continue the upward arc. The blade sank up to the hilt into a point just below Gant's breastbone. He stared disbelievingly at Steadman, his fingers still curled around the dagger's handle, the investigator's hand still gripped around his wrist, and there was a moment of absolute silence between them. One side of Gant's face was popping and blistering, a scorched eyelid covering one eye; the gaping wound where his nose had once been was weeping fresh blood. And then the arms dealer screamed and fell forward, his chest coming to rest against his knees, the dagger's hilt between them, his forehead touching the cold stone floor as though he were paying homage to the victor. Blood gurgled up from his throat and created a thick, red pool around his head, and he died in that position, his body refusing to topple on to its side, escaping gas from his abdomen taking any last shred of dignity from his dying.

Steadman stepped away to avoid the spreading pool and leaned against the wall, shock and weariness overcoming him. He looked down at the slumped body and felt no regret nor any gladness that the man was dead; only relief that it wasn't himself crouched there.

The throbbing in his arm reminded him of his wound. He touched a hand to his injured limb, flexing it at the elbow and wincing as the pain flared. It wasn't too bad, though: he could still lift his arm so no muscles had been torn. He glanced back at the dead arms dealer. Was it all over? Had the death of Gant signified the end of the new Reich, or was the net too widely spread, already too powerful to falter just because its leader had been killed. There would be chaos upstairs, the injured and the dying screaming for attention, Gant's soldiers searching for Holly and the man she had been with – had it been Baruch? Perhaps they were already dead. The idea that Holly might have been shot filled him with a new desperation. He knew she had lied to him, that somehow she was deeply involved in the whole affair, and he was angered by the deception; but stronger feelings overrode that anger, feelings he had thought burned from him with the death of Lilla long ago.

He had to go back and find her even though it was probably hopeless. He turned towards the curtained doorway. It was finished down here. The arms dealer was dead, there was nothing left. It was over.

But the sudden stillness, the sudden thick, cloying odour, the sudden drop in the already cold room's temperature, told him it was not over. Not yet.

The presence seemed to be everywhere, filling the gloomy underground chamber, and it was a familiar thing to Steadman now. The same feeling of intense pressure, the awareness that something unseen had manifested itself. Unconsciously, the investigator had backed himself against the curved wall, his eyes darting from left to right, searching the chamber, trying to *see* the presence and not just perceive it. They came to rest on the figure in the centre of the room.

The hermaphrodite was rigid, no longer swaying, no longer moaning. Kristina's lips were open wide as though mouthing a silent scream of agony; her eyes were tightly closed. She was still in a kneeling position before the high-backed chair, and the ancient spearhead lay on the stone floor where she had placed it. It seemed to quiver slightly, as though a current were running through its black metal, and Steadman felt, rather than heard, its vibration. He knew he had to take it from her, away from that dark room, away from the forces that were using its power . . . and he wondered at himself for believing such things.

Sounds seemed to be swirling around the circular chamber, soft voices that laughed and called, building to a crescendo as they had in the room above. The crucibles were burning black smoke and the wind swirled the smoke around the room, weaving dark patterns in the air, and Steadman imagined the shapes were lost spirits, twisting and writhing in a secret torment. Cold air brushed against his face, ruffling his hair, tearing at his clothes, seeming to beat against him, forcing him to raise an arm to protect his eyes, willing him to fall, to cower against the wall. Abruptly it ended, and silence returned to the underground chamber.

Only *the* presence remained.

The investigator forced himself away from the wall, dropping to the lower floor-level, crouching for a moment. He retched at the overpowering stench, the terrible smell of corruption, and his body felt leaden, the weakness spreading through him, drugging his brain, dragging him down. He tried to rise and staggered against one of the small pillars set around the arena. He saw the metal plate on the stone pillar, bare of any inscription, and he suddenly knew the reason for the twelve pedestals facing the room's centre: they would bear the ashes of the members of the new Teutonic Order as each member died. How he knew was no mystery to him: the presence had made him aware. It was telling him the truth of the Spear's legend, the power the holy relic held, the power that could be used for good or evil. It taunted him, cursed him, reviled him. And it feared him.

The knowledge that he could be feared drove Steadman on. He stumbled across the room he now knew was a place of the dead – a crypt – feeling his energy draining from him, forcing himself onwards to reach the Spear, resisting the urge to lie down and rest, just for a moment, just for one sweet second.

He fell, and began to crawl, one hand before the other, one knee forward then the other, one hand, one knee, one hand, one knee . . .

Kristina watched him, a tremor running through her body with a ferocity that made her shape blurred. Her mouth was still wide, and black smoke from the low flames in the crucibles entered her throat, descending into her lungs, filling her.

Steadman was near the spearhead, his hand reaching out, meeting a force that pushed his grasping fingers away. He looked up at Kristina and her eyes were straining against their sockets as she stared down at him, the pupils glazed yet strangely filled with life. Her body convulsed once, twice, became rigid again, her back arching but her gaze still on him. One more convulsion, this time even more violent, her hair crackling with the tension, her grimace stretching her lips and tearing them in several places. Then, with a long rattling exhalation of air, she fell backwards, and life was drawn from her body.

Steadman closed his eyes and rested his head against the cold floor for a brief moment, wanting to stay there, to sleep and so take himself away from the malevolent force in the chamber. He resisted, knowing to succumb would mean his death. Forcing his eyes open again, he saw the slumped form of the hermaphrodite, her tortured face mercifully turned away from him. He twisted his head, not wanting to look at the miscreation, and his eyes fell on something far worse. He faced the husk sitting in the high-backed chair.

The rotted corpse wore the faded uniform of the Nazi Schutzstaffeln: the brown shirt and black tie, the tunic with three silver-thread leaves enclosed in an oak-leaf wreath on each lapel, the sword-belt with ceremonial dagger attached, the cross-belt passed beneath silver braiding on the right shoulder, the swastika armband on the sleeve, the breeches tucked into long jackboots. On its head was the silver-braided cap with the Death's Head emblem at its centre. The whole uniform was covered in a fine layer of dust and hung loosely over the still form, as if the body had shrivelled within it.

It sat upright as though locked in position, and Steadman's horrified gaze travelled up from the jackboots, across the body, to the shrunken head that stared sightlessly across the dark chamber. The flesh on its face was stretched taut, greyish cheekbones showing through clearly, huge, festering rents in the skin alive with tiny, white moving shapes. The yellow skin at the throat sagged over the shirt collar, a shrivelled sack resembling a balloon that had been punctured. The lower lip had been eaten away revealing an uneven row of teeth stumps, and white, wispy hair clung sparsely to the upper lip. The face appeared chinless, as though the jawbone had receded back into the throat. One ear was missing completely, while all that remained of the other was a remnant of twisted, dried flesh. Thin strands of white hair hung from beneath the cap, whose peak fell low over the forehead, several sizes too big.

Peculiarly, pince-nez glasses were stuck firmly against the

bridge of the nose as though permanently glued there, and one eye had escaped from its retaining socket and pressed against a lens. The tip of the nose was missing but the rest, although wrinkled and pitted, was intact. As Steadman watched, something black crawled from a nostril and scurried down the lower lip into the gaping mouth, disappearing from sight.

The investigator's stomach heaved and he could no longer control the bile that rose in his throat. It poured from him in pain-wracking convulsions, steam rising in the deeply cold air. He pushed himself away, away from his own sickness and away from the vile, stinking creature they had kept embalmed in the underground crypt.

He knew, without any doubt, whose mummified body it was: the Gestapo uniform, the pince-nez, the remnants of a moustache – their Reichsführer, Heinrich Himmler. The stupid, demented bastards had kept his body all these years!

He shook with the horror of it. They had continued to worship not just his memory, but his physical body as well, hiding it here, a corrupted husk of dried flesh, an abomination which they could idolize as though he were still there to lead them!

He looked at the skeletal hands resting on the cadaver's lap, withered and yellow, conscious that they had written the orders which had sent millions to their deaths: the hands of a clerk, the hands of a murderous butcher. And as he looked at them, the fingers began to move.

'Oh, sweet Jesus,' he said as the head slowly swivelled round to look down at him.

23

'And the devil that deceived them was cast into the lake of fire and brimstone, where the beast and the false prophet are, and shall be tormented day and night for ever and ever.'
THE REVELATION OF ST JOHN THE DIVINE: 20:10 (RSV)

'Quickly. In which direction is . . . the launching site?' Baruch's voice was raised so it could be heard over the sound of the Gazelle's engine and the whirring blades overhead.

'It's too late, Baruch. There's less than twenty seconds left,' Holly shouted. She sat next to the Israeli in the small cockpit, tugging at his arm to make him understand.

'Just point,' he commanded, and she did so immediately.

'Towards the cliffs . . . there, you can just make it out in the moonlight . . . that bushy area!'

Baruch weakly moved the collective pitch lever upwards and the helicopter began to lift; he pressed the foot pedals, changing the pitch of the tail rotor blades to swing the machine round so it faced the direction they wanted to go. It was a jerky ascent and the Israeli concentrated his mind on controlling the engine power with the twist-grip throttle, thinking only of flying, shutting the nightmare from his mind. The machinery around him, the smell, the noise, brought him back to the world of the normal and he adjusted the cyclic control stick to speed the helicopter towards the cliff-tops.

Dark clouds scurried through the night, hiding the bright moon for long seconds, blacking out the land below them.

'I've lost it!' Holly cried, her head craned forward to look through the cockpit's perspex dome. 'I can't see a bloody thing down there!'

Baruch felt himself spin and he knew he had hardly any strength left. 'It . . . it must be somewhere . . . below us. I will keep to this area.'

'It's no good, Baruch. Even if we find it, what can we do? They'll be under cover down there. This gun won't stop them.'

The Israeli was silent, his head beginning to loll down on to his chest. The helicopter began to weave dangerously close to the ground. Suddenly, the moon appeared again and the grassy slope below was bathed in its silvery light.

Holly gripped the Israeli's shoulder. 'Over there! The small building – the outhouse! It's near there. Yes, I can see it, that circle of undergrowth. They've cleared the opening.'

Baruch's head jerked up and he looked in the direction the girl was indicating. The helicopter veered towards the spot and Holly was thrown back against her seat. They reached the shaft within a matter of seconds and Baruch hovered the machine before it.

Without turning towards his companion he yelled, 'Jump!'

Holly regarded him with astonishment. 'What are you going . . . ?'

'Jump!' His voice had reached a screech and he shoved her roughly towards the door at her side. Then she realized his intention and knew it was the only way.

'Get out! Now!' Once more he pushed her, and this time she reached for the handle and threw the small side-door open. She tumbled to the soft grass eight feet below and lay flat, unhurt but the wind knocked from her. She raised her head just in time to see the helicopter surge forward, hover for a brief second, then plummet down into the deep, brush-surrounded hole in the grassy slope.

Major Brannigan waited patiently for the second-hand to reach the appointed time, his body and brain keen with the excitement of a military operation that would alter the course of history. He and his staff were tucked away in a small alcove set in the side of the deep circular shaft, a thin metal partition erected at the alcove's entrance to protect them from any back-blast of the missile. The sound of crashing waves was driven up from the beach by the wind, along a winding tunnel, and the sea tang was strong in Brannigan's nostrils.

He quickly looked over the metal barrier's top to check visually that everything was in order. The stone staircase built around the shaft's circumference was free of personnel, the missile, bathed in a dim red light, was poised, waiting for its thrust into the sky. The surface-to-air missile stood only ten feet high and resembled the Soviet Goa in design, but it had been manufactured in Edward Gant's own weapons' factory, and to his specification.

'Broad Band Jamming in action?' he asked over his shoulder.

The technician seated at the control unit gave him a thumbs up and was immediately relieved that the Major had his back to him: such informal gestures were frowned upon by the stiff-backed officer. 'All's fine, sir,' the technician answered quickly. None of the nearby radar stations dotted along England's south-west coast would pick up the missile's flight path.

'Target on screen?'

'On screen and our beam locked in.'

Brannigan grunted with satisfaction. Their missile would home in on the US Secretary of State's jet like a needle drawn to a magnet. They knew the exact flight path and time schedule thanks to Cutbush. He looked up at the circular area of sky, the inconsistent moon a silver bright circle encompassed by the larger black circle of the shaft's entrance. He listened intently for a moment. He thought he had heard the whirring sound of rotor blades, but the crashing sea echoing up the long cave and swirling around the shaft's walls made it impossible to be sure. He glanced down at his watch. No time for pondering now. Only five seconds to go.

'Right,' he said, crouching down.

The technician was intent on the dials in front of him, his finger poised over a particular button. He had his own timer and that alone would give him the signal to press the button and not an order from the Major. Two of Gant's special militia stirred uncomfortably behind the technician; they didn't like their confinement with the missile, even though they had been assured there was no possible danger.

'Three. Two . . .' Brannigan's index-finger ticked the seconds away on his knee '. . . One. Let her go!'

The technician's finger stabbed at the button as Brannigan spoke and, on the other side of the metal screen, the surface-to-air missile roared into life, vapour pouring from its base and filling the sunken cavern with its flames.

Just as it began its ascent, Major Brannigan looked up through the gap between the top of the screen and roof of the alcove, and had time to frown and wonder what the huge object blocking out the round circle of moonlight was before the helicopter plunged down the shaft and met the missile on its way out.

There was not even time for the men inside the deep well to scream their terror as the explosion created a massive ball of fire which swept around the shaft, filling it completely, and searing their flesh and bones to charcoal.

Steadman stared at the obscenity in the chair and felt every hair on his body stiffen, a coldness running up his back and clamping itself against his neck. His skin crawled with revulsion and the urge to urinate was almost irresistible. He tried to push himself back, to get away from the decayed creature, but his strength was drained, there was no power in his muscles. Kristina's energy had been taken completely by this dead thing; she had not had the power to control its ravenous demands and now it was feeding off her psyche, had become a living entity. Now it was drawing on his, Steadman's, spirit, sucking the life from him as it had sucked Kristina's.

The head leaned forward, and Steadman shuddered as tiny white crawling worms were dislodged from the cavities in its cheeks. He saw one shaking, skeletal hand reaching down, flesh flaking from the fingers, and he drew in his breath at the thought of being touched by it. But the hand was stretching down towards the stone floor and he realized it was reaching for the ancient spearhead lying near the jackbooted feet. Steadman knew, beyond all doubt, that if the monstrosity grasped the Spear it would derive more strength from its strange power, and the weapon would once again be used against him, used to take his life.

With a cry of desperation, the investigator lunged forward and grabbed the spearhead just as the corpse's fingers curled around it. As he pulled the ancient weapon away, one of the creature's fingers fell to the floor, the rotted skin and brittle bones unable to resist the sudden movement.

Steadman drew the Spear to him, clasping it to his chest in both hands. He felt new strength coursing through him and though the pressure still drugged his brain, he was able to fight against the sensation, was able to rise from the floor and stagger away from the moving carcass. He backed away, stumbling over the dead body of Kristina, losing his grip on the spearhead, feeling the weakness again, crawling after the talisman, gripping it tightly, turning to see the dead thing rising from the chair and walking towards him, one arm raised, mouth gaping open, willing him to return the Spear, urging him to come back and be embraced.

Steadman screamed and staggered to his feet. He found the

stairs on the opposite side of the chamber's curtained entrance and clambered up them, the weakness making his movements slow, his footsteps leaden. He reached the door and slammed against its rough surface, one hand scrabbling madly for the handle, sensing the figure was behind, mounting the stairs, reaching for him.

He pulled at the handle, but the door was locked. He half-collapsed against it and, as he sank to his knees, he saw a rusted iron key projecting from the lock. He tried to twist the key, but it was jammed and his strength was useless. A shadow fell over him and he refused to turn round, too frightened to look into the corrupted face again, knowing the sight would paralyse him with its closeness. The foul smell swept over him, drawing his senses with its stench, and he wanted to close his eyes, to roll himself into a ball and hug himself tight.

Instead, he dropped the Spear and used both hands to turn the key, praying to God the mechanism would be released. His hands and arms shook with the exertion, but he felt the lock give, slightly at first, only a half turn, and then completely. He swung the door open as a hand grasped his shoulder and he pulled himself away from the deathly grip, scooping up the ancient weapon as he stumbled through into the black passage beyond.

There was no light. Only the freshness of the air drew him on, for it had to come from above ground, from the world of the living. He had no idea how long the passage was for he could see nothing ahead, only total darkness. Soft, tenuous material clung to his face and he thrashed wildly at the unseen cobwebs, smashing through them, revolted by their touch. His flesh crawled as tiny legs scurried across his cheek, and he slapped the spider away, shuddering at the sensation as its fragile body popped against his face. The floor was wet and he slipped, crashing painfully to his knees, his hand reaching out and scraping down a slimy wall. He turned his head as he rose and saw the corpse silhouetted in the doorway, a black shape growing larger as it moved forward. Then the door, urged by the breeze flowing along the passageway, slammed shut, and he knew the husk was in the darkness with him.

A sudden muffled sound came to his ears, the noise of a distant explosion, and the earth beneath his feet seemed to tremble with its force. He slipped again before he had fully risen, and heard the metal of the spearhead clang against the wall, nearly falling from his grasp. He gained his feet and forced himself on, a sudden thought bringing him to an abrupt halt. He wasn't sure in which direction he was headed. In the panic-stricken moment of rising he had lost his bearings; for all he knew he was running straight back into the decomposed arms of the corpse. He held his breath and listened.

A shuffling noise to his left sent him scuttling away, once again using his hand as his only guide forward. The slowness of his actions taunted him, but he could not make his limbs move any faster. It was only his greater fear of what stalked him that made him progress at all. When he stumbled into the stone steps ahead, it was his own lethargy that prevented any serious injury. The freshness of the air drifting down seemed to confirm that the stone steps led outside. Steadman began to climb, his breath escaping in short, sharp sobs.

As he climbed, the effort became greater, as though the creature below were using a stronger force to prevent him from reaching the surface. He fell against the stairs, too tired to move, too exhausted to try, and the shock of clammy, cold fingers entwining themselves around his exposed ankle made him scream again, sending the blood pounding round his system, releasing the adrenaline that sent him crawling upwards, tearing himself free from the loathsome grip.

The husk that had once been a living being followed.

The stairs ended abruptly and Steadman knew he had reached ground-level. A thin silvery bar lying horizontally before him made him halt; then he realized it was moonlight – beautiful, silver moonlight – shining beneath a door. With an exclamation of hope, he rushed forward, crashing against the wooden structure in his haste. But this door, too, was locked. And this time, there was no key in the lock.

He looked around the room, searching for something with which to prise open the door, but the silver bar suddenly vanished as clouds obscured the moon's rays. He groaned with frustration and footsteps made him look towards the stairway he had just emerged from. Even though he could not see in the dark, he knew the corpse was mounting the steps, was near the top, its head level with the room's floor. He turned back to the door and banged against it with the spearhead, striking out in anger, fear, dread. The sound of the metal against wood brought him to his senses: he was holding the tool for his escape in his own hands.

He felt again for the lock, then moved his hand to the right, feeling for the gap where door joined frame. He found it and inserted the spearhead's tip into the narrow gap, pressing his whole body against the rest of the blade, praying it wouldn't snap with the force. Fortunately the wood was rotted and the lock none too strong.

The door flew inwards with a sharp cracking sound and fresh night air flew in as though to do battle with the nauseating stench of the thing that was now on the top step. Steadman rushed through the door and the cruel wind whipped at his body, unbalancing him in his weakened state. He went down and, in a night of bizarre sights, his eyes focused uncomprehendingly on yet another. In the darkness ahead, huge flames leapt into the sky, flames that seemed to spring from the very earth. It acted like a beacon to him, for it was light among total darkness.

He clutched the Spear to his chest as the corpse appeared in the doorway of the strange, vault-like building, the black uniform now blood-red in the glow from the fire. Steadman sensed that this creature – this abomination – wanted not just him but the Spear also. It needed the Spear to exist.

He lurched to his feet, the drugging sensation making his head reel. He staggered towards the flames, the corpse of the

Reichsführer following, the wind tearing strips of parchment skin from its body, revealing the bones beneath.

The grass beneath Steadman's feet was soft, sending new life into him as though the earth was trying to help him escape the unnatural thing. The fire was close and he swayed like a drunken man towards it, feeling its heat, welcoming its attack on the abnormal coldness behind him. His legs were in quicksand, but he forced them on, each step a single battle, each one taken, a new victory. He finally reached the brink of the pit, swaying dangerously before it, the heat singeing his hair and eyebrows, his skin reddening and beginning to scorch. He turned his back to the inferno and faced the advancing demon, knowing he could run no further, that if he could, he would drag the thing down with him into the depths below, back to the hell it had risen from.

Then the creature was before him and he was gazing into one sightless eye, the pince-nez torn away by the wind, the eye that had rested against the lens hanging down on to a flesh-less cheek. The mouth was open wide as though the creature was screaming at him, but no sounds came from the lipless gap. Loose skin hung in flaps, breaking away, flaking into swirling dust. The corpse of Heinrich Himmler raised its withered arms to take Steadman in its embrace, the skeletal hands reaching behind the investigator's neck to draw him forward, to touch its face to his. And Steadman was powerless to resist, mesmerized with horror, feebly trying to twist his head away as the skull came forward, a small cry of terror his only sound.

He felt his senses swimming and though he turned his head, his eyes refused to look away from the terrible face. For a moment, he thought he saw the images of Edward Gant and Kristina in the hideous features, screaming out at him from their new-found torment. The skull seemed to grow larger, to fill his vision completely, the eaten-away features sharp in detail. He knew the creature wanted to drag him back to the crypt, to take his will and exist on it. The thing pulled at him and Steadman was powerless to resist.

The ravaged head suddenly burst apart in a hail of bullets, exploding into a fine powder, the remnants toppling from the corpse's body and rolling in the grass at its feet. Steadman drew back and felt his strength return, surging through his body till every nerve-end tingled with the sensation of it. He saw Holly on her knees no more than four yards away, her arms stretched before her, the gun she held in both hands aimed at their swaying figures. He called out her name, the relief of seeing her alive almost too much for his battered emotions, and her face was a mask of fear and incomprehension.

Inexplicably, the headless corpse remained erect, the hands having dropped from Steadman's neck to its side. It stood like a statue, the howling wind whipping at its clothing and threatening to disintegrate the frail body completely. Lights in the distance distracted Steadman for an instant and the crackle of gunfire came faintly to his ears, telling him it really was all over for Edward Gant's macabre New Order. He saw figures scurrying around the house and heard shouted commands, the breaking of glass as they forced their way into the building. Other figures had broken off from the main body and were hurrying towards them, towards the blaze.

He felt the vibration running through the spearhead and looked down, the power from its black metal seeming to course along his arms, penetrating his bloodstream. Then he felt the weakness again, the dragging sensation of energy being drained from him, syphoned from his body by a magnetic force. He fought against the sensation, against the power from the Spear. The headless figure before him reached out, the withered fingers grasping his wrists, and Steadman felt the strength in his arms begin to leave him, to flow from the Spear into the body of the dead Reichsführer.

Steadman screamed in rage, pulling away from the corpse, twisting his arms to break the grip. He staggered and the corpse lurched forward, almost toppling on to him. The investigator turned his body, the heat from the fire burning into his face again, his eyes narrowing with its intensity. In a last desperate effort, and with the agonized cry of the near-defeated, Steadman raised the ancient weapon and plunged it down at the figure's chest, aiming at the heart that had long ceased to beat. The spearhead sank deep, seeming to melt into the rotted flesh. The screech that tore into Steadman's mind was from a tormented creature, a piteous soul suffering the final torture.

Steadman pressed the spearhead in even deeper, pushing the body back towards the flames, ignoring the fresh screams that came from it, closing his mind to its beseeching, wailing cries. They were at the edge of the pit and he saw smoke rising from the black uniform as it began to smoulder. The pain was too much; Steadman knew he would soon collapse with it. But then the body was over the edge, the jackbooted feet scrabbling against the shaft's side, falling away from him, a black shape disappearing into the inferno below, to be devoured by the fires. Consumed into non-existence.

Steadman swayed on the brink, the full power of the Spear now flowing through him. Something had made him cling to the holy weapon as the corpse had fallen away from it, something that had told him he was now the bearer of the ancient talisman, that he now held the key to revelations sought by those who yearned for power and glory. In the flames he saw a mighty battle taking place, a cosmic war between hierarchies of Light and Darkness, a mighty struggle · between Good and Evil powers to control the destiny of mankind. It waged before him, a battle that was eternal, neither in the past nor in the future, but always in the present.

Holly screamed his name, seeing his body sway on the edge of the pit, knowing his skin was already being seared by the fire. She tried to reach him but found it impossible to move. She could only watch as he raised his arms above his head, holding something that had a tapering point, something wicked. A blue glow seemed to effuse from the object, an energy she could see clearly against the background of roaring yellow flames. It moved down his arms, flowing like incandescent water, encompassing his body, spreading to his lower

. limbs, and she saw his body quiver with some strange elation.

Holly called his name again and tried to crawl towards him in an attempt to drag him back from the fire. His body became rigid, and she wondered if he had heard her. She heard him shout as though in anger. He stretched his body back and with an effort that seemed to take all his strength, he hurled the object into the pit.

The flames swallowed the Spear, and Steadman knew it would melt in the inferno. He prayed its powers would melt with it.

The fire suddenly lost its intensity, became cold, frozen yellow tentacles rising from the deep shaft, the wind scarcely influencing their straight path into the sky; and it was the chill that drove Steadman back from the edge, not the heat.

Holly ran to him and for a moment his eyes were strange, looking down at her as though he did not know her, as though he did not know the world she was in. Then recognition flooded back and he held her to him in a grip that threatened to crush her; but she held on to him, returning the pressure, loving him and feeling his love.

The blazing heat returned, pouring from the pit like an explosion, and they moved back, away from its scorching blast. He leaned against her, now feeling the pain in his blistered face, the wound in his arm. But it was welcome pain, for it was real. It was something he could understand.

They held each other close as the first of the soldiers reached them, watching the flames rise into the sky, and they were suddenly aware of the distant droning of an aircraft in the deep, night air. The Marine Commando wondered why the dishevelled couple's upturned faces were smiling.